# THE RAT HUNT BOYS

## Anna Mockler

UNBEARABLE BOOKS / AUTONOMEDIA
Series Editors: Jim Feast and Ron Kolm

# THE
# RAT
# HUNT
# BOYS

## Anna Mockler

Autonomedia

Front Cover Art: Anna Mockler
Cover Design: Jim Fleming

Anna Mockler
www.annamockler.com

Unbearables
www.unbearables.com

Autonomedia
POB 568 Williamsburgh Station
Brooklyn, NY 11211-0568 USA

info@autonomedia.org
www.autonomedia.org

# TABLE OF CONTENTS

# Book One

# Ashes of Burning

*Is it chance or scheme when a seed breaks its coat and spreads its wings? There's a consideration. Many in Charnholm ground the question to dust once the seed took root and flowered too, once the rats ran nose to tail on the plaza and the shadow plays rose off the screen and this tale had come to a close. Was it a lucky thought spun from moon or wave or who knows where, or was it years of preparing the soil so close and careful there was breath in its crumbs; six of one, half-dozen of the other, said most at the end. Certain, it rose from the M'Cools, from a morning when two of them strolled out, past the tinker on his cart, past the ropewalk, past the jigging footless beggar.*

PAST THE TINKER on his cart, huge arms beating dams over potleaks, pausing to scratch his long-gone leg. Past the ropewalk where a few dregs hunched to their plaiting while a one-hand read loud from a crumble book, *lowest and most jected thing of fortune / Stands still in esperance.* Past the ratskull belt of the man who jigged on the corner, who danced on his stumps and grinned neath his round blue hat while the woman sat on a stonechunk, shaking a few chits in a yellow bowl. As they passed, Mary Katharine M'Cool tumble and clutch at her brother Finn's hem, the jigman's woman called to them, "Jig for a jug? nobbut one jug and he'll jig," but Mary Kath nor Finn never had the what-for in their pockets.

"Where?" said Mary Kath, *pompompadom* her heels on the stones, her head on one shoulder to turn the world sideways.

"To Rose Marie," Finn answered short. He slowed, tapped the back of her hand, "Walk like you know where we're going, like we've a chit from Gov Don himself to go there," said Finn, and Mary Kath followed him toe first and head up, their yellow straw brims gliding steady down promenade.

"Rose Marie?" said Mary Kath.

"We're going to Rose Marie."

"Why's she no come to us?"

"Housebound," said Finn, short. He backed Mary Kath into a doorway. "You've to shutter up and mind me till we're there, hear?"

"Why?"

"I'm the older."

"Nobbut two years," she said. "I sha be five soon and you're nobbut six." The morning sun could no get into that street. The stones was cold gainst her back. In a gap tween the houses, the ships nodded on the harbor below. Whitesail, redsail, mustard-yellow sail, all furled, down to the smallest bark with its handker of sail was close-hauled, and all of them nodded at Mary Kath as Finn shook her and shook her.

"Natheless," said Finn. "You're to mind me." He held her by her shoulders till she nodded, making the ships nod too.

Toe first and head up to the corner, where Mr Inkwhistle's knees loomed up. He cried, "Doves here, doves here, flesh of the sweet breast only, get your doves here, pale perfection onna stick, doves here," as they passed, but Cider Mother darkled on the dove seller, "Put your tusks to a one of Inkwhistle's avians, you'll tend night soil for a week, full," so Finn and Mary Kath nobbut touched their brims with their right hands, respectful, to Mr Inkwhistle, and swung round the corner in pace-form, Mary Kath gripping Finn's coattail, right feet forward together and then left, side to side rolling. Tween two strides their street vanished cepting Mr Inkwhistle's cry, "Fresh-caught doves, stoned on the wing this morning, doves here," till even his cry was vanished.

The noise and the people all died off together when they come to Dead Horse Moraine, one of the flat humpy lands made all of block stone and round stone, carven faces and wings leered and flew from mounds of rubblecobble, the whole dusted with coarse-grit grey sand. Mary Kath's toes stumped to a halt when the smell of the place come up her nostrils. Finn pulled a straw out his pocket. There was no use shoving Mary Kath one way or another, she'd nobbut dig her heels in. He whistled down a straw tween his thumbs. "A good thing Mary Patricia's no here," said Finn, casual. "She said she stopped home to help mam with the brewing, but I lay you it was cause the moraines fright her."

Out of course, Mary Kath moved forward at that. Moraines was fine adventure, and she'd no need to hold Finn's hand, though she did to show him, kindly, she was no dot afraid.

The rubblemounds rustled and slithered on their approach. Finn wrapped rags round his palms and grabbed a shivered pike from a stack by the entry gate to pound the stonewrack at their feet.

"They want to meet you so much as you want to meet them," Finn said.

"Everybody knows that," said Mary Kath.

"Sure," Finn said.

On the far side he laid his pike on the far stack, hung the rags from the fence, and they stuck their chins in the air as they walked on the balls of their feet into Yellowbrick.

Yellowbrick was everyways different from their side of Dead Horse. The buildings was four floors high, for one; a few windows on the first floor had glass in them, for another; each yellow building made one side of a green-yellow square, for a third. "Grass!" said Mary Kath as she stepped on the green-yellow. She reached out to grab a handful, Cider Mother said naught flavored a soup like grass, but Finn grabbed her hand away. "They squat on it, here," he said, "it's that keeps it so bright." She kept her hands at her sides after that, carrying them palms-out of course, as is proper mongst strangers, and they crossed the grass square to Rose Marie's yellow-brick building. Cept for one place above the third landing where Finn had to jump Mary Kath cross the gap, the stairs was all in one piece to the fourth floor where Finn knocked shave-and-a-haircut.

Finn had rehearsed what he'd to say to Rose Marie so many times it was spurting out his mouth fore Mary Kath had both feet on the landing: "Cider Mother's so deep in brewing that she's both mash-tuns going so we come here stead of you coming to —"

Rose Marie spoke right through him.

She said, "Now is this nice." Said it straight into Mary Kath's hairs. That was how high off the floor Rose Marie's mouth was; a drib of a thing wound in a black shawl with red fringe, a gold dragon flying round her head, a green pig-dog barking off her shoulder. "Now is this nice, the both of you come this long way when I'm homefast. I'd come to your place to mind you, like usual," she said, "was it no for my leg. It's hollow, see?" lifting the limb out from its shawl tangle, "So I'm glad you come to me. I've herbs for you to drink and we'll play pick-up, hmmm? Do you come in, you Finn, and you, Mary Katharine," turning on them her great green eyes and blinking her smoke lashes three times, "I'm main pleased you come. Lay your left palm to the door-scroll, yes-ss, and scrape your boots on the mat. There now. Come in, and we'll have a nice tittle-tattle."

Rose Marie snuggled into a pile of nappy velvet pillows, their grimy fringes flopping dust as she plumped on them. "Now you come for mugwort," she said. "The kettle's through the green porty-airs, cups beside it." Finn walked through the archway's velvet curtains and tangled with their muffly tatters till he beat his way through. Rose Marie said, "Trust a male to pernk through to the sweet," and the cloth over her belly rippled where she laughed. The porty-airs swaffled and bulged and then Finn was mong them again with two cups in his hand. He sat down next Mary Kath on the floor and they drank through their teeth, so to strain the chunks, till Rose Marie was done laughing.

When she was done: "Tell us a story, Rose Marie," said Mary Kath.

"Shall I tell you how the pig-dog got its name?" lifting it off her shoulder.

"Something scary," said Mary Kath. She crossed her black plaits neath her chin. "Something as'd fright Mary Pat."

"Well, Mary Patricia, she is a bit chilly-spined, for all she's older nor you, Finn." Rose Marie leaned forward to pat his head, disarranging her shawls considerable.

"Nobbut two years," Finn said.

"Natheless," said Mary Kath, and poked him tween the ribs. Finn grabbed her arm and made to bite it.

"Mmm, ayuh," said Rose Marie, busy draping the dragon so it once more covered her bald scalp. "Or maybe you'd like to hear of the king who lived in the leviathan? He'd his table and his cloth and his victuals three in its maw, same like you've in your home. Shall I tell you that one?" She retied the shawl firmly neath her left ear. "Course, that was fore the burning," she said quiet.

"Tell us of the burning, Rose Marie," said Finn.

She spoke right through him, "Or I could tell you the tale of the boy who cried 'School!' till the ship's crew, zausted with pitching their nets for naught, tossed him overboard where the deeps ate him up snip-snap."

"Please tell us of the burning," said Mary Kath.

"Well," she said, and they cozied gainst her heap of pillows. "That's a tale we maun tell in a clean room, dearies, so if you two spawn play pick-up tween these walls, when you're done we'll see."

"*We'll see*," whispered Mary Kath to Finn as they bent and stashed and cleared and folded. "When I'm grown I sha' never say that to —"

"Mary Katharine?" said Rose Marie. "Is the play too tiring? D'you ruther sit mumchance?"

"No'm," said Mary Kath. When Finn judged the room was tidy as the brew-cellar fore straining, they stood fore Rose Marie, who tilted her head and smiled, and they cozied — slower — gainst her heap of pillows.

Rose Marie said, "Well. Sure you want to hear the tale?" When they'd nodded their heads near off their necks, she sat up, crossed her legs, and leaned forward. Then she belched and laid her stumpy right hand, its first two fingers missing, on her rolly belly. "I should have a little drink fore I start on that," she said, "to put us in the spirit. Get it?" she bounced off the pillows and rubbed their heads with her palms, "in the spirit? Ha!" and was off through the porty-airs still laughing.

The sun was starting to come in through the rents in the west windowblinds and Mary Kath looked at Finn and the sunsplotches on the rug and back to Finn. His face was smooth as wet stone, there was never aught to be got from him when he looked so. Mary Kath played the figures in the rug was meeting each other in a garden bigger nor the orchard, bigger nor all Charnholm, like one group stood at North Point Light, and the other waved from the richard compounds up South Point; they climbed down and met by the jetty and was just started playing bowls long the promenade when Rose Marie come slither through the porty-airs. Finn and Mary Kath sat up soldier but Rose Marie wandered round the room touching this pile and that, smoothing the pillows' grimy fringes, looking out the west windows at the ships nodding in the harbor. Mary Kath made to open her mouth: "Shutter up," Finn hissed. Finally, Rose Marie swished her shawls and plopped her duff on the pillows. Mary Kath held her thumbs, but Rose Marie tilted a green-chased flask to her mouth. She sucked at the flaskmouth a time or two, her eyes whirling in her head, and then she sat up sudden and looked straight down Finn's eyes and said: "My granmam Livy was about your age when the burning started."

My granmam Livy was about your age when the burning started. She lived in a great walled compound, and at the gates was tiny men in peaky houses who ran their eyes all up and down your frame when you knocked; did they know you, you was in; did they no, you could stand there till your fingers fell off. (Finn and Mary Kath shivered and tucked their fingers neath their legs. "Go on," said Finn.) My granmam Livy's mam and dap and her two brothers lived in a house of their own behind all those big safe walls, they was musicians but no like what you have atop the Hunt Wagon these days, no, my granmam Livy's family played in richard halls, so they did. (Rose Marie took a long suck at the green-chased flask.) The richards they had back then liked their music so much they give them a house of their own behind those big safe walls — like what compounds the richards has today, maybe — behind which my granmam Livy's mam let Livy run round everywheres for there was naught could harm her. My granmam Livy played in the gardens making chains of flowers and friends of squirrels. (Seeing Finn and Mary Kath all puzzlement, Rose Marie explained: "Squirrels was near big as rats but with cute faces and all furry, even their long tails fluffed, and they liked you, squirrels, they'd no bite a friend." Rose Marie took up again her tale.) Livy'd invite 'em to tea with her, set out flowers and ask them how their families did and what dances they was going to that night. My granmam Livy never told me any too much of how her family lived inside the compound, maybe she could no remember or maybe she would no remember, it comes to the same thing, but this much she did tell me back when I was tall as Mary Katharine, when Livy and me pretended we was squirrels together having biscuits and sherry.

So one day my granmam Livy she tells the guard in his peaky house she has to go outside for a couple special flowers, she tells him it's desperate important, she's hostess to a annversary breakfast for all the squirrels, and he laughs and flips a hand and opens the wicket-gate for her and bows her out and down the drive she runs to the entry posts, her yellow party dress flouncing out behind her.

Livy hiked up her skirt so it'd no get grass stains ("What a priss," said Mary Kath. "Shutter up and listen," said Finn.) and she knelt by the drive's entry picking flowers. She pinched off each one zackle thumb-length, snipping them with her brother's knife she borrowed for the day, and tying them together with grassblades. She was a long time about it cause it was so important to get everything right for the annversary breakfast. ("I'd like to see one of those squirrels," Mary Kath whispered to Finn. "Shuh," he said, out the corner of his mouth, his eyes straight on Rose Marie.)

My granmam Livy told me she heard a crack and then a crackle and then a shouting 'Hoy! Hoy!' but that was how boys done when they made bonfires. That was going to be the big treat for the squirrels, see, they was going to their first-ever bonfire. ("But if squirrels was like rats, do you think they'd liked fires?" said Mary Kath, and Finn and Rose Marie both laid a finger cross their lips.)

The crackling and the shouting went on while Livy made dozens of bookeys of all kinds of flowers, pink stars and red foldy-overs with gold tongues and white overlappers round yellow buttons and orange daylils (they was smaller, then) and laid them careful in lines on the low stone wall that flanked the entry posts. The drive was mostly empty so late in the morning, the deliveries made, the olders at their work, the spawn with their minders, the sprats at their lessons, and this day everybody else was getting ready for the bonfires. The guard he must natural of figured she'd come to no harm there. Which that come true. (Rose Marie tilted the green-chased flask to her lips and swallowed three times.)

The crackling got louder and there was more shouting and bells rang *Ka-long, Ka-la-la-long* and Livy hurried up with the naming of each bookey for which squirrel it was meant for and gathered all the bookeys careful in a bunch and trotted up the drive to the wicket. She told me she rang and she rang and she knocked and she knocked on the wicket, but nobody come.

Even at seven years old my granmam Livy was a sensible chit. She sat on a bench by the wicket and counted her bookeys of flowers and practiced the speech she was going to give the squirrels at their breakfast. That's what she was doing, she told me, when the trees inside the walls shot up in the air in flames, their roots draggling rockety behind them, as they turned orange somersaults over the rooftops that flipped inside out, their eaves folding up and their spines collapsing in. She could see no more of it, no matter how she jumped: the gates was set so you could see nobbut the peaky guard-shacks, all but the rooftops of the houses was well hid by the fence from peery eyes. My granmam Livy ran up to the wicket and screamed loud as ever she could but nobody come. The metal fence was red-black and smoking, her palms come away burnt when she tried to climb it, she tore her yellow dress and wrapped it round her hands but the cloth burst to flame on touching the metal pickets. She ran round and round, trying to climb the close-laid stones of the fence or squeeze tween its iron gates but she could get no toehold in the stones and all the four gates burnt her crisper till the dress shredded off her and she ran in her white shimmy and her white drawers that went grey and then black and the screams died away altogether, nobbut flames and ash and black smuts falling from the sky all oily, sticking to her skin, burning oily there. She lay up at the back gate, prying its posts with her fingers.

That's where she was when the fire come out from behind the gates. It come in a wave taller nor the tallest mast of the longest ship, pus-yellow curling round a blue center, pushing a ship-long wind before it. It rose up gainst the walls of the compound. My granmam Livy cowered all her front in the dirt in the lee of the wall. The earth rose up neath her in a wave of its own, and another, and a third shoved her back long the fence away from the gate. She opened her eyes to see the line her body'd made in the dirt. She closed them again when the wave of fire crashed over the walls.

Fire skips like spawn skip, hippity-hop. The fire skipped hippity over my granmam Livy, a lick ate the hair off her nape and a leaf of flesh off her shoulders. No more. It went off on its business, which was to lick up all it could find of Charnholm. It pushed wind before it and it sucked air behind it. When the sucking come to an end and the air was still, my granmam

Livy crawled forward to the gap in the stone fence where that morning the back gate'd been.

She held two dirtclumps in her hand and stared. Near the back gate gap was the pond where her mam and her dap took her down to sail twig-boats. There was swingy trees all round that pond. They was charteeth now. She tried to call for her mam and dap, but her voice made a rasp, no more. She lay there as ashes drifted from the sky and settled. There was no breath of wind of any kind. At last, my granmam Livy saw a person coming, all stumble and tearing at a tangle mass of smoke flailing off its head, a grimpy robe hanging off it, carrakeening from side to side toward the pond. Stars shot from its head as it come through three pillars that was a gazebo just two days before when they all ate Livy's mam's pie by its shores which her dap called delicious and her brothers hollered for more but her mam ducked her head and said it was a little burnt; it was a gazebo then but now it was three cracked pillars as shot off stars as felled the stumbling body, its skin blacked and cracked and peeling, twenty foot from the water's edge, which could no been a refuge, any road, due to it was steaming and popping like breadknots frying in Livy's mam's blue kettle, and the crumplebody lay there with its eyes running down its face like smashed eggs and stars danced on its scalp till hairs, scalp, and stars was all gone to cinders, and the cinders gone to ash, the ashes gone to dust, and the dust blew off; and that was the only person my granmam Livy saw at all, at all, from out the hundreds who'd that morning called her Livy, Live-it-up, who'd wished her happy annversary and told her to come by, later, for little nut-cakes they'd made for her squirrels.

My granmam Livy walked away from that while dust fell on her bald nape and her charred shoulders and her boiled palms, scuffing grey dust behind her as she walked.

Rose Marie's lips closed over her flaskmouth.

"Scuffing grey dust behind her," said Finn, encouraging.

"Then what happened?" said Mary Kath.

The sun was striking the west window-sills.

"A wind come up," said Rose Marie to her flaskmouth.

"What'd the wind do?" said Finn.

"It come up strong," said Rose Marie.

"Land breeze or sea breeze?" said Finn. He threw out his chest on that; he listened to Daniel talk to their dap; he listened close and careful when James A told Daniel how to tack gainst a cross-wind.

"It come from everywhere," said Rose Marie. "Remember, she'd a knife with her."

"Well, now, how could that be?" said Finn. "Wind can no —"

"You'll have another cup of mugwort fore you go. You'll want to be neath your own roof come dark," said Rose Marie, and they could no winkle another word out of her.

They went stumble home from Rose Marie, after. The carven stones in Dead Horse Moraine was scorched and dusty from the Burning. A brown jaggedy half-bowl in one rubblemound maybe come from Rose Marie's gran-mam Livy's kitchen. A bleached bonepile jutting from another mound was maybe Livy's dap, or her mam, or one of her brothers. The mugwort that grew in the ashpockets maybe sucked its leaves out of some stumblebody's smashed-egg eyes. Mary Kath took tight hold of Finn's hand. Finn walked one-two one-two, looked neither right nor left, strode double-time to get home ahead of the dark, with Mary Kath dragfoot after neath a bled-out sky, their gullets stapled flat. When the rubblemounds slithered, they did no shy, they walked on. They'd no startle left in them. When they tried to speak they could make nobbut a raspy whisper.

They could no open their mouths sufficient for the evening's gruel, neither. Mary Pat taunted them, "Rat got your tongue?" Dan hushed her, tipped their bowls into his, and swallowed every last drap. Finn and Mary Kath could scarce drag themselves upstairs to their pallets, what with every shadow rocketing out the wall and somersaulting, but once they reached their ticks, they fell on them boots and all, still mute.

Cider Mother, though, she'd no short of words, later, when they was up all night and half the next day spewing. "Whether it's you two or Rose Marie who's the least sense I've no idea soever; giving you mugwort steeped in pondscoop, likely, no better; if she's roofcatch handy, the which I doubt, she's no spine enough to fetch it down for you pair of lackbrains who've potable enough to home. Have I no told you day in day out you're to drink nobbut potable, or is it you want to grow to Rose Marie's height only? that you pour liquid down your gullets no questions; there now, heave it up, mind your sense does no follow it." So she scolded as she held their heads over basins, as she wiped their faces with clean damp cloths, as they spewed their guts over and again.

It was gloaming of the next day fore they was settled flat on their pallets. Cider Mother sat on the windowledge, then, turning a mug of scrumpy in her hands, watching the other dregs on promenade. Another bakedust evening in Charnholm. Dregs are near turned to light by time they come to promenade. Rise fore the sun clears the limestone cliffs, swallow a cup of hot and slice of bread, then it's haul, mend, make, and scrub to scrape the day's meal from the day.

Cepting Marian, who sat by the empty window frame and read her crumble books to the spawn, in order: first the comedies, then the tragedies, then the historical plays. Cider Mother's mam had known Marian as a young woman, her scholar husband crushed neath blackened timbers of the summerhome, reading the comedies, then the tragedies, then the historical plays, as her husband's flesh melted slow off his bones, as his bones crumbled slow to dust. The books was scorched, pierced by thin flaming splinters; Marian read them, in order, so long as there was light to see by, and spoke them, in order, long past that hour:

P.    I'll deliver all,
And promise you calm seas, auspicious ga
And sail so expeditious that shall catch
          royal              chick
charge          – then to
     free and      fare well!      Please you, draw near.

First time any spawn was took to Marian's, that's the bit she read out to them. Marian. All the spawn sat round that littered room, wide to the winds, their chins propped on their fists, as Marian read aloud to them:

P.    *Sir, I invite your Highness and train*
*To my poor cell, where you shall take your re*
*With such discourse as I no doubt sha*

Likely had no need of those books by then, cepting to teach the spawn their letters. Marian dried to dust in place, long since. One morning when they come they found her in her chair, a book open on her lap, her eyes wide open.

They burned her. A new reader took her books and led Prospro's chant as the flames turned to coals, as the coals turned to ash:

*Ye elves of hills, brooks, stand*
*on the sands with print*
            *for I'll break my staff,*
*bury it certain          in the earth,*
*And deeper than did ever plum*
            *drown my book.*

Cider Mother repeated the lines from the windowledge overlooking the dregs on promenade; walking dust in one light, mud-smeared glorus stars an you looked at them with Marian's believing eyes.

⌣⟶

Dregs shuffled up cobbles and down, from North Point light, a stone heap set with spag lamps, to the ancient baulk, enamel in barnacle, glisten with salt, that long since leapt the jetty wall. Brackish harbor water nosed aside the jetty's grey-green mantle of slime and lapped up under those skirts and listless sank, its exhales rank with piscine slurry, spitting the pips through the jetty's scuppers.

On promenade the dregs hug what thin shade the locusts throw where they thrust from dusty gaps in the cobble walk, leaves sparse on spindle branches, sputtered with grey dust. The dregs are thin as the shade and the locusts, their scalt skin equal painted in grey dust as they ease their slippers up cobbles and down. In pairs and threes and solitary, they shuffle north, and turn, and shuffle south, and turn. They rest betimes gainst the jetty walls, pressing their bare legs to its cool stones, lifting a wranked hand in greeting that falls back to their sides like grey dust settling.

The promenade's punctuate by dustclouds that, on close approach, resolve themselves into spawn who run circles round their begetters shrieking *wantIwantwantIwaaant*, fresh from sleep they squall, blood fizzing in their veins, *IwantIwantwant*. Thus the spawn. Thus the most of them. Some few have no words on them. Their swollen heads loll gainst the mam-thighs they clutch with shrunken arms, they gape and gawp till some rising lymph forces a great roar from them, which done they slump jelly-boned, eyes rolling in their sockets, their paws weakly kneading the mams who hoist them to better catch a sluggish breeze.

Thus the promenade as long as any can remember and then some. Cider Mother'd seen it ten thousands of times by time she bore her first living child. This night, short of sleep and potable, her stomach past growl or ache, a numb kettle neath her lungs, she was wrung-out to that extent it all went distant on her, the commonest shapes a marvel or impossible odd, the hundred-cubit jetty a wall could wrap South Point. It was this night she got the unaccountable itch in the palms of her feet. It was this night she started again to rub her thumbnails together in slow circles, looking at nothing a half-fathom off the while, which James A could and would told you was a scheming trouble on its way. Maybe the scheme'd end up throwing a few extra fish in the pot or maybe it'd oilsoak every pallet in the house: it's the not knowing as wides my eyes, said James A.

*But there was none by that night to notice the sudden bloom, and indeed the scheme fruited slowly over eight long summers before it loosened keystones from their mortar, before it began the toppling, before the rats ran mad, before the squalling babe was pulled from its most unnatural womb, before all the world, from North Point to the burned city, began to grow new flesh over its suppurant gashes, before the set enduring mouths of the women broke into new grimace, before the hunched shoulders of the men went slack in pure surprise.*

# Courtyard Brangle

MARY KATHARINE M'COOL woke at dawn to a courtyard full of screams as she'd woke every morning for weeks. She covered her head with a corner of straw tick. Morning breeze slugged off the harbor, so hot it could nobbut drag itself in scorch pulses through the front shutters and out the back, into the courtyard where it swirled a half a time and sunk down mong the dust and bones. The woman cross the courtyard was screaming. Her screams clanged the hot stones and sank and rose again. Those who screamed usually stopped after a time. This one's man rumbled back at her now and now, or a justborn pitched its wails into the stew, or all of them to once. Naught to be done about it. In summer, did they no keep the shutters open, they'd all cough worse and Nora'd bring up blood again. No matter how thick Mary Kath stuffed the bedcloths in her ears, the woman screamed that her flesh was drapping down, she'd no never be the hollow-bone girl she once was, and there'd never be more nor what there was.

Mary Kath gave up sleeping as a bad job and threw back the cloths.

Mary Patricia snored lady-gentle in the next pallet; she'd a power to sleep you could nobbut envy. Her hand had slipped off the brass-hinged box their dap gave her for her Seventh. Mary Kath stuck one stealthy hand neath the lid and easy pushed it back. Mary Pat snored on. There was gleam inside —

"Mary Katharine M'Cool! Get out of that!"

"Now, Mary Pat. I nobbut saw your box lid was open, which I thought you'd maybe wake in a fret off that so here I am, quiet as sand, tryna set it back right and what do I get for my pains? A fearsome screeching in my ears. Catch me trying to set your heart easy again, oh no, next time I'll —"

"Shutter up. I'll flat your nose an you touch my brass-bound again."

"As you like, queen of all, you've but to speak and I obey." The screams rose up again and Mary Kath took it on the heel and toe down stairs.

Mary Pat slid her hand inside the box and come up with a shard of clear rock, spock of gold at its heart. Dan said it was the lost eye of a deepfish, but Cider Mother said it was glass, like what used to be in windowframes, as had melted on itself. Like spag does, said Cider Mother. Mary Pat laid her eye to the glass eye. Towers leapt out the earth in cartwheel and all flames licking, the while a handful of ships flicked this way and that on the seawaves halfway to the sun. The Burning again. You'd think it'd sometimes show aught else. Mary Pat laid the glass eye back in its nest, rolled over, and wrapped herself again in sleep.

Cider Mother was in the kitchen, Nora on her hip, cutting bread quiet. The screams pullulated. Like to knock the sieves off the wall, they was. It come hard to them as once was horii when their breasts fell and their waists went square. This one wailed for what was gone, what was left: her man's few zausted pats and the spawn wailing, and still the porridge to get in the morning's hot stench. Cider Mother shrugged and cut another slice. They come to terms or screeched theirselves hoarse, whichever, as this one would. Mary Kath burst down the kitchen stairs: "Mam, Mary Pat's a monster of selfish, she —"

"Good morning, Mary Katharine. Did you sleep well?" Cider Mother carried on slicing the bread. "There's bread. And jam over."

Mary Kath sat down to table and ate her bread and blackberry jam. She told Cider Mother of the screams as she stuffed two slices down her. "So why's she every morning scream and scream?"

Cider Mother cut another four slices of bread. "There's Dan and Finn stirring," she said. "Fill the kettle, Mary Kath."

How could you tell a spawn (as Cider Mother spread jam on four slices, as the boys clattered down) that age and decay bring some to scream in hopes the peristalsis will shiver the aged carapace and bring the gone years back? You could no tell them.

"That's enough of the potable, Mary Kath. Put a roll of spag in your ears and the screaming will no wake you." Cider Mother wiped her hands on her pinna and settled Nora in the hipsling.

Dan and Finn burst in the room. Dan could burst into a rainstorm; when Finn was by him he was zactly twice as loud; and now young Mary

Kath'd picked it up. Well, it was better they burst than slunk into rooms like some did. Dan and Finn grabbed the bread fresh off the knife and crammed the slices down their maws, push and shove all full of theirselves and the day upcoming.

"Great rudesby," Mary Kath muttered towards Danny.

"What's that, our Mary Kath? Doost speak up now, Mary Katharine, elst we'un can no hear thee."

Mary Kath told him to shutter up, she was no cave cowering shallop as'd slum through her tongue, and he said yes she was, and she said she was no and give him a clunk on his kneecap, and he pulled her backhair. "Shutter up, each and every one of you," said Cider Mother. "Mary Katharine, call your sister. Daniel, four bowls for porridge. Finn, only so much applesauce in each bowl as fits on your thumbback," and they was quiet till the trumpets blared. Dan and Finn was already shoving back their chairs as Mary Pat took her last dreamy lick off the steel spoon her dap brought back from his last scavenging mong the stone scrapers. "People used to live in the scrapers," James A'd told her, "looked down on the street from four and six floors up, through windows made all of glass."

"Like my eye," said Mary Pat, gone back to her dreams.

The boys was near to the door. Cider Mother tapped the porridge spoon gainst the kettle rim. "Boys, walk out that door and you'll feel the flat of my hand. Mary Patricia, rouse up." Finn spoke back to her:

"But mam, it's nobbut the trumpets gone so far. We could easy make out we did no hear them, they'd but chase us in, we could see the Wagon once quick —"

"Finnegan M'Cool. I'll thank you to remember you're a month past your Seventh, no mewling justborn. Think the trumpets a joke? A jape? A merry ha and a ho and all laughs together, buckies? Trumpets march flanked by glassies, scutmen, and yoorawls — scutmen cried the five-minute Shutter-up and you sha' heed that." Cider Mother scoured the porridge bowls with horsetail brush. "Scutmen owes their very eyes to richards. I gone to a shock of trouble to raise you this far, I'll no toss those years to vain letting you make part of a scutman's haul. You four sha' stay in this house till the first rimer sets foot on plaza, and that's flat."

Finn whispered at Mary Kath, "I could go in and out so slick they'd never see a hair of me."

"Course you could," said Mary Kath. Finn could lift the kitchen through the roof, and he'd a mind to, did you ask Mary Kath.

Cider Mother hefted Nora on her hip. James Aloysius had to give her a break from all these spawn. Soon as he come back she'd tell him straight. Say a week or two after he got back. Sure a month after. "Now what do we do come Hunt Day?"

"Shutter up," said Mary Kath, looking sideways to see if there was trouble coming off that.

"Yeah, shutters closed, what else?"

"No peeking!" said Dan and Finn in a one voice, "We will no peek nor pry nor elsewise part the shutter slats!"

Cider Mother nodded. It was lovely how spawn learned to talk, but the dark of it was, they never, after, left off talking. "A bit less noise'd come welcome, but you've the stem of the notion. Mary Pat?"

"Mmmm?"

"Mary Pat, did you hear an any word of that?"

"Mam?"

Cider Mother sighed and tucked the flannel a bit more round pale Nora's throat. With spawn, you'd to say the same things over and over and then once more. "It's Hunt Day, Mary Patricia. Now what do we do?"

"Go up garret and watch the Hunt through the scope you set up special for us," said Mary Pat.

"Mary Kath, you're of age now to watch." Mary Kath did no squeal, a dozen points in her favor over Mary Pat, but then Mary Kath was no weighted with being able to see down a crystal eye like Mary Pat could. "Dan, you're to mind she calls down no doorbang scutman."

"Now, mam, is it likely?"

"The one time you did it —"

"One time!"

"They took every last crumb of provender from out the cupboard."

"Mam, five years ago! I was six!"

"I'll give you six an you bring down a scutman on us. Off with you!"

Dan was first up the stairs with Finn and Mary Kath close behind, Mary Pat slinker slanker last, her fingers petting the plaster walls as she mounted. Cider Mother shook her head and tossed the scrubbed porridge bowls in the drainvat. "Passel of feckless shabrags," she told pale Nora, who coughed in answer.

It was no the cough was so loud, it was how it rackled, like a pike-end rattling iron pickets. Nora's face was pale blue; she weighed half of naught, slept all the day, waking only to cough, and twitched in her sleep as well, whether shutters was open or close. Cider Mother gulped air, gripping the table top. Trust James A to be elsewhere when it come to mucky jobs. Well, it was time to give Nora the medicine. The other four'd tear their livers did they catch her dying on them. Cider Mother shifted the spawn closer to her heart, the way it'd keep quiet till Hunt passed. The least rapple-tat'd was enough to draw down scutmen, lately. Scutmen had so little work, these days, all the richards hiring privates since they come up from their shelter caves; no like when she was a spawn; then, each block ponied up for its scutman; scutmen these days was anxious at an any sound to prove their valor. Down cellar Nora could make all the sound she needed, and the brew vats needed checking anyhow. Small sense letting the business fall apart, now when she'd most need of it. Nora coughed a plotch of blood on her shoulder, her ribs heaving with the push of it. Cider Mother stroked Nora's sweaty crown and whispered, "Hush now," the spawn's hair rough neath her palm, "Hush now."

Up garret, Mary Pat showed Mary Kath how to peer down the hagioscope. It was nobbut drainpipe caps pierced a many times so you could see out, but scutmen could see no crack from the cobblestones below. The trumpets blew *Alors Alors* so the dregs'd know the Hunt was coming, "Like we was deaf stupidos, like we'd no figure it, othergates," said Finn.

"Like we never seen a Hunt before," said Dan.

Mary Kath said no word. She'd both eyes to the hagioscope in the lee of Mary Pat's shoulder. "You said the wagon's red but it's all rusty color."

"That's the bloodsmoke, know-naught," said Dan from his lofty.

"Well, she never seen it before," said Finn.

"Right aright," said Dan. "Step on my knee up to here, Mary Kath. Here from the roof lion's mouth you can see the Hunt whole." She clambered on his great bronze leg, thick with muscle cord. He lifted her to the thin gap at the shutters' top, the way she'd a straight view down. She was on top of the world now. "You can see from here the whole of the Wagon, any road. See the wheels? They're picked out in gold." Mary Kath shook her head the least hair. "Well they are, so, whether you see them or no. It was me painted them, last month as ever was, brushed gold along each spoke and hub, gold as gold. It's gone dim already now. That's from the bloodsmoke."

"Bloodsmoke? From where?" said Mary Kath.

"From the crematoria," he said. "The door's on the far side from us, but I'd my hand on it when I painted, a gorry iron stove is the Wagon belly, to be sure. See the fine haze rise up from the Wagon's far side? See the smoke, now?"

"Yeah," she said. She held tight to Dan's hand as the squealing rose.

"That's nobbut skirling, Marekat," said Finn. "That's the dancerats scarpering out from the bag of pommy-mash they been gorging on all the night till they're stumbledrunk. Yoorawls dump them into the pen, round which they'll caper till the richards lean from carrychairs to spike them with their long brass poles."

"Poles three fathoms long, some on 'em," said Dan. "They're terrible frighted of rats, is richards."

Mary Pat tossed back her hair. "Those richards got no more notion how to spike than does pale Nora."

Dan leaned down to Mary Kath, "The richards poke and poke; they've no the training to spike: that's why the rats squeal so. Do you listen for how different they squeak when a Hunt Boy spits them," and Mary Kath made no sound, though Dan poked her onefinger in the ribs. "They poke them neath their tails," said Dan. "They poke them where they live, you see," at which she did let out a small skreel.

"Bite it off," said Finn. "She's no need to know where they poke."

"*I* already knew," said Mary Pat.

"Did no," said Dan.

"Did so," said Mary Pat. "Since I was old as Mary Kath is now, so there's for you."

"Right aright," said Dan. "You known since you was a puling milkfed justborn, if you maun have it so." He leaned down to Mary Kath again. "Hunt Boys poke the rats neath their tails till the ratguts seep out, then with cramp on cramp and awful squeal their eyes fill with blood. When they're rosy full, they snap stiff still forevermore. Toss them in the crematoria in the Wagon's belly. Then the richards laugh, slap each other's back."

"Richards is full of laugh," said Finn, low, to Mary Kath.

⟋

Down cellar, Cider Mother set a pot of spiced cider on the hob. She pulled a twicefold bag of crystal from the lowboy, and measured two spoons into a mug. She crooled, "Doost willun craig a benno? Doost willun?" holding the spawn close as close till pale Nora's coughs quieted some. The trumpets passed, and the pacing rimers.

⟋

Mary Kath said, "What's all those in white?"

Finn told her they was rimers as walked before the Hunt to lull the rats in their tracks with verse. Mary Kath nodded; it had to make sense when it was Finn speaking.

"That's the skin of the burnt dead they walk in," said Dan.

"Dan! You'll scare the spawn out her own skin," said Mary Pat.

"She should know what's what in this world," said Dan, giving Mary Kath a lollop ride up and down on his knee, shtomp shtomp. "You do no want to be a ignorany, do you, Mary Katharine?" pitching his voice high as Aunt Connie's.

"No," said Mary Kath. She could trust her voice to be steady on a short sound like that.

⟋

Cider Mother felt careful neath Nora's jaw. The lumps was coming. Did she leave it to tomorrow, they'd turn blue as her cheeks, swell to size of her small, dimpled fists. Next they'd spew at touch and it was spew as'd kill the others. Now was the time. The cider was reduced to thick syrup. She poured it in the mug of crystals, and fed Nora the syrup, spoon on spoon down her stiff throat, pucking the small mouth open to each spoonful. Hunt beaters shoved their poniards at cellar windows, but theirs was well and truly shuttered.

⌐

Mary Kath poked Finn in the ribs. He said naught, his head on a slant, listening. She poked him again. "Beaters, Mary Kath. They flush the anathematized rats to the road verge. They're beaters. Now leave me be." He returned to his still posture, one ear cocked towards cellar.

Dan said, "Can no get lower nor a beater. Hunt Boys novices as can no make it, them they turn to beaters."

"I'd fine talk with a beater yestermorning," said Mary Pat. "Asked me what was up of the clock and I told him it was near sundown, and he said, 'Sure, is it? By the light of your eyes and your glory copper hairs I'd thought it bright noon.'"

They was silent a minute, for that, and then said Finn, "And you nobbut two years past your Seventh? Stopple your gab, Mary Pat."

"I'll tell our mam!"

"She's down below with pale Nora," said Finn. "I'll blunt my tongue when you mend your flissome ways."

"I'm no flissome, Finn M'Cool." Mary Pat flounced. She could do that, sitting. "Was nobbut a pleasant chat."

"It's so they start," Dan nodded solemn, "the hip-swayers who stroll up jetty and down again of a fine evening. Yes," he said, "they start out smiling to some boy's honey words. You best take care, Mary Pat."

"Was nobbut a pleasant chat," she repeated, wiping her eyes with the back of her hand, "no more nor that."

⌐

Nora stopped coughing. Then she stopped wheezing. Her breaths come slower and slower till the heave was altogether gone from her. When she was every speck blue, Cider Mother lifted her in her arms and cradled her, so, to the kiln. The mad violist sawed at his strings in the Hunt Wagon's prow.

⌐

Mary Pat said, "Did you hear that cry?"

"That was the viol," Finn said, knuckles to his teeth.

"He stands at Wagon prow," Dan said, staring straight at the garret ceiling and the webs cobs had wove there.

"What's all the fire?" said Mary Kath.

"That's the crematoria, as I told you of before. Get down from off my knee, Mary Katharine, you're too big to be light on me these days."

"Am I grown so big?"

"You are and all," he told her. "Keep it up and you'll be a fine figure of a girl. Why, they'll cast you for a prowwoman, all streamy hair and double size, on the lookout for reef or rock, your eyes large as my head, each shoe long as a Hunt pike; and you'll need those shoes for you'll be too large to fit withindoors, up and down jetty you'll trample all your days, wheezing, 'Ah, and if only I had no stealen the porridge from neath my brother's nose, I'd be still a decent dreg-sized being!'" He pushed Finn's shoulder, here, and Finn he pushed him back, and they two tussled on the floor while the sisters pressed their eyes to the hagioscope. It was full of flames that licked the Wagon's iron belly, orange and red and deep blue at the base.

⟨⟩

The flames leapt, ate flesh, left bone-ash behind. Cider Mother stepped back from the kiln, and wiped her palms down her pinna, over and over. The flames leapt high. The bones whined as they cracked. The horns blew, the viol sobbed, the drums rolled on, rolled on.

⟨⟩

"What are those atop the Wagon?"

"Musicians, Mary Kath," said Dan, his hands over his ears.

"Listen close," said Finn, his ear gainst the windowsill. "That's drums. *Tappita-tappita*, quick as rat hearts beat, hear?"

"They say Musicians is good value," said Mary Pat, buffing her nails on her thigh.

"Oh shutter up," said Dan, and Finn he said the same. They and Mary Pat stared at the cobwebs above them like they was studying to weave them.

"And there's the viol in the prow?" said Mary Kath.

"Yeah, you can hear him thirling from up the orchard, even, he's a sound on him," said Finn, his eyes fixed still on the webs.

"Drums, strings, and the brassy horns, all that's Musicians," said Mary Pat, her eyes never leaving the cobwebs a hand's reach from her.

"Never heard it when I was down cellar with our mam. Down cellar you can no hear it separate like this," said Mary Kath.

"Cellar walls is solid thick," said Dan, pacing the garret's length. Two strides and turn, two strides and turn again.

"Down cellar you can no feel the heat, neither," said Mary Kath.

"The crematoria puts out a good blaze," said Finn.

"Takes a good heat to render those bones," said Dan.

He and Finn and Mary Pat was still eyes fixed on the ceiling webs. Looked like the three olders could drawn every web in the attic, strand for strand accurate. Mary Kath shrugged. No accounting for what olders got up to. Sides, the music was main lovely. "Musician," she said. "That's what I sha' be when I grow up."

"Always say, *should* I grow up, Mary Kath," said Mary Pat, absent, counting strands.

"Yeah. It's bad luck to say *when*," said Finn.

"Sides, females can no be Musicians," said Dan.

"Can too."

"Can no."

"Can too," till they fell on each other in tussle. It took Dan nobbut four heartbeats to pin Mary Kath's arms to the garret floor.

The flames fell in on themselves, their yellow and orange rinds fallen away, their blue hearts swole and steady, ranging over the last shreds of meat, hissing as they turned the last shreds to smoke and fat that pooled mong the ashes. The flames licked the meat and drank from the fat pools. Tween the blue flickers the bones shone white, and the ashes grey, and then all went dim in the bloodsmoke. The viol rasped and screeched as the foul flesh pulled away from the bones.

Dan pulled away off from Mary Katharine, and helped her to her feet. "Put your eyes to the scope," he said. "Comes now the scavengers — you do no want to find yourself alone with a scavenger. Richards let them out the stone scrapers just for Hunts, to pulp what's left behind, toss it in those sacks, and carry them to the richards who give them potable same as the bag weighs."

"You can get potable, so?" said Mary Pat.

"You can," he said, "if you're agreeable to sleep in a straw pile foul with your own wastes." The three youngest shuddered. "Right aright, then. We'll keep getting potable like we been doing," and turned away from the scope. "They're done now, any road."

"But what of the rest?" said Mary Kath. "What of the tumblers, the dancers, the shaggy fur as walked on long sticks, I did no ask you —"

"There'll come a next time, Mary Kath," said Finn. "Live long enough, you see everything, mam says."

They walked down stairs slow, coughing a bit on the smokecloud as hung dank and low on the cobblestones.

⟋

The smoke turned white and then blew off altogether as the last of the flesh burned from off the bones. White bones lay mong old ash. The howling neath the music died away. Cider Mother wiped her damp face on her pinna.

⟋

The Hunt Wagon passed.

# Up the Orchard I

OUT OF COURSE, James Aloysius can no come up the orchard. Off scavenging with his passel, James A." Cider Mother stompled up the stones, digging herbage out the cracks with short, precise jabs of her stick. "Come *long*, Daniel, and you Finn," she shouted downpath.

"Well, Gov Don does think the world of James A," said her sister Constance, shoving some foliars off the cliff. "Could make a *book* out all these," shaking a stone at Olympia.

"Ayuh," said Cider Mother, "or a beheader," miming the quick backhand toss as'd send the thin leaf downpath. She grimaced.

"Ought no twist so rapido, Olympe, at your time of life you did no ought."

"Willa stopple tha' chuntering, Con."

"Willna."

"Best!"

"Shanna."

"Was the spawn to hear us ... These cliffwalls shed so quick," said Cider Mother, shoving a spall offpath. "Gov Don thinks the world of James A, he does and certain. Reckons his worth so high he lists James A for any farflung scavenge passel."

"Mong the stone scrapers?" Cider Mother nodded. "Well," Connie said, "it's good fortune, then, he never thought much of my Kevin."

Cider Mother plucked a cress from a stone-edge. "Willa look now, Con, gone already to seed, this has." She shook the seedheads round them. "You're right there. Gov Don he's such regard for James A he lets him off home but three-four times in the year."

Connie shifted her basket further up her back. "Well, is that no the way of it for scavengers."

"Since James A come off the ships —"

"Since his dap died."

"There's that. Anyhow, since he went for scavenger, James A comes home for reaping," said Cider Mother.

"Mmm-hmm." Connie grapped a blackberry ramping over path, took it careful tween its thorns, and bent the woody back on itself. "You've the two floors out of it, no? ... come *long*, Mary Patricia ... and you've most months out the year when James A's out from under, no? Not to say the potable as flows to the M'Cools, eh? What of that now?"

"There's all that," said Cider Mother, heavy.

"Keeps the spawn well-spaced, does it no?"

"Shutter up, Con."

"Canna make me."

"If tha doesna ... come *long*, slugleg spawn," said Cider Mother. "This is the twist, here."

The blackberries was higher nor Dan's head and went onandon far as the eye could see. Far as Mary Kath's eyes could see, any road. "We're going in *there?*" she whispered to Finn.

It was Mary Pat as answered, a workaday Mary Pat, her copper hairs wound up off her head in cloth strips, a tea-color pinna stiff down her front and back, thick brogues on her feet. "Fore we can celebrate your Seventh, Mary Katharine, we plant you a tree." she said, "Naught to fret on. We done this a dunnamany times."

"I been coming up the orchard since fore you was born, Mary Kath, and I come back each time scatheless," said Dan.

"I'm no *fretting*," Mary Kath insisted. "I'm nobbut *asking*, is all."

"I see," Mary Pat took her hand. "Next year, come your Seventh, you sha' be crowned so, Mary Katharine M'Cool, bravest of dregs, the —"

"Shutter up," Dan suggested. "We come to the twist."

Mary Pat paid him all the mind she ever did. "Richards can no do this, Mary Kath, too swolegut to slither tween the brambles, and their clothes catch their fine threads."

"Can they no wear spagcloth?"

Mary Pat shook her head, grave. "They can no. Their least clothes, their rags, even, is silks and velvets; likely they'd perish was they to slip

inside spagcloth, their skin'd clamp up on them and the poisons rise to
their heads and —"

"Mary Pat! Come *long!*" shouted Cider Mother.

Mary Kath shuffled long in their wake, last cept Dan who brought up
the rear. The blackberries was overhead and all round and she could no stop
lest Dan think her frighted by a mess of blackberry. So she went on. The
vines was thicker nor her neck and bristling with thorns; they ranged fierce
towards her, appearing to favor her face and ankles, closer and closer as the
tunnel narrowed and again narrowed as they pushed forward. They none of
them spoke, though Dan grunted up in his nose a few times when Mary
Kath held back a woody vine for him just long enough for it to slap him
cross the hatbrim. After they was gouged a few good times, and was forced
to crab sidewise so to slip tween the vines, the blackberries ended, sudden,
and they come out under the sky, their brogues crushing mint as they shuffled forward. They paused in the lee of the brambles till their eyes narrowed
down to the bright of the day, the sun throwing down its rays in furious
shafts as spiked them soon as they come out from neath the thorny hedge.

"The orchard," Dan waved his less-gouged arm with a flourish. "Orchard, Mary Katharine; Mary Kath, orchard." He raised his hat and pushed
his black hair off his face. The sweat gleamed on his high bronze cheekbones; his dark blue eyes was black in the sun. Finn's eyes lightened from
calm-sea green to leaf-green as he moved from the sun to the spockled shade
of an apple tree. Cider Mother, deep in the grove, unwrapped blanket-rolls;
her eyes was dark brown in the shade, but their green flecks danced under
the leaves. Mary Pat's eyes was the mirror of them, kelp floating on their
green pools each time she stepped into a sun-shaft.

"What color are my eyes?" said Mary Kath.

Cider Mother straightened, a hand to the small of her back, and
cupped the girl's chin in her hand. "You've gloaming eyes, Mary Katharine,
as match the last light of the longest day." She stepped back, tilting Mary
Kath's eyes to the light. "Are they no, Con?"

"Dark blue I'd say, with a green streak for good luck." Constance patted Mary Kath's head. "Green in the sky means rain's coming, Mary Kath;
good luck altogether."

"Why?" said Mary Kath, but Connie and Cider Mother was airing the blankets on the lowest branches. The apple flowers was tucked inside themselves like old dregs drowsing in narrow jetty shade, arm thrown up to guard their heads at midday. "Why'd we come up here in heat of the day?" she asked till Mary Pat answered her: "So's to scape notice, Mary Kath."

"Why'd we no come up —"

Daniel sat crossleg on the springing mint and hauled Mary Kath to anchor gainst his knee. He played clap-hands with her: "Stars is out, scutmen about; break of day, dregs haul away; sun falls down, promenade round — but midday heat is time to snore; streets is empty, none ashore." Mary Kath clapped hands, laughing. Dan looked up to get Cider Mother's smile smack in his eye and looked down again quick, fore Mary Kath could see. "So," he continued, "when streets is empty, there's no eyes to look on and *was* they to look on, they'd suspicion naught. 'What? The M'Cools gone picnic? In heat of the day? Those fool M'Cools,' is all they'd say." He folded her hands. "Whenever you've aught to do you want no eyes on, Mary Kath, do you set about it in full glare like you'd every right to."

"Like we'd a chit from Gov Don himself," she said, and Dan picked her up and swung her round. "But why'd we come up at all?" she asked, and Dan set her down.

Cider Mother held Mary Kath's chin: "We come cause here's where we get the wherewith for two squares a day and potable enough for all. Your Seventh's later down the year, Mary Katharine; we come up to plant you a sapling, like we done for Daniel, and Mary Patricia, and Finn—"

"All of them stayed living," said Mary Kath.

"Ayuh. Lucky chance, that," said Cider Mother, still holding the girl's chin. "You'll start work in the morning, Mary Katharine."

"Real sprat work you'll be doing," Finn encouraged her.

Mary Pat and Daniel jigged round singing: So *spawn become sprats, so sprats turn to work* —

Finn joined them: *Work turns sprats to dregs, then turns dregs to dust* —

Cider Mother let loose of Mary Kath, who leapt up and jigged:

*Dust blows through the town, then dregs chew it down, they fuck till they're blown, then new spawn is born ...*

Round and round they jigged, trampling the dry grass, till the heat of the day felled them. All of them huddled in the orchard shadepools for an hour or so, the olders drowsing, the rest blowing grassblades held tween their thumbs. Finn and Mary Kath rolled downhill, crushing mint as they neared the wall of blackberries backlit by the dropping sun. In the brief cool of twilight, the olders paced mong the trees, planning the morning's work. Finn, a year past his Seventh, was old enough to pace longside, waving his arms as they did, pointing his finger a beat behind Cider Mother's, shaking his head beat for beat with theirs at the profuse of blossom.

Mary Kath wandered off to pluck danlions. She was weaving a wreath of them when she heard the squeaks. She got up to vestigate, as any body would, parting the long grass clump by clump till she found them.

A nestfull of flat-nose round-eye pups whose ears flopped anyhow, who somersaulted for no cause, chased their tails, tumbled in wrestle till they dropped by ones and twos to sleep in soft piles of pupfur. Mary Kath made of her lap a mountain range the pups scaled, chittering, their feeble claws snagging her pinna as they slid in squeaks off her knees; squeaks that brought their mam raging. Their mam froze in drawnback lips and yellow glare when she saw Mary Kath. Her mangy fur twitched on her skin erupt with larval burrows, her bitten tail lashed dust, her face was all mouth and her mouth was all rotted purple. A few draps of bile trailed from a corner of her swole gums. She dragged her bloated dugs, each ringed by pus-seep petals, through the dust zig and zag to her squeaking pups, her eyes steady on Mary Kath's the while, till she was nobbut a cubit from them, at when the pups stampeded the crawling rat, knocked her sideways with their hunger, palpated her belly till it flowed with milk and pus. Their mam craned her drazzled snout over her back and snarled. As the pups sucked, the yellow eyes kept Mary Kath in glare as the girl rose easy and slow from the ground, as she walked backward slow and easy, till she turned and raced toefirst to the pacing olders.

When she told Finn of it, later, when they was cocooned gainst the nightcold atop a heap of dried grass, he grunted and rolled into sleep. Mary Kath harrumphed; that ratmam could return and snap her long yellow teeth closed in their flesh for all Finn cared. Well, Mary Katharine M'Cool would stay awake all night long till the moon went down, she would, till the moon went, she would, so to keep vigil lest, she would, till the moon, she.

Seaward breeze woke her, lifting the hairs off her scalp. Cider Mother and Constance was already up and about, pulling ryecakes from tins, carboys from baskets, spawn from their cocoons. "The trees is lit with seashine," said Mary Kath, but Cider Mother said they'd no time to stand gawk, there was the pollen to dust on pistil so fruit'd come, "The tall ones is sprat work, Mary Kath," so the girl trotted after her mam, sticking her nose in every blossom she could reach, while Cider Mother twirled her pinky round each swole pistil faster nor eyes could follow. Finn, Mary Pat, and Dan was up the treetops, likewise nuzzling blossoms, when the sun inched over the sandstone cliffs.

The first light and the first crack come together. Mary Kath flatted to the ground, "It's nobbut a limb broke neath Dan's weight," said Cider Mother, and handed the girl a second ryecake. Mary Kath snatched a bite tween one apple tree and the next, rubbing sleep out her eyes with the back of her hand, getting her nose far down in each white blossom, her nosehairs gold with their pollen, "Get your beak down in there, Mary Kath," bite of ryecake, shuffle shuffle, next tree, swig of potable from Cider Mother's carboy and dip the nose and breathe and dip and —

Crack. "Go on to the next few thout me," said Cider Mother. Mary Kath pattled up hill snuffing blossoms till she was gold up to her gloaming eyes, while Cider Mother coaxed Dan up off the grass. "Your second Seventh's two years off, Daniel M'Cool," she told him, "and already you're too big to climb these trees," and suchlike crooning till Dan was mawdled back to upright shape. When he'd some spine to him, Cider Mother led him to the shinegreen mint patch at slopetop. On the humps of that patch, the most stubborn enduring of last year's apple seeds had took root. Cider Mother emptied her pockets of ryecake crumbs, absent, near a hump of dusty turf. "It's no just the weight, Daniel. It's the nose."

"I got a nose," all offended, twelve years on him and look how good he was at that already.

"You've a nose and a fine one, sure, that weighs one gainst the other. The spawn snuffle up whatever's in their path and they're invaluable, so."

Cider Mother stroked his cheek in a rare caress. "Con and me, we could use you down on the ground, any road; our knees —"

"What's that squeaking?" said Daniel.

"Squeaking? I was saying, knees start to give out past the fourth Seventh, and your —"

"I heard squeaking plain as plain."

"Did you now? So, with the height on you, we could use you to pollen the mid-tree flowers, then me and Con we could —"

"Coming from that dusty turf-hump," said Daniel.

Cider Mother raised one eyebrow. "Pay it no mind," she said. "We got today and tomorrow, only, to pollen all these flowers, so let's take the stoutest of these chance-sown, plant it for Mary Katharine, and get on with the work." They knelt and prised one seedling from the mucky loam. "Keep a clump of muck round it, so it feels the shock less," said Cider Mother, a hand to the small of her back as she stood to watch him carry it downslope. The ryecrumbs was all gone from round the turfhump. She emptied her other pocket's crumbs before she followed Dan.

As she walked downslope she paused at the chest-high sapling they planted for Shanny, who drowned, and at Brendan's small tree, who got the buboes on him and was burned therefore. Nora'd no tree, the poor creature'd lacked the strength to live till her Seventh. Constance stood by her side as Dan held the seedling upright, as Mary Pat showed Mary Kath how to ease the soil round its roots, as Finn patted the mounded loam. When they was done, they turned to Cider Mother to give the blessing. She raised her eyes to the sun, clear of the sandstone bluffs, to the sea, dull green and white patches above the blackberry thicket, and lowered her eyes to the four bronze spawn round her and her sister's runneled face and the small seedling quivering in the morning breeze and the apple blossoms unfurled to the muted, early sun and she said, "This one's for Mary Katharine. Take hold and grow strong."

*So spawn become sprats, so sprats turn to work, work turns sprats to dregs, then turns dregs to dust.*

"You're in it now," said Finn.

"You're in for it now," said Mary Pat.

# Spag Diving

WHEN THEY WAS SPAWN, the days rolled by like midsummer waves. Mary Katharine and Finn worked at their studies; cleanhand hours bent over crumble books, taking it in turn to be Henry and Romo and Rosali and Julet; and they worked at their chores after a fashion. When they was put to grinding rye, crushing the kernels with a watersmooth cobble in a scoopstone tween their short legs, they rolled ryeballs and shot them cross the wonky floorboards. Mary Patricia raked them down for their lackdaisy sorting: "The rocks and shells? Those are the bits we take *out* the kelp." In the back of all, Cider Mother hummed down-cellar mong the mash-tuns, while the mornings rolled by, and nuncheon came and went, and they lay on their pallets through the heat of the day, and rose from them when the sun come through the shutter warps, and swept or ground or scrubbed as their mam directed till the sun was dropping low and fiery, when they ran circles round Cider Mother long the promenade, then scappered upstones home for ryegruel, then lay on their pallets *again* though they was no whit sleepy, talking soft while the olders sat round the kitchen table talking and talking in pullulate waves that rolled and crested and gathered themselves and crashed gainst the shore, and one wave darked their eyes, and that was sleep, and so the days rolled by.

Cepting sometimes. Sometimes, Cider Mother broke off humming, Times she'd resume the hum, but othertimes she'd call, "Spawn!" It was no a shriek like many mams give out; what Cider Mother needed you to hear come to you low and thrum. Her spawncry was a drop-all sound that she gave only when it was needful, absolute, that every spawn in hearshot come on the quick. Times it was a treat as'd spoil easy, times it was a rat in the arras — either how, did they hear it, they ran hotfoot.

Times it meant they was near out of spag. Finn and Mary Kath had watched out of window as Mary Pat and Daniel sledged off with Cider

Mother at first dark and come back fore the sun did. "They're getting spag from out the stone scrapers," Finn said. Dan told him more nor he'd say to Mary Kath. You had to have spag, Dan said. Spag made light in dark places; they lit themselves upstairs after gruel by spaglight, while the older ones chuntered on belowstairs by spaglight. Mary Pat and Dan got to gather spag cause they was always, always older, though still light enough to walk downtilt the fallen stones to the spag pool in the cellar of the cloaca publica. Finn should gone a couple year since. Cider Mother said he was slow getting his growth. Mary Pat said he was a dwarf changel, a knee-biter to his bones; she said the gobbles laid stones on his head while he slept, cramping his height, so. But Cider Mother said to pay no mind to Mary Pat. Finn said naught, but when they two was alone he spent hours hanging from the doorframe with Mary Kath pulling down on his feet, so to stretch himself.

Which must, finally, done the trick. Because one morning, when Finn was ten and Mary Kath eight, Cider Mother let out a spawncry and it was them, she said, it was to be them on the sledge, it was them as would gather spag for the M'Cools.

Course they asked the why of it. How'd spag come to the cloaca cellar? Cider Mother lied to no-one, but you could walk from sunup to full dark and still no find a body as could circle the truth like her. Cider Mother told them the spag came there long since, it was there a long time, and speaking of time there was none to waste if they was to eat a special dinner of carpball stew and applecake, and if they was done screeching the roof off the house, she said, they was to wipe their hands and come to table, for they'd need to sleep straight from midday to sundown so to be fresh for the expedition.

Course they did no sleep. The sun dropped out of the sky summat jerky, maybe, and they did rest their eyes betimes, but who could sleep on the cusp of an Expedition? So Finn and Mary Kath drowsed away the sledge-ride to the city of stone scrapers, cocooned in wraps, and woke full when the sledge juddered to a stop at the stairfoot of the cloaca publica.

Cider Mother kept vigil out in the air while Dan led them the most of the way down, that first time, and it was he told them.

"Mind the slab," said Dan. He was three weeks past his second Seventh, already tall as the mash-tun and straight as a spike, he was oldest son, responsible and warmheart son, his black hair falling in his dark blue eyes no matter how often their mam cut it with her sharp paring knife. He balanced on the tiltslab that filled the building's maw. "You got to walk this line, else it shifts neath you." Mary Kath and Finn followed him neath the arch, wriggled tween its gaping swordpoint bars, shuffled long the sill inside the stone wall thick as they was high, and down the stone stairs set by joinery into the wall. The most of the stairflight was still joined to the wall.

"Where's spag come from, Dan?" said Finn.

"From the burned dead. Now there's gaps —"

"What, from the crisps?" said Mary Kath.

"Yeah, it come from out their bodies."

"I sha' move no step till you tell all, Dan," said Mary Kath. She haunkered down on the step, and Finn he did the same.

Dan sat two steps above them. Even then, he liked to be up high as he could. "Well. I have this from dap, which he said he got from his grandap's voice. In the Great Burning, a dunnamany people worked in the cloaca publica. They was most of them lardass, nobbut chairdust, tosspails for food and then more food which they slung down the gullet maybe three four plates a day —"

"No," said Finn.

"Dap said. Said his grandap's voice told him clear as you hear me now. They thought they could waddle down-cellar of the cloaca publica and there lie safe through the Burning. Lookit all what they left behind them, which we been mining since dap remembers, and you'll see that their leavings prove past doubting that they was swoleguts one and all. Anyhow, all them lardboys and oleogirls waddled over here to keep safe, must been packed tight as nestlings when the flames come through. Dap said the flames was so hot they burnt quick as you can chant summer rats from out the grass; one second they was sighing, may be, next the fat was spooling off them and rolling downgrate to the undercellar."

Finn and Mary Kath was silent, hunched on stone steps worn low in their middles off years and years of use, feet going upstairs and feet coming downstairs, all those feet as once trippled up and down those stairs now gone to spag.

Dan said, "Mind the gaps to these stairs. Best no fall tween —"

"No," said Mary Kath, looking through a three-stair gap at a jumble of rusty bars, four fathoms below.

"So you help each other. See? And remember, there's no rats to fear; spag's death to them as it'd be to you did you put the least speck in your mouth. Mind, now." (Back then it was common for Dan to speak kind. In after time, Finn reminded Mary Kath that Dan was once their shield.) "Me and James A laid this cable. There's two loops near this end of it, see? Finn, now, slide your bony ass into the larger loop, and put your hand through the smaller loop at cable's end, so. Grab the spaglamp. You've to mind it, now, none can aid you do you set fire to the spag. All right?" Finn nodded. "Good boy. Now hold fast. Are you ready?" Finn nodded. "I'll ease you down, now."

Finn's knuckles gleamed in the spaglight as Dan let him down, hand over hand. Mary Kath clamped her tongue tween her back teeth. Dan's nose was pinched thin as a knife till Finn landed safe and hollered up: "Come on, Mary Kath." Dan hauled up the cable, Mary Kath fitted herself in its loops and lifted her unlit spaglamp high. Dan's nose was gone pinched again, eyes wide on hers as she swayed down past stumps of stair-joins till she landed next her brother all laughing.

"Good enough," said Dan. He drew up the cable and lashed a brace of pails to the loops. "Stand away," he said.

"But what of you, Dan?"

"I remain above. I'm too weighty for the cable, now. I'll talk you through the rest; it's no hard for two so canny and spry as you." Finn and Mary Kath tried to look unco' canny. "You've but the one small rubbleheap to climb — now up and over — now that was naught, am I right?"

"Naught, to be sure," said Finn. His voice rang flat on the stones.

"Now head back towards me neath the stairs, there's a bit of an alley, like, see it?"

"Yeah."

"Keep coming ... yeah ... watch that spar; it longs to spill on you, al-most did for me, first time ... okay ... you done that lovely, better nor I did, first time in ... now you pass through that square hole, see it?"

"Leads to t'other side of the wall the stones is sunk in?" said Finn.

"That's the one." They raised high the spaglamps as they eased long the alley to the square hole that led away from Dan's voice. "Listen close. You'll be out of hearshot soon as you do what I say next, got it?"

"Yeah."

"You'll no be able to hear me once you're through the square hole, so if you've any question *soever*, one of you'll come to where you're right now standing. Got it?"

"Got it," said Finn.

"Okay. Wriggle through there and scoop the clear only and lay it in the pail, then come straight back to where you're standing now. Got it?"

"Got it," said Finn. He went through the hole, then Mary Kath passed him the pails, then she wriggled up to the ledge. She was about to turn round and lower herself when Finn, inside, raised his lamp high.

Through the square hole was a room made of pillars connected by arch on point-top arch as folded in above the pillars like hands covering a bowl, forming a dome of blue and white all burnt black round its rim. Each arch was carved in shape of leaves, and all the stone ran with blue veins like the veins in their palms. Rusted grates tween the pillars, from a few of which still hung the iron pipes, all burst and splorn, that was set to drain those grates. The pipes was swole with spag, encased in spag, as shining free of rust as they must been in the moment of their burst.

The pillars nearest the square hole was scraped clean of spag to their bases. The yellow spag stretched off from that half-circle as level and smooth as the harbor after storm, near as high as Finn's shoulders. Mary Kath let herself down off the ledge and wiped her hands on her tunic. "Best spag's the top spag, Cider Mother says, and I'm lightest," she said.

Finn nodded. They'd had this out before. He ran cable through a ring in the wall, and hooked one end to Mary Kath's belt, the way he could drag her back out did the spag suck her feet from under. He handed her the pail and ladle, and squatted for her to climb his back. He stood, easy, and she climbed, easy, off his back and onto the spag crust. Her landing, light as it was, set the spag heaving; its blistered crust folded in corruscate, its carmine underlay shuddered like a stiff kelpmat, floating on the underspag that quivered and pouted and wept a few plotches. "Lie down on it like it was low-tide muck. It'll hold you better, so," warned Finn. She stretched herself careful on the spag crust and set her pail by its edge. Swole-bellied darters hovered, viridian and fuchsia, over the crust. Fly hum danked gainst the old cold stone walls. She sliced into the crust, easy, and folded its rubbery stiffness back to expose the topspag.

There was all marvel of stuff inside the spag. Once the thin crust was breached, the spag was yellow-clear; as Mary Kath's eyes adjusted to the dim light, they could make out bulk shapes and then the scroll and line of them. There was vacuoles where other creatures had tried to cross the spag crust and sunk deep, great hairy legs and long thin bones in clouds of pale brown. There was wormtrack through the fresh-mined spag where the motion had jagged it just so loose that a mindless creature with hooks on its mouths could get a purchase.

Mary Kath took a first scoop of the clear stuff neath the crust. She plopped it in the pail, tapped the ladle's handle on the pail-rim to expel the full takings, took a breath, and scooped another. And another. When she'd half-filled the pail, she eased it, crawling slow on her belly, to an arms-length from the crust edge, where Finn swapped it for an empty. Then they did it again. And again. While she ladled, he poured one half-pail into the other, and set the full pail on the ledge. He would no leave the dome while Mary Kath lay balanced on the spag crust. When the full pail was set on the ledge, Finn hollered up to Dan to lower the hook-end by its cable. Finn hooked pail handle to it, called "Hoy!" and ducked back neath the square hole while Dan hauled up the bucket. Then they did it again. And yet again for an hour, two hours, three; no way to tell time's passage in the under-cellar far from sky or wind.

So there was no way to tell how long they was in to it when the ladle thwocked something hard. Finn and Mary Kath looked at each other all thrill; well who'd no be thrilled? Mary Kath scraped all round the place with the ladle till she uncovered a crumble book from the spag.

Mary Kath sighed, "All that for naught."

Finn come down off the ledge and took it out her hands. "Some part's still good," he said. Inside its spag skin, the book's boards was scorched black; when they parted its boards, the burnt places went to crumble in their hands, their edges black. There was whole places mong the blackened pages. Finn's nose was down mong them, his spaglamp held high, but Mary Kath was full of scheme.

"Those are *stone* shelves gainst the far wall," she said. "Must be, else they would burned. And there's more of these books on them, Finn."

Finn nodded, rapt in a blackfringe page. "Listen to this. '*No marble, nor the gilded monuments / Of princes, shall outlive this powerful rime;*' wait, there's more ..."

"If we could get cross the room we could have *all* those books."

"Something something '*unswept stone, besmear'd with sluttish time.*'"

"We could *read* the more, could we but get those books to home. Look at them all!" Mary Kath wranked her hands together. "Could we but get to them, we'd be rich as —"

"Can no cross spag, Marekat, you're no to even think on it, see what happens an you do," pointing to a worm track long as his arm. "I'll holler Dan to raise us do you take one step that way."

"No need. A fearsome end, that, drowned in uncured spag," and they come close together, imagining the stuff sucking at their feet, slowly drawing them in. Flies and darters hummed in fatbelly circles neath the dome.

"How beautiful it must been here," said Finn.

"Sure. Look at those pillars. But they dislaid it."

"They what?"

"Maybe that's no how you say it. But I been staring down its face for a good time now. Can you no feel it through your skin? How the people was, here, fore the Burning? Passing neath these dreamwing arches; the swoleguts spat pits on the floor, scrawled mustaches on the faces" — strange bloated faces magnified by the melted fat — "do you no see? but *they* did no see the place. They come rushing down here to lay one lot of papers atop another, slammed close the doors, and rushed off again, knuckling cobwebs out their eyes. Can you no see them, Finn? Those swoleguts waddled downstairs to this carved beauty like we dive into a Moraine, like we can no skip out that skank fast enough; pile our drap of rubble on the nearest heap and we're away."

Finn rubbed his hands together. "You think they brought *on* the Burning by their ways? Think if we —"

"Finnegan! Mary Katharine!" Dan's holler come in zigzag bounce down the stairwell: "Have you made up your minds to live down there? Shall I tell our mam there's two stewplates the more for the rest of us?"

Finn laid his hand on Mary Kath's shoulder, "Come long now. We'll talk of this with Cider Mother."

"Mmm. And Dan," said Mary Kath. Finn nodded and ducked back through the entry with the crumble book and hollered Dan they'd nobbut the last pail to fill, and he should take what's in this pail and keep it safe.

Mary Kath filled the last pail with quivering spag. Well, it was all safe enough down here, it was no going to melt or shab off, and surely tween her and Finn they'd figure how to walk cross the spag crust and grab out all those books. There was dozens of them and then some; the richards themselves could no have so many. The crumble books she'd seen from out the spag cellar was lists of numbers going left right and up down with a few squig letters atop each column, of which they none of them could make a scrap of sense; or forms, lots of forms, each sheet same as the next cept the spaces on them full of the hot round writing of hands that now was ash. "Ash!" she shouted. "Did the either of you remember we was told off to gather three-four buckets of ash?"

There was more hollering tween Dan and Finn to which she paid no mind as she plopped scoop after viscous scoop into the pail. The spag was dead smooth just here, if she'd a knife stead of this blunt ladle she could carve it into blocks or pyramids; well, time enough to ponder that when she was to home again; she and Cider Mother could sit round the kitchen doing 'gorry frissome slaving' as Mary Pat called it, and carve spag as they liked, fore they tossed it in the copper. She swung the full pail towards the entry door but could no lift it over the lintel by herself. "Finn!" but no answer. "Finn! Last bucket's full!" but no answer. She counted the books she could see cross the undercellar. There was twenty-six for sure and certain, and likely more on shelves neath the spag crust. "Finn!"

"The both of you thinks hollering shoves the sun through the sky," Finn grumbled. "Time moves the same pace for us all, fret and holler will no change that," which was their mam's slow morning grumble since they could remember. "Ash does no leap into buckets by its lonesome, me and Dan pulled up four buckets, and sieved ash, mind you, no a bone to the lot." He lugged the full pail to Dan's cable and come back for her. "Come now, Mary Kath," he said. "These things will no shift once we take our eyes off them."

They clambered up the cables, past the stairgaps and over the tiltslabs to the corner where Cider Mother sat in alcove next to Dan. "You're back, so," was all she said. "Give me a hand up and we'll haul this good work home." Dan had the gurney loaded ready. They each grabbed a carrypole and wrassled the pole to a shoulder and set off on the long walk home. They sang as they walked, 'like a bunch of coulees,' Mary Pat would said:

*The yellow down runs down, runs down / The yellow runs to clear / What burns away is dust in ground / What's left sha' see us clear*

"Where's that song from, mam?" said Finn.

"I dunno," she said. "We always sung it, coming back from spag diving." She nodded with the motion of their hauling. Dan shifted more of the weight to his own shoulder. They trotted forty-seven huffs fore she spoke again. "There's stew to home."

"Mary Pat, too?" said Mary Kath.

"Yeah, even our slackwaist Mary Patricia sha' have stew. She can no help how she is, Mary Katharine. It tires a body down to the bone, seeing the days to come. It's no steady, you know. The come and go of it rasps her considerable."

"I know, mam. But why is it she never sees aught of interest?"

"She'll grow into it, Marekat."

Mary Kath gave a small sigh. But then she gave a small skip, for was she no out in the dark of night alone with Finn and Dan and Cider Mother? Was it no Mary Kath as had swung down stairs and filched the spag? Had she no seen the days gone by all buried in the spag?

They jogged home quiet, passing the rubble piles of Dead Horse Moraine in the hour fore first light, back when they was young, back when everything was known or would be.

# The Shingle

MARY KATHARINE M'COOL walked the wrack-line, kicking stray flints at the incoming tide. Thud, on the strip of sand tween high and neap tides, thud on the smooth ribbon above the muck and below the shingle, the waves mumbling over the muck like an old mouth gumming its porridge, thud on the sand the only soft sound in all of Charnholm, may be, cepting a nine-flail whopping on some bare ass-cheeks: what else was soft on this harsh day? Cider Mother's breast dropping on James Aloysius laid down in the front room. That was a sound as had no sound at all to it. Nobbut silence where James A's breath was used to be. Mary Kath turned abrupt and paced the wrack-line back towards Charnholm, but that was no good. Charnholm was full, just this now, of big tearsoak eyes and downturn lips and *there there*; there was no place Mary Kath could walk in Charnholm proper as was free of wide wet pity eyes, so no; she spun away off from Charnholm. She walked down to tideline and let the rivvels swish round her heels in chuttering white foam till she was ankle-sunk.

Why would Mary Patricia choose this of all days to throw a frense, tears out her eyes, sweat out her pores, snot dreeling from her nose, probably pissing herself, what with every spout thrown wide; why today? Today was a plaster clump in a loosewove box, crumbling away to naught as you breathed on it. But for Mary Pat today was the day to roust up the drama — Mary Kath spat at a clump of flotsam — till it was more than a body could stand up to. She kicked a flint all the way up to the jetty, till she was sneck in its lee, back against its stones, naught in her eyes but sea, naught in her ears but promenade voices chuntering on like always:

*Where's Inkwhistle?*

*Too zausted for promenade, this night*

*Inkwhistle, he's past it*

*Fore the Burning, he'd been a Smith, likely*

*Yeah, and fore the Burning potable flowed out the rocks, likely*
*There was more Smiths fore the Burning, certain*
*Oh ah? And chalders of grain dropped from the sky?*
*Shutter up*
*Shutter up*
*Shutter up, richards coming*
(*Shammajank, shimsham, shuffle tug.* Kneeling dregs pull their forelocks.)
(Coulee grunts as they set down the palankeen on the cobbles.)

"Good evening, good people, Lady Mandra and myself hope to see you at the coming Rat Hunt."

(*Jamjan woolshtenap bolla bolla nake.* The dregs shuffle their feet in gratitude.)

(Coulee grunts as they hoisted the palankeen again to their shoulders. Coulee feet *shuffle shammajank, shimsham.* Song.)

*The fat cat / On a mat / Who be gone to eat him? / The fat cat / Can no spat / He sha' be our meat then / The fat cat / On a –*

The coulee song receded.

There was pictures of cats in some of the crumble books Mary Kath and Finn had pulled out the spag. Toothy creatures they did look. James A's lips was drawn back off his teeth that morning. His lips was spag to eye and touch. Cider Mother kept stopping to pet them as she bustled round the front room, setting Daniel to take every last crumb of putrible out the house, out out, the while Dan nobbut stood there, arms hanging off his shoulders, till Finn and Mary Pat stepped up to his chores. She shook her head to get the picture out of her eyes, the heap of Nora's clothes toys blankets (and Brendan's fore her, and others, and still more after her) and Cider Mother drizzling spag over the heap and dropping a scoopful of hot coals on the spag and the whole going up hot and quick and blue like an arm punching from below — Mary Kath saw this wheresoever she looked, that morning, the sun burning her eyes something cruel each time she set them anywheres, the heap burning blue till she shook her head and cleared her eyes a bit. She looked up at the jetty where Nora's blue wrapper had burned, back years ago when they was spawn, where James A and all his would soon burn, and shook her head, and there was Mary Pat.

Mary Pat looked down from jetty at the short square determination that was Mary Kath, pacing the wrackline, getting her good boots all salt. Going on nine years old and the sense of a wet spawn. Course, it was no like sense came with years, you'd but to listen to these dregs shuffling their aches up jetty and down on nightly promenade, right out there in the open where richards could get at them with their patronize till your usual dreg was panting for richard stuff and wadding — which a lot of it was lovely, mind, the hat perched on Lady Mandra's head sucked the bags out from under her eyes till all you saw was the pool-blue of them, you could feel the soft of her lap-robe from this far down-jetty. But did these dregs feel the hooks in their flesh, or yen for what was, after all, nobbut fripperies? They did no. Shuffle, shuffle, up jetty and down, spouting.

*He's off the rope-walk?*

*Been a good while since Inkwhistle was on rope-walk*

*Seen his fifth Seventh come and go, he has*

*Be nobbut a dove-seller soon, Inkwhistle*

Mary Pat leaned over jetty to make sure Mary Kath was all of one piece. She'd gone to considerable trouble to get the girl out the house; Cider Mother said Mary Kath was too young to stand up to the busywork of death; Mary Pat'd had to throw a hiss and spit fore Mary Kath was roused sufficient to slam out the door; leastwise there she was now, walking shingle, she could hardly come to harm that way. Mary Pat straightened, and bit her teeth with the yank pain of her muscles. She and Finn had covered for Dan that morning. All his chores *and* theirs. And him just past his second Seventh, there was considerable heft to his chores. Mary Pat stretched and watched the passing male dregs eye her, stretching. *They* knew she was hori to come, right aright. Next spring, after pollening, she'd go for hori, finish her nova year by her second Seventh. She jumped up on the jetty wall and sat there, swinging her legs, craning her head over her shoulder betimes so to keep one eye on Mary Kath. Her long legs made the jump in one snatch, her copper hair sweeled round her head as she leapt, her bronze arms was covered in silver down, and all the world was right aright. Well. Was it no for their dap lying dead in the front room. Was it no for that. She stretched her long bronze arms overhead and watched necks crack as they took her in. Her arms ached down to the bone. Dan roused, finally, and took Finn off to snare the rats to lay at James A's feet, and it was good to see Dan come up behind his eyes again, but it was Mary Pat as swept the floor and masked the mirrors and ground the rye and shaped the cakes and lugged firkins of potable and carboys of scrumpy up the cellar stairs to the front room and swept the floor again and swaddled the dinner-bell and filled all the spag-lamps. Cider Mother kept saying they'd do these things together, and she'd start off fine, but a couple swipes cross the floor with the broom straws and their busy mam was gone stone again. When Mary Pat finally sent her down-cellar to stir the mash-tuns, Cider Mother nodded, cupped her swole belly, and sidled down the stairs. Mary Pat swept the floor again. It was no wonder she'd a band round her chest off all that sweeping and what-not.

> *Fore the Burning, Inkwhistle been a Smith, likely*
> *Fore the Burning potable flowed out the rocks, likely*
> *There was more Smiths fore the Burning, certain*
> *Shutter up*
> *If Inkwhistle can no stand up to it, who can?*
> *Shutter up*

This was Finn's fervent wish. That they'd shutter up. They would no. But he wished they would. Dan might wish summat, who could tell? He was a rat-slay automan this morning, he was, snatching them by tail and whirling them gainst stones, singing *James A has gone to clay*, till they was snuffed, no word passed his teeth's barrier cept, *James A has gone to clay*, as he slew them one after the next, bashed their brains out, white pulp all over the stones, *James A has gone* – Dan spat on the pulp mass and up again and took another. Finn clutched his cramp gut. Enough to turn your stomach, like he'd swallowed one of those whitepulp stones. He'd killed two rats for every three of Dan's; he'd no disgraced himself, but when you'd no dinner no breakfast no nuncheon, out of course the gut cramped. Their dap, James Aloysius, been off scavenging since fore Finn could remember, coming home some few times a year to sleep long next to Cider Mother, to wake to hold a cup of hot in his two cracked hands, to stare at the plaster lumping off the walls, to wander off to Gessel's shop where Finn was sent to gather him home for nuncheon, the men leaning gainst the shop walls, arms cross their chests, grunting at sight of Finn, at last coughing up James A. His dap walked home with Finn long the path, breathing through his clench teeth when he'd to haul his left leg up a rise, laying a gristle forearm over the boy's shoulders now and now. At table, James A squared his shoulders, said little, watched Cider Mother, who looked back at him tween spooning stew into bowls; they was in each other's eyes fore and after and all the while they cuffed Dan, laid spoons, cut bread, tilted the kilderkin of potable to fill the spawn's cups, drove a shim neath a table-leg; all the while they was rope-dancers on a single cord, from her eyes to his, and what was his mam to swing on now their cable was cut?

*Inkwhistle, hammp, he been all times peculiar*

*Snuffing round M'Cools now, likely*

*Can no abide a empty hole, Inkwhistle*

"Shutter up," Finn hissed through the fist he held gainst his mouth. "Shutter up shutter up shutter up." Course they'd no. Promenade dregs chuntered onandon like pus drooled from a rat's gash, slow, steady, death of a hundred drops.

Mary Pat strolled downjetty to where Finn stood hunchback, fist to mouth. They could none of them care for themselves thout she was by. Mary Pat sent him to tend Mary Kath, then leaned gainst the jetty, peeling orange mold from its lip. Finn, like a blade walking, balanced cross the shingle's angle stones to where Mary Kath was building a sand compound in spite of outrider waves off the rising tide three cubits short of washing her toes. Mary Pat peeled mold. Finn helped Mary Kath pack the sand tighter, build the walls higher, plant a kelp frond either side of the gates. Mary Pat tore mold peel into fine strips. Finn bent to Mary Kath's ear. The two of them strolled off. Well, good enough. Maybe they'd do some of the dunnamany chores Cider Mother thought needful. Mary Pat cut the head off each mold strip with her thumbnail. It was no like James A was home much, and when he *was* round he was flat-eyed by day, making sure the pallet had a good sag to its middle by jouncing on Cider Mother deep into the night. Mary Pat tossed the mold chips in her palm. On her Seventh, starched from one end to the other, James A took Mary Pat by the hand downpath and out the pier like she was Lady Mandra herself, walking a stair or two below her so she could lay her fingertips on the crook of his arm. But that was so long ago it might never happened. Dan said James A was used to be wily and strong and full of laugh, back fore his own dap died; Mary Pat had no recall of it soever. No matter. Sun shone out James A's eyes so far as Dan was concerned, always had; he was likely off mooning over the *Hail Janus*, burning stray hairs off the hawsers or summat. They'd know naught of James A's death on the *Hail Janus*. That'd be a comfort to Dan. Mary Pat shook out her copper hair and jumped down off the capstones. Finn and Mary Kath was near to the house. Time to go homewards herself. Probably no one emptied the tin of phlegm James A'd coughed up over the past three days, and there'd be the sheets to wash his sweat from, and the brew ready in the mash-tun needed pouring into carboys what with people coming by to weep and replace the liquid lost with Cider Mother's best scrumpy. Mary Pat laid her hands on the hot stones and arched her back and let her hair spill out — like shining from shook foil, James A said — and watched every male eye on promenade stop and stare, no more than her deserts! till she'd her fill, when she glided up path and so to home.

Finn and Mary Kath was still climbing at Mary Kath's short-leg pace. "It was close enough to shingle that tide would *no* have reached it," she said. "Well, at spring-tide mayhap," she added, being a truthful person. "But tonight it was safe as —" Her throat caught on itself. There was no safe, nowhere.

"Safe as can be," said Finn, smooth. "Come *long*, Mary Kath," tugging a fold of her pinna in his hand. He was to care for Mary Kath; well, all of them. James A was no pap-mouth as'd come out and say so, but Finn knew it for sure for all that. When James A come home this time, thin as a mast and heaving long coughs, he took straight to his pallet. The first tea seemed to ease him. It was then he said Finn was making to be a fine and a upright — the rest lost in cough. Enough to go on with. "Come *long*, Marekat," he said. Mary Kath slipped her hand in his and they walked up path quiet as leaves falling.

There was no warning of their arrival, so. The house door was wide to the wind. Cider Mother sat at table in the front room. Though James A's candles was guttering, she made no move to snuff them. She twirled a metal band round and round on the table. She tried to roll it a few times, but it was too lumpy to roll. James A found that band and her own when he was scavenging up the old scrapers to the north, back when she was heavy with Brendan. She was always a bit restive when he was working in those high, hollow places as rose dozens of fathoms aboveground, where what more likely than a chunk'd fall from the roof smack on James A's head? Yet it turned out that was no danger at all, at all. She twirled his metal band round and round her fingertip. The metal made a quiet scrape gainst the table boards. A dunnamany things needed doing. The mash-tun; the sheets; the spawn'd need gathering and cosseting. Right aright. She'd get up and tend to that in a bit. Always good to sit quiet with James A when he come back from up north. She twirled the metal band. The candles guttered.

Finn drew Mary Kath back down path. They stood round the corner, quiet as stones on the seafloor. Finn petted her fine black hair. "I never saw our mam thout she was working," said Mary Kath. "Shutter up," said Finn, and petted her hair. When Mary Pat come up, Finn leaned to her ear and whispered and then said loud, "Come long, Mary Kath." When the three of them showed at the door, Cider Mother was bustling mong the pots in steady candlelight. "You're in time for stew and cider," she said, her back to them, "Where's Daniel?"

Daniel was up the sandstone bluffs. It was a long climb up the zigzag path that turned to grains where and how it chose, so even if you'd walked it every day for years, it could easy slide away neath your boot. Dan come up the path while the sun was still falling, nor he'd no plans to descend that night. He hugged his knees to his chest. The fine red dust blew round him. The orchard below was huddled in its blackberry mantle. Even with knowing it was there, he could no make it out from the bluffs. Neath its thorny cover it sucked at its spring. There was water wove all through the rocks neath Charnholm, James A said; he said first thing richards did when they come surface was set dregs at digging wells down to the sweetwater web. A half-dozen dregs died off the bad air fore they come to water, their bodies stacked aside till there was enough of them to warrant burning. Said James A. At last they hit water, when four dregs died off drowning. "Was that no peculiar?" said James A, "So deep in the ground to die of water?" The water gushed out the hole for a half-day then went bone-dry altogether, like skin closes over a bloody cut. "It's no like richards care a ratbreath for a handful of dead dregs," said James A; had the water lasted they'd been digging still. "That's when they set up the Potable Works," said James A. "Richards offered all the potable and beans any able body could put away, to build fence up on South Point. Once that was done, the richards come mong us again," said James A. "Fine prospects they did offer. We did no say 'slave' back then for richard work, we said 'prospect'. Ha!" Here James A stopped to cough, drained a perry flagon, went on. "Richards said it was job of a lifetime, which was true enough. No dreg come back ever to Charnholm from behind the fine fence."

Dan put his hands to his ears to stop the ringing. Which dulled it some. James A said more, great heaps of words he'd said, but Dan could no bear to recall another word just then. "I'd wallow, was I any heavier freighted," he said aloud to the dry red air.

He'd promised his dap to say naught to any, till the time come, of what all he'd told him. "Right aright," said James A, and eased his bones joint by creaking joint onto his pallet. "Yes," he'd said, and closed his eyes, and coughed. "Lay a quilt on me fore you go, Daniel."

Dan tucked his knees to his chest, wrapped his elbows round his knees, his hands over his ears. He rocked there, high above Charnholm, till first light.

# Junk in a Squall

"DAP! STORM'S BREWING!"

No answer.

The boy paced the deck from bow to stern. He held fast to the man rope every step of the way. Of a calm morning, the sea a pond, he could saunter that route—now he'd to hand-over-hand it, now the sky'd gone green and black and the waves gnashed white as their crests flicked the scuppers.

"Dap! Looks a big one coming at us!"

No answer.

Palan yanked open the midship hatch to the familiar stench of tarpon oil, sulfur, and alum. "Dap!" he hollered.

"Mm-hmm, hoy-hah?" the below-deck mumbled. "Storm, eh? Do you get the curtains rolled up."

"The sails, dap?"

"Hum, hah, sails, yeah out of course, furl them sails. This brew's on the turn but so soon as it steadies I'll be above deck looking for your assistance most able."

The boy replaced the hatch. Assistance enough to fill a teacup, may be. Did his dap know he'd rigged the ship so he could sail her single-handed, he'd never come up for air. The *Mam Can Cook* was a nearshore junk made to be crewed by a man and a boy, cepting that Palan had hardly never a man awake enough to help him sail her. It was on his dap's account that Palan had set the square sails on jacklines that went end-to-end of the yard, a design he pinched from smiths; later, he was to see these in richard window curtains. He could slide the sails apart or together with a tug on the line same as those; he unwound the throat- and peaklines from their pins and with one tug narrowed the squaretop to a third its full width. This was a tricky coastline, with rocks enough to stove in a brace of strakes with one roll of the sea, yet did they get too far offshore, the open-sea winds'd slam the junk sidewise. Palan's dap believed the winds got angry when they could no knock the *Mam Can Cook* gainst the rocks as they tacked round the point. Palan let his dap's words blow overhead, too busy tacking into come-and-go winds. There was usually deep water in the lee of a point. The *Mam Can Cook* had a blunt bow and a flatcenter hull, she'd swing considerable in deeper water, but green waves'd no bury her. Tack on tack, he steered the luggish ship to safe berth neath the point. She was unhandy with so little mainsail but he could no take the chance of a sudden gust. When she was placed just right, he dropped the foresail in its lazyjack sling. Palan hauled up the dozen rockfull cages from the bilge, a bit of extra ballast, and dropped each laden cage to the seafloor. The junk tugged at her anchors, then settled to place.

Belowdeck, Fergus heard the filled cages bounce off the junk's hull as they sank. He paid it no mind, out of course. Fergus held a black cube tween two metal rods precisely one thumbwidth above a thin blue flame. He'd drawn his thumb-trace on vellum that morning so the scholars who came after him could repeat his results. Palan had been calling him again. So soon as he finished this bright, particular brew, he'd assume his duties in the world, he'd roll up, batten down —

The brew curdled. It curdled! The horizoscopic floor, some affair of the boy's with springs and counterweights, clean outside Fergus's line of work, swayed level gainst the ship's rocking. In all history tarpon venom had never curdled before: this must be entered immediate into his notes. Fergus headed a fresh page in his lab book: Venom Curdles! He dipped his left least fingernail into a small silver box. He inhaled one scoopful. There. Precisely the right amount. He wrote steadily by light of a spag lantern set in its sand bucket at his right elbow.

Palan stood to the wheel. No need for that soever with the sails furled and the rudder raised up into its trunk in the poop and the twelve full cages resting on the seafloor, but it was his place on the ship. When Palan's at the helm, his mam said, all hands may rest easy. Which she should known. Even back when his mam was alive, his dap was champion at resting easy. Since her death, Fergus'd got even better at it so you'd no thought there was any room for provement, yet Fergus had found a way how. Palan ran his hand down a wheel spoke. At the wheel, a body could brace for what was coming. There was no escape; they was the storm's to sport with. The sky struck sparks from the sea. The waves rose straight up and crashed down on themselves in orgy of self-flagellation. Palan lashed the wheel to its post and crabbed back to the stern, hanging to manrope and taffrail with his two hands. "Dap!" he shouted once more. No answer. "Dap!" No answer. "Dap!" he shouted a third time, tossed aside by the wind's paws: "There's a big one coming, a maelstrom. Sha' I step the mast?"

A direct question drew a direct answer. "Carry on about that directly, young Palan. Do you run into difficulties, you've but to call. As well you know."

Fergus leaned back in his chair. Every flask and alembic was safe stowed in nets swaddled in batting. The venom was sealed in a vial plugged with paraffin that swam in a ratskin bladder floating in a wide-neck firkin. All was well with his works. He'd climb to the deck so soon as he finished noting the color changes as the curdling venom simmered its dross away. "O piscine poison, loose thy surly bonds," sang Fergus tween his teeth as his left hand held steady the blue flame neath the curdling elixir. He treated himself to another few grains of tarpon venom from the silver box, tilting his head gracefully so to deliver equal amounts to each nostril.

Palan slid the topmast the first notch down in front of the mainmast. Housing the topmast was a chore he always done with his mam, they two laying her down, gentle, long the junk's length. When she started in to ail, he come up with this stepping. She looked on from a perch by the wheel while he first slid the topmast down like a telescope. *"Now that's elegant,"* his mam said. Palan shook his head and stepped the topmast its second notch, and paused to take the heel aft, and socketed it home in the third, last, and final notch. The air crackled of sulfur; the low bell of sky flattened gainst the sea, stuffed with dank wadding. Palan's timpani rang in muffled peals. The ship lurched to the left and righted itself. He crouched gainst the deckhouse, fingers limpet round its iron rungs, and hand over hand crabbed long its length to the door. It took some wrestling gainst the wind to prize the door wide enough for his snaky hips to pass through, but closing it was easier nor winking.

Palan lay in bunk on his stomach, the ship's log spread out on his pillow. He'd no horizoscopic floor as it betwaddled his sea legs to pass back and fro from level floor to swaying deck. The log said they'd had fine catch this trip; there was half a dozen tarpons in baskets in the hold. "My dap's a simple fisherman," sang Palan, "who sails upon the sea." They was due in Charnholm harbor some later this month. "Charnholm!" his dap said reverent after they hooked the last venomous fish. "With a haul like this we can put you down to land, my boy. How sha' you like that? An end to slipping round Smith caves by darkness but into the sunlight with Palan Fergusson! Time for you to get out your galanty show, stound the richards; *they'll* see your worth. Ayuh. No scorning the dregs' thin mite, neither; heap it up enough and it'll tell, indeed it will, indeed," he said. "You sha' have all the tools of a great town to hand. Finest maker and fashioner of all the ages, proper heir to your dap, you are. All my labor sha' fetch at last its price and Palan, son of Fergus the Fisherman, sha' be known and reknown throughout the land."

"Ah, right enough," said Palan. Galanty show. All bollock and hot wind. Course he could do it and get gain by it, but his dap wanting reknown for his heir? Ha. His dap wanted to ease him off the ship so's he'd no have to see his dead wife in Palan's deep green eyes. "It's like you stole those eyes off her corpus," Fergus said, and each time he said it he'd trip downstairs, and snuff, and snuff again. Later would come the bellering from below-decks: "Caro Caro Caro Caro Caro-line. An you'd believed in me, an you'd believed in the inventor that I am, an you'd believed, why you'd be mong us still. You near scuppered me, Caroline, with all your we'll-see ballast and your maybe-so weed on the hull, and in tryna scupper me, you sunk yourself. An you'd believed, you'd be sipping tea in a deckchair stead of lying on the seafloor, crabs making a fine snap and grubble off you. Everything had to be all your own way, did it no? Had to mark even your own son with your dark green stare-down prove-it eyes, well you sha' see, the same trap does no spring twice on a clever man. No on a clever man. Which I am, I am I am, more clever nor you could believed, Caroline, you sha' see it, mark me now." Then there'd come the clink of a vial, then a snuff, then another snuff, then the same voice, raised an octave and thinned considerable:

"Green eyes? Green eyes be damn. Vast heaving! So close. So close but how can I go that last step when every move's dogged by those dark green dark green eyes?"

It was clear as shoal water: soon as Palan was fast aground, his dap would heave a sigh and clap hands with some Sal or Simeon, one of the old staggerer Smiths who kept him company through the long nights while Palan rolled in his cold damp blanket.

Palan rolled onto his back and laced his hands behind his neck. The ship was battened as he could make it and it was the wind, now, as'd choose to leave her afloat or no. He stared at the low arched ceiling. Fergus was still ranting belowdecks. Lovely green eyes his mam did have. Wind had laid still so long you could be sure a dacious pounce was coming. His dap meant him to gain sufficient off the galanty show to buy a place in a mechanics krewe. It'd no be so bad to join up with other mechanics. There was all manner of joinery to learn. Wind was coming up to blow now. He shifted to his hammock and let his mind rest on a tube of lens and mirrors he once saw in a crumble book on the *Roger Roundly*, a dockbound ship. How'd they grind the lens? Mirror, now, he could make mirror by coating a sheet with dollops dug from fishgut, quivery balls that shone yourself back at you. But how'd they make glass, even? Their mirrors was finer, too. It was in those mirrors he'd first seen his dap's work clear for what it was. Till he looked in them, he'd seen his dap down below to mend net, gut fish; to go about the work of the boat. Till that night when he'd looked up from the crumble book and seen the hunch of Fergus mirrored by two hunches, drool spilling from a corner of every mouth. Each time the *Roger Roundly* swayed gainst its moorings, the viscous drool lengthened.

Fergus generally met his landmates in caves built by smiths in the lost days fore the Great Burning, who carved them gainst the coming days of wrath out of the sandstone and cobble hills. Those old Smiths cut the stone clear-edge, and victualled them gainst the wrathful days with dried foods and sealed hogsheads of potable and sealed carboys of scrumpy. Every meal Fergus ever had with Smiths, any meal Palan ever grabbed crumbs of, started with a grand toast to these dead smiths from whom the toasters claimed descent, by blood or by possession.

Smiths gathered in their caves at the dark of the moon, which they done, they said, since fore the Burning. Fergus said their choice of gather-time was a straight gift, being as the *Mam Can Cook* could slide in and out of coves round North Point in the dark, proferring tarponesse. Dozens and hundreds of times had Palan watched Fergus lay out his black case on one central stone or another while smiths gathered round, fingering their cheeks, their nostrils flaring, as Fergus opened, slow, the black case; as he showed them, vial by vial, what marvels it contained. Very hail fellow well met was the smiths at such showing, and all the more so as the night wore on and samples disappeared up their flared nostrils.

Once they'd snuffed a few spoonfuls, they was jig-limb and near flight. Tarponesse! It made the snuffer the man he could been. Large, generous, altogether grand.

Fergus stayed belowdeck for a week or more after any of these visits. Snorting and groaning in the hold, he rued his ways, made vows to change them, oh for poor spawn's sake, oh for his dear Caroline, oh for the man he might been.

Once he'd done whining, Fergus was back in his works, slicing, meas-uring, sifting, distilling, and what all. Palan expected no different. So it'd been since he was too short to get his chin on the taffrail. He used the time to fashion gaskets for fastening sails and lines and this and that, sail-raisers and rye-cookers; narrowed his dark green eyes and made sure the *Mam Can Cook* was a ship as'd carry him safe, till such time as Fergus remembered he could no stand the look of Palan, and started muttering how he'd put him offsides soon as he figured the how of it.

O Childhood! O Happy, Happy Time!

Palan could see why they'd let so many books crumble to dust in the Great Burning, such lies as they did tell.

# Danny Boy

WHAT I GOT ON ME, I never asked for. I got a bequest is a lamprey on my throat. Could you think about aught else? Say you prayed for a good catch and you got it, all right; got it flapping its gills foot-thick over deck and you neath the pile gasping. Would you be, then, off wandering mossy philosophic halls? Nah, same as me, you'd curse your fate.

I know how the fishcake crumbles. Kin, mates, travellers; they every one slide off soon as they see me coming and why? For they're death afraid. Course I know that. Even flies flinch down in a corner when I fume past.

It's my damn dap passed this on to me. May he rot. No, wipe that off the slate; I loved my dap for true. He went for a good man in the catalogue. He meant it for the best. It's me, what it is. I'm no built right for the job.

He's the one passed on to me this burden when he got too thin to hold it up, fore he slid out this life. In his last hours he was calm as a wet stone, smiling like I never seen him fore and now I know why: once he shucked this stinging load he took breath easy.

I shake, my nose opens wide for more air, my fists clench and slam, my lips bleed gainst my teethpoints, I shake with it I tell you. "Control your mad wrath," Olympia says. What's she know? She knows to be Cider Mother, all she knows. Wake up and sweet round the house, whistling, pays us no mind, brews and cleans and jigs the justborn Suellen on her hip. Control it? She knows naught. What's in me's no mewling pup you can sweet with candies. What I got's an old lord protects its turf. She think I'm a control that? With how? She shuffles herself and the spawn from one day to the next and thinks that enough; wake up hale every morning, drop to pallet full-belly every night, she thinks that's enough.

It's no enough! By the first rat's last yellow tooth it's no enough!

I work it off as best I can. I been down the docks since my second Seventh, since I was old as Mary Pat is now. Since my dap snuffed. Started out

I mended net, coiled rope, scrubbed down the fish decks. Poop decks got to be bleach white fore our pier's captains will set sail. I spent a plenty time on my knees pushing hot soapy into them boards with a brush. Alone in the down below I scream it off, then as now. All of it. What James A said to me fore he went and how all I got to keep it close and how hard the days go by. My brother Finn, he's a good boy, works hard for all our shoes and cabbage, but he's no, by the king of rats to come, he's no least notion. "Keep it from Finn," my dap said. "You the oldest; you got to keep this to your own self. Somebody got to take care of them," he said, "and you the one luck picked." Be damned to such luck. In the hull I scream it off. When they send me out alone in a curragh to dislade the deep boats, alone on the harbor waves, ah, I let it off with screaming then.

But it's all here the next day. I swim in the same rank waters then. That's what staps my vitals.

"You know there's words you can no take back, Daniel?" James A said to me. I nodded cause he was black with sweat on his last pallet, but I'd no least notion of it. Clear to me now, out of course. There's words you can no stop hearing after you hear them once. Try to stop waves.

Bang my skull gainst the mizzen; I'm too heavy freighted. I wallow in the water where another craft would fly from crest to crest. I push my brains together with my hand-heels to make room for something else, gravel me, aught else, but they'll no squash, the hold's full up, I got to make my voyage with all this on board.

An I wake in the dark and grab a cocajava off the shelf and glutting it come quickfoot to the wharf to break a sweat by heft and by scour, by climb and by haul, an I do that I can bear it.

I'm mostly on the rigging these days, three-minute climb above the scrubbing boyos. Careful you got to be, up there. Boat tilts and you're belly-flat five fathoms up, all's water below you, the which you do no want to fall upon. My dap was a full fathom high. I'd fall five daps an I fell. Water's rock an you fall that far. Rigging shakes you like a rat on a Hunt Boy's pike; where your decklegs feel but a shiver, in the ropes you quiver like dustspeck; oh you got to hold on up there. Balance alone's no good. You got to be all times fastened and you got to bounce off what the ship does, dance with it, like.

I scrub and mend and furbish up the crowsnest all times I can. It's a good place. You can see the far sky from up there. See Charnholm spread round the cove if you look that way; I never do. Gulls circle my head — I seen a picture once in crumble book of all the once-was birds, herons and osprey and kingfisher and that, it must used to been lively up here — gulls they got the water to themself to scoop into they gullets, like rats got the whole land. Long the jetty you'll sometimes see gulls scrapple with rats, teeth gainst beak, but from up here it's the draggled birds only, looking to make the trouble they live for. Up in the crowsnest, whirled by gulls, I can stand up neath what I got to carry.

How I got this laden on me: Couple days fore he conked, I was sitting with James A racked on a dank straw pallet, lighting another candle every time his eyes come open and he said the dark was dripping water down his clampshut throat. That's when he told me. That's when he passed it on. "Danny boy, you're the one to be the voice," he said. "I was Dap's voice, and he his dap's; he the third-born, you the first, it goes by no rule, the voice, it goes where it lists." I figured he was rambling neath foggy trees. It was gone dark and he'd the black sweat on him and could get down nobbut a spoonful of potable at each giving and his frame clutched up on itself now and now; I was no attending like I should. Well, should-have places last in any race; it was me as I was then sitting by James A while he blatted out what he had inside him.

It's my great granddap's voice James A gave me. The voice remembers the burning. That's the quick and dirty for you. He told it to his son, who told it to my dap, who told it on to me.

Great Granddap's voice is standing out to sea, climbing rigging while his mates crowd the starboard deck as the city slides below the water's edge, slides till only its spires and towers are showing still, and they only from crow's nest. It's six bells, the sun rounding to its apex, shadows huddled round the sailors's feet. The gobs they cheer and the bosun he lambastes them for the lazy dogs they are and the tars turn slow-handed to what work is next and they're still turning round when the voice crooks a elbow round the crowsnest —

(James A give a scream, here, as laid him flat gainst the pillows. I'd give a year and a arm to hear that no longer, but who takes such trades?)

The voice from the crowsnest screams when he sees it. Like a galanty show in tempest, all the ziggurats and pyramids and towers red and gold somersaulting, the heat tears them out their sockets and they stand on their heads, shaking their roots at the sun straight above, then in a slow cartwheel making like darts for the compounds and plazas and chockablock dry-mud house groups; whole blocks turn to jelly and melt in place, only the voice mong all that crew sees it and his cries tatter on the wind and reach the decks below in shreds, in rags, in dust.

From the decks the tars see nobbut spires and towers rising and falling tween the waves, enough however to stap their vitals. The steersman lets loose his hands and says, *I shot an arrow to the air / It fell to earth I know no where*, and he stands slackwrist while the wheel spins mad. The bosun stands at gaze, a rope crushed to his lips throttles speech, his toes curl back on his heels.

And then they see nobbut smoke. The bosun rouses and barks the crew alive to luff and tack gainst the land wind back to harbor for all they're worth. The voice up the crowsnest sees horrors still, hollers himself hoarse and keeps hollering when it's nobbut air whistling into his lungs and out again, as the fire so hot skips cross the city, leaves a block here and a half-street there, blasts warehouses to silt, turns on its haunches and spreads its wings and obliterates with one open-mouth outbreath the gold dome of the cloaca publica; it launches itself and leaves standing a tower, then bowls a meet-hall sideways down the university commons, splatting heavy-lidded students in its wake. Orange and red with a blue heart, it leaps about at its pleasure till it's sated, yawns, and curls itself to sleep, tail on its tongue.

Ten thousand spurty fires burn and the smoke that therefrom rises blows to sea on the landward wind, carrying stray black-curl pages and rags and shoebuckles in mongst its dust and ashes. A bone here and a doorknob there, a gold pen and a red dishpan, all these scraps the seagoing wind drops down mong the rigging of the voice's ship. The wind now brings the homebound ship the wailing. Each cry they hear spikes the silence. The silence throttles the voice. (And James A left off telling to fall silent his own self.)

Should I go on? I can no go on. This I've said is but scrapings off the tale the voice tells and tells, never stops, every hour of every day it sings and talks, rants and stalks; it'll go to mutter, mayhap, for an hour or few; then it's up twitching its tail again.

It says: The richards in their shelter caves knew all about it. The voice says this soft and whiskery, says: they knew it was coming in time to scuttle belowground with their silks, their silver, their pomanders. They lounged five fathoms down on cush recliners while the city burned, while dregs and toilmen ran mong falling slates and flaming boards, holding their hand-bones over their heads as they ran and weeping their eyes down their faces.

The voice says the dregs was stunned from the getgo, see, already squashed in toil, a few dullmetal coins was all their magic carpets. Burning but changed their cribbed bones to ash. The voice says remember, remem-ber. We'll all of us turn to salt do we forget: dregs died like so much soot you'd brush off your eyes. Now, did richards pluck their soft hands from a tree? Clouds parted and golden hens dropped on richard shoulders and there laid golden eggs? No, and again and also no. It was dregs drained the marshes, dregs who raised towers on the claimed land. It was dregs who was left topside to live or die like so many midges swarming round a corpus. Dregs with their callus palms ground wheat fine as dust to make richard loaves. Dregs are the pumice as make richard palms soft.

How are we to turn time backwards, drag what is through a mirror till it shifts shape to what ought to be? The voice says, cup the remembering in your two hands and walk with it forward and justice like a mighty sword shall flood forth from mountains; iniquity shall vanish like smoke and error be no more. Someone sha' drink that cup and all this come to pass. It could been on James A to drink it. Could be me. The voice nobbut repeats how we're to remember, remember, pass it down.

Then it guffaws, near choking on its own clever. It says it has no least notion what use is remembering.

I've all I can do to walk upright with this on me. There's so much the voice saw and tells me inside my head, it drops me to my knees; such things it saw, I can no stop thinking of them nor can I give them away. I've tried, no fear. Couple-three times I launched the voice on a following wind, but each essay keeled and jibbed and sank prow-first. I can no get my tongue round it so any other can hear it like I hear it. Fish can no make chowder, for all they've the ingredients so handy. I'm a dreg of flesh and bone, no more, made to build this day on top of days fore, to clap loud at passing flags; I'm no framed to carry one. Wake up hale and drop to pallet full-belly, that'd be lovely. As it is, I can no shuck the voice nor get my shoulder neath it. My life but uses me to carry the voice on to the next one. Which how can I get born a son with all this choking my pipes? How find a woman willing to spend her time undersheet with a man who shakes atwitch from shuteye to dawn?

Did spirits help I'd be sunk to my eyes in a firkin of scrumpy fore my eyes opened of a morning. Working helps. Rigging helps. I'm a man of one piece when I'm weaving slings to hoist dunnage aboard, mending net to catch deepfish in our meshes, climbing high to mend a stuns'l or a jib, lashing down, making safe.

But when I stop I flail about me. Since James A screamed it down my ears, I can no close my selvages long enough to take a look on it. I know the other dregs run from me for how I am neath this. Do I no run from myself? And I know running does no good. But it eases me considerable to feel my hairs stream back for a bit, like I was a spawn again snagging ratpups with my brother Finn in moldgreen culverts, running our spikes long their metal ribs and raising a joyous noise. Soon as I stop running, the voice comes out of my eyes my throat, my hands thwack fore I know what they're about; if there's a body near it gets thwacked, what can I do but keep to my lone?

It's like this: Set a ship's sails for come-and-go breezes. Take that ship and whallop a hurcan out of a sky gone green from blue in a headturn, so it runs fore a wind as tatters its sails like skin crisping. It'll founder and wallow and spin round. A case like that, it's no on the captain she's so unhandy. A crew's hands can act but only so much.

I take a dunnamany curses for my rampageous ways but they're no on me; it's but the past blowing through me towards a time to come as slams my ears all times regardless.

# Book Two

# As It Begins

*And so the M'Cools passed from year to year, as they neared or passed their second Seventh, the time when a dreg sits up and takes notice and chooses the way to lead life, or, more like, slips in anywhere they can find a berth. For the living desire to continue living, so that mostly the question of living on one's feet or on one's knees, now, is a question few ask, for the clamor of the empty maw drowns out the question, the parched gullet strangles it, the routine of the day dulls its edged point. Is it when there's food and potable enough that the matter takes on import? Or is it when the knees can bear no more? simply can not bend one heartbeat longer?*

THE DREGS ON PROMENADE shuffle up cobbles and down in the gloaming, from North Point light, a stone heap set with spag lamps, to the ancient baulk, enamel in barnacle, glisten with salt, as long since leapt the jetty wall. Brackish harbor water noses aside the jetty's grey-green mantle of slime and laps up under those skirts and as it listless sinks, its exhales rank with piscine slurry, it spits the pips through the jetty's scuppers.

The dregs hug what thin shade the locusts throw where they thrust from dusty gaps in the cobble walk. The locust leaves are sparse on spindle branches, sputtered with grey dust. The dregs are thin as the shade and the locusts; their scalt skin as covered with grey dust as they ease their slippers up cobbles and down neath hats of plaited straw. In pairs and threes and solitary, they shuffle north, and turn, and shuffle south, and turn. The wrung-out slump on the jetty's slick walls, cool stones gainst their bare legs despite the filth, lifting a wranked hand in greeting that falls back to their laps like grey dust.

The promenade's punctuate by dustclouds that, on close approach, resolve themselves into spawn who run circles round their begetters shrieking, *wantlwantwantlwaaant*, fresh from sleep they squall, blood fizzing in their veins, *Iwantlwantwant*. Thus the spawn. Thus the most of them. Some hide in crannies, their swollen heads lolling gainst the mam-thighs they clutch with shrunken arms, mouths slack till their rising lymph forces a great roar from them, after which they come back to slump, eyes rolling in their sockets, their fingers kneading their mams who hoist them to better catch a sluggish breeze.

Another hot gloaming in Charnholm. Dregs rise fore the sun clears the sandstone cliffs, swallow a cup of hot and slice of rye fore they set out to haul, patch, mend, make, weave, scrub, scrape the day's meal from the day, the which they eat at sun's height, then fall to their pallets, and wake when the sun's half down, and lay into their work again.

This evening, hot and dry as skull teeth, two-thirds of Charnholm's dregs scuffed up and down the jetty. Another few score dregs in their houses yet, too busy at their work or too worn by it. The promenade slowed when the sun fell into the puce haze over harbor. A low junk tacked round South Point, its dark red sails puffing and slacking fore a come-and-go breeze. A young boy leapt from the rigging to the bow. An older man come on deck, waving his hands, tucking up his bags, his mouth moving, his eyepelts twitching. He shook himself, wiped brine from his cuffs, ran his tongue back and fro cross his lips; his mouth still moving, he pointed the boy back towards sea. They rounded the point again to disappear in shimmer heat, the boy's gold hair glinting through it as they passed.

The most of the dregs turned away at this, rejoined the promenade, shuffling weary their grass slippers from stone heap to beached ship and back again; the lovers of course continued their ways oblivious, the roarers lifted their mouths and howled to their own peculiar beat; but the spawn shouted *Whozzat? Whozzat?* and when their elders shrugged in answer, ran round and round with greater speed as stirred up greater clouds from the harborstones. When one such dust cloud settled, it revealed a woman coming up on her last days and her daughter, halfpast labile, who was troubled with sight. Cider Mother and Mary Patricia M'Cool.

Finn and Mary Katharine M'Cool, lean and bronze and wiry as the rest, their short hair mica in the falling sun, craned over the sandstone jetty for a last glimpse of the redsail junk.

"The craft is named *Mam Can Cook*," said Finn.

"See that well as you," said Mary Kath. "The boy had gold hair, did you note that?"

"I did so," replied Finn. "Gold from out the sea. That one's come for a Hunt Boy."

"Rat Hunt take up a incomer?" said Mary Kath.

"Did Mary Pat no see it in the cards last Sunday."

"Mary Pat sees a dunnamany things in the cards that the cards no got in them."

"She saw it in the cards," said Finn.

"That was rubbish what she saw for you," Mary Kath laid a hand on his arm. "You'll make a fine Hunt Boy. No goldhead will divert that."

Ambrose and Matron shuffled the promenade arm in arm. "A rare night out mong the people," he said, waving a lit pessary neath his beak.

"Stopple your gab," she said. "You seen that crystal eye looker, that Mary Patricia? I'm taking her in as nova soon."

"Her mam was no ill-looking," Ambrose said, and looked out to sea.

Cider Mother waved Mary Pat off to join Finn and Mary Kath. Her sister Constance come up alongside, height enough on both of them to see the last glint of the redsail junk. "Fergus," said Cider Mother.

"Mmm-hmm," agreed Constance.

"And his spawn."

"Mmm-hmm."

"More gorry work, and in harvest season, to boot."

"Well, Olympia, it's Fergus. Naught else we can do," said Constance. Her sister nodded.

Governor Donal lowered the glass from his eye. "*Mam Can Cook*," he said, and spun his lady round. "*What* a Rat Hunt we shall have. *What* a Hunt Breakfast!"

"Stop that," said Lady Mandra, twitching her taffeta back to shape.

"You like it well when the footman does it," said Gov Don, furrows down his nose.

"That's another matter altogether," she said. "I am fatigued with these stones and this watching." She motioned to her parlogal.

"Yes'm," said the parlogal.

"Call up the coulees. I shall take the palanquin back to the compound now."

"Yes'm," said the parlogal, and glided off the ramparts.

⟶

Max had slipped away from his mam and dap to play for the lounging coulees. They'd every means and all intent, but no word could they say while he bowed the viol tucked to his shoulder till Lady Mandra's new parlogal come hotfoot down the burren: "Shutter up, Max," she said, "lovely and all, but these coulees need to be uphill soonest lest milady soil her new slippers stamping impatient the fort stones."

⟶

Daniel M'Cool stood on deck of the *Hail Janus*, torn nets at his feet. Hands over his ears, he shouted, "Yeah, they toppled. So they toppled in the Great Burning. What in gorry can I do about that?"

# Some Born to It

WHEN JAMES ALOYSIUS DIED, Suellen was growing inside Cider Mother, then Suellen got born, then Suellen was a plainty justborn. Through all, Mary Katharine kept to a small round of chores. When she could break free, she crept downstairs to sit tween the cider vats on the cool cellar floor. She'd a handful of crumble books she paged through; mostly she sang, her bare feet on the cool floor. Mary Kath sang tween the cider vats, her voice ringing off stone walls and metal mash-tuns.

*The Rat Hunt Boys / With eyes of flame / Strode whistling through the howl-ing streets / And slaughtered as they came.*

She was singing, so, on a still day in early summer, when the front door banged above, prompting Suellen to wail, then feet plogged cross the boards above, and Cider Mother said, "Morning to you, Max, and these?" Nobbut Max the violist come for his mam and dap's cider. Mary Kath went on singing:

*The Rat Hunt Boys / With pikes of steel / Pierced living rats and spilled their guts / And strode off toe and heel.*

It was the smell as turned her. Their feet shuffling down-cellar she sang through; their smell she could no disregard. They stank like the cellar the morning after she saw Max play viol at Wagon prow, morning after she saw her first Rat Hunt when she come down the stairs and pale Nora was gone, leaving behind only this smell as rankled high up in the back of the nose. Their dried-up faces matched their smell. Mary Kath left off singing. The man put his hood back and said, "One sweats to excess in these white gowns. Dearest, may I present you to Mary Katharine M'Cool, sister to our Max's colleague, Finn. Mary Katharine, this is my gentle Goodwin," the woman simpering at that, making her look more like a withered pippin than ever, "and I am Bran." He stepped back like Mary Kath needed time to recover from the blow.

Goodwin put off her hood. "Pleased to make your acquaintance," she said, and sat, in all that white, plop down on the brew slab, mong peels and sour mash and pissdrop and all. "You have an exquisite voice."

"Delectable," Bran agreed.

Goodwin followed Mary Kath's eyes and said, "These gowns take no stain. They are fashioned from the skins of the burnt dead."

Mary Kath was still waiting for Goodwin's dry bones to snap when up piped Bran: "The traditional garb of anathematizers."

"Traditional," said Goodwin, in a hot outbreath as'd melt spag.

"Oh yeah," said Mary Kath.

"Rimers you may call them," said Bran.

"Of which august company —" said Goodwin.

"We think you might make one," said Bran.

"Which that would be *what* when it's at home?" Mary Kath asked. Course she knew, any dreg breathing knew, but these two got up her nose.

"One who strides out before the Hunt Wagon to lull the rats by anathematizing them; by cursing them in verse."

"One couldn't call it poetry," said Goodwin.

"It seldom is, dearest, though we have had moments..."

"Exactly," she said. "Moments."

"Which shall increase under our tutelage, dearest," said Bran.

Mary Kath hummed quiet to herself tween the vats. These two pippins had no need of her. They was stuffed full of crumble book, which she, sudden, yearned for. First thing she yearned for since James A died. She knew every crumble book in her store by heart. These rimers must have crumble books past count. They tossed glass balls of language back and fro for a while and then they said about the training, and suitable reimbursement in portable potable, and generally choked themselves on chandelier words till they took breath when Mary Kath said yes. She said yes, she'd frame songs for them, right aright.

⌒

That night, Finn drowsed over his chowder while Cider Mother joundled Suellen on her hip, buppety-bib. When Mary Kath come in, her mam's lips was parted, her grey hair damp gainst her skull, her nose pinched to its bone. "Mam," said Mary Kath, and there was no turn nor quiver in answer. Cider Mother was away off like this most of the time when James A was fresh dead, but it was rare these days; "Cider Mother," said Mary Kath.

"Hmmm?" said Cider Mother from inside her pinched nose.

"Mam, they picked me for rimer."

"Hmmm?"

"Rimer, now," said Finn, strooling his spoon round his bowl. "That's fine, that is."

Cider Mother woke for a beat and looked round at Finn. "Why're you no on the promenade?"

He shrugged. "I'd no feel for it."

"Eleven years on you and you've no feel for it?"

Finn shrugged again in answer.

"Mary Patricia's up-jetty for us all," said Mary Kath.

"Willa shutter up on Mary Pat," said Cider Mother, thout heat. She stirred the pot. "More chowder?" she said. She paused and stared at Suellen's closed eyes like the blue veins on their pale brown lids was so many words. "More chowder? That's fine, Mary Kath. Bout the rimers and all." She turned to Finn. "And what does tha' plan for thysen, Finn?"

Finn slammed his fists gainst the tabletop and shoved back his bench so hard it flew in crash. "Plan? I? Course a body feels the dark coming, even as us boyos ponk the ball for one last hoop, we know the dark'll soon muffle the sky. Think we're lackbrain ignorami? No notion of what's to come? That in a few years time we'll huffle round snotdrip as coulee, yassuh massuh neath some richard's palankeen; or walk everyways stiff like smith, hand glued to the small of the back fore our youngest spawn's walking; by the rat's snotstiff whisker! Course a person turns wood past his third Seventh. My skull's full to bursting, I tell you, with what all I got coming in through eyes and ears alone, and you think I'm a sit down and tell you one word lock to another what all I plan? I plan? A dreg plan? So yeast may plan or a bramble bush for all the good it does. The ground'll swool out from under, pitch me into darkness soon enough. No point *planning*."

They sat quiet round the table, dipping their spoons into their bowls.

While they sat so, Mary Pat was on the promenade. She was swinging her hips arm-in-arm with Galyse and Chrysta. "In a month's time, we'll be novae," said Chrysta.

"All the potable you can drink, in harum," said Galyse.

"Potable? You've a mind to potable? All the Hunt Boy I can swallow, that's what I'm ready for," said Chrysta.

"It'll be nobbut novices at first," said Galyse.

"Novices and beaters," said Chrysta, and the two of them said "Eee-yuuu, *beaters*," and Mary Pat said, "Eee-yuuu," a beat after them.

"Hunt Boy spurt's a specific gainst buboes," said Galyse.

"It's good for what ails you," said Chrysta, straightface, and the two of them bent double laughing.

Mary Pat laughed with them. Out of course she did. She and Chrysta and Galyse was flexish trout who schooled and turned and darted as one. Their bronze arms was thin and supple as hawsers, their footsoles smooth, their hairs plump, the way before them clear: they'd be horii as Sharna was hori — so lacious that thirsty men set aside drink for her embrace — their flesh, like Sharna's, would burst from their frames as barley from its husk.

Some born lacious, some learn it, some get the knack thrust on them. Some, like Mary Kath, never learn. Stuck whooling to herself tween the mash-tuns, she'd no notion of how to grease herself so's to squeeze forward through the tight places. Mary Pat, lone mong the M'Cools, was any good at that. She'd her obligation clear; one body mong them must swim forward lest all of them run aground and seagrass grow out their ears. She gave her fins a shake and darted back to her place, her silver scales gleaming.

"Only a month till harum," said Mary Pat, and "Harum," Galyse and Chrysta echoed. "Out of that house all day and all night," Mary Pat continued. No more bowing and scraping to richards. Never no more.

"Pallets soft as milkweed," said Galyse.

"No grissom, darkling eyes," said Mary Pat.

"Sweet oils," said Chrysta.

"No harrumph and sigh when you nobbut look in a mirror to check your hair," said Mary Pat.

"The pole," said Galyse.

"The pole," Chrysta agreed. The sun touched the harbor, turning their skin from bronze to copper. Galyse and Chrysta sighed as one: "Chores," they said, and with a flurry of embraces all round they flicked their tails and was gone.

Mary Pat dawdled up-jetty. In harum, there'd be no-one mawking back at the past; if she never heard more of the Burning, it'd be too soon. Nor there'd be none chiding her to see forward; she'd keep that close, at harum. It was no like she could see clear what'd happen next. It was no steady. It was only after James A died that she'd made sense of what she saw a year beforehand: forge bellows creaking and wheezing in the front room, a tinfull of viscous slime beside them. Who could known that was the sound of James A dying? Who could known he'd cough up such a tinfull? What was the good of such fore-knowing? No good soever. In harum, there'd be no-one pushing her to make sense of such stuff. She'd float in the present time, and the waves'd push her steady forward till Sharna herself'd curl in the dust at the feet of Mary Patricia M'Cool to learn the curve of her fingers, the shimjig of her hips.

When she reached home, Mary Kath and Finn and Cider Mother was sitting round the table as she'd known they'd be, rimming their empty bowls with their spoonbacks. Foreseeing that took no special powers.

# Stealing Fire

S O THEY CHOSE MARY KATHARINE for the Rimehouse. Chose her to stalk at head of the Rat Hunt in a rimer's white skin, those skins loosed from the frangible dead, to pace mong the rimers who anathematize the rats in verse. She trained for that up one year and down the next, while Mary Patricia left for harum, while Finn went stragglefoot off to dockside barracks where Rat Hunt Boys was made, while Daniel lived, far as any could see, in the crowsnest of the *Hail Janus*. Cider Mother, only, continued on in the house two-up two-down with Suellen, humming round her cider vats, pouring her brew into pipes and carboys.

Rimer training was a great thing in the new Rimehouse compound planned and built by Gov Don. Rimers trained in rhetoric and rhyme, in strophe and antistrophe, in clausal syllabism and suchlike, behind closed shutters for years in the stone and tin hossles near the foot of South Point, in the lee of the salt-glisten baulk, handy for richards to lean their heads out their windows and listen down to prentice rimers nunciating, or prentice musicians scraping tunes. One day Thorn, Mary Kath's bizzled tutor in rodomontade and parlay-fair, started on how there was fine tales in the days before the Burning — we was walking in the footprints of giants, said Thorn, and did the prentices know any olders who'd tales to tell? Mary Kath spoke up as how Rose Marie'd maybe know some tales. So one noon after she slipped off her whiteskin robe, stead of going home to rest on her pallet, she crossed Dead Horse Moraine to knock on Rose Marie's door. She carried a carboy of Cider Mother's best in her elbow crook.

Rose Marie opened the door and took the carboy while nattering on of how Mary Kath'd grown. Rose Marie had no changed since Mary Kath and Finn last came. Her smoky laugh was the same, her pig-dog headscarf the same, her nest of cushions the same, the porty-airs the same, like time stood still; which out of course that's the one thing time never does. While

Rose Marie tipped the carboy down her green-chased flask, Mary Kath looked round the place closer. Well, she was wrong and Rose Marie had changed, changed considerable: the grime as once lived on cushion fringes only had marched over every plane. Every surface was coated with spagfume oil and dust and oil again and more dust in layers you could see clear near the windowtops, say, or anywheres else the drib Rose Marie could no reach. Mary Kath cleaned off a cushion for herself on the quiet while Rose Marie was whirling bout to no clear end. She said she needed tales, old tales, to use up the Rimehouse, and waited for Rose Marie to indicate she was ready for tales to be teased from her, but no. The word "Rimehouse" was like throwing dry grass on a brazier. Rose Marie's hands fell apart on her lap, her lips quivered but no sound came from them. After a time Rose Marie heaved up and started talking, no havering nor shill-I shall-I now, she spoke like a bloat gut bursting.

"There's vats of stories but there's one I never heard told. It needs someone to remember. They tell all round it but never direct to the grain. Scoils my mind like a army of one marching round and round a tree till it turns to spag. I'll tell you what the Burning crimsoned to ash and how the richards sprang from the dead earth to stand mong us."

Mary Katharine sat next Rose Marie on the grime-velvet cushions. Her lips drew back off her teeth at the foul of them, but no matter. How could this old dreg remember aught of things as happened when her granmam was nobbut a spawn? Still, no matter if the tales was true, so long as they was good. That was a thing they said up the Rimehouse that Mary Kath agreed to wholeheart. She waited while Rose Marie tipped the green-chase flask down her throat, and wiped her lips with the back of one grimy hand, and parted her damp, blistered lips. "How they tell it is this."

How they tell it is this: after the Great Burning nobbut we dregs lived on the surface mong the sticks and bones of the old days, charred sticks they was and white the bones, at first there was maggots bubble neath flesh but when flesh goes maggots go and it was silence clamped over the dregs huddled flank by flank in the rubble and the dust of the stone scrapers, towers high as five masts end to end rising hollow to rusty windvents creaking useless on their roofshards. After a while some few dreg eyes come open with hunger and they looked round and saw a dunnamany skellingtons round them. But *they* was no dead. Those few dregs stood up out of those shards and blinked and foraged on the crust while far below the richards opened tins with silver knives, lounging on down-stuff cushions, holding lavenda to their flared nostrils, fanning cool air with languid wrist, well content to do naught. They say many crust-stumblers lost their wits from the airvents creaking as they turned; bleeding from the ears, the unlucky dregs leapt from the stone jetties into harborwater that ate them down to bone, if indeed there was so much left. But there was no short of ways to die then; water etched away the spawn's guts from the inside, hands flamed to dust did they touch some certain instruments, and did you lay aside your mouthcloth you snuffed up lungfulls of smucky ash; oh there was no lack of ways to die slow and naught to be done about it. There was body-heaps burning everywheres, and more stacked ready for the flames.

While richards waited in their snug caves, we dregs scuttered on the crust. The Burning rasped its long tongues wheresover it chose and puked up foul vapor that pocked skin, corroded grout from tween the bricks, melted innards to black lumps. Even the rats would no touch those charnel innards. The Burning snaked inside safes, cellars, cisterns, cesspools; pus drained everywhere from open sores; oh Charnholm took a time to scab over. Those dregs as could walk walked careful but their empty flapping maws pushed them to look and keep looking. There was gems and gold coin and clockwork of a marvel but none of that feeds a body; they shoved it to one side and scrabbled mong the rubble and refuse till they found sealed jars, but they was cracked, and found beans, but they was pulsing. Rats writhed in heaps and dregs pushed away the rats to find a half a face or a thighbone judder with worms, its moldfur a scanty blanket, and the emptygut dregs pawed all that away, they gave over any niceness in their tastes and shoved down their maws rice that squirmed, and barley that blew up their guts when they poured ale on top of it.

Rose Marie tilted the flask down her throat. Mary Kath said, "Did they no die off that?"

Rose Marie sputtered, near lost a thimbleful, so, but lapped it careful off her lips, wetting the dead white blisters. "Die?" she said. "Course they died. They died like rats, on their backs squeaking. They died easy, the dregs, they died like winking." Rose Marie distangled her hand from shawl-fringe and spread her three fingers. "If you walked surface those days you likely died off," she bent back a finger, "the air," bent back another, "the drink," a third, "the food," and so made a fist of that hand as her clogs beat gainst the floorboards, raising puffs of dust and what-all else. "Who walked surface? Us dregs. There was no walking round back then, no *promenades*," she spat, making a clear space mong the dust, "there was cuzzling down in sack nest, feather nest, nest of hair, and in those nests there was fucking. Ah there was palaces of fucking while dust blew and chunks skattered in the streets; in the cellars and lockrooms they fucked themselves sore and salved their parts with a dollop of spag grabbed off the nearest melting body; while outside hail dust rampaged cyclonic, inside dregs brushed grey-green slime from their eyes and come back to fucking. In, out, upside down, backwards; wheelbarrow races there was up and down the marble halls of the cloaca publica where Gov Don these days dispenses half-bakes on spear-point. My granmam Livy's gardeen Nan was champion wheelbarrow three times running, fore the sores come on her lips and her asshole, fore the sores opened and spread up her belly and down her neck, fore her fingers stiffed up and dropped off and her eyes poured out they sockets; fore that she'd some glory on her."

Rose Marie refilled the flask. "So there was for a long time fine fucking or anyhow plentiful. Those who was bound to die got on with it and those left over fucked and scratched and gulped what they could find while dust blew down the streets and up the vents and settled on eyelash and turnip alike. Till at last the down rains came. Oh they'd wished for those. Till they got them. The rains first settled the dust and then made mud of it and last sloshed the dust downstreets to harbor where it snagged on the drains and clogged there; the mash of dust and water backed up and rose gainst the stone jetties till those dregs as could walk yet rose from their floaty beds to wade waistdeep to the jetty where heel and toe they wraggled clumps off the drains, singing the while, O *The Muskrat Ramble Ramble O*, and then come the rushing of many waters and so the dockside rinsed and so with the dry wind, after, the dockside dried."

Rose Marie poured cider down her. "All that dryness," she said.

Mary Kath blinked as a few spocks of light pushed through the raggy windowblind. "How'd the Great Burning start?" she said.

"Ah, well, start," said Rose-Marie. "Take rumor, now. How's that start? Enmity's easy tracked but how's love begin? Why do the good die young and who killed Cock Robin? To start some questions, Mary Katharine, is to stick your head down a sinking porthole; grand view at first, later considerable damp to drown in."

Grown-olds seldom pass the chance to pour their wisdom down young ear horns, like that bottles it and lays it down cellar. "Do you know, Rose Marie, how the Burning started?" Spag makes the wheels go round, Mary Kath repeated to herself.

"There's a tale for another time," said Rose Marie.

As to say she'd no least notion. Mary Kath leaned back on her hands and blew out her held breath. "Well, what come after dockside dried off?"

"Rushy, rushy, all you spawn is rushy." Another slug from the green-chased flask opened her eyes wide and yellow. Rose Marie curled herself into a yellow cushion striped drip-drap vertical with stains of rust, tea, soup, and what all else — Mary Kath closed her magination to it — tucked velvet tatterdemalion round her ankles, and steepled her fingers fore she spoke. "Dockside drained and dried, now I told you of that? Yes. No point rushing on some tales, bad news keeps.

"Dry wind baked our dockside; a raked pile crisped quicker nor one left aclump but elsewise no matter, whatever dripped was that wind's fair suck. It drove before it dust so fine it passed through your eyelids and ground your sight away grain by grain; so parching that waves changed mid-crest to steam. Ships that lay at anchor when the Burning come, which sunk them two fathom solid down, now rose up from harborwater and lay aground as they sprang at seam and peg; their planks bowed and cupped and sang parting songs in screech. No matter how a dreg hammered his fists bloody at the hatches of the richards' shelter caves, answer came there none, and while they begged, their skin cracked and their innards withered till the dust breath come out of them and they fell in pile of salty dust the wind scooped and carried down away the dockside."

She went silent, the flask at her side. "How'd any live to tell the tale?" said Mary Kath.

"Luck of the draw," said Rose Marie, still flaccid mong the cushions. "Some had cunning as their luck, pulled skin after burnt skin over them and breathed what mucal lay inside those cocoons; some had lucky noses to find a cranny of sweet air; some was born lucky, did naught and come through scatheless."

"How'd your granmam Livy live through?"

"Dying teat's how she made it. Nestled on what breasty pillow she come across and suckled there. Hands wrapped her round in crackle skin stripped from where found, leaving her mouth outside, only, and as she drained one dug of its milk she was passed on, hand by hand, to another."

"What of their own spawn?"

"Think an armheld child lives through that? No."

"And their mams' dugs held milk yet?"

"They did, else my granmam Livy was a liar born, by life perfected."

Mary Kath said she was sorry. She said it up one side and down the other. Rose Marie inclined her head, gracious, slupped from the green-chased flask, and went on.

"After a long time passed, that succubal wind come to an end. As all things do for the living. When it blew itself out, the dockside lay calm neath a ratgrey sky. Waves slapped planks and bones gainst the jetty. The brooms swept to that beat, *shashish, shashashish, shashish, shashashish.*"

"Brooms, what brooms?" said Mary Kath, snapping away from contemplate of a squirming dustheap.

"First thing they did, the living, was sweep away the fine dust so they could see what lay neath it. Any whole corpus they found, which there was few enough of those, they sent to sea. All the while the living kept on sweeping, like a clean floor could make things right, like an the floors was swept, those who once walked them would come back. When you're no certain what next to do, you clean. *O a new broom sweeps / O a new broom sweeps / O a new broom do sweep clean-o!*"

Mary Kath looked round at the squirming dustheap, the grime, and the tatter blinds, and she breathed. "So what happened after they swept away the dust?" she said.

"You're living in it, no?"

Mary Kath asked and asked again but Rose Marie nobbut waggled the empty carboy. Her eyes dropped shut and her bit of a frame went flat gainst the cushions and there was no more to be got from Rose Marie.

Mary Kath slipped out the door to the wide flat dry flat creakjoint town, and slipped mong the starveling dregs that was, and were, to the gate of Dead Horse Moraine as quivered in the gloaming, and slipped through dusty pots and socks and ring fingers, smacking often the ground to warn off the slithers and rustles in the piles, till she reached the far gate and slipped through it, till she reached her old house and slid through its door and down stone stairs to her old nest tween the cider vats where she sang through the night, sang quiet, punctuate by long silences when the songs abandoned her in clench fear and pity of those who scrabbled neath the stones for any ease, and got her breath back, and sang again.

# Cider Mother Morning

WITH ALL THE SPAWN BUT SUELLEN out the house, Cider Mother come downstairs humming, trailing her fingers down the iron baluster, trailing stairdust on her house-shoes, and trailing likewise the same morning thoughts she had every morning of her life: You got to eat your peck of dirt fore you die; life is dust revealed at death. Cider Mother opened the cellar door, humming still, her rosered lips vibrato in her copper face framed in nightblack hair. Come close. Her face is ordinary bronze dreg flesh. Come closer. Her hair is grey with threads of black. Look close into her green-brown eyes. She is lean, like all the dregs, but straight neath forty-some years of hard work, an age when most dregs are wrung out or dead. She has sun-squint lines in her bronze dreg face, deep rays round her eyes and mouth, like all the harbor people. Come close to her mouth. Her mouth is truly rosered. A thread of a sound issued from her rosered lips unceasing: *Full fathom five thy father lies.* She sings in hum all day except for when she sleeps, which by the nature of things she can no testify to. *Of his bones are coral made.*

You do no want to let your voice ring out or leap, o ye high hills, if you're a harborside dreg in a two-up, two-down as you got with great luck, and with room enough for your mash-tuns down cellar. In that position you want to sing in hum.

*Those are pearls that were his eyes.* Cider Mother hummed down the cellar stairs.

Now, if she could sing out, she'd have trumpets and drums to back up her song; they'd toss tones like richard ladies toss sacks of gold from their palankeens (well, every Hunt Day richards talk of the tossing, though no dreg's seen it ever), and goldsack largesse'd fly through the windows. It'd be the crumble books coming true, that say "*Profusion* is Life's most prominent Characteristic." Cider Mother snorted. That's so far off the mark it might as well be sun's home over the water. Those books come to crumble in the Great Burning, that's to say, every single thing those writers thought they knew was wrong. *Profusion;* that's no the way of it. Life's made of dust as for a moment trembles in the shape of a soft palm in yours or a cup of tea, then in a blink returns to dust. Since all is dust, dregs'd fare better could they make cold hearts for themselves, hearts as'd beat steady and slow while dust took one shape after another, and then collapsed in pile while coldheart dregs leaned gainst the jetty chatting of "dust up to its shenanigans again," but such cold hearts they can no make. Cider Mother gave up long since on other dregs seeing the dust. She makes her brew, tends what she's inclined to tend, hums down the days.

*Nothing of him that doth fade / But doth suffer a seachange / Into something rich and strange.*

She waited. Times one can do naught but wait. *Let time pass, it is better than much thinking.* Some queen said that long ago. Now time's passage had set most of the spawn on their own feet and none other she was bound to (James A and all those others gone, gone to dust); Cider Mother let herself be Olympia; she let that ropeflying girl come out of storage. Olympia did no let time pass. Olympia cleaved time. Cider Mother floated on it.

*Nothing of him that doth fade / But doth suffer a seachange / Into something rich and strange.*

Cider Mother put Olympia back in her deep cave and went about her business. She inspected her mash-tuns from bottom to top. She raked out the coals and laid new fascines mong them. Once the fire blazed up, she lit a spag dip and set it by the near vat's bunghole, which she opened half a turn till it guttered but stayed lit. Next she climbed the ladder and sniffed the working mash, no rot smell, good; crust was thin and liquor still a bit mucky, good; say a week till this vat needed racking. The far vat, though, was dead ready to rack, it stinguished the spag lamp soon as she gave it a quarter-turn, its liquor bright neath a thick crust full of pulp chunk; well, there was her day clear ahead of her. Cider Mother sang out — that was safe tween the vats — loud as the sprat Olympia running barefoot down jetty stones: *Sea-nymphs hourly ring his knell / Ding-dong / Hark! Now I hear them / Ding-dong, bell.*

There'd be cider and scrumpy enough to swap for potable, comestible
— Cider Mother tapped the words gainst the vat-sides — enough to fill five
hungry maws.

Five.

*Full fathom five.*

Since the Burning, few could blossom, fewer still could bear ripe fruit.
Olympia and James A made no provision for spawn; then five years after
they took house together, whoomp her belly pushed out and that was Brendan, who died at nine months, and then Dan, the end of her beginner's
nerves, hoop-la! and then two come at once as died before they'd names,
then Mary Patricia, then Finn, then Seamus who died while birthing. James
A was walking Mary Pat downpath on her Seventh fore Cider Mother
trusted the girl was come to stay.

*Full fathom five thy father lies / Of his bones are coral made.*

They'd been far enough ahead to make some splash for Mary Pat's
Seventh. Every manjack of the dockside guzzling her good cider, singing
*Welcome welcome Mary Patricia M'Cool to life, to the life, the life of a harbor dreg,
hey hey, to the life of a harbor dreg;* Cider Mother'd looked askance at how
rapido the brew slid down their throats but what matter? Mary Pat had
made it to her Seventh. In seven years the girl had made for herself all fresh
blood, the which August Inkwhistle showed the crowd: one careful slit back
of Mary Pat's left knee. In fat red drops the fresh blood ran down her calf
while the dockside hollered *Spring it, spring it, spring it rare.* Mary Pat's eyes
rolled white, wide, the sweat stood on her, yet she did as her dap'd told her:
*Keep a straight spine and a fair tongue tween your teeth.* Mary Pat thanked the
harbor dregs, "Thank you kindly," she said. Dan leaned gainst a piling,
every inch indifferent, yet smack where Mary Pat could all times see him.
James A drained carboys with the best of them; "What of Finn and Mary
Kath," Cider Mother asked him, and he waved at the two smallest propped
in a half-keg, Finn's scant arm over the little one's shoulder. Cider Mother
reached to shake James A's arm and he raised her on it and sang *A fine
bookay you sprung, my cabbage, but twas I twas I as watered them,* and the sun
shone and the rats was nesting so richards would no hunt that week and
she danced with James A on the pier...

No profit in that memry. Cider Mother hummed a bit and got on with racking the second vat. She gathered her hotwashed carboys round the spigot and turned it and filled them each to a thumbwidth shy of their rims. The fire roared a bit in the braze; she raked coals to slow it.

The roarers was fewer now than when she was a spawn. Back then, the roaring spawn was many, lurched up jetty and down: they roared out of the good side of their stove-in faces, from tween their tiny earflaps, out of throats lumpy with red-black clots big as a justborn's fist. A few of the young ones who roared made it to their Seventh, but none was welcomed in ceremony. They crept on neath some wing or another till they was found one morning stiff in rigor, nor did the dockside come to their burning; nobbut the people of their own blood stood round while the roaring flames licked the misshape bones to ash. You had to be grateful you was no dealt a hand like that. Plain as tides there was no reason to who delivered a roarer and which hearts kept beating and for how long; spawn did no cling to bellies cause they was warmheart nor slide out from the careless; spawn come and stayed and throve without regard to kind or cruel or hopes.

After filling the last carboy, Cider Mother straightened creak by creak. Now *there* was a sound from the dung heap of the past. Open the door to one memry and a host'll crowd through, certain. Creak creak creak. The old couple on the roof of the world.

When she was still Olympia, two years past her Seventh, Constance pulled her out the side door while their mam and dap was having their Hunt Day lie-in. "They're grunt and snore for sure, come *long* Olympia," and led her cross the moraine, past the horse skeleton and through the iron gateposts to a yellowbrick four-story that they climbed and they climbed till they come to the tower on the flat roof. All Charnholm was spread out below them, sun glaring off the glassy dust. It dazzled Olympia some, so she was slow making out what lay behind the tower door. Inside, a little old wizened old monkey couple, the man and the woman side by side on a padded bench all flowery in a room with every tall window darked by red velvet porty-airs lined with tatter silk that hung in long fringes. The old monkeys directed them to the galley where Connie made the tea, proud of knowing the place to a faretheewell. "Carry this," she told Olympia, and shoved her out the galley with her handker full of mangel-wurzel cubes. Connie followed after with a tray of teapot and chipped handle-lack cups on mismatch saucers. The old woman wrapped ten hairy digits round the teapot's handle when she poured them out their tea. Constance and Olympia perched on a hard bench, sipping tea, chatting small about the weather; it was hot, and it had been hot, and it would be hot. Olympia swung her legs and kept her tea neath her nose to mask the tidemarsh smell of the monkey people's den.

Suddenly the old man leaned forward, creaking louder than the clink clink of Olympia stirring her tea. He whispered harsh through his used-raw throat cords:

"It was right, what happened. They was right to burn it. There was naught to be done but eat it with flame, every last office was foul rotten to the heart; they was right — *do you hear me?* — to burn it."

He sat back, creak creak, and sipped his tea. His monkey wife creaked her monkey skull in nod after his every creak and one more for good measure. "Right to burn," she said, "oh all to the good; can I press you to another cup of tea?"

"But what of the richards?" Olympia said. "How'd they come through scatheless?"

The old man nodded to his own creaks as he leaned forward again. "Richards come out of the ground like locusts. Every nineteen year," he said. "Come out, devour our substance, then it's back down in the ground with them. This too shall pass, and the righteous triumph, and the meek shall inherit the earth."

"It's good for the crops, actually," creaked the old woman. "Eat them back to the root, stimulates their growth, actually."

"Is that so?" said Olympia, polite. She looked to her sister for aid, but Constance sat prim beside her, her longer legs planted to the floor, sipping her redbrown tea.

"It is, actually," said the old woman. "So there is naught to worry about, naught at all, all's as it should be, service serves the good. Can I urge you to a nice salt biscuit?"

Connie cleared her throat and sat up straight, pushing her new breast nubbins out from her chest. "So," she said, "the richards will someday crawl back into their holes?"

Both pairs of monkey lips opened and spoke in staggered chorus:
"Oh yes they will my dear
    Of course they will my dear
        You have naught to fear
            All shall disappear..."

"It will have been one long bad dream," said the old man. He creaked upright and spoke more brisk than at any time since they walked through the door. "By my calculations, there are nine years, six months, and three days remaining to their reign. On that date, at 10:54 a.m., their iniquities shall be made known and they shall vanish like smoke."

The old woman spoke up from deep mong flowery cushions of ease. "Dearest, are you no forgetting that they've been here now already for twice seven years and some?"

"Homp, homp," said the old man's gums. "No, *dearest*, it is you who neglect to take into account that we seen three separate, unequal batches of these richards, spawned by the heat of the Great Burning which accrued unto them strange powers, powers that doubled their pleasure in copu- copu- copu-lation; those batches are the two-headed calves of the Unseeable Dairy, launched into being through a window we can no imagine; did we see it we should die on the instant. The richards who move mong us are sports of Nature, and with their passing shall come a return to the rhythms and the certainties of days gone by. Fear no darkness! The light of the burning shall be rekindled! Great swords of lightning shall flash from the heavens to sever the dappled and the ring-straked from the earth that abominates them! The burning shall come again and its Great fury shall cleanse every filthy soul from this the chosen World!" He'd been on his feet, shouting in his harsh whisper these declamations, but at this he sank, creak creak, back onto the cushions till he was near prone, from which position he creaked, "These times significate that we who remain on the surface are worthy of the final test. Remain upright; honor the dung pile as you honor the blossom; sing without ceasing; and some one day the Hunt

Wagon's passing shall spawn the great Gathering, wherein you and all the righteous shall be granted life while every blackheart coldheart richard is gathered to the airy vastness and there dispatched by giant strangulating hands." He closed his eyes. Creak creak.

"It's been a great pleasure to entertain you," said his wife. "What a pity you must go now." She did no rise nor wave but watched them, only, as they backed out the room and closed the door behind them.

"Is all he said for true, Con?" Olympia said as they repassed the horse skeleton.

Constance shrugged. "I've no least notion," she said. "But is it no lacious to think the richards will one day be scoured off the surface? Picture it was us had the potable. Picture it was us as had it."

"No more louring uphill downhill lugging great firkins."

"Did a richard ask, 'Where's my little truckling dreg?' we'd spit."

"We'd say, 'Gone where the sun don't shine,'" said Olympia.

Cider Mother straightened creak by creak. That was the last carboy filled. That old couple was dead now, certain, gone to moldy bone with James A and all. Time distilled days and years; you pressed gathered apples through cloths and made cakes of the pommace, you poured the mash into the vat and you racked and you racked while you let time pass for settling, till at last you'd your essence. *Those are pearls that were his eyes / Ding-dong.* The used mash mulched the apple trees and so around and so time moved long. *Eppur si muove,* it does indeed move — did she read that in a crumble book? Or was it a tale from her mam's bent knees? The man the richards threw down for his learning, who gave them the lie with his last breath, *Eppur si muove.* So much went to ash in the Burning. Well, ash had its own uses, and psha, if she was no forgetting to water her own ashes in courtyard, tsk she clicked, they was short on lye to make up soap from all the fresh spag as was melting slowly in its buckets still. Cider Mother hummed in the stone cellar as she built up the fire, as she ladled here and poked there, as she wove a frail nest from twigs and crumbs, as she built a bulwark any richard blow could topple, as she laid it up natheless.

# Dockside Scutage

IGH UP ON SOUTH POINT, in the tallest, stoniest keep in the compound, Governor Donal bade farewell to his lady. "Reap Day," he said. "Off to reap the scutage," *harnxhh, harnxxh*, he laughed.

Lady Mandra had lived by him many a long year. "Oh yes, Reap Day," said she, straightening petals of her paper flowers. "Do remind the dregs that it's they who owe *you* the service, Donal. With all you've done for them, the mines and the potable and all, a few months of service or a modest fee is the *least* exchange they should make. Though I'm afraid they're inclined to think scutage unjust to those of straitened means." She stood back to judge the effect of the flowers in a tall bone vase. "Had the smiths sucked *all* the marrow from this, I could have made much more splash," she cavilled. "While the fact is, it's your kindness only as gives *any* dreg an out. We must all pull together for a better, finer Charnholm. Tell them, 'When the fee is mine, you're free of the mines.' Tell them that."

"That's catchy, that is," said Gov Don, admiring, and pencilled it on his shirt-cuff. Mandra was a fount unfailing. She'd other virtues, too.

Lady Mandra shrugged, raising and lowering two of her virtues. "Do make sure you wrap your throat well, my dear."

Gov Don cleared his throat. These displays of affection roused his *hrmph hrmph* gland. "See to the palanquin," he said.

Lady Mandra blew him a kiss off the back of her hand. As he walked through the garden, he glimpsed her skirts going round and round in the drawing room. These vitus bouts of hers came without warning; only twirling while strengthy footmen tootled their pennywhistles in any way calmed her. Whom she always assiduously summoned on the least threat of an attack, so careful was she of her health, so tender of her obligations to her position.

Gov Don hrmphed and stumped off to the stables. He favored his right leg, walking. "Old wound does act up," Gov Don told his headgroom. "Same night you got yours," he said.

"Ay, imph'm," said the headgroom. M'Donal despised the Governor. M'Donal was on gatewatch the night Gov Don tried to stick it to Mandra atop the compound wall. The lady'd have none of it, natural like, and a well-aimed kick tossed him to the stones below. Where he set up a wailing, *skree-eek, skree-eek,* till M'Donal cursed and unlatched the wicket door to raise the wailing bone sack. At which Gov Don give him such a lash-out with his good leg that M'Donal fell to the rubble and twisted his own ankle. They hobbled back through the open wicket arm in arm, last time he'd laid flesh to the Gov's. M'Donal soothed his soul by doing so little work for the Governor as he might and stealing what he could. "Ay," said M'Donal, "old wound. Right. Who'll ye have out today, then, gov?"

Gov Don gave it a think. "Oh, the usuals. Give them all a thick bran mash, there's a good man."

"Right," said M'Donal. He spat out a ryestraw and whistled three short and a high long.

Six men square and true rupted from the nearest stall. "Rations rations rations," they growled.

"Ghastly noise they do make," Gov Don said to his headgroom.

"Never notice it on m'self," said M'Donal. "Sit ye down on the bench, I'll have them harnessed in less time nor it takes to cut a whistle."

The Governor reclined in the grateful sunlight. So many obligations, so many dependents; the constant effort required to steward his demesne could tire a man. Lady Mandra, the compound, sundry administrative tasks. The House of the Teaching Anathematizers alone was a massive responsibility; his chest swelled as he contemplated what a legacy he'd there leave behind him. "Palanquin ready yet, M'Donal?" he shouted to the raw air to vent the swelling. He and he alone had gathered the finest rimers in a House devoted to edification of rimers to come. How they'd concentrate their knowledge beneath his benevolent eye. Anathematizing songs were tunelier and made good sense, these days. *Strike boys strike / and do not fail / kill the rats / by tooth and nail.* That was a pretty one. Not that they killed by tooth and nail any too much nowadays, except it might be at a jamboree. But that was no matter to a song. Good company, too, rimers, always lots to say once you got them out of those white robes; robes were tradition but tradition could mislead a man; you needed to see more than ankles to form a full and fair estimate. That's where he was so clever on the Hunt Breakfasts. Lady Mandra was all for any event where she might dress skin and skintight, and naturally she set the fashion; skirts went up, necklines plunged, garb clung, Gov Don reaped the benefits.

Reap Day. He was supposed, "Supposed to have left a full tick ago," Gov Don hollered.

"Coming now, Gov," said the headgroom.

Ca-lok, ca-trak, ca-lok, ca-trak.

The coulees sang as they ran beneath the carrypoles of his palankeen. Hard to get used to, that had been. Every now and now the Governor spoke to his headgroom on this subject. "Sure they're on the up and up?"

"Out of course!" M'Donal said each time. "It's the proxmatey to your honor makes them want to emlate your most excellent contribution to Charnholm by singing songs like rimers do."

"They're such ... mmm ... *bloody* tunes. Do you know."

"Pro-active, what it is, sir. When they give voice to any black spirits as might lurk within, they turn them harmless. Like upside down day, sir, ye know how ye like that."

"Once a moon is one thing. Need they exorcise potential demons every carriage day?"

"It's every week the men and I are meeting to work on better songs; they're working up to it, sir. It's they fear to give full voice to their gratitude, might grow weak neath carrypole and slow your stately progress. Sir, ye're a rare model for these dregs. I wisht ye could see how hard they strive to be worthy of ye."

"Ah. Well, hmmm. Well, dole a carboy of scrumpy for each of them to drink my health and I wish them the speediest possible betterment."

"I'm sure they sha' be the more speedy for that gift, yer honor."

Gov Don moved off after exchanging bows with his headgroom, who, soon as the Gov was round the corner, threw himself down by the First Six, the Usuals, where he shoved his snout in the straw to muffle his laughs. "Oh, oh," M'Donal gasped at last, "jack up tha' boots, boyos, for none here can better this," wiping tears off his cheeks. "I had just now some kindly speech with your master and preserver."

So Gov Don gave no worry to the songs his six square coulees sang as they trotted him downhill to the docks, for they were making strides to correct their poor performance. He leaned back on the quilted bench and inhaled a little tarponesse.

*Rats and richards / In their holes / We will find and spear you / Rats and richards / Come to sun / By its light we'll pierce you / Blood you / Spit you / Rats and richards / Show your snouts / We will kill and render / Into spag / Light and clean / Your bones we'll glean / Rats and richards / Hear our song / Poke your nose where we belong / And a one thrust / two thrust / three thrust / more / Run through / Spin round / Toss on flames / Rats and richards / Render well / Light and clean you'll leave us .... and a one thrust / two thrust / three thrust / more...*

Gov Don inhaled another pinch. Song like that should restore their blood. Going to be a fine Reap Day. A watching coulee tugged his codpiece in homage. Gov Don wished they'd stayed with the traditional tugging of the forelock but new times new ways as Mandra said. Coulees carried him smooth and came when he called; that doubtless stretched their capacities to the maximum. Small minds, small deeds. He stretched out his arms in the sunlight. He, the coulee governor, acted on a much, much larger field.

*Rats and richards / Hear our song / Poke your nose where we belong...*

Were there only some mind so wide as his own to appreciate the scope of his acts. Mandra tried but she lacked the necessary concentration. A pity.

*Puff a dick / Puff a dick / Puff a dick up / Still a skinny noodle / Still can't stuff a hole / Stick it in / Wiggle round / Warm her up / We sha' lick / We sha' lick / We sha' lick the bowl...*

Still, the work was its own satisfaction.

*Apple tart / Apple tart / Perry on the top / Sweet treats / Richards meat / Dregs eat on the hop...*

One performed one's role as best one could.

*Skinny dick / Skinny dick / Needs a pair of horns on / Give to him / Give to him / What he needs and that quick.*

*Rats and richards / In their holes / We sha' find and ...*

"Ha hmmph hallo," said Gov Don to the rigman who held open his carriage door. "Bosun?"

"No, sir," said the rigman. "Bosun's still up the formast rigging. Nob-but two snecks before he fetch here."

Gov Don snorted. Waiting was at all times abominable; worse in this fierce sun among all these smells and vermin.

"You come faster nor we expected, sir," said the young rigman. "Sharp time you did make coming atop these coulees. Fine backs and legs you got and fine matched, sir."

The Gov's chest swelled. He *had* picked a good coulee crew. "Sound in wind and limb," he told the rigman, and went on to describe how he'd bred them and how he trained them. "Bran mash once a week and double every hols day," the Governor was telling him as the bosun came bluster and sweat up the hill, "essential to care for your cattle." The rigman listened carefully and the bosun bobbed respectfully and all the while the sun shone on the harbor and Gov Don nodded through his tarponesse haze. A few sturdy smiths lined one side of the dais; best give them some honor said Mandra, seeing it's they put the sharp on the pike-points, and so he'd called up Drosh, Quix, and Innsmort, trusty men and true, to the first rank of the dreg mass. "Now now well now, hmmph." Gov Don took a deep steadying snuff of tarponesse. Dregs would soon crowd round him, breathing garlic on his lapels. Tarponesse made the smell bearable and he must bear it while dregs admired his leadership.

At last the comper of the dock scutmen came up huffing, a satchel full of scut-chits in his arms, followed by all the horii in the harum, each waving a barley sheaf over her head. "Ah," said Gov Don, and rubbed his hands together. He noted that the sheaf-waving was a trifle lazy-lax. He mentioned it to the comper when he took the satchel from him and riffled the chits. Must make a show of it. He'd go through them, later, with a fine-tooth comb. Ah, the barley sheaves were waving more energetically now. Gov Don raised his voice to the crowd: "Mustn't keep the ladies waiting," and moved towards the dais.

"Likely catch their death in those scants," said Quix.

"Takes two to catch a sneeze," said Drosh.

"Like to see my old woman in one of those," said Innsmort.

"See her by daylight at all be a change for you, apple nose," said Quix.

"Well then," Governor Donal addressed the massed dregs. "This is certainly a pleasant surprise." They were patently impressed by his costume and stature, for a hum of marvelment went round.

"How can it be anyways surprising?" said Quix.

"Every gorry year we do the same gorry thing," said Drosh.

"Memry like his, probably *is* a surprise," Innsmort told them.

"Well, then," Gov Don rubbed his hands. "I, I stand here, don't I?"

"Same place as every time," the bosun whispered to the first mate.

"If your honor'd be so good," said the docks comper.

"Must have the scutage or the service, you know," said Gov Don.

"To which your honor's surely welcome," said the bosun.

"It is not I but fair Charnholm requires it," said Gov Don.

"Snark me up the rump again, gormless fatbake," Drosh muttered.

"Ah-he-hemm," said the Governor, and lifted his voice. "I come before you this Reap Day —" The crowd was responding already.

"He did no come before; we was here waiting him," said Quix.

"Could he no come on his own?" said Drosh.

"Gov's main powerful. Likely he could come just pondering his power," said Innsmort.

Gov Don said, "This Reap Day, to receive from you, good people —"

"Ah, we're one and each good good people," said Quix.

"Never better," said Drosh.

"The due presentment of your yearly toil." Gov Don uncovered his head. "A mere third of your crops, your catch, your year's production. And all to keep fair Charnholm free. Free! Safe! Queen among cities!" The horii waved their barley sheaves over his pate in the seagrey sunlight. The bosun and his first mate hauled the burning brazier to Gov Don's side, and laid the metal rod in its coals.

"Enough to blind a man," said Quix.

"Hoy, hoy, eye damage! Waived scutage for these blasted eyes!" said Innsmort.

The horii danced three times round beloved Governor Donal while the mad viol played, while the massed rimers sang of wind and rain and the fat grains growing, while the first mate rotated the metal rod in the red coals. "Reap me reap me reap me," the horii sang, their frond skirts flying round their nipples as they high-kicked.

"Nice thatch, there," said Quix.

"Use a hank of that to patch my roof," said Drosh.

The horii sank to their knees before Gov Don. They laid their sheaves at his feet. "For these sheaves I thank you." He motioned the bosun to raise high the red-burnt rod of metal. "Step forward and present your scutage and I swear to you here that I shall this year, in exchange for scutage, remit the lawful obligation on each male hale in mind and body, to serve in the forces that protect Charnholm from enemies without and traitors within." The dregs jammed in a tight column to present their rumps for scutage. The bosun touched the rod to each cheek. Gov Don ogled the breasts of the kneeling horii the while. When all were marked, the bosun roused the Gov from his contemplation. "Harrumph, rump," he said. "I have received your scutage and found it good. I proclaim that each marked male dreg here today present shall be free of his requisite and due guardian service for the coming year. Your service has been measured and found wanted. Go in peace and may peace reign ever over our fair Charnholm."

"Huzzah, huzzah," they cried, and pressed wet kelp to their new brands.

"Whump, up the richards," said Quix.

"Round and round," said Drosh, "Scutmen gather chits and —

"Chits pay scutage," Innsmort whispered with them.

"Like to see, sometime, one of these here enemies," said Innsmort.

"Let me know an you do," said Quix.

"Some among you whisper!" Every pair of eyes looked up. Times, Gov Don'd spike up in a heartbeat, like a cracked bone poking from spag; took the dregs by shock every time. "Some among you good toilers do whisper of a better life did you have the trappings of we the serving class. We moil from first light to candle gutter that you good people may live carefree. Whispers of a better life? Heed not these whispers, my friends! Who among us has no dreams of a better life? None. All of us dream these dreams. Yet you will not achieve that better life by opening your ears to the sly voices of troublestirrups." Gov Don drank potable and spat and dried his damp mouth with his hand. "Your sinews are strong and your backs are broad; you stride the earth and sail the seas; you are the pride of Charnholm. A few who cannot muster the small scutage fee; pallet pounders, limpnecks, gutless marvels; these few murmur of softer lives to be had by running counter to Charnholm's laws — only a ploy to weaken you, my friends! Their envy knows no limit, and in that limitless envy they desire to pull you down to their own flabby level. These whisperers want all dregs to crawl in the dust as they do. Pay no heed to whispers! Keep yourselves strong and proud and brave, you incomparable, inconquerable men of Charnholm!"

The scutmen cheered and waved and twitched their unburned ass-cheeks. The other dregs waggled, once, their wet-kelp poultices. The smiths raised their gloved right fists overhead.

"Clap clap, yay yay," mouthed Quix.

"Shutter up, else you'll get one of them flat-top necks," said Drosh.

"Y'honor, I take my head in my hands—" said Innsmort.

"To thank you for your sound advice," said Quix.

"A sound I can no more hear," said Drosh.

"Hold hard, here he blows," said Innsmort.

"And now — thank you, thank you — and now, good my people, let mirth prevail! Welcome to these laden boards, come and have some cakes and ale. Let each scutman take a hori and proceed. When every scutman's taken his fill, throw ope the boards to all Charnholm!"

There was cheering at that. A bit feeble, mayhap. Guzzling scutmen leave small crumbs behind. Still, "There you go then," said Quix.

"A full belly slaps a smile on the mug," said Drosh.

"Open wide your rye-hole, smarmy mates," said Innsmort.

"Stuff, lads, stuff," all three chanted underbreath.

Gov Don took a ceremonial bite and a ceremonial swig and shook every man jack's hand. "Make sure the coulees get their plates full," he told the bosun. The smiths approached to deliver their plaudits.

"Aye aye, sir," said Innsmort.

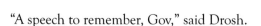

"A speech to remember, Gov," said Drosh.

"Rare job, sir," said Quix.

The smiths' hands were stronger than they knew. They crushed his slim digits with their rough affection, slapped his back so hard his teeth jostled. Gov Don sighed over leadership's fierce obligations. It was good to see their brawny spirits advance on the food and drink and sweep all before them; thus would they demolish any threat to the public peace. Gov Don shook out his mangled fingers for another few dozen hands to shake. The fleet's sails hung slack from their furlings. The harbor lapped the stone jetty. The men advanced and took his hand and crushed it and bobbed their heads and strode to the table and reaped its fruits. The horii, their crowns askew, served the finest provender to his coulees. Everyone was having a glad and easy time. A pity Mandra was rarely strong enough to stand beside him at these affairs; the very notion set her spinning. Here came another pair to wring blood from his hands.

"Taller far than a tall tops'l, gov."

"That was giving it stick, sir."

It seemed they approved his speech, though their parlance was obscure. Well, the bosun would report any malingerers or false speakers. He could rely on the bosun.

"Pleasant as it has been to bestow upon you this small portion of what you deserve, I must leave you now, good my people, and return to the never-ending work of ensuring a better, finer Charnholm. Give yourselves three cheers and hooray for scutmen!"

"Stick it down solid, gov!" said Quix through his full mouth.

"Reap me reap me reap me!" said Drosh into his perry.

"Who'll help the horii home?" called Innsmort.

Gov Don heard them not. His palanquin cantered uphill as he snored among its cushions, deaf to his coulees singing:

*Rats and richards / Stuff their maws / Rats and richards / Sheathe their claws / Fat tum / Soft foot / Roll them over / On their backs lay / Give their guts some air / Oh / Poke their guts a hole / Ha / Spill and snarl and tangle / Innards curl and mangle / Bellies fat / Spew on hats / Stand back from the spray / Oh / Stand clear of the spout...*

Lady Mandra leapt from the tapestry bench by the window, tossing her broidery frame aside. "Oh how was it my dear Donal? No, take the big chair, yes, did it go well? Careful of my hair, the new parlogal just now got it straight, shall I ring for a nice hot cider?"

Governor Don settled himself in his chair, which would have been more comfortable without the half-dozen small pillows Lady Mandra adored. "Hrmph, hrmph," he said. "They liked the speech. I gave them a bit of the what-for. Well received, that. Cider, now. Cider'd go down nicely. Hmmm," and then he told her all about it.

# Lady Mandra

I KEEP MY LIPS CLAMPED SHUT lest what I know escape them. This is my advice to all the plangent young who scurry, feathers flying, through their glossy days. Your lips long to part in confession; do not permit them. Keep your green soul in its shell. Strengthen the carapace that keeps the tender soul secure. Secrete layer upon layer upon layer. Spare no effort to encase that pearl.

Once you open the hatch, every virtue and every ill flies out of your magic box, scatters like ashes, becomes a part of everything and thus nothing. Keep yourself to yourself, keep your face a great mask, ignore no chink, be at all times vigilant.

This lesson my own mother never learned. Nor any of her set. When shelter caves were all the go, all of them built shelter caves, the season's venue for the weeklong galas of ether and tambour till dawn, laughing in bejeweled gowns, tapping cross stone floors in crystal heels wherein one goldfish swam. Clare was seven and I a year younger when flunkeys lifted us from our warm beds through a puff of cold midnight to our warm carriage. Hot bricks at our feet as Nana and the footmen and Anthick the butler dwindled away. The carriage was full of jasmine and honeysuckle as it swayed over quiet streets, the scent wafting from where our parents sat in front with the driver, and we'd been promised cake and orange at journey's end. We clambered down stairs until we reached bottom. Clare always claimed she felt the whoof of air but I did not notice the hatch close overhead. Cake and orange! We girls sat on the Ashkbez green and blue carpet while our parents brought and served us that illicit meal. What fun! we thought, having our parents drudge for us. What fun!

I held that night between my breast and my pillow for twenty-one years. For that period we orbited our parents. In pairs, in threes, and all together we discussed Mamé's changes to her exercise regime and Dadda's fly-tying;

and whether long overtunics were permissible as evening wear if draped over silk trous. It was a long dream in the shelter cave. For years we made and remade beaded drapery. Then with a clap that long dream ended.

It was a hot night. Clare and I were suffocate. We climbed to the hatch and she pushed it open. We balanced on the hatchring. Clare pushed her neck and shoulders into the opening. "What is it?" I asked, but she would not yield me her place. I heard chanting, and a viol playing, and grunts of effort, and squeals I felt in my very spine. At last I could not bear it. I pulled Clare aside and raised my eyes above the hatchring.

A red-orange moon shone full upon the Hunt Boys' risen cocks that swung at turgid length as they marched, as they chanted, while the viol played behind a trundle cart. Their bodies were red-orange as they speared and turned and thrust spitted rats into the cartbed.

All this I saw in a glimpse. Voices rose below us and Delphine let the hatch ring down.

Perhaps? Yes. That Hunt peep is why I chose Gov Don. Yes. He is six inches shorter than I and stout as a bolster; he cleans his ears with his pinky in a vigorous, stirring motion; he is nearly bald and in each wrinkle on his pate a little dirty wax resides; he snorts in his sleep and he sleeps for many hours. Awake, he has no conversation. But when he is by, the world is back-lit red-orange and marvelous and new. How unchancy that it should be he who opens that hatch.

How can one (one cannot) forsake that person (one cannot even imagine forsaking that person) who unlocks the hatch? One cleaves to that person forevermore.

# Galanty Show

WITH MOST OF CHARNHOLM up the Reap Day tables, few saw a redsail junk draw up to the shingle of North Point. The women down the sour crags half-heard its rigging furl as it rounded the point and nobbut pulled their stippled reedticks the closer; mensal bleeding does chill a body. The North Light comper was up-jetty guzzling provender from horii hands, leaving a skeleton scut-patrol behind to stretch pout-mouth on their pallets.

As the *Mam Can Cook* reached shoal water, Palan steered her mong the saltgrass tussocks into shelter. When Palan had lowered and laden the reed curragh, Fergus come above deck, grunting and cursing down the rope ladder to the waiting curragh, much hampered by a large square case held tight to his chest, the which he placed on his knees once his duff was secure on the curragh's thwart. "Palan!" he shouted. "Hustle your stumps. Hard work never killed no one."

Palan walked the junk, re-checking every hatch and batten. Below-deck, his mam's deep green eyes looked out from a corner. "Come *long*, Palan!" shouted his dap. Palan swarmed down ladder. He paddled the curragh to shallow water, leapt out and towed her inshore till Fergus could step out dryshod. Fergus snapped his fingers soon as he was upstanding. "Dislade the rest, get the curragh in cover, then it's home to our grotto."

Grotto? Palan had no expectation Fergus would explain, which expectation was fulfilled entire. Palan dragged the curragh in mong the bog and rubble at the harborside foot of North Point and carried gear back to his dap. To where his dap'd been; Fergus and his large square case was halfway up the shingle, so Palan shrugged and hoisted and moiled up slope in his dap's wake.

Fergus pushed through a bramble thicket and Palan followed after, stooped as he stooped, the cases clanking on his feet some, to tumble forward through an arch a fathom high that opened into the sandstone cliff.

Fergus set down the square case and threw out his arms, his long nails touching the walls: "Our grotto," he said. "Make yourself to home." While Palan spawn-handled cases and canes gainst the far wall, Fergus sat crossleg on a bench scraped from the north wall. He opened the large square case a handswidth and peered inside. No clouding in the vials. Fergus took a sniff of tarponesse, careful like, lest the spawn see him and clamor maybe for a snort of his own. The vials was all intacto. A good thing, when you looked at what store of edibles they had. The spawn was a born forager, sure, but he'd no brought the spawn ashore to forage. That knackiness of his should be turned to fine account here in Charnholm. The spawn, sad enough, had naught of his dap's skill with dregs nor richards; he hung his head mute-tongue when backs needed slapping and virtues was sore in want of magnification. Fergus shook his head. No, the spawn'd never have skill with making nor doling tarponesse. But enough Smiths owed Fergus a favor, yes they did, Fergus nodded his head, sure one would take the spawn neath his brawn. "Spawn neath brawn," he chortled.

Palan paid him no mind. He'd enough to do sorting the galanty show. Canes unrolled easy; though there was a few wet spots on the canvas, they'd dry soon enough in this wind as come off the harbor steady here. He crouched by the grotto-entry and looked round. Walls of red sandstone pocked with glintrock, dry red gravel and sand on the floor. The walls was carved by some sort of wedge, the edge-marks clear in the growing light. It smelled like any smith cave, reft of even the least breath of a fish-fin. Land smells every way round him. His dap was nodding in tarponesse haze gainst the far wall. Palan pulled a crumble book stealthy from his pack. The ingenia of Leo a Vinci. He chewed a hunk of salttack, turned the pages careful with his right hand. A lens; now where'd they get such — he near ripped the page when Fergus beltered sudden.

"Now den!" Fergus on his feet, his gutball rising and falling as he spoke, out-thrusting off his lean frame, "Galanty Show! I'm off for spag and provender. Do you rest here, naught to busy yourself with but gentle tinkering and get your land-legs. Scrabble and grive, that's all we olders is good for; pull out our own tendons to tie up better lives for spawn! So while I toil and moil, you'll stretch at your leisure, work nobbut your brain-pan."

"I've no spag to make a light with," said Palan.

"Work by light and sleep by night," said Fergus, the gutball leaping neath his skin, "There's naught healthier for you young spawn."

"I've eleven years, dap."

"Can pass for nine with the small height on you," Fergus assured him. "Oh they sha' be cowtered entire when you come from back of the galanty screen; the pixie with the pictures, they'll say. I'm for forage; stay close within till I return."

"Aye aye," said Palan. When his dap was clear of the brambles as concealed the cavemouth, he muttered to the dry red gravel: "Pixie with the pictures. What a soak of a notion." He shrugged and set out the spin-lantern. One by one he drew in poke-ink and kelp-ink the images for its frames.

⌒

Fergus lay up mong the rubble till nightfall, snuffing tarponesse, sleeping and scheming by turns. Come moonrise, he paddled the curragh long the jetty and round South Point. What he did there he did by quarter-moonlight. He was back fore sun-up with three bushels of edibles, two kegs of potable, and a cask wrapped round in spag. "Who takes care of his boy, eh?" said Fergus. He and Palan lay up in the grotto a good long while. Fergus ate till his gutball swole, Palan studied and tinkered. They'd no more to say to each other on land than they'd at sea. "What do we wait for?" Palan asked round the first half-moon. "Light at the dark of the year," was all the answer he got off Fergus.

⌒

The days got shorter quicker and quicker, like the nights was nudging them aside to reach the dark of the year. There is a pause, then, when it seems the tide'll never turn, and then it turns. Day swung round night easy, slow, till day got its strength and night began to wither.

Gov Don proclaimed a hols day on the first full moon following the triumph of light over dark. "He does love a proclamation," Lady Mandra told the other ladies over tiffin. This hols day was one they none of them could escape. She and all the tiffin ladies braced for a long spell on the bleachers in full rig-out. "Headdresses and all," Lady Mandra assured them, and plonked her broider needle through stretched canvas with more force than necessary.

The Governor and his Lady set out from South Point early one morning, the full moon still hanging faint overharbor. Lady Mandra's hat lifted from her head as she put one copper-toed boot on a coulee's laced hands. "Oh, oh!" she cried with vexation, snatching it from the air with her finger-tips and resettling it to its 20-degree tilt.

Gov Don looked straight ahead. "Make a fuss in public, hmm, hmmph," he said.

The Governor and his Lady stepped into the ceremonial palanquin. "Hmm, have you checked carry poles?" the Governor said to headgroom M'Donal.

"All righty-okay," the man answered, pulling his forelock the least amount.

"Hmm?" the Governor asked his lady.

"Mm-hmm," she answered.

"Forward!" Gov Don told his six coulees, who hefted the chair's poles to their shoulders and trotted downhill to the harbor. Their feet slapped to the beat of their song:

*Fat cat, got a rat, how now sha' he kill it? / Fat cat, squashed flat, in his cave he's buried / Fat cat, thought he's smart, now he's neath the rubble / Bite black, breath snaps / Don't be coy, who's the boy / Choice is made, what'll you do / He is, he is, y – o – u !*

Lady Mandra poked her husband's eye with a hat plume. "Should they?"

"Hmm?" said Gov Don.

"They be singing that?" she said.

"Keep your veil round your mouth, Mandra. Kept me awake all night last time you breathed lowland. There. Now, hum, what?"

"Singing."

"Ah, hmm." He listened to the coulees singing, their chests thrown well forward. "M'Donal says they're working hard to better the songs. He says we intimidate them."

"Ah," she said.

"Mm-hmm," he said.

*Downhill, don't spill / Fat cat and his lady / Richard kill, pay the bill / Fore you are ready...*

"That last one don't roll smooth," said near hind coulee.

"You're a socket-yanker, you are," said off hind coulee.

"More trot in time, boyos, and less chatback," near fore coulee hollered over his right shoulder.

"Clam yourselves on my solo or I'll stripe it off your skins," said the head coulee, looking leftways at near fore.

"Hear that?" near fore hollered to the sweat shiny hind coulees.

The head coulee sang: *Pikes and spears and piercéd eyes / Fat rats will be dying / Crisping in some Wagon maw / Meanwhile I'll be crying?*

"Ha / ha / ha / ha" sang all six coulees together, and ran faster, ran heats with their own heeldust, down, downhill.

They outraced their own shadows coming down the final fathoms above the harbor, the coulees chanting below, the deadweight blinking above. Flags snapped in the stiff salt breeze. Lady Mandra clapped her hands.

"I'll give you summat to clap about," off hind coulee hissed.

The clouds opened and closed like mussels feeding. Hundreds of Hunt Boys in polished corvisers gleamed in the sunbreaks. Flags snapped, and coulees stamped their feet as they off-loaded richards onto the viewing bleachers. Horii caressed Hunt Boy backsides with oiled palms, their shoulders and calves glittering mica in the morning sun as they worked.

"Lovely day for a revue," said Lady Mandra.

"Simple necessity," said Gov Don. "They're mad for this kind of thing."

⟋

Hols Day! Hunt Boys gleamed and horii glittered, richards watched from bleachers and dregs from the jetty bankmen; flags waved and musicians played; the Hunt Wagon's keel glowed blue. Hunt Boys drilled and horii danced, tables groaned neath fragrant platters, kegs of Cider Mother's best perry flowed free. In holes and sumps and nooks and crannies, ratpups tugged blind at ratdugs, tumbled half-grown in play, leapt out at their olders and was cuffed for their pains. And all the living scratched at fleas, even those who laved their toes in basins of wormwort tea.

Finn M'Cool prowled the jetty's harborside with his clanch of boyos, slinkstep paddywhack full of grig, chasing each other with bullkelp whips. Mary Patricia and Mary Katharine, cleanfoot and skirt-tucked, kicked their heels gainst the bankmen; Mary Pat preening her outthrust chestnubs, Mary Kath's skirt hiked and clumped. Cider Mother seldom laid any charge on them, cept they was to stay behind shutters as a Rat Hunt passed, keep their tongues behind their teeth round scutmen, and drink nobbut the potable she gave them. So long as they did all that: "You may scamper up and down *Hail Janus* mast all day long, for all of me," said Cider Mother. This morning she'd buttoned them into clean pinnas *and* longskirt tunics. Ton of clothes to lug round, did you ask Mary Kath. None did. They sat on the bankmen watching Cider Mother by her kegs, doling cider and stronger to all comers, a smile for any and speech for few. "Ambrose won a few words off her," said Mary Pat, which they tucked away to consider later, like so much they saw. "Likely asking him can he take Finn for next round of Hunt Boy training," Mary Pat said. "Don't *squirm*, Mary Kath. You — hold on now. What's he?" said Mary Pat. She leaned back on her hands, like she was zamining the sky for spots.

"You can quit off now, Mary Pat. I think every male of them's got a good eyeful of your charms."

"I atching is unn," said Mary Pat.

"You're what?"

"Oook at inn!" When Mary Kath kept up looking blank at her, Mary Pat opened a corner of her mouth. "He ull see an I oove eye ips, ackbrain."

Mary Kath twisted round. A compact male spawn trudged long the shingle, a bundle of rods and a roll of cloth neath his left arm. Where his black knit cap rode up on his crown, gold hair sprung thick as bog-moss. His skin was pale bronze; his eyes was some kind of dark in the noon light as made no shadows, no surprises to none of that, but "Gold hair," said Mary Kath. "You ever —" Mary Pat shook her head, and Mary Kath continued, "Got a spring to him like a tumbler, hmmm? He'd hold up well on a long haul."

Mary Pat sat up straight and faced the horii passing. "Was he to get his growth, maybe. Hair's a glory, though."

"One of the small sprys they send down mine?"

"Or a rope-dancer's toss."

The boyo clanch spied the gold hair at the same time. "Chalybeate!" "Catch that!" "Lick the wax out my ears!" "Tin tin tintin tintinabulation!" as they advanced on the half-size, whirling bullkelp round their heads the while. The incomer stopped, laid his long bundle on the sand, and planted his feet. Finn hung back while the rest of his clanch harranged and spat. Times, these slung-from-elsewheres washed up on hols days but this one was out of the common. He'd his own balance, like he could glide on spag. Finn started to move forward, his palm outstretched, when he was thrust aside by a pair of burly Smiths. "Come long," said one to the gold-head. "Show time," said the other. Their quarry picked up his bundle, placid, and walked forward tween the two Smiths. The clanch floated off to the tideline. Finn watched the trio till they climbed up jetty, then raced in great flails of sand to rejoin the clanch, who was vigorous splaining what they'd done to the incomer had the Smiths no been there.

⟨⟩

Ambrose walked away from Cider Mother with a drap of perry. Tomfool to call her Olympia front of all those know-naughts. Small wonder she gave him a bit of hiss. As the sun rolled down slow off the top of its arch, he tried his luck again. "Olympia," he said.

"No," said Cider Mother.

"Do you remember —" he said.

"No," she said. "Perry?"

He let her fill his cup. "Remember when —"

"No."

"When Akrim was first training us?"

"No."

"You did fine but I fell off the rope two out of three times, remember?"

"No."

"Then one day I give up, tossed my balance swag at his head, 'I'm done,' I told him."

"Oh?" Her face moved so much as a spag lump might.

"I was boxing at him from the hawser, remember? How he grinned?"

"No," she said, but this time she'd to clamp her lower lip tween her teeth. What a gawk he'd looked, his feet every which a way but all times somehow on the thick rope, black with their sweat.

"I told him he maun be glad. 'Can sleep all your mornings away from this day forward,' I shouted. Remember?" She refilled his cup. "He said: 'How goot you dense,' " Ambrose said, sipping his fresh perry. "'When forget. When yell. Is goot, vare goot.' "

She smiled. "You've Akrim to the life, there. He was seldom so kind to me. He —" She turned away to serve some richard's coulee come up for his perry. Ambrose wandered off; coulees stank of the smuck he'd pulled his boots right out of. Comp-major of the Hunt Boys. Gov Don even tipped the hat to him. Your most of the coulees plain ached to rase all that. To pull you back down mong them.

Gov Don was just slipping his feet from out their buskins and into a basin of wormwort tea when Fergus come sidling up. "Gov, I've —"

Gov Don stamped his feet back into their husks. "Later," he said.

"But Gov I —" his black hair falling in oily lanks over his eyes, his long fingers twitching. Gov Don waved him off. Fergus backed away a step, near treading on Lady Mandra's robe, pedaled his feet in air, like, drove a hand neath his tunic and come out with a small stone box. "Present for the Gov," Fergus wheedled. "Come now, can no turn 'way my scutage, Gov, tardy though it be, still, you're 'bliged to gracious ceptance, no?" The Governor nudged the lid open with one large square thumb. "Ware wind!" said Fergus, and Gov Don moved the box to the lee of his cloak.

On the dais below, two Smiths cupped hands and blew: *Hallooo! Halloooo!* the hams of their hands opening and closing. *Galanty Show!* they shouted. *Galanty Show!* the dregs hollered back.

"Ah," said Gov Don. "Well, I accept your hmmm, your timely hmmm, yes, gift." He cleared his throat and looked round. Every eye was fixed on the dais below where some sprat was unscrolling a wide sail framed by two long poles. Out of course, the dreg mass standing round the dais would no dare to lift their eyes to Gov Don, or maybe it was they cared no jot nor tittle when there was this new show going forward. That was the point, no?

Keep giving them new shows. Only got themselves in trouble when they lacked employment or entertainment. Small brainpans, small power to govern, couldn't even govern themselves; fallen to animals, really. They needed a model, someone they could raise their eyes to. Gov Don himself had eyes only for the small stone box of fine tarponesse in his hand. He made room for Fergus aside him on the bleacher.

Fergus looked at Gov Don. His face a disk of dirty spag-ends, his eyes grey slits sunk in a pair of spag hollows, his lips a trough of spag-crust, his nose lump on lump of spag.

Gov Don looked at Fergus. A long thin snout, two button-black eyes set in yellow drooping flesh, cheekbones raked above the sunken cheeks, a long thin chin tipped with a tuft of black.

In the lee of their cloaks, they bent over the stone box, sampled and chaffered; the tuck at the corners of their lips the same, their eyes intent on the box the same.

Time to time, while an offer lingered in one pair of ears, they turned to the dais, where shadows now danced on the white canvas. A dancing figure unfolded to reveal two smaller figures aboard ship — "Willa look on those waves!" cried a dreg — crossing the water to a new land. The man, his great cock springing, and the woman, her great breasts swinging, walked cross the water to the land.

"Ah, well, seeing you've a nose for quality, Gov, take a whiff on this," Fergus proffered another box.

Gov Don tapped a few grains to the hollow of his thumb, tipped his cluster of spag-lumps, and inhaled. "Is that your best quality?"

On the white sheet below them, shadows flew off the water to the land. Once on land, they turned to each other. A drum beat. And again. The shadow figures merged on the white sheet, and thrust, the woman's legs round the man's, and thrust, her arms flew up to the sky while his cupped her normous bottom, and they thrust, drums and thrusts faster and faster, till on a sudden the white sheet cast nobbut shadows of spray, and a reed-flute sang.

"Well," said Fergus, "there's this," proffering a box of emerald-green, "better nor what I use my own self."

Gov Don inhaled a few grains from the hollow of his wrist. He exhaled slow. "Ah. That's the rosy rictus," he said.

The spray flew on the white screen. From that spray the man and woman rose, and kept rising, flew to the top of the screen and swooped back down, the flute swooping as they rose. Then up they swooped again, huge, their faces filling the screen, then dwindling to twice dreg-size, then half as large, then nobbut big as a thumbnail till they flew off altogether.

"That's the fine kind," said Gov Don, and led the clapping and stomping in the bleachers.

A small figure, a black knit cap pulled firm over his gold hairs, stepped out from behind the white screen. He bowed, and raised his arms, and clapped back at the crowd clapping before he slipped back behind screen. Though the clapping kept on, he did no reappear.

"My Palan," said Fergus, thumbing a sheaf of Gov Don chits into a pocket of his cloak. "A handy boy. Maybe of some use to the Smiths, hmm?"

"Smiths!" ejaculated Gov Don. "Make a Hunt Boy of him."

"Well." Fergus mulled. Hunt Boy. There was opportunities to Hunt Boy. "Tell me more," he said. Eager gets you naught, he was all times telling Palan. Gov Don maundered on as the sun fell red into the harbor, as the tumbling krewes danced on their ropes, as the Hunt Boys gleamed copper and the horii glittered rose, and the rats stole to the mouths of their burrows, spittle flecking their lips as they sniffed the crumbs and waited for the dark to cover them, and Gov Don tipped grains on grains from the emerald box to the hollow of his thumb, and tilted, and sniffed, and chuntered on of the fine life of a Hunt Boy till Fergus let himself be suaded, and Palan Fergusson was down on the lists for Hunt Barracks, with a two-room for he himself and his dap while they waited for next training to commence. Fergus made no mention of the grotto. That'd be a de facto.

Mary Pat skipped up the stairs to home, jouncing every which way she could. Mary Kath lingered on the bankmen till Finn come long in the thick of his boyo clanch. "Finn," she said. First he did no hear her. "Finn," she said again. He slapped a few backs and slid out to her. The clanch shouted after, "Slap streets with your boy pups, Finnegan!" and "You've to rank it up with tha' clanch!" "That's the billy!" Finn waved over his back, and they tumbled upstreet, shouting still. Finn leapt and turned in air and landed next her on the jetty stones. "What's towards, Marekat?" he said.

"Did you see the Galanty Show?" she asked, and he nodded. "How'd he...?" she waved her hands in the drowning light.

"He was back of the sheet, Marekat," Finn drummed his heels gainst the stones, blew tween his thumbs like the Smiths did, splatting where they'd hallooed. "See how my ears move when I do this?"

"Ayuh," she said, though they moved nobbut a hair. She waited.

"The goldhair was back of the sheet, dancing, and —"

"How'd you —"

"We was all to one side of the dais. The goldhair danced tween the falling sun and the sheet, and was he threw shadows on it. Then he grabbed a couple figures —"

"Figures?"

"I've no least notion," Finn admitted. "They was maybe long as your arm, wrapped round his hands, and he danced them tween the sun and the sheet, to and back, the while he jerked a cord with his left foot as drove a rod gainst a drum. Closer he got, smaller the shadows."

"And the flute?" The cliffs glittering lit up Mary Kath's eyes a treat as the sun drowned in harbor. Finn made no mention of it. It'd be a sad day did Mary Kath get so full of her looks as Mary Pat was.

"The flute?" he said. "No least notion. How could he play flute —"

"With both hands wrapped in figures?" Mary Kath ended.

He shook his head. "Who lives, learns," he said, in their mam's gone-quiet voice.

"Aaaxxxxh," groaned Mary Kath, and cuffed his ears. She took a long jump off the jetty and long strides up the stairs, but he caught her up by the first landing. They made the rest of the climb with her head tucked in the crook of his elbow, Finn drumming on it with his knuckles.

# First Night in Barracks

THE MORNING WAS CRISP, the air blowing fine out to harbor. The novices shuffled on the cold pierstones. Hunt Barracks hulked at the pier-end over the greygreen slap of wave on wave smucking the furry algal mats into gapes and swithers as'd trance you did you look at them too long. Fore any eyes could get tranced, so, Ambrose barked: "Eyes front, novices." Ambrose said tween his teeth, pacing back of the lines, his voice lighting romanfire up their spines, "Eyes up and on the gov while he talks or you sha' swill gruel, I tell you, gruel; one shift one snort one snigger and best brace for a week of wet shitting." Twenty-six novices jerked their chins, shuffled their stonecold feet. Long the jetty a couple hundredweight of friends, relations, and bypassers pressed round the braziers of the hot-dove sellers.

Gov Don spoke from the dais, backed by a double-line of shivering horii flanked by Hunt Boys. Finn stood eyes up and on the gov. Last hols day Mary Katharine snorted: "The gov ought set up house on that dais." Best keep that out of his mind for now.

From the dais, the horii whorling and shimmying behind, Gov Don commanded: "Remember this, Boys:" (Finn strove to forget.) "The Rat Hunts are the forge wherein your manhood's smelted."

"Pie in the sky when you die!" someone hooted back of Finn. Ambrose slid cross the pier and scratched a backface "R" on the hooter's cheek fore the echoes was done, his shale blade flashing downstroke from cheekpoint to lip-end, and up, easy he curved from that cut a left-facing cup, and below that a jutting leg out, blood welling up after, slow, drop on drop. Twenty-five novices did no shift their eyes one hair, what with Ambrose standing near and his breath coming short, but their lips drew up from their teeth with the sweet bloodfug steaming off the novice as'd hooted. Who'd stopped hooting. Who stood knifestraight, eyes clamped to the dais like jaws of a singed rat.

Gov Don rolled on. "For in the blood and soot of your thrust and carry is found the beating heart of Charnholm. Tonight you novices enter the Barracks; in three months you shall emerge as Rat Hunt Boys."

Tremendous cheers from the novices, specially the carved and dripping novice. Gov Don bowed toward the loudest cheers, turned round to bow toward the watching dregs by jetty. Cheering was, to be sure, spurred no little by Ambrose's krewe wielding their staves: "We're nobbut tickling, boyos," they hissed when some novice twitched at all, at all. Gov Don walked through wiggling horii and stonestill Hunt Boys and down off the dais. As he strolled down-pier, gripping a few chosen hands, the coulees started to sing, *Fat cat / Got a rat / How sha' he kill him? / Fat rat / Bites the cat / Buboes then sha' fill him / Ha - ha - ha - ha - ha.* Soon as Gov Don was out of easy ear-reach, the cheering stopped in novice throats. The novices knocked gainst each other, full of sport, while Ambrose strode long the line with a grim whisper on him (none could remember his words, later), like a rat in a locked coop Ambrose paced their backs, they could feel it in their spines (they agreed, later). From the pier-end, Gov Don turned and give them a smile, like we're all lads together, no? but it was the Gov so the novices and their friends and relations give up a cheer. With Ambrose stompling at novice backs, oh yeah, they cheered something roarful.

When Gov Don mounted his palankeen, the novices gave a final shout of *Rat Hunt!* at when the watchers shouted back, *Rat Hunt!* and went off bout their business. The novices started for barracks, push, scrum, and a grim forward, all together now, knee slammed knee. The old lags, Hunt Boys made and blooded, roared *Who's for supper?* from the balls up, at which a thin voice piped — there's always one mong the lubbers — *I'm for supper!* and the old lags set their teeth playful in the piping throat and slung him on their shoulders to the barracks, calling, *Who has an apple for his mouth?* tween plucks at his ribs they called, *Have to fatten you up a bit, noodlekin,* the pup squeaking a bit as his nose scraped the keystone of the entry arch, but no harm, no harm.

Ambrose paid no mind to these old scenes. He could cued the breakup shout from his cozy nook in Matron's parlor at the harum's plaisance two piers over. He was busy about the next day's set-up, stacking and folding and coiling in a dark corner. Let the old lags handle the novices, this round; they'd no need of him, though it went ragged if he was out of earshot. Ambrose rolled a smooth hawser tween his palms. A nice bit of round plaiting with little stretch to it. Once strung, it'd hold its shape. He stared at the back of his eyelids for a dozen heartbeats and blinked and went on with coiling it, length after length, hand over hand.

Gov Don cantered off homeward. These ceremonies for the novices, hmm, hmm, quite the bore, but necessary, ah, keep their spirits up and all. He hoped Mandra would have remembered he was coming home to supper. If it was one of her spinning days she could still be whirling round the footmen and the table empty as a dreg-pocket. He leaned forward. "Step it up!" he told his coulees.

The coulees grunted and picked up the pace. They sang:

*Run your feet / To smithereens / Run your feet to bone*
*Haul his fat ass / Uphill downhill / Haul his fat ass down*
*Bleed for glory / Boys and menfolk / Spilt blood shall soak stones.*

Finn hauled the squeaking pup to his feet after the old lags'd dropped him and caromed off. "Ease off the noise and they'll no remember bone nor hair of you come morning."

The small figure pulled a black knit cap down over his ears. He eyed Finn, wary. "Strangers are natural targets. Seemed they'd give it me worse if I did no squeak."

"That's sense," Finn agreed.

*Bleed for glory / Boys and menfolk / Spilt blood shall soak stones.*

"What's that?" said the boy.

"That? Gov coulees." Finn shrugged. The boy looked blank at him. "Never heard coulees?" The boy shook his head. "Carry Gov's palankeen, sing the while," Finn explained. "Where you from, bantling, you never heard coulees? What's the name?"

"Palan," said the boy. He did no move out the shadows. "I'm to doss at the letter O, they said."

"Well, you're next me, then," said Finn. "Come long."

Palan set his duffel at the foot of his pallet, an O drawn in coupled, hissing snakes on its head- and footboard. Finn's doss, a bedlength away, was similar marked N, a thin pallet flat on its swingy ropes, one in a row of twenty-six as lined the west wall. Over each footboard a thin quilt was folded, gainst each footboard stood a tin coffer with no latch, and facing each coffer, a bedlength distant, was a porthole in the east wall, one of twenty-six portholes shuttered tight. "Someone has an eye for the exact," said Palan.

Finn laughed. "Someone has an eye for the spare, more like," and Palan grinned a crack. "Hunt Boys spoil easy as fish, mayhap," he said. "Keep best in cold and salt."

Finn looked at him. "Where you from?" he asked again. For answer, the sprat unlatched his porthole. They looked out at the cold scum harbor roiling gainst itself like rats fighting in a sack. Palan shivered and jumped down. "How'd you come here?" he asked.

"Harbor give you a chill, bantling?" said Finn. "Ought see what's past horizon. Waves tall as cliffs, out there."

Palan shivered again. "I know," he said. Finn raised an eyebrow. "I was raised shipboard," said Palan.

"Well, I come here off my dap's wishing, and my mam's brewing," said Finn. "How'd you come here?"

"Your dap wants you to be Hunt Boy?"

"He did. Dead now. It's my mam, more like. There's none can brew cider like her."

"Has none tried?" said Palan, watching the light play off the harbor gainst the roof timbers.

"Course they have," said Finn. "Cider Mother says —"

"That's your mam?"

"Ayuh. She says the richards took her vats and froth-rakes and bungs and all, years fore I was born. Going to brew their own, they was. Keep it to themselves, see, like they does the potable." Palan nodded. "But they could no. Cider Mother says it'd made a rat laugh to see the swill they brewed."

"I'd like to watch her," said Palan. The light come off the sun, then off the waves, then like thrown pikes each streak went its own way.

"Mmm," said Finn. Cider Mother did no just care for watchers. "Raised shipboard," he said, "How'd you come here?" Easier to nudge rats out their burrow than to get answers from this sprat with his calm ways, no way to poke him off his balance, he — "Wait. You're the Galanty Show," said Finn. "Saw you the last hols day. You was main good, bantling."

Palan bowed. The light streaks as came through center of the porthole went straightest. The ones as came in round the porthole edge bent most.

The other boy was still talking. "How'd you come from Galanty Show to Hunt barracks?"

"My dap." Palan dragged his eyes from the porthole to Finn's eyes. They was green, paler nor his own. Finn's was the color of a cold, windless day, out of sight of land. "He's a fisher, my dap is."

"I see, then," said Finn. "You was out striding the high seas when one fine morning you woke to gulls screaming and decided you'd go for a Hunt Boy, 'Captain, steer for Charnholm, I'm mad to be a Hunt Boy,' you said, and the Captain said, 'Aye aye,' and you come straight to harbor here, couple of scrub boyos rolled out a red carpet for you and you strolled downplank in your broidered cloak and said, 'Ambrose, my good man, put me down all to be a Hunt Boy, there's a fellow,' and Ambrose went down on one knee to you." Finn cuffed the boy's shoulder blades, easy. "What's the true tale, scrap?"

"My dap asked Gov Don. Gov Don fixed it."

Finn weighed that. This Palan had a dap who could win boons off Gov Don. Was that true, the rest was true. Still: "Best no give tongue to that here," Finn warned. He walked round Palan. "Galanty Show. Think on it. I watched you from harborside of the jetty, do you know?"

"Course I knew," said Palan.

"Then tell me. How'd you play the flute while you was dancing those figures?"

"No flute," Palan said. He whistled round and bass, sharp and treble; he whistled the love-plaint of the couple rising up the sheet, and rising close, and closer still —

The entry doors clanged iron gainst the barracks walls as two dozen novices stomped in, all braggadoce and flared iris.

"Shutter up," Finn hissed. "Stifle your gaum till we're lone."

Palan was quick. The Rat Hunt took none but the quick; they chose good dancers and those as could see a storm blowing up from three pink, fluffy clouds. He nodded, slammed and hatched the porthole, slid to O doss and stood there soldier as was Finn. Two dozen Hunt novices blustered in, their eyes shifting side to side, their hands on the twitch as they slung their duffels on each their assignated doss. "Do look a happy party," Palan said out the side of his mouth.

"Shutter," hissed Finn. The novices' shout and blab rang off the stones.

"Willan, begunt a sze!"

"Slive dan fur begunt drain prohole."

"An dreep swallow, murr treep a blanken."

"Ol isht punt ar fayge, bo beep da fool imp trank perffer?"

"Willan, drape's a grobb nissen!"

Finn stood next his doss, eyes front, mouth straight. The barrack walls dripped seawash. After a time the bluster wore off the incomers:

"Must think we're training for compound step and fetchits, all a-line this way."

"I got doss S. Where in this gorry spag-heap's that doss?"

"See that? The hole. The hole with the pole."

"Whooo-eeee!!"

"An that drone had no shut his clap, I'd spitted him. Practice, like."

"You and whose scutmen was going to spit the Gov?"

"They've *pallets* atop the bedropes!"

Finn looked straight before him at his hatched porthole. The tide'd be on the ebb now, each wave swallowing the former, leaving more and more shingle wide to the wind. James A all times said Finn'd go for a Hunt Boy. Cider Mother said Finn'd be a piscine scupper did he no roster himself for Hunt Boy. Mary Kath leaned out her nest tween the copper vats long enough to mouth an *as you think best,* her eyes gone gleam fore-seeing Finn a Hunt Boy. Dan said little but then that was how much you got off Dan since James A passed; soon as he woke, he rolled off-pallet and slid out of house. Mary Pat giggled but since Mary Pat was made hori you could tell her the house was afire and she'd nobbut cover her teeth with her palm and giggle. Since, since, since. The changes come with James A's passing and they'd no let up since then at all, at all. Finn shuffled his feet beside doss letter N. Might's well be Hunt Boy. What else was he to do? Siffle round after Cider Mother, tending the vats and the orchard? He pulled weeds and seedlings in the same fistfull and his brew-ups was good for vinegar only. Down to the sea in ships? The harbor and the sea beyond was good to look at from the stone solid jetty, but he was a landman, root and branch.

Something slammed his chest from the inside like Suellen kicked the tea off Cider Mother's swole belly, a fist slam to the plexus made of: how Mr Inkwhistle cried his doves; how Mary Kath went small tween the vats; how the sad sunk feet slapped the cobbles in promenade of a morning; how James A coughed at the last; how Aunt Con brought tea to table tween her wrists when her fingers would no close from plaiting rope; how the coulees shouted scraum rimes while blood dripped from their noses neath the weight of some fat richard at lounge; how Gov Don waved his hand and dregs trembled neath him like grass; how whether they lipped him or no they trembled; something made of all this slammed gainst Finn's ribs unceasing. Morning, evening, through his wakeful and dreaming nights, it drove up from below till he ofttimes could no get his breath. When he did, it stank of fish. First time Finn smelled fishstink, he was nobbut a spawn. His mam had brought him up the orchard for harvest; they woke and slept neath applebough for a week so's not to show too much come and go about the place. When they come laden back to Charnholm, the fish smell hit him sudden. For the first time ever it was a separate odor; for an hour he smelled fish and then naught once more, like steam goes off into the air. How could you get outside the air you breathed? Might as well go for Hunt Boy till he could get his breath. Till he could get his feet under him. Some had it. You could see it when they did. Say now Max. Max stuffed food in his maw to keep the corpo going, kept his eyes open so he'd no stumble, but he walked on stone, every step on stone; there was playing the viol and that was all there was and so he'd all times stone underfoot. In fog so thick your own hand was a stranger, Max trod the dead middle of the path. Now that Mary Kath was going for rimer she could thread Dead Horse Moraine, even, with her nose in a crumble book. Whereas Finn walked like cloud, like mist. It was a startlement some times that his shoes left tracks.

Finn shuffled his feet beside doss letter N, his eyes fixed soldier on the porthole while the most of the novices roared, tossed each other about, crammed duffle contents into tin coffers, jumped into the air, slapped each other's palms. There was Bannock who'd snared doves for Mr Inkwhistle; Lebone who got his jollies off spiking hawser coils with shards till the captains traced him, when he only scaped drowning by a promise to go for Hunt Boy; Clarch who nobbut followed his boot toes through his days, so those boots must've led him here; Stampel who liked to pour sand down fish gills, and stand back, and watch; Thursgood the streetsinger who could rifle a resting sack in the time it took the owner to wipe the sweat off his face with a handker; and —

Into the barracks come Ambrose.

"The bloody suck of you turns my gut. You stand *straight!* on the beat you hear me through that door. Nor do you give me lip — skip down off that hook fore I spit you on it, my little prince — as to how you did no hear. You are *always!* hear you, *always!* on the listen. Need I say it twice?"

"Nossir," said Finn.

"I can no hear you boys! Do I need to say it two times?"

"Sir, no sir," said the boys. Each had come to soldier, just like Finn, next his lotted doss.

"Five minutes. I'll be back. Every coffer square to its doss, every novice mong you heels to your coffer. *Now!*"

Ambrose walked out the door. Lebone tried to pull a punch on the boy one doss over; Stampel hissed him and they all fell to.

Five minutes later by the big clock over the barrack doors, Ambrose was back. Though every ear was on the prick, none heard him approach.

"Now good evening to you, boys. Welcome to the Rat Hunt Barracks, and may each of you" — staring a bit hard at Lebone — "prosper fine in the months upcoming. Are there any questions?"

Thursgood stepped forward. "What sha' we be doing?"

"You call me 'sir'," Ambrose said, quiet, like it was a secret.

"Sir, what sha' we be doing?"

"I am main glad you give me the opportunity so quick to tell you," still in the soft secret voice; "I. Will. No. answer such poking prying questions, now nor ever. Any more questions?"

Finn shuffled his feet. "Sir, can we anywise prepare for the morrow's activities, what or when they may be?"

"Now there's a good question. Boys, listen up to this fine and clever questioner name of Finn." He wandered down the doss line, kicking a few coffers as was a hair out of place, pointing a finger at the end of his out-stretch arm at each offender, right up to Finn's face. "NO!" he shouted. "When I am done with you lot, you'll be ready for whatever comes, which that'd lose its surprise was I to tell you first what was coming. You are no at home with your mams dripping pap down your dreaming tongues, do you hear me? Hunt Boys are no made from porridge, am I clear to you?" He got down off his toes and strolled off.

Ambrose bit down hard. "Does a one of you fuckers know what a rat is? Did you ever even pick the shit out of your own crack? Has a one of you done aught but suck his mam's pap? You, eyelash boy," he picked up Lebone by the scruff and shook him. "Ever done a hand's turn since you come pul-ing out your mam?"

"Hand's turn what," Lebone stiffled. "Sir."

"Ah may the last rat choke on my toenails. A Hand's Turn of Work, you worthless sack of seeping shit. You ever?"

"Sir, yes sir."

Ambrose fell back gainst the barrackwall, back of his hand to his brow. "I can die happy, so," he said. "Now, eyelash boy, you, Lebone. Tell all of us here present just what this back-breaking work of yours was like."

"Sir, I beat shutters back in true. Shutters as got shammered off the scut-patrols."

Ambrose bowed his head, quiet. Mayhap he'd sucked all the blood he could get off this one; mayhap Lebone's was a right answer. The boy's arms was proof of how hard it was to beat shutters back to shape.

But Lebone did no leave it there. No, he'd to toss more coals on the brazier. "Sir, I did it with my dap, was he showed me how."

Ambrose pushed one lazy foot gainst the barrackwall, then flew over doss C to land his nose gainst Lebone's. "Did it with your dap. With your *dap*? Dap-bugger, are you? Or was it the other way round? Was it your own dap thought you'd a tasty bung, just right for his size?" He spat and shoved Lebone aside. "Does any other have a yen to tell me you done scutwork any hour of your lives till now?"

There was enough silence in the barracks to balance the chatter of a covey of midwives swapping tales. "Right aright," said Ambrose. "Tomorrow, dawn, *sharp!* your training starts. You'll learn a gorry thing or nine of hard work. Listen now and listen good: no dreg walks out these doors till training's over. They may carry you out, but none sha' walk. Hear me?"

"Sir, yes sir," said the novices.

"Right aright. Now I know every pup mong you wants to piss his pants, so throw wide your porthole and fill up the sea. Lights out in five minutes. Them as has no finished by then sha' be left with their working parts dangling in the breeze." He turned on his heel and walked past the pole-hole to the door. He closed the door quiet.

The novices pissed out the portholes with no glance sidewise. Finn and Palan swapped looks, no more. Who knew where Ambrose and his eyes was.

In the dark, Finn played back the day. Starting from morning bread with Mary Kath —

"Hssst." Palan was a sideways hump in the next doss.

"Shutter up," Finn said through his teeth.

"Here."

"Shutter your gaum, I said."

"We sha' do fine," Palan whispered.

"Ayuh." Finn lay on his back and looked out of porthole. You can get used to aught, even hanging, Cider Mother said. He summoned the mad skirl of Max bowing his viol till the sound faded and sleep took him up.

# Ambrose on the High Wire

I COME BY IT NATURAL. As a sprat, my crib was a hawser coil. Mam dropped me in the middle and went on with her crying, "Flapping fresh off the boat!" Dap slept round the coil's strands all day; he was a night-worker, my dap. Soon's I could crawl out of the rope coils, he snatched me straightway off to help him in his work. "Any boy worth his salt says yeah he wants to help his kin." Mam said no but her nos melted quick, she being all twitch for boats coming in and what their docks held, produce and producer if you get me; "I love a good haul," my Mam said and often, though fair enough, she kept one eye and a ear on me while the fishermen bounced her; our Mam was careful enough of her young till we could hook and down our own victuals.

Balance is what it's all about. Balance and you do no think what might happen. You think where your next step's going and you shut firm the door on a slip or a slide or a slack in the rope. Those things will no happen. Last thing you think of's the pay; you'll fall, sure, that road.

Balance I learned first from Dap in the shiny hours when richards sleep deep, fathoms down, richards who never have to worry, who snort the night through while the harbor makes ready, wharf rats scurry to coil and tie off and net-mend, while captains stalk in white boots the piers, smell the wind, feel the tide on their tongues and calculate the day's run according, bark hurry-ups to the wharf rats trembling. First I was nobbut a lookout, my eyes jammed open by Dap's thwirling stick, haunkered in a doorway my ears all up and both ways looking. But only till I learned the rhythm of it. Fifth time out Dap give me a high hoist and a tilt of his stick to a handswidth ledge I scuddered round to a fire window. Skinny arms can reach tween the mesh and slip a padlock off its hasp as quiet as a flea biting. Sliding back the gates quiet was tricky but it's a great motivation being some fathoms up and your footsweat slicking your grip; you want to lift and ease them open. Metal's got its own notions of how it wants to move; when your belly's pressed gainst the lintel is no time to show it who's master.

Once I was in I'd grab and bag and slide swag down the stone walls to where Dap stood, spats and tophat, whistling like his palankeen was tardy, like he'd all the time and reason to be out and about in the shiny hours. Toff he did look. From twenty paces with his bass case leaning, he looked like he'd played some richard bash and was off home to a bit stew and flagon of cider. Swish the swag come down and slick my dad snapped ope the case and slid it all inside and wheeled off whistling. Careful workmanship, my dap said, always pays. I'd slide shut the gates and rehang the vain padlock and inch the ledge round to the alley side, turn myself and grab by my nails and let drop and stroll downstreet with my dap. *Grand to see a spawn take interest in his dap's work*, one time a flic said to my face. We was bent double laughing round the corner off that.

Later Dap learned me to climb corners. In the shadow of the stone scrapers, where I come yelping to life, richards they live in stone buildings, ornamentation up the wazoo round the doors and window and neath the roofline. Lot of them has spikes at their wall-ends. It's like they *want* you topside. There's always a fingerhold in rough stone. I'd keep tied to the roofline graspnel Dap threw up and hooked, but I never put much trust in it. I seen those come out. I used my weight and my fingers and toes and I stayed balanced.

It was me figured the roof to roof rope. Me. There was this one building had no ledges, its gates oped from inside lock, and they had — this was slick — oil dripping down the corners so you could get no hold. Seemed no way to crack that place thout you had a helpful bird. I went up on the next-door roof and tied a rope fast to the parapet. I tossed the rope to the next building over where my brother Nelson fixed it down. Casual, I walked the rope cross the alley to the roof's trap door, snicked it open, and strolled on down the stairs. That was it. That was how I found my calling. I had to give Nelson half the swag; catch him doing the fair thing, "I didn't ask to be your kin," he said, but I still come out enough ahead to get a room of my own and study with Akrim Mandonovich, the guy who walked the Not Our Dame in Paris. He said.

I learned *everything* from Mandonovich. I learned how you got to keep them guessing you're on the edge of spill, cause the suckers don't come back to watch you do it easy; they want to see you risk a dive. When you stay balanced, their mouths hang open and their brains fly out those holes. Akrim taught me to carry lots of what does no go together: a rocking chair and a picture hat and a rubber hose and a copper u-joint and a potted plant; us up there care only what it weighs and how it balances, but it draws the suckers. They walk if they not stounded.

I learned everything from Akrim. A business arrangement. For five years I gave him one-third of everything I made. He banged my door every morning at ten for us to go out and get up and walk it. You got to do it every day. You got to be routine. That's how it sinks into your blood, so every morning your body wakes and it does no think on what's coming next, slings itself out from the sheets and splashes water on its face and does a few stretches all fore your backbrain comes awake to sing those golden oldies: it's hard; I'm tired; my left knee's pulled; everything has to rest, look at how rope goes bad if it's not let go slack sometimes; I got a bad feeling about today; I'll have more spunk if I swallow a steak first — these gold songs are unco' easy to dance to. They'll get your limbs twitching fore you know it. You got to start work early, fore the songs start you jigging.

Anyhow, I come by it natural. Those years with Akrim went by like a song. Every week we'd sit sweatstuck together after we worked and he'd say, "Ambrose, you fuck up this two week. No practice. How you think you great if you no work?" shaking his head. One week I dropped my swag on the floor and danced up and down rope waving my hands shouting, "Akrim I'm done." I shouted, "Akrim I give up! What's the gorry point to lugging all this shit around?" dancing and shadow-boxing on the rope. Akrim stood on the platform grinning. Grinning? You could shoved a carp down the wide mouth on him. "What?" I shouted. "You happy cause now you can sleep away your days? Cause now you've no gorry student you got to wake and stir his lard around?" which was things he'd said to me, actual. He stood there grinning. He said, "Look how good you dance. Is very good."

There is no better in this world than you're good at something; you got a natural inclination, like, and you got the longing, too. You make the time to work hard and you keep it up no matter how sweet the gold songs come in your ears, and your hard work pays off, and you get good. I mean good. I mean really good. There's no better nor that. We come on some luck and when it come we'd did the work so we could run cross-harbor on the crests of the waves, near about. Dancing on top of your form and the suckers gawking up so you want to drop rat scat in they mouths (that's fore you start dancing up there; once you're dancing you see naught, you walk cross air and the rope's aidful therein, no more) the suckers looking down throats of they own deaths, seeing they own lives turn all to dance as your feet dance, hearts turning over, gulp and delight like froth on the waves inside them, they for two heartbeats quiet and then kalashazam they shout and slap hands together, oh there's no better. When you're up on the rope you see no death; you see naught, like I said, but they see it and it gets them all alive. Naught could be better nor that.

I worked with Olympia mostly, and her and me had a kind of a thing going. We slept inside each other but we never had much to say. Who else was we going to be with that knew about dancing like we did? Plus it paid off on the rope. It was the natural thing and I was all about natural, floating on my belly on my talent and my hard work and my good luck, letting the clouds take me where they chose.

I come by it natural, and I lost it natural. One day I was five fathoms up doing a fancy routine outside in the dark red sun. Me and Olympia was hitting it good; doing it sideways, carrying each other on chairs, balancing on one toe. Grandstanding but we'd the stomach for it. I was doing a 360 on my right toe, right round the rope and everybody but me holding they breath and I was on it. On it. Halfway round I seen on a slant inside one of them shelter caves. These two girls was brushing their hair. Richard girls with naff teeth, too young to know there was different luck for people, richard girls brushing they long red hair, quiet as incoming tide, glad in their fingers. I never seen it before. Quiet like that. I never seen it before. A fish worries more about its next minute than those two. They was quiet off themselves; they was made of it. I swayed to my left and I swayed to my right and I saved myself by inches, grabbing the rope. Olympia almost got her death off the rope so shaking.

I got off it after that. I got off it and I never got back on. Once you fall, you never get back on. I drank Fergus's rotgut for a couple months till Akrim huffed by with a couple casseroles which he pushed down me; he rummaged through my trunks and when he saw what little coin I got, he waved his hands round and shook his fist in my face. "Goddam catapillah," said Akrim. "Fokkin slug," on and on till I stood up and threw a bench at him. He ducked and stood and said, "All right then now. You alive, I make you a proposal."

I signed on to whip the Hunt Novices into shape. I run the Barracks. Teach them everything cept how to slide the pole. I get an old Boy for that. Everybody got certain limitations. Mine is I keep off heights. On the ground I'm fine, I snuff up blood and I put up with no weakness, but I climb no ladders nor stairs nor poles. Like Antaeus, I draw strength from the ground. It's what I tell them.

I can pick up a brace of cubs and shake them like paper; they got a good healthy fear of Ambrose. That makes my job easy and that makes their training go good. My pups is good pups with a strong bark on them. I'm fine saying the same stuff over and over. I'm fine with routine.

Olympia one time asked me do I no care there's no applause. No, I said. It was no for the clapping. That was no why I rope-danced. I did it on account of I was perfect. Now I'm naught, I'm a drainpipe; you got to have it but you'll no celebrate. Better I work, less you think on me. I'll no dress it up with pretty: I had it, now it's gone.

It passes the time, what I do. That's it. It passes the time. I do the work that pays for the space I take up. Then I go home. I stretch on my pallet and watch the sun move. I go for a walk when the stars come out. My days are flat rocks in shallow water. I keep walking through and the waters keep sliding underfoot, away.

# Why the Richards

IT WAS RIGHT AFTER FINN COME BACK HOME, fresh kicked out from the Hunt Barracks, no word of why off him, that Mary Katharine paced home from rodomontade class, her shadow hugging her feet. She pulled her nose out of her versebook at a shout. Cider Mother yanked Suellen from out the road fore a palankeen full of Gov Don and his Lady could tromple her. Gov Don lashed his coulees on like they was wind. Like they was no more to blame than wind. Once Suellen had left off wailing, Mary Kath asked Finn the why of the richards. He was fathoms down in silence, sunk in his pallet from meal to meal, so she got no answer from him. Small use asking Cider Mother, she in full thirl, both vats brewing and Suellen, bruised and frighted, cranky at her hem. Mary Patricia, who come dragging a sledge for the harum's cider kegs, raised her eyebrows in graceful arch at the question and bleated, "We got to learn acceptance; no point kicking gainst the pricks, only wear yourself out an you do," said Mary Pat, and hoisted the sledge yoke to her shoulders away off downhill.

Mary Kath mulled it for a time, then stepped upstairs to where Finn was stretched on his pallet, a light stubble on his lean chin. He did no turn nor blink when she blocked the light. Natheless, she folded her angly limbs on the next pallet, where Dan still sometimes laid himself, and asked him a second time: "Why the richards?"

Finn turned his face to the wall. "I've summat slamming in my chest," he said, and no more.

Rimers stuffed prentices with books of fine verse to anathematize the rats, lull them fore the Rat Hunt Boys come striding with their pikes and their Wagon's iron gutfire. They studied fine speeches out of the past and listened to crumble-book scholars who could read the burnt pages easy as reading the sky. Mary Kath read the books frontways and backways and surely they'd some words inside them as would stir Finn now. She asked:

"Are we no the many, they the few? Nobbut a few dozen shelter caves and hundreds of dregs?"

Finn said naught.

"Which the many could snatch those silk comforters off adipose richard flesh and wrap them round our Suellen, times she chokes, shakes with cold, and naught to warm her but wool scraps pieced and scratchy. Snatch their filter caves for all the Smiths who cough blood."

Finn said naught.

"Great Burning might been a great change for the richards but shook no stone neath our houses. Wanting then and wanting still. Why want when caves are chock-full?"

Finn rolled his head toward her a quarter-turn. "Might as well grab the potable works while you're about it, Marekat."

She'd the wit to keep silent. Turned her palms up, only.

"Where they make the potable. Up South Point."

Mary Kath took a deep breath. "Well."

Finn returned to staring at the ceiling. "Zackly. Dunnamany scutmen as owe their swole bellies to Gov Don pace those walls day and night. Maybe a hundred scutmen altogether. And we're to take them." He shook his head the least bit on his grimy pillow.

"They're our own!" Mary Kath was up and pacing at this. Finn wished she'd settle again. "Scutmen was born dregs!"

"Ayuh," said Finn.

"Listen, Finn. Richards keep us down with potable, thout which most dregs'd die roaring. They keep us tame and pressed-down with scutmen. Rat Hunts is nobbut the shiny as turns our eyes away from that plain fact. Could we —"

Finn spoke on shallow breaths, like grunt haulers who ease themselves to pallets at nightfall, too tired to eat the slice of bread in their hands. "You know Janko who mops the bathhouse. Cider Mother says he was once a full man with blood in him, a tiller-maven who bred a household stuffed with mischief. Now he's a half a sack who drools when he stutters and nods more than speaks. He got the change a decade since, when he worked coachman while the ships was winter idle. The richard did no just like how Janko geed the coulees, spoke him a bit sharp about it, and Janko answered like he'd answer any man, polite, sure, but fixed as a mainmast, whereat the richard took him down the stables for a bit of correction and redirection. Janko come out from there like you see him now, cramped over a place in his right side where something needful's gone missing. Ask him, he'll no tell you what happened. Gimps through his days. Cider Mother says his wife come down soon as word passed where he was, spoke in his ear, spooned gruel in his mouth: naught. Puling sprats and heelstanding spawn come down, pulled his sleeve: naught. They leave him be now."

"But what's that to —"

Finn went on. "Take Ilis on our own street. You know Sharna?" Mary Kath spread her palms and shrugged. "Course you do. Cider Mother says Ilis, in her day, was a sun to Sharna's moon. Look at now. Is there a lousier skivvy than what Ilis got? Picking up nightsoil and fish guts all so the Gov's Lady can have *a splendid array of blossoms*, that's what her cronypaps say, they ask her "How *do* you do it?" Ilis skives upstreet downstreet from doorlatch to cockcrow, tipping skanky housepots into her wheelbarrel, singing "*Cockels and mussels, alive, alive-O*" – then wheeling that barrel at last to her curragh and she gets *in* to that curragh, right down mong the foul, and come first light she paddles cross harbor to the marshes. Ilis paddles to the island mid the marshes and how she dumps and how she gets that hull anywise clean is anyone's guess. She's back by half-rise to lie in what lee shade's handy till moonrise."

Mary Kath nodded. "Inkwhistle the doveseller says Ilis once was a fairy queen, angel of light, tricked belowground where she was fed twelve pomgranate seeds as bespelled her so she never can return to Overworld." She looked hopeful at her brother.

"Ayuh," said Finn, and closed his eyes. "Got to study richards in their compounds. Figure their ways." He was silent a while. "You're looming at me, Marekat."

Mary Kath sat down, finally, and quivered. "They'd spit a dreg soon as look at one, Finn."

"Mmmm," he said.

"They'd spit you, sure as check."

Finn's head went up and down the least bit. His eyes moved neath his sun-starved lids. "They'd spit me, out of course. You, too. You can no more keep your tongue back of your teeth's barrier than you could dance hori."

"Could and if I chose I —"

"Could no," he said, and opened his eyes. "Of us all, Mary Pat's the one to go up the richards."

"Mary Pat's hori. She'd no leave harum for aught. Cepting maybe one of us." Mary Kath tucked her knees to her chest. "She'd shovel the cloaca publica for Cider Mother, sure. I think. But they'd no let her leave harum, even an she wanted it."

Finn got up on one elbow. "No one's hori forever, Mary Katharine." His eyes was green as a cold sea. "Mary Patricia's the one," he repeated.

The wind shifted. Old, hot, crawling kelp filled their noses. A boyo clanch passed by, spiking clumps of dry as had dared to roll out on their passage. Finn pressed his lips together, squinced his closed eyes. Max's viol skirled on the rising wind.

# A Dinner of Herbs

MAX LAID HIS VIOL on the marble hall table. He hung his grey fur-trimmed cape on his hook. "Hello the house!" Max hollered. Silence answered. He poked his long nose into the kitchen; wild garlic strings waved in the doorwind; in the tablinum, screeves and paperstacks rustled on every desk and draft stand. Again he shouted and again silence answered. Viol underarm, he wandered upstairs; the big room held its bed under eave, red silk and blue sack quilt drawn up to the brass headboard, two rushbottom chairs, three trunks, and a washcloset. Max opened his door on his own arrangements, his own fug of sweat and outbreath. No one had touched his desk or his clothes or his books or his trunks. No one ever did. That was no where the shoe pinched.

Max laid his viol in its nest and flopped on his pallet which crimpled neath him and exhaled wormwood; he flung one arm over his eyes and went waterside. The marshes just past the sour crags where wind soughed through reeds, where tide lapped mudflats; a world of air and water. When he gagged on how much fire and dust this city dished up spoon by leaden spoonful, the marshes eased the peristaltic cramp.

Max lay on his pallet breathing the salt and sulphur of the marshes. Rushes blew mong sweetflag, high-tide bush pushed small, fragrant, yellow flowers from out mong its thorns, and fiddler crabs waved their one large claw at his approach. He spent time enough crouched in thickets of pipes skirling and flames aleap, of brass *ba ba ba banxh* hornblare, rasp of Ambrose hollering "*Now*, you lacklusts, spit 'em *now*," smack and jolt of tin-hoop cart wheel clampering over stone and rut, snap crackle pop of fat melting in the cart's keelfire, and he above in the wagon prow drawing his bow cross strings E-A-D-G keening, fatspit on the fingerboard, bowsmoke rising off his strings, oh now rising ...

"Max? Come to table."

... and rising ...

"Ma-aax! Come now."

... and rising ...

"Maxie! Provender for the willing!"

... and gone as gone as dockfog by mid-morning.

Max propped himself on his left elbow and hollered: "Down in a tick."
A couple-three later, he slap-soled downstairs to fetch up in the kitchen.
Bran and Goodwin was doffing their skin robes. "Ah, Max. Hands clean?
Daresadear," said Goodwin. She laid the whiteskin robe over his arm, kissed
the air beside his cheeks. "Did you pass a pleasant day?"

Max hung their white skins side by side on the cedar branch. Bran'd
sewn a withy cross into the robes. "It keeps straight the back and square the
shoulders," he said, which was true but what point? anathematizers walked
that way anyhow, their legs swung out and round to make of each step a
circle, Bran's grandfather's invention, of which was he proud? To be sure.
"Sphere, sphere, sphere," said Bran, "our every stride must remind us that
life is a circle."

Their voices droned droned on. Behind the wall, Max smoothed the
skin robes long their dry cracks, creases, the shiny lapels where gloves
clutched close, the ovals where sweat leapt sudden long their spines, the
stains where green spittle fell from their mint-chewing mouths. Oh they
were cloaked in lyric enough to cleanse all Charnholm. "Excoriation!" Bran
thumped his fist on the table, wincing short as pain shot up to the shoulder;
"Rasping away hypocrisy through excoriation, the outer image and epitome
of our culture's desire for real surfaces. This is echoed in our practice of
full-body depilation, when we scrape down, scrape *down* to our real skin;
we are but naked creatures who arrive howling and depart howling; we have
no *time* for pretense."

"Doesna think the Rat Hunts pretense, Dap?" Max had been calling
his father 'Dap' for years now because he so hated to be called by a toilman's
title; Bran knew he ought no hate it but it gravelled him sore. He winced,
now, as Max went on. "Are'na the costumes, the masks, the armor, the
music — let alone the Hunt Wagon and its fires — a bit *more* than necessary
to kill the rats? Is it all no a bit pretentious?"

"It was you who desired to be a Hunt Musician," Bran said. "*I* never suggested you take that trade in hand. You're quite good at it but what is it to be good at? Such music."

"Such music," chimed Goodwin.

Bran gave his wife a sidewise look but she was scrubbing greens like vegetable cleanliness was her all-in-all. He continued, "Lie down with dogs, get up with fleas, that's what I say. But to say the Hunts are made of pretense. Pretense? There? To what greater use might we put our skills and talent, our craft, than in making the songs we sing into the people? It is when their hearts are cracked wide to the bloodletting and the naked flesh – you see how we come back to that, always coming back to that, yes – and when the music of the Hunt Musicians opens wide their listening ears as well, yes, oh the Hunts open every sense, *every*, and it is just then, while the soul gapes through its five open doors, that through those doors we can sing beauty down into their bones. We wake them to beauty, we instill thoughtful ways and appreciation. Let the people learn to give *way* to their gratitude; let it flow up like mighty waters; let it light up the sun; let error be no more. Oh the Hunts are but a *tool*, surely you know that by now? only a tool to augment human evolution."

"Bran," said Goodwin.

"Should that theory prove true," said Bran, staccato. Then, in largo, lento, lentissimo, "All of us want the same thing, Max. We all want our people to grow straight and beautiful and fruitful beneath the sun, we all want better lives for our children. The people are our children, Max. They need our tender, loving care, these poor stunted survivors of catastrophe unimaginable. Who are in no way to blame for their circumstances. They need guidance, succour, *kindness*–"

"Such as they find in our songs," said Goodwin.

"Yes," Bran cast her another sidewise look. "By our songs we guide them gently to full humanity. Someday they will achieve it. Someday they will reach that goal. Neither in my lifetime nor in yours, but Max, I truly believe that some day you will be the proud grandfather of the man –"

"Or woman," said Goodwin.

"Or *woman* ... who can stand shoulder to shoulder with a toilman–"

"Or —" said Goodwin.

"Or toilwoman ... and proudly claim that they two are *equals* ... oh what a glorious day that will be." Bran sank his face in his hands to recoup his forces. "But until then," he said from the cup of his palms, "We shall give our all and our best to this great mission, raising up benighted souls," he stood here to his full height, his fingertips brushing the rafters, "to the highest we shall raise them, from whence they can openly and without hesitation display their gratitude in full to we their teachers and their preservers."

For a full minute Max said naught. Goodwin hummed a massing chant. Some women mong the rimers went early to the massing place and there spread out provender upon the verge and there, while waiting for the rimer men to march in upon them, they filled their now-empty baskets with sweet rush, plashing through the tidepools in oilskin footwraps as they sang. *Herein come / and welcome / rise up now / and enter / have no fear / we're all here / bestir now / And enter,* Goodwin hummed.

"What a soak of a tune, Mam!" said Max.

"Language, language!" said Bran. "You know," laying a hand on his wife's shoulder, "women have their ways that men can never master." He looked flat-faced at his son, "It behooves us to remember that women's dark intuitive wisdom is of a different quality. Difference is —"

"ToBeHonored. Right. Sure. But Mam, you do surely know it's a gorry slag tune?"

"You have been long with Hunt Boys, Max." Goodwin dried her hands on a red cloth tucked at her waist. "Your language suffers therefrom."

"It's a bad song, Mam."

"It is less technically proficient than many other —"

"It's a *bad* song, Mam."

She smiled and patted his shoulder. "Yes it is. However, its words are easy to remember, which is what such songs require. A woman at her first massing needs songs she can sing straightaway. Thus we enfold her."

"But maybe they'd *like* it to be hard. So it'd be more beautiful."

"No, Max, that has been tried and found wanting. The people wish to advance no more than one small step at a time. Thus they walk always on solid ground." Goodwin hummed as she placed spoons and knives on table. "Most mortals crave continuity. Only some can fly," she said. She brought the platter and set it at Bran's left hand. "There," she said, "a fine fat fish and a grand bowlful of greens spiced with the year's first succory and a loaf of saltrye. Sit down to it."

They drew rushbottom chairs to the table. Bran and Goodwin found benches common. "I don't wish to squish my bum with every other one," Bran ofttimes said. Lavanda candles flickered on the copper surface. "So, Max, how was your day? It was a Hunt Day, yes?" Goodwin snapped her lapcloth open.

"Yes, *son*, tell us about it. Your *mother* and I were in Gov Don's archives," Bran said, "In his shelter cave. At his request. How was the Hunt?" Bran said. He cut a bite of fish, evenly covered it with greens, and carried the spoonful to his lips.

Max opened his mouth to tell them of it, tell them all about it, the Sulfur Pool where the Boys was first baptized, and the flames as kept the Pool hot, hot, hotted up; the raw klaxon voices of Matron and Ambrose hustling horii and Hunt Boys through their paces, screaming tween the pillars as the fire sank, "Emptyhand lackbrain worthless ratmeat, *Stoke!*"; the feel underfoot of the clausatorium, marble slick with ratblood, humanblood, dried come, rancid oil, and spilt perfume as rose from the mezzotint of shaved hairs; the cold slick sliding tween palms of the brass pole; how the brass was covered at base by oiled horii three-high standing on each the other's shoulders, hands linked, backs to pole; how long it took to wipe from his hands their scented oil — which out of course was needful, could no play with oiled hands — how the oil clung and how the scent clung even after his fingers was dry as dust; how Ambrose from pole-top tossed him his viol while he was still wiping, how it was only grace he caught it at all, at all; then running on the crouch down tunnel and down, boy scent breast-high, behind him corvisers clacking and leather straps squeaking and boysweat huffing in pack and shove down tunnel and down and how the sky smacked when at last he reached it, oh now how light and wind stung his eyes when the Hunt Boys came armored into the day, open, electric; how the viol leapt catlike to his shoulder, rising; how his right hand curled round the bow; how it stroked of its own, how it played him and all the whirl in cyclonic rising, oh now rising; and from the bowels of the earth came drums rapid before flames advancing; and from the rimers' careful study or the sky's faulty memry came herons came flutes in flight exulting as trumpets blared *Charge! Charge!* and horns wailed *Abandoned! Bandoned! on these dry rocks*, and again the drums pulsed their blood higher, hotter, cracked the earth with it till nightdreams walked mong the waking; and the Musicians rose, oh now rose to stand compressed atop the Hunt Wagon, from where, ensemble, they breathed in blood and rut and ensemble breathed out triumph, albeit triumph with a worm in it; and ensemble they played time past, long gone, and to come; and all this while fat drops from cremated rats spat up and danced on the viol's strings, speckling his fingers with pin-blisters; how he tossed sweat and fatspit hair out of his eyes and played himself out of himself, and again played; how the rimers stalked fore the Wagon's narrow prow, chanting words tossed them by the small cluster of anathematizers at their core, all speaking words they forged from crumble books and old tales and the ore they mined from inside their ribs and from every particle they breathed; how their chanting lulled the red-eyed rats to pause, raise themselves, one foot tucked to their chests; they paused and in that pause some Hunt Boy lunged and pierced and thrust the spitted rat mong the flames in the Wagon's keel and turned and again paced forward, gleaming, armored; all this while the music skirled overhead and he the viol skirling at the Wagon prow its figurehead and point; how the blazing sun made silhouette of the Boys' tendons and of the three locust trees on the hilltop, shone through flesh, flashed off eyes behind shuttercracks he dared no stare at lest some scutman mark their door with a halberd's point and maybe split the door and stride over threshold and spit a child and toss it with the rats mong the flames, calling over shoulder to some keening Mam, *if you can no stand the heat, get out from the kitchen*; and Max at the Wagon prow played on, shifting from foot to foot as the Wagon roof heated neath his feet; how the music played him till it was done and then dropped him with a flick of its jaws, snap; and next he knew he was on the grass verge, elbows on his knees, head sunk to chest, viol cradled in his lap, weak as milkwort; waking somewhat when the sun brazed the harborwater, waking and stiff rising and creak walking overcobble out of dockland and uphill to this stone house built gainst the Governor's compound while sprats ran round him taunting, *Softhand, softhand, have you any brawn? / Softhand, softhand, it will no take long / to skin you, and grin while / We eat you, eat you, crack your bones*; and walking still leftfoot rightfoot to the compound gate while the sprats skuttered pebbles at his heels, only to scatter when the gateman rolled from his keep and bellowed "If you come to be richard's slave come in then," at which every last sprat blew away downhill as Max stonkered up the stone flags to the house door and opened the door onehand with his viol still cradled to his chest neath his vest and at last closed the door on the gateman's laugh and the sprats screeching, and he closed it on silence, and on silence, and laid his viol on the marble hall table and took off his cape and clomped upstairs clutching the rail with his right hand for his left hand ached so; and at last flopped on his pallet in his own room all lone and lay flat on back, roaming the marshes in thought; and he was coming on to rise when they yanked him; as he began to rise his mam and dap cranked the reel in his plexus that whirled as they pulled him in to their skein of words that threw a pretty coverlet over all this their life and they reeled him down the stairs and there in their clutch they flayed him —

"My day?" said Max. "A bissump Hunt, bare two dozen slangered. Same of a sameness, nohow spank nor fresh."

"That docktalk —" said Bran.

"Well, that's grand, Max," said Goodwin, nibbling succory, "I was walking in the garden with Lady Mandra last night and we both thought your playing had quite a sweet tone. Marked, definite talent, that's what she said to me." Her voice went on, and on and on, pouring sweet over troubled waters, drowning them; her voice sinking, oh now sinking...

# Up the Orchard II

FINN AND MARY PATRICIA tossed their pecks and themselves to the grass with a whoof. Mary Katharine wandered round the orchard with her share still on her back. The gone-yellow apple trees bent neath their own load. Lodged grasses shed their awns in long dry tangles round the trees. In cover of the grasses, and in the brambles' lee, even now in the dry of the year, a few bright green mold splotches marked where springwater hung just below surface. *"Yellow leave, or none, or few do hang / Pon bough which shake gainst the cold, / Bare ruin'd hoirs, where late the sweet birds sang,"* Mary Kath sang through the first fallen yellows and browns as she laid her pecks ceremonious at Mary Pat's feet. "Think they're somewhere, still?"

Mary Pat opened one eye. "What?"

"The sweet birds. Think they somewhere sing?" Mary Kath knelt on the grass tween the other two. "Feathers flying through the green trees singing. Would that no lift you up?"

"Should get your nose out the crumble books," said Mary Pat.

"The crumble books, now. They're curious. They go on and on over some justborn's wailing, yet treat it like it was no more nor sun rising or tide making. Think they was heartless?"

"Sure," said Mary Pat, pulling buskins on her feet.

"Or maybe it was regular for them?"

Mary Pat shrugged. "Might been."

"Only time I ever heard justborn wail was Nora, time or two before."

"Well, I heard Nora, and I heard Seamus, and Dan heard a brace of them fore I come." Mary Pat wiggled her toes in the buskins, tucked her long copper hair neath a widebrim straw hat. "Justborns keen when hungry, wail only when death pokes his long nose at them. Crumble books is foolish. Ought get your nose out them."

"Think I got boosted to Rimehouse off putting my nose up some richard's brown ass stead of tween pages of —"

"Oh hold hard, Mary Katharine." Mary Pat rolled to her side, her forearm resting on the slim curve of her waist. "Get your shimmy in a twist off naught. All that sweet birds and bare ruins is fine, fine enough, but where's your own songs? Where's your own verse?"

Mary Kath stretched out long side of Mary Pat, face to face, square to slim; where Mary Pat was ovals from crown to soles, Mary Kath was built more angular-like. "Now they'd never boosted me to Rimehouse off my own verse," she said, sturdy elbow planted mong the grasses that was once flexish, now sere and yellow. "All that's supple one day withers," she said quiet.

"There you are now. That's your own, innit? Now look at me. Am I like to anyone?"

Mary Kath laughed out. "You're like to none, Mary Pat. Sure even the great Sharna never dored herself so much."

"Out of course, and off that I'm dored in return." Mary Pat plucked three dry grass blades and began to plait them. "Love my bubble, I do. Laugh so much as you list, Mary Katharine, but it's for a short time only I sha' be sleekskin." She wound the plaited grass blades round her wrist and held it at armlength. "Crack soon," she pursed her lips and nodded. "Should I spit out the kernel and swallow chaff till then? May the last rat share my pallet an I do. Till the bubble breaks I mean to sup at the high table."

"And then?"

"Life's shortness breaks the wisest hearts, Mary Katharine, so it does." Mary Pat stood, dusted the awns from her pinna, stretched her arms overhead. "Finn? Dost plan to sleep the day gone? Leaving we two frails to bear the brunt?" Finn rolled his eyes behind his closed lids. "Too proud off Hunt Boy training to pluck pippins, Finn?"

Finn was on his feet at that and oped his mouth and filled his chest — and stopped. He grinned. "Dost keep that tongue back of your teeth's barrier when you speak with Hunt Boys, Mary Pat?"

"Out of course. Think it's kindly speech they want of me?" She tossed him a sack. "Light's a-wasting, fair Corinna," she said.

Finn and Mary Kath in the trees, Mary Pat on the ground. Out of course. Though Finn was getting his growth, wrists gangling out of his sleeves and his ankles similar stretched, Mary Pat was still the taller. And she was Mary Pat. While the other two clambered mong the treetops, Mary Pat undulated in and out of the low branches, swaying from one ripe fruit to the next. What she reached for fell into her palm.

Mary Kath ofttimes lost her footing in craning to reach far, or her hand slipped off a ripe fruit and knocked it to the ground, or she scraped an elbow when she clean forgot she was up in the air and a handhold needful. When she'd her mind on the work, she tugged at an apple till it gave or tore, sometimes bruised it with her grip; no matter, these was cider apples; she chunked them in her peck, shoved the peck neath an arm, climbed to the next branch, went on. Sweat come off her. She went on.

Finn scorned pecks. He'd a jute sack cross his chest. He ran at a tree, grabbed a low branch, pulled himself up, and turned mid-air to end sitting on the branch. His toes clung to the bark as he slithered to the top, plucked two apples at a time, and slung them down the sackmouth. When a sack was full, he hooked his feet-tops round a branch and swung head-down, let the sack drop easy, pulled himself back up, and drew another sack from his tunic. Whistling all the while.

When the sun was nobbut a handspan above harbor, the yellow leaves flushed orange with its falling light, they ranged the day's catch mid-slope. Finn and Mary Kath tossed smashed apples down slopefoot while Mary Pat laid the rest in safekeep casks.

Come dark, they ate bread and smoked fish at top of the orchard slope. "Apple?" said Mary Kath, and Mary Pat shuddered all down her length but ended up eating four or five, same as the two youngest.

Sprawled on the dry grass, they talked idle of the haul, this year's harvest larger than last year's, last Reap Day, next Reap Day, the Galanty Show. "The one as did the Galanty Show? He was in barracks with me," said Finn. Mary Kath gave Mary Pat a nudge in the dark — first time Finn's spoke of the barracks since — and Mary Pat nudged back. "Was he?" said Mary Pat in elaborate unconcern, "What's he like?" "Palan?" said Finn, "He's good. Get your back for you and keep it. If you lie, he'll swear to it." "A friend, then," said Mary Pat. "Yeah," said Finn, slow. "No?" Mary Pat tossed an apple core far over the brambles. "He's a friend so far as you can catch his attention," Finn said finally. "He studies on mechanics, most times." "Was that what he did up the barracks?" said Mary Pat. "Mmmm," said Finn.

Mary Kath, impatient of all this back and fro, said, "What was it like up the barracks?" and Mary Pat gave her a nudge — shutter up — but though Mary Kath did no nudge her back, she let time pass. She sang them of the fish the high prince caught, and how he let him go, and what wishes the magical fish did grant him, and how all come to smash when the prince reached greedy far above his head, and how the fish swam round and round, after, tirralirra, swishing its silver tail through a greencold sea thick with princedust.

The moon was clear of the sandstone cliffs at their backs when Finn spoke again.

⟍⟋

He told them of Palan, and Ambrose; he told them how they melted Varik for scrap; how laughter come on him when they first slid down the oiled horii pole ("But that's main solemn!" Mary Pat said, "When they set you in position they *chant*, by the kingrat's hind foot, and old rimes at that. And you laughed?") cause their nipples tickled his feet, their tongues tickled his armpits; he told her how laughing took him, again, when Ambrose showed them how to spit a rat.

"Which me and Dan was spitting them when our gills was still wet, yet here come Ambrose all roar in our faces. Shoves his chin up sudden neath my pike arm, 'Lagless gormless spunfish wickerboy,' he says, and what would you? I doubled, I spat laughing. Out of course Ambrose turned purple off that." Finn dug a hole with his bootheel. "Ambrose. His roaring. Mmm. It got in among you."

"He said I'd a nice ass," said Finn. "Well there's naught to that. He called me assboy. It's no the words, it's him." His voice went thick, rough, high; Ambrose to the life: "'Spawn of ratturd! I can no gorry believe I shown you a hunnert times already and you spleenards stand there like ye never held spikestaff in all your life before now. You with the nice ass. You go through the drill for me one time maybe get it right. Say you see a rat do ye run back to your mam? Nah, ye spit it! Ye spit the fucker! It azzna so gorry hard, cause they're lulled by the Rimers. What Rimers? Is those ears on your head for decor only? The anathematizers! Who practically do your job for you, is there *any* storeroom in your mind soever? I got to tell you how a ship floats? You, eyelash boy, tell me on the quick, what's their task, the anathematizers? Right, somebody's listening; they walk ahead of the wagon and curse the rats in verse so they're like, stunned, exactly. Everybody scrape the wax from out yer ears, got that? Back to the mechanics, how gorry hard is this? Ye spit the fucking rat and then ye turn — faster nor that, assboy, an you want to keep that pretty ass all in a piece — like this, okay, you got it, you're on. Now this next part you got to do it fast, hear me? Do it slow and pitflame burns the fingers of you clean off, the way your mam'll need to spoon your pap to your paphole for you all your days. So what ye do is — yeah, assboy, right — ye flip *up* the pitdoor in the wagon keel, ye push *down* the spikestaff, *snatch* that rat into the flames quick as you can, you step *back* and *away*, you got it. Okay, next.' "

Finn rubbed his hands together. Mary Kath reached a cup of cider through the dark into his hands, which he downed at a gulp. "Afternoons we polished our corvisers. Our grated helmets and our breast plates and our loinguards had all to be gleam or Ambrose set us to porthole guarding. Now that sounds scant, but come time the moon goes down, your legs buckle under from standing there in the dark with the dark stones itching to come out their grout, and all the while twenty-five dossed-down novices eager to snap from sleep and snatch rewards for tossing the news to Ambrose of how a porthole guard had come apart at the knees. So we'd good reason to stick to the work. While we polished, he'd say, 'Lappish sluggards, this is no a party as you come to dressed in seawrack. Novices lack eyes in the backs of their heads so they've no natural protection. You got to keep your corviser's shine on so to blind them. Hear me? Blind them and they're fuddled. Corner a rat and it leaps a fathom high maybe. They can eat through metal; you got to think what they can do to your flesh,' Ambrose said."

"That's a fact," said Mary Kath.

"Seen them do it at Reap Day baitings," said Mary Pat.

Finn snorted. "Those rats you see come Reap Day? They're naught, shadows, broidery thread to a mainline hawser. Up the barracks they've some rats." Finn's words rolled off his tongue like each added weight to a fishline. "Well, when he was done cheering us, so, we'd pole practice. Shoved round the pole for first go, fore the oil wore off the horii standing one hand-joined rank on the next one's shoulders, three ranks high of oiled horii had our cocks standing pretty good, I tell you —"

"I know," said Mary Pat.

"Yeah. Out of course you do. Anyhow, Ambrose come up roaring —"

"Is he ever other?" Mary Pat flicked her long copper hair, a comfort to her in the dark, even.

"Ambrose he'd roar, 'By the first flea, lay off crowding the musicians when you go slide this pole. It's musicians first and yeah they get the first oil but come time they're done, them horii's warmed for you. Cause are you no warriors? Ones as ought get it?' That's the way of his speech. He roars like no richard can touch him but he maun be a dreg, am I wrong?"

"No," said Mary Kath.

"No," Finn agreed. "But he talks like no dreg I ever known. They say he was a ropedancer one time."

"Yeah?" said Mary Kath.

Mary Pat tossed her hair. "Uh-huh. He was our mam's partner back when she was Olympia."

Mary Kath said "Hold a —" but Finn ran right over her.

"They say he'd a good big fall and never laid foot on it from that day to this." Finn went quiet. "Up the barracks, Clarch said our mam used to toss her whole soft front at his waiting hands. Clarch said he heard it everywheres how our mam and Ambrose split a carboy after every show; he said all Charnholm knew where she hung her tunic." He paused to dig a new hole for his heels to rest in. "Clarch said everybody knew."

"Oh may plague fleas bite your nipples!" Mary Kath exclaimed. She looked up quick at the scudding clouds come all over the stars, and wiped her left palm over the back of her right hand, quick, and her right hand cross her front so to cancel the wish. "Sorry. I take it back," she said. She turned to Finn. "May the plague flea leave you and all your parts most strict and punctilio alone. But may a one-eared rat climb a house-front an sense could get a echo off you. Think dregs got nobbut to think on than what our mam did in time past? She's Cider Mother as mashes apples and makes of the mash the finest cider any dreg, yeah, nor any richard ever drunk. That's all they hold to. Think they cast their minds back, back, far as last week, even?"

"They ought," said Mary Pat.

"But they do no."

"No," said Mary Pat.

"Two days back's a stretch for the most of them," said Mary Kath. "Was it no for the rimers, they'd forget where they woke of a morning."

Finn said, slow, "Would no be a bad idea and they *did* think back."

"Potable ought flow from the ground and fish flock to the seines like homecoming," said Mary Pat. "Talk sense. What Cider Mother was or will be's out of our hands. So Ambrose, once a ropedancer partnered to our mam, roared at you. So, then?"

"You ever seen the land fall away from itself?" said Finn. They said no. "Up the sandstone cliffs, past where Lady Mandra picnics, the land goes to heath with white stone outcrops. Shell-studded it is. I was up there one morning scavaging with a few from the clanch when there come up a roar from out the ground and a chunk of that heath sunk out of sight. Like that," he snapped his fingers. "Where there was hill there was hole, dust rising therefrom. Ambrose roared like that, like the ground fell out from under tween one heartbeat and the next. Leastwise in my ears."

He asked for potable and they gave it him. He drank, and wiped his face, and went on. "So my heart broke. The night it broke I was lying on my doss, Varik melting to scrap behind my eyes, him and Ambrose roaring gainst each other in my skull," said Finn. "Fortnight into the training, dawn scrabbling at porthole, Boys A-M to the right of me, O-Z to my left, there I was, pinned down by my plexus, like the saddle Gov Don straps round a hori belly, but mine was made all of stone. I could no move nor breathe neath it. I knew well it was no any real stone saddle got slapped on me — when Ambrose punishes he sets his own boys to strap you round with hawsers — even half dreaming I knew it was no real, what of that?

"I jumped slank from my doss and stood cold and tremble (but soldier still) on the cold stones, and like that," he snapped his fingers, "my heart cracked, broke, leaked clean out of me, slid downdrain. Till dawn smacked the portholes, I stood soldier, not from will but from its lack. My ears roared and my tendons. Us novices, A right through to Z, was nobbut toys moved round the floor by a bored sprat who clapped us up in box for the night, the better to preserve us for the next day's sport. You remember Dead Horse Moraine?"

"Out of course," said Mary Pat.

"We was there together last week," said Mary Kath.

"Ayuh? An you say so." Finn gulped potable, "Each of us novices was alone in a waste as made that look a garden and I knew the coming day he'd toy with us again, rub the salt well in, and me thout my heart to warm me by its throbbing. Like mash turns to cake off the weight above it, so the roaring mashed me solid, too small a vessel to hold a heart and its beating."

He spat in the fresh-dug dust. "It's lighter, lacking a heart. So light seems I need stones in my boots to keep upright. Too light to make a Hunt Boy of. Seems. At end of training, Ambrose named me beater."

Mary Pat stretched one long leg straight up her front till it pressed her nose. After she counted twenty, and repeated with the other leg, she sat crossleg, topsoles on her thighs, and said, "They do like to break you. Ambrose and Matron both. When you're nova hori, first thing they do's break you. Mmm-hmm."

"Tell us how, Mary Pat. Finn, rest your tongue behind your teeth's barrier. How do they break you, Mary Pat." Mary Kath leaned forward, pushed her black hair out of her eyes. "Up the Rimehouse, they *want* your feet off the ground, always pushing you to fly and fly higher. I can see why richards break a coulee, a hauler, but why horii? Why smash a Hunt Boy?"

"Made finer by beating maybe?" Mary Pat shrugged. "All I know is Matron joyed to do it. Dis-cip-line, she called it. Always took us to the pool when it come time for dis-cip-line, rat and stake it were better she poked you with a trophy ratpaw than she threat you, '*I'll put my hands on your skin for discipline.*' So for fear, purely, us horii stood our two hundred sixty bare toes in a line on the pool edge while Matron strolled long, brushing our bare backsides with a fascine of willow twig. Which that was all for show, that was, Matron punishes in her own rooms, ofttimes boasted how she did her best work all by hand. First afternoon I was there," Mary Pat moved her shoulders like any old hauler once the yoke's off, "Matron come up breathing down my nape; out of course I stood straight as spine can be while that acidlated breath told me I was dreg of dregs, vinegar lees, abscess drip, worse nor useless, poking me everywheres the while. Then she led all the horii in chant, *Dry crotch, nary splotch, how you goneta please them? / Pair of scones on your chest bones, how you goneta please them? / Drap flesh, spag at rest, thick neck, lips that peck, how you goneta please them?* and like that they went on till the sun was deep down the harbor's wide legs and dark stained the portholes and Matron's belly growled for its supper. Then—" Mary Pat quit speaking.

"Then?"

"She sent us to our broodwar. Summat like your barracks, Finn, cept we'd our two and two dozen headboards rayed out from a round mat, each pallet six and a half hands wide and equal distant from the next hori. After we got customed to harum, we stayed up whispering, swapping tricks and machinations, it was all, '*He did and then I did and he asked and I said maybe and then maybe yes and then yes and here's how he sounded then*' — but none of that my first night." Mary Pat stretched her arms overhead. "The most of the horii cried."

"*You* cried?" Mary Kath near toppled on her nose with surprise.

"I did no."

"Well then." Mary Kath leaned back. "Out of course you did no."

"I was broke, though," said Mary Pat, cheery, like that was a most desirable end. "Lay there hollow as a gull's yellow egg. The eye of eyes'd looked me over and said I'd never crack nova. Said I was no framed to please. That drained my sap, I tell you." She paused. "I'm main tired," she yawned. "We've the pecks to haul out to the road come dawn."

"Mary Patricia M'Cool, you can no sleep yet," Finn said. "How'd you get sap back in your veins?"

Mary Pat shrugged. "Hard to say. I'd a dunnamany foresights since fore my first Seventh of how I'd be hori complete to a shade. Lying there, I decided to trust those foresightings, for even an they was wrong, they was better nor listening to Matron. Smelled better, too. So I crawled out of pallet come morning and hung my head and caved my breast for a couple-three days and that was enough for Matron. She was used to us horii break-ing. Had no shelf in her mind to lay the notion that we might bend and bounce back. Took the shadow for the substance, eh, Mary Kath?" She nudged her. "Am I wrong?"

"No," said Mary Kath.

"Eyes see what they spect to see," said Mary Pat, and yawned again. "Most all of them, any road. By the sucking flea I'm zausted. May your dreams flow wide and clear," she said. She was rolled in her blanket and sleep-breathing in the time it takes to tell it.

Mary Kath nudged Finn aside and spoke in his ear. "Was it that bad?"

"Yeah and it was. Shutter." Finn gripped her shoulder in goodnight. He wrapped himself in blankets. Was it that bad? Yeah and it was. Worse nor what he told them. It was grateful to be up the orchard. Even his sisters' snores made good hearing. He'd likely no startle awake in the night, here, remembering Ambrose. Remembering when Bourke was set to flight. Off the cloacal roof, off a hand to the small of his back. All the novices cheered Bourke's flight cepting him and Palan. Palan, now. He ought seek out Palan. Palan could spend a day and a night concocting a machine as'd core apples, though all the scutmen in the world was galomphing down on him.

Ought track that boyo to his lair. He grinned in the moonlight, pic-turing the gold head bent over some mad project in a shack, Palan blinking as Finn filled the door sudden. Bring Dan to him. They'd lug a carboy down the stone pier. Finn stretched inside his blanket. His tendons sang gainst his bones, his heart beat steady in his chest, his tongue was plump in his mouth. He took a long breath and slept.

# Book Three

# Even Mud Will Squeak, Given Time

*A spark here, a spark there, a good breeze, fuel sufficient: will the timber catch fire? Will we continue in our dreary round, pushing uphill our appetites, that disparate heterogeneous bundle in all its disorder, stuffed with known and unknown, vital and peripheral, tools and dross, its elements liable to tumble by the way and we to hold the upheap steady as we stoop to recover, muscles straining. Or will the sparks remain alit, catch hold, burn, sear, consume.*

DREG SPENDS HALF AN ANY DAY WAITING, walking harborside, kicking coil, what's else to do? Naught. Dregs prop elbows on stone jetty, half-mast eyes watch waves come in, come in, again; greygreen water smacks the jetty, shtreels away, half-mast eyes watching. Dregs have gumption enough to scoop porridge down their maws; enough and no more, says Mary Patricia. Mary Katharine says they're building their strength; she says when you can no see where you're going it's cutest to halt, snuff the air, look round. Mary Pat let it go till now; in the first place, rimers maybe knew deeper; in the second place, she did no care. But now she asks, is that a fact? Who halts when checked mid-stride? Do we no, likelier, grope forward, cursing as stones trip us, muttering; do we no by nature *keep going?*

Mary Pat mutters to her ownself a gracious plenty now. She's time for it now she slaves in a richard compound. She dusts Lady Mandra's mantelknacks and plumps her many cushions; she says "Yes, m'lady," or "No, m'lady." When Lady Mandra asks is she doing well here at the Governor's Compound, Mary Pat answers "As you say, m'lady." Three weeks it's been and Mary Pat answers honest for once because she's no least notion how she's doing here. She's nobbut a doormat you shake on the stoop, how should such judge?

It was always Mary Kath asked the deep questions; now it's her words roll on Mary Pat's own tongue. Why do richards float through their days while dregs flail, each new wave leaving their mouth filled with salt? Why do shoals rake dreg keels till they beach broken on the shingle by their seventh Seventh, while richards tack, and come about, and sail on and on? All her years to now Mary Pat shrugged in answer: *things are as they are and that's that*; she waved off the notion that lives could be otherwise than they are; an they could be, they would. Now, while Lady Mandra twirls in the next room on the spindle of the tallest footman's long arm up her skirt, Mary Pat asks what quality makes this woman her mistress? She maun clamp her teeth down hard lest these questions scape her teeth's barrier.

This morning, Mary Pat dusted scrollwork dragons' tongues and stretched her jaws gainst the ache from long clamping ... to snap them together sharp enough when Lady Mandra swirled through the doorway.

"Ah, Mayry," she said. "Isn't it a beauty day?" parting the curtains and mashing her hot breasts gainst the cool glass, "Don't you wish we didn't have to work on a day like this?"

"Yes ma'am," said Mary Pat, smearing a little nosedrip into a dragon's eye, "surely does seem a shame."

Lady Mandra turned sharp, hooded eyes on her. "Now Mayry Patriza. You have been here a fortnight, which should be long enough, surely? to have learned that I do not keep around me those who speak as though gruel stops their mouth. Do not do so again. You were an hori so I shall forgive your mealy ways this once, but take my warning now. Stand up straight and breathe through your nose; take pride in your work and precision in your words, and we shall never quarrel. Do I make myself clear?"

"Well, ma'am," she could no keep the words back of her teeth's barrier once she unclamped her jaws, "I can no say we sha' no quarrel. If a straight back and straight chat you must have, then soon or late my road and yours will crack heads at a signpost. Quiet dreg? Meekmouth? There's a role I've my whole life trained for, play it for you in my sleep, I can. Now if you're wanting pride and naff, the mix is new to me; I could well stumble, spill the new mix, stain your pretty robes."

In the silence after, Mary Pat dusted the dragon's ears. A breeze through the open window rang gallywhamp in her ears. Her heart slammed gainst her ribs, dark purple as any risen cock ripe for oiling.

Lady Mandra opened her mouth a time or two; then her lips found speech. "Ha!" she said. "You appear to believe that I will not explode in fury against you. Were I you, however, I should not take the chance."

"That's as may be, my lady. You was born with a freshwove net neath your every step. With me it's walk the rope or crack the pate."

"Perhaps," her eyes narrowed lizard again, "my husband, Governor Donal, has informed you that he 'likes a girl with spirit,' has he?"

Mary Pat stood up soldier. "My lady, what'll I reap do I tip a wink at a fixed-down man older nor my dap would been, easy rest his bones. The gate's my harvest an you once saw a coveting eye in my head. You can no think me so lackbrain as to toss aside this sitation for which you hired me your own self. Chose you so poorly?"

Lady Mandra coughed behind her tiny coral nails. "Ah, yes, mmm," she said. "Well, Mayry Patriza, I believe I shall postpone, probably forever, the day when I shall ask you to assume the role of — what was your phrase? — quiet meekmouth. The mirror above the mantel is streaky; attend to it. When you're done, get your amanuensis kit from Collins."

"Ama-nensis? M'lady?"

"Amanuensis. Chantal has one, and Thassy, but I want no orbiting moon who would take the shine out of me. Whereas you have absolutely nothing going for you but youth, and a certain stimulating quality of mind. Yes. I want you in grey smock when I go visiting, the amanuensis kit in a smock pocket, always. Yes. I think we'll have fun with that, don't you? Mayry Patriza?"

"Ah. Yes of course, m'lady." Mary Pat curtsied as her mistress swept from the room. "Nothing going for me but youth," she muttered to a well-polished dragon. "That wants carving in stone."

Taffeta swooshed gainst the door inlay. "Did you speak, Mayry Patriza?"

"No, m'lady."

"Ah. I quite thought you did. My error. Collins has the kit and smock," and whoosh went Lady Mandra's taffeta skirts through the doorway, click went Lady Mandra's glass heels cross the marble floor.

"Hmmph," said Mary Pat, main quiet. "No porridge lest I say porridge, but then it's I maun have three bowls hot, and sharp about it."

*Rats and richards / Hear our song / Poke your nose where we belong / And a one thrust / two thrust / three thrust / more / Run through / Spin round / Toss on flames / Rats and richards / Render well / Light and clean you'll leave us .... and a one thrust / two thrust / three thrust / more.*

Governor Don's coulees was singing short as they hauled his palankeen up the last rise. Mary Pat shoved her dustrag neath a cushion and slid down bannister to the servant cave. Servants had their own *cave*, here in Gov Don's compound. Its fans was ratchety and its stones leaked, but it was a cave sure enough, and did he no joy to remind them of that? To make sure they was sufficient beholden? Oh, he took considerable joy in it. Collins the housekeeper ruled the servant cave. She swanned over it, preening her fat neck like she dug it out from the stone with her own blunt beak. This morning she was missing, must swooled upstairs to welcome Master Gov, *oh the poor hardworked beastie, oh the blood he sweat for others, oh.* Soon as he brushed Collins aside and stampled off to find his twirly lady, the fat-neck'd tromple down the narrow backstairs to take up her rule again, to grab her long spoon and shout for her dregs, *Am I to get the supper and run this compound all my own self?* Soon as they was dripping sweat at their slave, Collins'd shift some of her tonnage off her feet and onto a bench and sigh and tell them, once more, how they was gorry fortune's spawn, one and all, to get three bowls a day of richard leavings down their maws. Oh, she'd sigh, oh mercy, pressing her thick fingers to her dentable breast, oh that a one of them survived at all at all was by richard contriving only, each sigh setting the flesh to romp on her frame.

Collins was the first dreg Mary Pat saw ever with flesh on her for two. Matron was ample round the hips but Collins was size of a mash-tun. She ladled it in, hand over fist, of an evening while she diddled her count books at the broad plank table, one eye to the dregs clearing away.

"Who's been at the apple butter?" she'd say, and all the dregs'd look nohow. Collins chose who'd no jumped high enough that day, and mark the value of the maginary apple butter gainst that dreg down in her count books. Collins shilled for richards, pure and simple. Mary Pat had tried telling the others that, got the same blank wide look they gave Collins in return, like she was nobbut a carp opening and closing its lips.

Mary Kath could hold to it that such dregs was husbanding their strength; she could make rimes off it till she was blue-face; but these dregs in Gov Don's compound nobbut skated through their days, pupils wide, smashed to pulp. You could tell them the world was up-ended, and it was richards down, dregs on top, they'd turn no hair (how could you turn a hair? another no-point proverb of Cider Mother's), only stand and gawp till some click in their skulls sparked them to some no-thought task like restuffing a tick, straw by straw. A passel of spineless bobanks as could make a job of work off strolling jetty on a Hunt Boy arm.

They none of them could made hori. No chance soever.

Mary Pat'd be a hori still an she could. But you can no kick gainst the pricks; there was a Cider Mother proverb with point to it. You was a hori till the end come, which did no creep up on a hori; it come final to them, four-star, blaze cross the sky.

Mary Pat's end come during monthly peer review, which was Matron walking up and down to peer at you real close. No oil on you nor naught, even was it your time you'd to stand there dripping scarlet down your thighs to pooltiles. "M'Cool! Step front!" Mary Pat had stepped fore Matron was done speaking. She was long enough in the harum to be scarum, she knew what welts would rise did she no snap when Matron said pop. She stood there in her altogether while Matron walked round and round her. "What's this? What's this I see?"

"Can't say, ma'am," said Mary Pat tween her teeth.

"This is FAT! This is CELLULITE! This is Fleshy Degradation! All you girls gather round and look at the top of M'Cool's legs here. Yes, right here beneath her well-curved ass. M'Cool, there is no quarrel with your ass. But beneath it, beneath it ... oh and it's on both legs, what a shame, what a shame. Girls, look here. This, now THIS is what I want you all to watch and ward for. These is marks of a *former* hori." Matron paused a moment to let that bit sink in. "Touch it, go on, squeeze it good, learn you the feel of it. Because THAT is the feel of good-bye. All you girls has gone lax lax lax in feeling yourselves. Have you no? HAVE you no?" Twenty-five heads nodded up and down.

Mary Pat stood soldier while two dozen and one hands squeezed her thigh tops from behind. She'd felt it, right aright, she'd kept slap up with nightly feeling, but speak of it? She'd no speak up for a mash-tun of potable. Tick, you spoke up; tock, you started the long walk out the harum, and Mary Pat liked harum fine. There was food and what to drink and for certain plenty proper bathing; there was watching the new Boys find nooks as was safe from peepers; plus she'd her metyay, training up Novices in the way they was to go on; you'd never go blind off dulldom in harum. Nobody in the horii krewe ever lambasted her for letting her brains relax and assume their natural level. Think she'd give up all that easy? Out of course she'd no let on what she felt in her nightly self-probes. Meanwhile five-and-twenty heads kept nodding. Mary Pat smiled dark. Called themselves friends, did they? Nod away, little lasses, you'll catch your dropdown soon.

"I want you gerruls to drop and give me twenty; make that thirty. Shout after me, now, 'I will feel myself each night / I will feel and probe.' Great laggards that I should be divagating you like a bunch of comestarts. Louder, please, gerruls."

*I will feel myself all fore I sleep / Probe myself all over / I will feel myself each night / Lest I wake to cellulite.*

"Now THAT is more the way of it!"

*For if I swell up fore I wake / I pray some girls my clothes to take / For I sha' no need them, wandering lorn / Wishing I was never born.*

"And now, the rousing chorus!"

*I'll wander naked as a cloud / Beyond these well-loved doors / And take my sad and aged place / 'Mong sweepers, drabs, and –*

"That's right, that's right, and a good solid rest on that last beat. And *eight* and *six* and *eight* and *five* and *rest*. Gerruls, you may assume the upright position. You have ten minutes by the pool clock and then I want you back here shining, SHINING, do you hear me? Every crack and crevice glisteny with oil, no shirking, and DO NO forget your backs! On the double, now." The girls slithered off, their soles slapping. Chrysta and Galyse waggled two fingers behind, but Mary Pat made them no return. Safest for all, that road.

"Now, M'Cool."

"Yes, Matron."

"Who'd you think you could fool?"

"Sorry, Matron."

"Now we've got on fine on the whole, so I will no give you a scold, but I want you to know, the time has come to go."

"Yes, Matron."

"What do you say?"

"Thank you, Matron." This was always safe. There was all times summat you should be spouting thanks for. You'd likely no least notion what it was; Matron kept a eager and a running tally.

"You're welcome. You been a good, bedient hori, but here's the end of story, you may run back to the dorm, say farewell to the swarm, course you'll smitter while you pack but — M'Cool! — in fifteen minutes I want to see your back."

"Yes, Matron. Thank you again, Matron."

"Best luck all future, Mary Patricia," and Mary Pat curtsied and backed out the door and that was *that* sorted.

A quick whip-round mong the horii yielded three fat dangles, one silk handker, and a flash casket of scented oil, and that was that for the harum. *Next!*

Mary Pat loafed on her pallet for nine days straight. "My young dreams is used up, spilled like potable down a piscine," she told Cider Mother, who hummed and brought a slice of applebread and hummed away to her brew-vats. Mary Pat lay on her pallet. She'd her makeup kit and ten learned fingers and she knew fine what to say to a heartslammed Novice or a burnt-eye Hunt Boy; she'd a year's cache of potable for the house, and she'd the plaque. "Make a fine trivet, that will," Cider Mother said. Finn and Mary Kath took it in turns to chunter on of duty and responsibility and the rest of her life and the position of the dregs and who knew what all else. Mary Pat let them go on. They was beside her full of speech and then they was gone and the room was empty of words, no matter. Mary Pat laid there for the lotted time.

On the tenth day, she rose up, fluffed her hair and donned her clothes, went out walking and smack into this slave she walked, or *this sitation* as

Lady Mandra called it. House dreg. It was better than a peck over the head with a sharp rock. There was potable and provender enough, if no more. She could go off-compound after a full month work with no complaint. Till then, there was work enough to fill the hours tween dawn and midnight; in the chinks she burrowed down in this corner of the kitchen where the dried herbs hung.

The only spag in the gruel come just then grousling down stairs with a bumpf each time one flat foot landed, "These dregs're gorry fortune's spawn to get three bowls a day, do they preciate? They do no. Vaporate like harbormist at noon." Mary Pat ducked under table with her rag fore Collins burst through door.

"Nuzzin but scamps in this lair, lash and skinnings, fish to fry and no hands round, lazzible goutrumps," Collins eased her lardly ass to her cushion bench. "Cussle of brainmills with no one grain to grind," and shifted to roar easy as kiss your hand, "Mercator! Spindrift! Punzelmane! Dazymare! Get your gorry stupid branks on deck fore I suds your soupplates!"

Mary Pat popped out from under table. "Yes, ma'am?"

"Dazymare, right. One brand snatched fro burning. What was you doing all creep underfoot?"

"Dusting, ma'am."

"Dusting my ass," said Collins, comfortable.

"Could do that an you wish, ma'am."

"Shutter up."

"Exist only to serve, ma'am."

"Shut your gorry pie-hole, broomhead. Where's the other gorry useless dregsweeps? Hah? Gone to shore up harbor jetty?"

"But for their support, those walls'd tumble sure, ma'am."

"Oh, less of it," said Collins. "You been routering with yes my lady by sound of you. She tell you off to ask me for the am-an-u-ensis kit?"

Mary Pat dropped to her haunches (Collins let no dreg sit till she invited them). "Rat and spike, how you come to guess that?"

"Guess? *Guess?* I guess I do little guessing hereabout. I got capacious *reserves* to lug about, would boiled away like cabbage long since did I no keep my ears on the listen. You the Parlogal. I seen a dunnamany Parlogals, and every one, after a time, Lady M goes twirly round roundabout, *Oh I got to have a amanuensis like Chantal and Thassy got.* Tell you off for the grey smock, did she? Visiting wear, was it?"

Mary Pat shifted her thighs gainst each other to rub up a little think-juice from her fork. "I'm no Parlogal," she offered. *Vamp till ready, girls, then forward with the oil!*

"Tssss," said Collins, shaking her head all sad. "Stifle them antic pants; sit down and give your brain a crank, willa? Make a nice change. You was hired as Parlogal and Parlogal you been. Opens door, dost no? Dusts cushions for my lady's tender butt cheeks, dost no? Wears a bliddish starch on brow, mmmm? Or is that nobbut my lying eyes?"

"Parlogal," said Mary Pat. "Right aright. Well, give over the amanensis and I'll start in on it."

"I will no. There's two bushel carrots need scraping, and then —"

"Lady M said amanensis kit, on the double. I shudder to think —"

"Now *that* is true as live."

"What all she'd say did I no spit-spot with the doings. Give over, Collins."

Collins rummaged in the spice cupboard; mint, garlic, best-quality tongue-stripping peppers. "Amanensis. And no binnock neath *this* roof calls me other than Mistress Collins."

"What name could be better?"

Three wormwood sachets and a yarrow wreath was tossed to floor. "Saw it here just the other day," said Collins. "Saw it plain as I'm looking at you now."

"I could mention that you are *no* looking at me right now, but I sha' hold off on account of us Parlogals is noted for our courtesy." Mary Pat sat on the kitchen table, swinging her legs crossed at ankle. Matron was strong on her girls crossing their legs at ankle. *Yer street girls crosses at the knee, tucked sideways for a lady, a girl who would good hori be, for Boy assault she's ready.* First time Matron spieled that Chrysta piped up, "Sha' we cover Frog Position later in this course? Is that what Boys prefer? That why we got to be ready crossed at the ankles, so to sume the position with no blink nor shicker?" All the horii laughed. There was a fine passel of easy laughing back at the start. They was all laugh till they learned the many, many ways as Matron could take the laugh right out of you.

Collins finally dug out the amanensis kit. A leathern purse, all it was. Size of Mary Pat's spread hands. Inside the purse, a bound book and three leads in a brass tube.

"Right aright," said Mary Pat. "Am I to write on paper? Likely! Where's the slates, Collins?" who shrugged in answer. "Look at this kit. What, by the last rat's singed whiskers, am I to do with it? Does Lady Mandra think I'm to *write* on *paper?*"

Collins shrugged. "I've no least notion. Who am I to know what you're to do with with it. Draw their robes, likely. *Write.* Think any Parlogal can *write?*"

"Out of course —" Mary Pat took a breath. "Out of course they can no. Gown sketching, now, that's what I'm framed for."

Collins aimed a swipe in Mary Pat's general direction. "Get along with you, out of my kitchen, less you want to scrape carrots."

Outside the door, Mary Pat held the kit to the light. The leather was stubbly in her hands; close to, it was a field of nicks, pricks, piercings, what? Mary Pat held it closer. The pricks was tiny, mayhap done with a pin, and made a schema of tanks, pipes, and coils neath a small fierce sun. Stamped round the edges ran two words repeated: *Aqua Pura.* She looked at it for a time, then rolled it in her handker and stowed it in her pocket. "Right aright," said Mary Patricia M'Cool. In two weeks she'd have an afternoon's leave. She'd show this to Cider Mother then. For now, there was more dragon eyes to wipe.

# Water Lap Stone

FINN WALKED HOBBLE down the stone pier. Even a flexish beater tips to one side when he's a full carboy tucked down one pantsleg. *Stump calatter stump* went Finn long the cobbles, a whistle on his tongue, his hands at sway, the last of the hot day's light flushing his ears.

No one gave a blind bit of notice to the long skinny dreg staggering down pier. Was the morning tide on the turn, there'd been a handful of quaymen to spit and mutter how they'd never ship nohow so lank a boy, one as'd crack his chin belowdeck with that length on him, but it was near sunfall so the fishboats tugged at their pilings. Idlers and dreamers — that is to say, the most of the harborside dregs — leaned their elbows on the jetty but there was little to mark in a blackhair bronzeflesh green-eye dreg walking to water's edge. Once past the shallow-draught nobbies snubbed to the shoalwater pilings, lading rigs coiled in their bows, Finn was safe enough. It was no profit to any dreg to take heed of what went on mong the deep-water craft; richards owned them, scutmen patrolled them. Best to turn a blind eye. Which dregs was main good at.

The pier-end pilings come close to him and closer (Finn had snaked his long tongue a few times down the carboy's throat) till, of a sudden, they jumped at his eyes. Due to him turning clever in mid-air, the pilings could no land a kayo, though the acrobatics did shake up the carboy some. Finn propped up the far piling, off his own deciding entirely, for prudent he was raised; taking the strain off his left leg, he was, so as to raise it perilous high and to ease, easy now, the carboy out from his pantsleg. Triumphant carboy! The far piling come apart as he watched; from one section mussel-laid and dulse-bedizened rose a dreg dark as wrack and solid as the salted piling. Finn set the carboy down, prudent-like, and turned to face the other.

"You're ashore, then, Dan," said Finn.

"I am no," said his brother. "What've you there?"

"Our mam's finest scrumpy," said Finn. "You *look* to be ashore."

"There's manifold illusions rise from the dusty earth, that's why I remain afloat. Cider Mother give you a whole carboy to your own?"

"Well, as to say *give*, sure she *would* given it to me and she'd known I needed it so."

"Then hand over what belongs to the needful, you splatted sprat."

"You'll say that less easy once you're outside this brew," said Finn.

They drank turn by turn. Waves lapped at the pilings, dulse fronds intertwined and slapped the stones as one, the strong cider sloshed in the jar, their throat apples gurgled, the warm air billowed over the water.

Finn kicked his calves gainst the pierstones. "So how come you ashore, our Dan?"

"I am no ashore nor am I your Dan your Danny your Danny Boy, I'm my own and no man's else." Dan'l drank off his brew and returned the carboy to its place tween them. He flicked his black hair off his wide shoulders. "You want a story? I've a story for you, *our Finn*, as've been a needy widemouth since you slipped from out our mam, bellering and frackish, drove even the midwife to wring her hands and sigh, *Our wee prince, now, we've no cloth fine enough to swaddle him,* and what've you come to off that? nobbut a beater."

"I chose it, Dan." Finn linked his long hands round his bony knees and stared at the sea boiling round the pilings.

"Chose, got chose, the gap tween's no wider nor a hair. You want a story of how a choice is made? I can tell you a story of that." He downed a healthy slosh. "What would you say to a voice as came in your head, will you nill you, even was you up the rigropes, five dap-heights above the waves, no matter; the voice in your head took no thought to how you'd splat did you fall from that great height, how dock or sea would splinter your bones inside your skinsack the same — maybe the dock'd be kinder, think — a voice as come rearing up to tell tales of the Great Burning, only and always that one tale; call that what a man chose? Who mong us'd *choose* a voice to ring gainst your ears from their insides, caring for you no whit, was you to slip or fall or holler betimes its own tones was all its concern and it going on, and on, and on and on, onandonand —" clouting each word into the piling with his fists, all the treethick of his arms behind them, his barrel chest heaving, "Onandon and onandon and —"

"Shutter, Dan'l," said Finn, and his brother went stone, toes to pier-edge, scraped knuckles raw at his side. Finn paused to pour some liquor down his gullet. "You been at sea a long time. Main long. They say that out to sea the whispering lies thicker nor fog, that past sight of land there's uncanny music."

"*I am no ashore!* You thickhead. I am all times afloat. Lodge that in your brainpan."

Finn got to his feet. The moon was rising. "You're past my depth with all this talk of voices; you say you're afloat when my own two eyes see you standing ashore. You been overlong aloft, where you should learned to con what you see by its edges. Instead you been rubbing your head gainst cloud bottoms as have pulled, like to like, the batting right out of you. Your skull's scraped clean within and now you wail, loud in that hollow place, *ah,* lost and lonely, *ah poor Dan.*"

They sat side by side at the pier-end, two dark men in the darkness, the moon flecting off their eyes and teeth. Kinship flickered tween them in the quick turn of their long thin beaks, in their spatulate fingers, in the hunch and ready of their shoulders. Kinship guttered tween them in their framing, Dan muscled tough as root and square-chinned, like their dam; Finn stretched out lean and wiry like James A. At the shoosh of footsteps down the pier, Dan haunkered pugnace, a solid mass, while Finn balanced on balls of his feet so to launch himself as called for. The footsteps come on, *plonk ta plonk,* heel and toe striking together, a scutman's walk, smack up to the last piling but one.

"Is that you, Finn M'Cool?" said the incomer.

"It's nobbut Palan. We was in barracks together," Finn said low. "He's closemouth. A great sea-goer by his own account." He raised his voice a notch. "Palan, keep mum till you reach us." The footsteps shushed over the pierstones. Dan breathed out long and soft.

Then Palan was tween them, strong with garlic, his voice in their necks. "Scutmen walking dark-lantern tonight; best fold gainst the pilings a while."

"Any why to it?" said Finn, already flat to a piling's harbor side.

Palan said, "Sounded like nobbut training, but who's to know?" He folded into the dark by Finn. "Stow your hair," said Dan, and with a soft curse Palan snuffed his pale hair neath a black knit cap. They lay close till the dark lanterns passed.

Dan had so melted to the far piling that his hair flapped gainst it like dulse fronds. The harbor glows lit his beak, picked out his long lashes as his closed eyes flashed open. He stretched and sat crossleg with them. "Training," he said. "I heard on scutman training. On the *Leda*, my relief watch, Lammas, used walk dark-lantern till he fled it for the gorry waves. You know Ambrose, up the barracks?"

Yes. They knew Ambrose.

"Ambrose keeps an eye out for likely boys, boys as stick a rat then stir its innards with the spearpoint, boys as like to stick them in the eye or up neath they tails; those boys Ambrose takes aside after a few weeks in barracks. There's a special krewe, he says. There's an over-krewe, he says."

"Well, overkrewe, right aright," said Palan. "We've met overkrewe. They've no objection to any flesh going, novice flesh no least."

"Seek 'em and spike 'em, that's their maxim," said Finn.

Dan went on like their words was nobbut a couple gulls fluckering by. "Overkrewe trains special. Sganal, the squint-eye, he trains them. Sends them up the Rimehouse where the tumbling meister learns them only leaps and clambers; musicians school them only to the zanghorn, tinny and shrill, as they wear round the neck. Gov Don takes them, even, down the filtration chamber of his own shelter cave, lets them hold in their own two hands the crystals as sweeten the water. So my relief watch Lammas told me. Sganal tells the overkrewe, Gov Don back of him, all this is nobbut first fruits of what they'll get when they're full-trained, so they'll swallow whatever's put before them to that end. Once they're trained, Sganal sends them down to Ambrose. Ambrose sets them to easy tasks as get them out of barracks and in mong the horii —"

"They've horii to their own?" said Finn.

"So Lammas said. When they're puffed full of what fine fellows they are, Ambrose leads them blindfold to the municipal cloaca's roof, leads their toes to the roof edge, there halts them and unbinds their eyes. There

they stand, Lammas said, toes six fathoms off the ground, a hawser taut
gainst their asses. There, Ambrose explains how wide's their freedom. Tells
them they've the choice; to live up to the glorus tradition of scutmen, keeping order mong the lesser dregs, or to learn to fly."

"We'd one in Barracks took it on him to learn flight," said Finn, quiet.

"Well, Bourke sweated night and day fore they took him up-roof," said
Palan, softer still. "He knew what'd come to his mam and dap did he refuse
the over-krewe."

"He got clumsy all on a sudden while he was waiting," said Finn.

"Stumbled over a block of thick air, did Bourke," said Palan.

Finn sang in minor key:

*Bourke's dead and gone / Left us alone*

Palan joined in:

*See how he dies / See how he lies*
*The tails he whacked roped round his throat*
*The guts he sacked made a tidy coat*
*The rats laugh last – ha ha! / The rats laugh last – ha ha!*

They bowed their heads for a long count. Finn poured first swig into
the harbor as Bourke's libation, and took one slosh for himself. Palan tossed
three drops over his shoulder — "Waste no lest you wasted be" — then
poured two handsfull down his gullet. It was full dark now and the moon
silvered the harbor. The stomp-stomp of the harbor watch moving away was
clear over the water.

Palan passed the carboy straight to Dan's moonwhite palms. Dan
tipped it down. "That's as may be. My relief watch Lammas turned his back
on flight, swore high tide ebb tide his whole desire was a good spot mong
the scutmen. Six months he stuck it. Six months of whacking senseless
aught that moved. Windy nights, he told me, plenty of his mates bloodied
themselves by thwocking leaves that fluttered in the wind. Scutmen want
every living shape to crawl from shadows as pantspissed fearful as they get
when a richard snaps his fingers." Dan spat. "Scutmen," he continued,
"nobbut richard eyes, what they are."

Dan paced the pier's width. Finn said, "Steady, Dan. Many a slip twixt
the brink and the drink," nodding at the silver water.

Dan shook his head, short, tossing it off, though he moved a handspan away from pier edge. "Scutage jobs. Let me get the faugh taste of such men off my tongue," he said, and took another slosh from the carboy.

"Well, there's such persons," said Palan, equable. "Always been, always be. No sense fretting over what's fixed." His grey-green eyes slanted neath his lids tween Finn and Dan.

"Met our Mary Patricia?" said Dan, once more on the pace. "You and her'd get on wonderful, so you would. 'Only those deserving feel the lash,' Mary Pat says. Though she'd maybe say they ought lash first and ask never, for if a boy's no committing devilry right then, he sha' be soon."

"Easy on," said Finn.

"Well, roll me on my back and spin me," said Palan, "you do rise up quick. I been too long mong landmen, maybe, a stolid clanch they are."

"At sea, were you?" said Dan. "How came you here?"

Palan rested his chin on his knees. "Well, it's curious you should ask. I been thinking on that all day. A voice — have you ever heard it? comes at you from every point of the compass? over the open waves? Ever lost your own voice, keening after it?"

"Go on," said Dan.

Finn said, "Strange things does happen when a man's too long at sea," with a sideglance at his brother.

"Go on," choked Dan.

"Well, it was maybe two years back, I was on my knees cleaning scuppers, mong the fish trails baked hard to each hollow, down on my knees and cursing quiet as I scrubbed, scraped, cursed, wiped my bitter eyes. Was then I heard a voice come singing over the waves, of flames, flames and tumblers." Palan stopped for a swig from the carboy wedged tween Finn's boots. "Tumblers, hmmm, saw them first time in the flesh when I come to give Galanty Show." He socked the vessel tween his boots and went on.

"Well, I laid down scrub brush when I heard that singing." Palan snorted. "Stood by taffrail while the voice sang over the waves of a tree shot from its roots; and I thought how? where? when?" Palan spread his hands. "Listen as I would, I could no make it out."

"Sound does change in travelling cross the water," said Dan, rotating his palms gainst each other, back and fro.

"True enough," said Palan. "Then the voice said 'Charnholm;' it soughed in the rigging, 'Charnholm;' full of longing it was, and terrible fearful, like a body lashed to the wheel in a hurlgainst, the winds snapping sail and timbers while the voice cried, 'flames' and 'Charnholm' and 'flames;' in come and go gusts it sang in a voice as'd pull your heart from out your —"

"Sang, did it?" said Dan, smoothing the pier-edge with his palms. "Come smack cross the waves, singing? A voice? Now, have you a witness to that?"

"Well, my dap was there, half-sides over then as now. Would you call him as witness, M'Cool? Seeing as you've no trust in my word?"

Dan snaked the carboy from Palan's feet. "One of Cider Mother's best bottomless, this," he said. "Now Palan, no call to rise up in the air over so small a matter. You come from who knows where; you come mong us blathering of a voice you could no understand as come at you cross waves we never seen. Tell me what welcome you'd hand a shipwreck as come aboard your own ship with a tale like your own, made all of cloud."

Palan laughed, short and quiet so not to rouse the scutmen. "*You've heard it same as me. Did you no?*"

"You gorry snotblind puse, clamp your trap," said Dan. "Frighting the crew with your tales. Was you on my ship, I'd have you dragged by the taffrail; I'd —"

Palan grunted like a cornered rat and backed gainst the near piling. "What then, Dan? Stow me midships? feed me on bread and water? give me the cat?" He squatted on his hams and spoke quiet, his palms dangling tween his knees. "Listen. I heard a voice sing in bits and pieces. Seemingly, you heard a fuller song. I'll no say, tell us and all will be well, for who knows that for certain? Sure there's no dregs living as'd listen as close as I and your own Finn here, but keep mute an you want. Your black bile, though, keep to your own self; I am no stone to suffer acid quiet, but a live man with vitals to me." He sat down on the pier edge, one leg dangling overwater.

The harbor papillated neath the full risen moon. "Tide's making fast," said Finn.

Dan's knees was drawn to his chest, fists clenched atop them. Palan swung his free leg careless, whistling soft tween his teeth.

Dan said, "Tide'll be high as she goes in an hour."

Palan said, "Land breeze freshening."

Dan's words was punched out his plexus: "The land stinks."

"Stinks?" said Finn. "What stench do you get, here so far to sea?"

Palan and Dan bent, laughing. "Send the lubber home!" said Palan.

Dan's teeth gleamed. "Send him up rigging to fetch a sky hook!"

Finn walked to the pier end and sniffed in. Brack smell, no more, neither piscine nor ratden. He bided his time. So they'd say of him when he was gone: *Finn M'Cool: He bided his time.* Out of course, by then the virtue might gone out of it, seeing how all corpuses was equal good at biding.

Dan clouted his shoulder. "You got to go to sea to get the landstink out your nose, Finn. You know how Charnholm has a rank smell to it when you come down off the orchard? That's naught, an apple peel to a doublepeck, to the smell you get when you're out of landsight, snuffing up air as has touched naught but seafoam for a million thousand leagues."

Finn clouted him back. "Right aright," he said, "you two mariners chunter on till sunrise an you like, but all the while scutmen are patrolling upjetty and down. They know where we are and they know where we'll be. The sea's as fresh and full of rare song as you like; we come back, always, to here," he waved at Charnholm sleeping neath the beetling sandstone cliffs. "Here. Where scutmen let the blood out our bodies so long as richards fill their pockets with the fruits of the harvest squeezed from dregs, down to the last drop of work in them, down to their last breath. Richards know naught and care less what rare songs may cross the waves to pour down some sailor's ear. What beats in their blood is 'How much will it yield?' that and no more. Have you never heard dregs shout on Reap Day? Gov Don speaks of troublestirrups who want to pull down, dreg and richard, rimer and smith, pull them all down to their level; and the dregs shout hoorah. Hoorah hoorah. To what? Who fed them this tale? The richards. Who reaps aught from such a tale? The richards. Who keeps that harvest? The richards." Finn slammed Dan's piling with the ham of his fist each time he said 'richard.' "The gorry richards in their shelter caves with their clean air clean water clean this that and the other. Do richards die untimely, buboes their necklace? No. Their women of fifty-some have a good sway on them and why? Because they got what to eat they got what to drink they got what to breathe. Their *leftovers* is enough for every dreg living. How can we eat up a minute, even, talking of aught else? Are we to put up with —"

"Can no be always on the stretch, Finn," said Dan. "More to this life than who's got and who lacks."

"Fine, then, fine: let's palather all the livelong day. After we depose these gorry richards."

"Best speak of this elsewhere," Palan shushed them.

"Sound does carry over water," said Dan. "Best we keep off it now."

Finn said, "An now's wrong, when's right? An it's we should no speak of it, then who?"

Palan gripped Finn's shoulder. "Well, three of us, that's too few to re-make Charnholm. We maun get this right or richards'll snap us like laths. It's late now and we're slag-tongue off your mam's scrumpy. We need to machinate some means of suasion." He rubbed his eyes. "I'm forgone. When sha' we three meet again?"

After some back and fro, they decided to meet up the lookout near the cliff edge, three days off, the first hour after noon, that windless hour when most dregs was at table. They parted, and made their solitary ways to their solitary pallets.

# Knock Knock

"WHAT'S THIS, DAY OF COLLIDING GIRLS?" said Cider Mother. Mary Patricia bluthered through her hand.

"You girls wanted flat noses, should told me sooner, all a matter of early training which I'd been happy to —"

"Ooh o-bed ore in by bace!"

"Used to be, a woman could walk out her own front door without smacking some daughter in the —"

"Right in by bace!"

"But no, first Mary Katharine come running to have her nose flattened, now it's you wanting the selfsame —"

"Bary Kath was heah?"

"Lay this cold metal to your nose, and speak up, Mary Patricia, none will hear you an you mutter into your palm, stands to reason you —"

Mary Pat let her hand fall from her nose. "Mary Katharine was here this morning?"

"What have I been telling you, else?"

Mary Pat followed her mam through the front room to the kitchen table gainst the back windows. "You say she was here this morning. Mary Katharine."

Cider Mother snapped her fingers in the air. "Mary Patricia M'Cool. You been drinking from piscines? You're addled as a shook ratpup."

"Mam."

"Mam, what?" said Cider Mother. She waited, her swole-knuckled hands folded. In the street, a hawker shouted, *Leaf drip, fine fresh leaf drip, get your leaf drip here!*

"Sha' we holler for a drap? My throat's dead parched."

"We'll drain no stranger's dipper."

"I've means. Three chits in my pocket."

"Mary Patricia M'Cool, neath roof of your own you may sip a strange hawker's potable. You've her claim for it, only, that it's leaf drip. Now, how goes it up the richards?"

"Mam, I'd a talk with Lady Mandra. Did you know she spins, mam?"

"Out of course. Always had roundbout ways, has Mandra. I'll make you some chamomile," said Cider Mother.

"I'm a *Parlogal*, mam. A gorry *Parlogal*." Mary Pat tossed her copper hair. "With talents on me as'd founder the white boat, on account of gorry *cellulite* I got to toss them over and be amanensis to my lady." She told her mam of Lady Mandra and fat Collins till the water boiled and her voice sank. "I was a *good* hori. It's no fair I was tossed for cellulite, only."

Cider Mother set a mug of chamomile by Mary Pat and took a sip of her own. "Fair, is it," she said. She closed the shutters, latched the door. Then she put back her head and laughed like Mary Pat'd no heard in time past count, shaking one finger at the girl, "It's no fair, she says, it's no fair time passes over me," holding her ribs with laughing till she'd no breath more.

"Right, mam, right aright," said Mary Pat. "Drink up your nice chamomile."

Cider Mother wiped her eyes. "Oh, she says, my terrible life, mam dear mam, oh I'm mured in a fine big compound with two squares daily and a gallon of certain-sure potable and oh the slave I maun be for that! Got to say yes m'lady no m'lady, wear myself out scratching notes for maybe four-five *hours* fore I can rest in a *shelter cave* where I dine off choicest *meats*, oh the terrible sad of it mam, oh how I suffer, here," swatting her bony chest, "Since I've no the full execution of my *talents*."

"Right aright. Still and all, it *is* no fair. I should be —"

Cider Mother sat up soldier. "Do I see you breaking your back hauling, dockside? No. Do I see you truckling your nose in the dirt when some richard sweeps through the gates? No. Do I —"

"*Would* see me truckle low an Gov Don was passing. He wants to see those aft-ends up, up, up." Mary Pat put palms to floor, spread her lips in smile, and waggled her backside, "Keep those sterns high and perky," she said in Gov Don's squeak tones. Cider Mother smiled up one side of her face. Mary Pat sipped her tea. "He says it's a con-di-tion of the si-ta-tion."

"Gov Don's nobbut one organ still stiffens, and that tween his teeth. What matter, so long as you've a soft berth in Charnholm? Did you want to make it better, now —"

"My sitation? Or the town?"

"Either. Either or both. Was you to put your mind to it. As you like."

"But, mam, what should I —"

Her mam clomped her elbows on table. "But me no buts, clamorous spawn. I give you food, a roof, clothes, and succor, which I sha' give you till I can no longer, which that could be tomorrow. Tell you the truth so far as I'm able, but only when you ask. More nor that's force-feeding. Your life's yours to make or to mar, and mine the same. I am your mam, no your gyre." Cider Mother pulled a bushel of apples out of the screenmetal food cage. "This batch is for drying," she said, laying a horn-handle knife by Mary Pat. They cored apples in familiar silence. "What sent you here hot-foot? First day off-compound, I thought you'd carouse some."

"The pricks I held in hand," said Mary Pat, setting down her knife. Cider Mother cut her eyes at her, and Mary Pat picked it up again. "The amanensis kit Collins give me? Leathern. I'd brought it you was the guard no on the watch. First home-going they search you to the skin and then some. The leathern kit was all over pinpricks, and mam, those pinpricks lined out some rangement of coils, pipes, some kind of machinery, and round the edge they said, over and over, *Aqua Pura*."

Cider Mother missed a beat in apple-coring. "Aqua pura, eh. Now that, that is summat to come home about. Your hair's in the apples, Mary Pat."

"Yeah, mam. Mary Kath sang an old song as had those words in it. She was here today. When?"

Cider Mother looked over her head, coring apples by feel. "Mmm?" she said.

"When was Mary Kath here this day?"

"She was here, yeah. Aqua pura. Certain sure of that?" On Mary Pat's nod, Cider Mother crossed to the back window and looked out at court-yard. Two wan locust trees hung their thin yellow leaves above the dust and wormwood crowding three lopside stools. "Aqua pura," said Cider Mother, laughing soft. "You're certain sure?"

"Was she sure?" Bedelia Coldhand asked. She moved restless in her chair, her swole right leg propped on three strawsacks.

"Aqua pura. Sure as I live," Cider Mother answered.

"The machinery. It was clear?"

"Mary Patricia's no brought it yet, but that's her word." Cider Mother filled Bedelia Coldhand's cup with her best perry. She tapped the table edge with the flat of her hand: "Remember? *The pricks go in the pricks go out / and how she flows, she flows, she flows* ... Remember, Delia?"

"Out of course I remember." Bedelia Coldhand set down her empty cup with a snap. "These bones is mayhap some older than yours, but they're no *ash*, Olympia. *Pricks go in and flows down hole, aqua aqua how she's swole.* I *taught* it you in this very courtyard as ever was. You fool sprats all times chaff your olders and for why? Mischief putrid in you's why. Course I remember. How clear was the pricks? Could build from them?"

Cider Mother bit the laughter back tween her teeth. It'd been a few Sevenths since any called her sprat, certain. She refilled Bedelia's cup. "When I hold it in these hands, may runt-tails be my portion if I'll no match you question for question. Look round, Delia. There's me and you, only, in this kitchen. Mary Pat and the leathern purse are ... lacking. Mary Pat and the leathern purse are ... where the clapping of one hand sounds. Mary Pat and the leathern purse are among those absent, in the rearguard of the visible, figmen of our magining, fish jewels, scutman's tears, rat pity, a richard's genrosity. Till we see it, Delia, let me comfort you with apples."

Bedelia Coldhand rubbed her right leg and winced. "She's a fleet girl, true enough. Well, stay me with flagons, Olympia, till we see it."

Cider Mother poured her another drap of perry. Gather, mash, brew, cork, uncork, pour; repeat. Well, there was worse slaves. She said, "Mary Pat's fleet enough, though addled off her time in harum; her very sweat's lascivous."

"They grow past it, Olympia." Bedelia Coldhand shifted her right hip higher. "This one'll come out the other side as well. Never fret."

"You keep thinking you can pour your learning down their earshells and bottle it, so." Bedelia Coldhand grunted in answer. Cider Mother rolled her glass back and fro tween her hands. "How to plant the notion in the girl's head, mmm, how to plant it so it grows, so it'll push the wax out her ears as its rootmass swells." Bedelia Coldhand made a grunt of disgust, brushed maginary foul off her tunic. "It's this. The girl can fix her mind on you for ten minutes hand-running and there's an end to it. Time's up and her eyes cloud. Holler her name, she may or may no turn her face to you off seeing your lips move. Her pores, some stroke conjuring, all abloom in desire."

"Call it up like it was yesterday," Bedelia mumbled in her empty cup. "I was lacious once my own self."

"She ties up to any dock for a quarter-hour, longest, and it's in that brief time, only, you can catch her dislades in your arms." Cider Mother straightened her elbow to fill the other's cup, hesitated, set down the flagon, and tucked her hands neath her crossed arms. "But you never know when she'll hove into view."

"Got to be ready natheless," said Bedelia Coldhand.

The women sat at the kitchen table coring apples while the courtyard bricks went from red to rose, till their skins tightened on their bones with the night breeze off the harbor, carrying salt, tar, corcach sulphur, knocking locust leaves gainst each other that spilled dust; sat on till the moon rose overharbor dark orange, flinging one milkwhite trail cross the harbor; they cored apples till the last dreg had left the jetty and sat to supper, bread and cider behind closed shutters, till spag lamps fluckered and the harbor watch leaned back in their chairs, picking their teeth, as slut dregs scurried to ready their night lanterns. In this pause tween one tick and the next when every leaf edge was outlined by the dark blue twilight distilled by the harbor; in this seam of the day, a clever dreg could slip off from the stragglers of the evening promenade, slink long the stones and mong the pillars, and so to a moraine below South Point, in the lee of the footpath up to richards' compounds, where cover was found gainst a standing stone crenellate with blunt carving gainst which rested an upturned wreck of a barge — the salt baulk, scupper-deep in salt-gnawed nets, its portholes gape, its keel stove-in, its ribs glistening in moonlight.

Mary Pat crept long the salt baulk's waterline, past its drape of fretted netstrings, making for the faint path through tumblestone up South Point the backway to the compounds. *Full fathom five / Thy father lies / Of his bones are coral made / Those are pearls that were his eyes / Nothing of him that ...* come bellering from the saltbaulk's far side. "That you, Finn?" she hissed.

"No other," he said. "And is that you, my dainty fine, making her way like a hobnail scutman through the gloaming? No, no, let us consider. Sha' we consider? We ought. Yes. Yes! You do no tromp like a scutman soever; you make riot enough for twenty! What hast brought thee, alone and soft desiring? What hath brought thee hither to tromple in the gloaming?"

"Shutter up, Finn. You're gorry smashed. You been into Cider Mother's perry?"

Finn reeled round the barge, his black hair spiking out from his head, his pants rolled to his knees like there was never no rat in moraines; no stick about him, even. His shirt billowed out round his chest, a white shirt too; he was a good wide mark altogether. "Mary Pat, Mary Pat," he sang, "how bout that? how bout that? I could been rimer! Did tha know that? Did tha? Did no!" he concluded triumphal. "Did no know! Thass a pun," he confided at the top of his voice. "A pun and a fine one. Hey! I made a rime thout trying. And there's another. There's no question soever, the fine fellow I am with the words, that sure a pity tis and tis pity, sure, that I'm nobbut a beater." He dove forward in a no-hands front-flip, and back again to land on his feet, hands outflung. "*Oh the beater's life is easy, oh the beater's life is free, let Hunt Boys cocks stand ne'er so high, who scaups the rats? Tis we!* Ever hear that one, Mary Pat? No! Course you've no. For why? Cause I just now spun it out of moonthread. Me. I did that. I'm a master, see, the unsung master of the song."

Mary Pat, who'd been all this while hushing and shushing to no effect soever, wrapped her arm cross his mouth. "Stopple your cake-hole, wretch," she said most sisterly. "Think cause you be blind, no dreg can see you? That tha deafness steals their ears? Stopple yourself and now, Finn; I got to slip up-compound." She took her arm from off his mouth, at when he commenced to yowling again, so again she clamped him down: "By the shriven Smith, put a cork in it!"

That stopped him. Stopped him cold and quick as stepping off North Point into the breakers. He sluffed off her arm like it was nobbut kelp and fixed her with his sea-green eyes. "How come you to know aught of the Smiths, Mary Pat?" he whispered.

She flopped down on a stump-stone. "Think you're the only knows how to open your earflaps? Down the harum we knew of it, and up the compounds there's no nightly chat but includes talk of the fools as gather in cliff caves dreaming of a time when they sha' follow their dreamed god Vulcan to rule all Charnholm, when peace and plenty and milk and honey sha' flood every home and justice pour down like mighty waters."

"Is it?" said Finn. He plomped down on a stone next hers only to rise up sudden on finding it thick with spikes. From a crouch, he said, "Well, that's useful to know and no mistake. How come you to hear that, Mary Pat? Are they speaking of them, now, up the compounds?"

"I've no least notion, Finn. See me here before you, dost tha no? Likely, I'd say." His eyes met hers, now, for all he was still smashed. Naught to be got from him till his head cleared. She tore him a hunk of bread from her sack. "Cider Mother's fresh rye. It'll soak up the poteen." Behind his head, pale masts swayed in the moon's light. "Finn, I found this pouch up the compound. Odd, it was. So this morning, first day of my leave, I went up the house to tell her. Cider Mother's so *practical*, is she no?" Finn nodded vigorous, one cheek swole with bread. "Practical's good, I like practical," Finn nodded again, "but she's no *vision* soever, know what I mean?" Finn shrugged. The masts glittered as some current pushed their prows south. "I mean, I *liked* being hori. I was *used* to being hori. I was *good* at it." Finn lowered his chin and gazed steady at her. "Which, yeah, right aright, better to been good at hori than never to been hori at all, you've the right of it. Look at Mary Kath, now will you, she never had least chance at harum; keeps a good front on her but you know she got to wish —"

"Put a cork in it, Mary Patricia," Finn suggested. "What you know on Mary Katharine'd fit in a libate cup. Never wanted to be hori."

So, good then, he was clear enough to go on with. "Back to our mam, then, eh?" Finn made no move and Mary Pat continued. "She has always the practical answers, mmm? She's no *vision*."

"Said that."

"Mmm, saying it again. There's pleasure to be gained in this life; there's thrill and the comfortable lie-back, after. Our mam's no taste for none of that. It's rise-and-work and work-and-work and eat-sleep-work all the day long for Cider Mother. What use having a body, even one less good as this one," gesturing at the series of ovals that she was, "an you do naught with it but slave? The thing with Cider Mother is, she'll no open herself to what pleasures we can scrape from our short lives. She's no eyes to see them nor skin to feel them."

Finn's head was down, sketching in the dust with a baulk splinter. "Know what she did when I come home from barracks nobbut a beater?" Mary Pat shook her head. "Took my face tween her two hands, what she did." Mary Pat spread her palms. "No more. Looked straight down my eyes till the wind changed."

"And then?"

"Gave my hair a pat and she said, 'You've a chance to keep a soft heart, Finnegan M'Cool,' and went down cellar mong the mash-tuns."

"What the —"

Finn shrugged, and stood, and reached a hand down to her. "I've no least notion. It's gone late, Mary Pat. I'll walk you to trailmouth. What's your errand up-compound, anyhow?"

"Skim their brew and bring the distill home to mam."

Finn stiffened his arm. "Easy over this bit. What's that mean?"

"I can see clear as cockstand that what I bring her sha' be lucky for us all."

"Can you see that, Mary Pat?" Finn stopped short, and Mary Pat perforce stopped too. "What of the lookout, Mary Pat? Do you see yourself up the crownest?" pointing at the flat ledge near clifftops to their north.

"Why should I go up mong all that dirt now, Finn?" She tugged at his arm to no effect. "I got to be back. Lady M made me a slot, all my own, amanensis I sha' be."

"Uh-huh."

"That's something, that is. That's my mounting-block, Finn."

"Uh-huh."

"Last time I went up the crowsnest, I was greenstain and sorearm for a se'en-night."

"No matter."

"No matter! Give *you* the creaks for so long time, see if it matters. Was you —"

Finn grabbed her by the shoulders. "See yourself up the crowsnest, Mary Patricia M'Cool? Give me a yes or a no."

"Well then yes," she said all in a rush. "Yes I do."

"See aught else?"

"Leave be, Finn. There's a grey-eye boy with a gold mane, lot of *stuff*, you know? Most times what I see, forward, gets all muddied up with the old tales from the crumble books; it's seldom I know what's foreseeing and what's remembering." She dug her heel back and fro in the dust.

"Mmm," said Finn. "Grey eyes and yellow hair, is it?"

"Most times I know what I seen after it comes to pass; it's no clear like first light, or kettle on the boil. Yeah, grey his eyes and gold his hair, I seen him up the lookout with some others, by the next rat's bad leap I've no more nor that, I got to be *back*, Finn." But she stood by him neath the moon, near the salt-glisten barge, mong the dust scraped grain on grain by the land's nighttime outbreaths, exhaled in fatigation after a long hot day of sucking in what vapor it could lap from the sea-mist.

"And the clouds parted, and the mist rolled away," said Finn.

"What? What are you on about?"

"Nobbut a song, Mary Pat, come into my head, like." He moved forward. "Here's trailmouth. Be up the lookout three days from now, hear?"

"But I —"

"Shutter up, Mary Pat," Finn said, brotherly. "Three days from now, mind."

"But —"

"Good, then. An hour past noon. All's quiet then."

"Shabrag dishclout," she said, tucking her arm in his.

"Whatever you say. Mind the hole by your left."

"Like I could no see it."

"You could see it but aimed to fall down it?"

"I was practicing my grace."

"Oh, sure. Practicing you was."

They disappeared mong the tumblestones. Rats crept from the salt-baulk. They snuffled up every crumb the two had dropped, padding forward and back. In minutes there was no trace of them soever.

# Heart Rime

"THIS IS GREAT HALL," sighed Dulse Geratty.

Mary Katharine sighed in answer. By the first curst rat's last tooth, the girl was misplaced mong rimers; she'd do better down the docks where ships crews'd thank her, fasting, for her strengthy sighs as'd fill the vastest sails, offset the fiercest landward breeze. Mary Kath fingered the leathern purse in her pocket. An Dulse ate up all their walkround in sighing, she'd be late up the lookout; which, seeing as Mary Pat come hotfoot from compound only to hand off this same purse, Mary Kath could no be late. What'd speed Dulse past her heavy-freighted outbreaths? Sigh sigh, like to die, that was about the right of it. Dulse used to be merry as a grig till she fixed her heart on Daniel M'Cool. A fool fixing. Dan twirled her round for a few months then set her back on her chair with a bow. Mary Kath could told her from launch what catch that net'd yield; no point setting your heart on Dan; nowhere to set it. What was tender in him went missing the night their dap passed, James A in the parlor, new-caught rats laid to his soles, Finn rats to his left foot and Dan rats to his right. They danced round him, Finn with 14 rattails round his neck, Dan with 21, while tears rolled sidewise from eyes to ears, dug long furrows in their fresh cheeks, left salt in those trenches. That was the last time Dan's eyes was live in their sockets. Dulse maybe thought she could light an empty spaglamp. She could no, and therefore sighed.

"The Great Hall [sigh] is a perfect oval. Its length [sigh] is twenty-six cubits and its width [sigh] is sixteen cubits. It holds 192 persons —"

"Even if they're size of Gov Don's fleshheap, Mistress Collins?"

Dulse nearly giggled but giggling did no consort with pale, droop, love-broke, thin; no roof could house heartsick and snigger both. She laughed hollow and sighed and spoke on, sighing: "Its proportions lifted direct from a moldering tome of enormous size —"

"Is that a big crumble book when it's to home?" muttered Mary Kath; Dulse nobbut chuntered on of the acoustics, the columns, the capitals, the dreg who laid on his back to paint the ceiling, oh on and on. Mary Kath decided to leave off counting the sighs. The girl had other habits as wranked her last nail-quick. Where a common dreg'd look at her face, Dulse had to dress it up, *search her features* for their resemblance to her beloved Daniel. Oh for a nostrum of toe-jam to give the girl! For a voice divine as'd rock the ceiling and bend her earbones back and holler: Leave off sighing! Mary Kath gave herself a bit shake. It was true that Dulse's sighs and lovesick countenance — that was a Dulse word for sure — had withered every last drap from Mary Kath's toleration. It was true, also, that Dulse alone stood forward when Goodwin asked who'd do walkround with the new girl, dripping it out like oh who wants most this treat? The tour was dull, all of them knew every word to it by time they was neath Rimehouse roof a month, yet it had to be ticked off by Goodwin fore you could pass from novice to Rimer. At Goodwin's asking, while the others nobbut stared at their knees, Dulse put up her hand, so Dulse was a good person and becoming a good person was next on Mary Kath's list of personal goals so soon as she could spare the time; till when Mary Kath ought no carp over sigh — there was another one! — upon sigh upon sigh. She really ought no carp.

"Now, let me show you the refectory," sighed Dulse. "I myself have little appetite," she sighed, "but you must be sharp-set."

No carping no carping no carping. Mary Kath tucked her tongue back of her teeth's barrier. "Oh I'm main eager to see the Rimehouse mainhall."

Dulse turned on her so sharp her heel spun. "*Outside* these walls, best use the full name when you name it, Mary Katharine. The House of the Teaching Company of Anathematizers. Withindoors, we familiars do clept it Rimehouse." Dulse led on to the refectory. Certain the hall had more and better food nor what you found at M'Cools, where they ate nobbut fish and bread and bread and fish and apples and bread and all washed down with cider. "Our fish is freshest in Charnholm," Dulse said, and sighed. "Daniel used to bring the fish himself," she said, and sighed.

They climbed a dunnamany stairs to the Choral Loft. "This is our Organ," Dulse sighed to Mary Kath, who nodded all attention.

"Organic Rim'us!" piped a voice at their elbows, his or her head wrapped in a pokeberry red cloth, a most precarious turban; a rollpaper tube stuck in her or his lips wagging as they moved again: "Kindly Organ! Gen-tal Organ!"

"Shutter up, Rimshot," Dulse said.

"Lost my insp'ration, have'n I? Got to fine m'insp'ration so's I can cre-ate. Who's the newbody?" The rollpaper tube danced in the corner of Rimshot's lips.

"Look neath tha doss for it, willna? Does Goodwin know you've scabbed off metric practice to come fret us?" Nary sigh come from Dulse's lips now, Mary Kath took note.

"Stress, stress, Dulse; hark at yourself! All shook up does no good so-ever to your e-nun-ci-a-ci-a-ci-a-tion." Rimshot lit the rollpaper tube from a spag light hung to the stone wall. The loft filled with acrid herbsmoke. "Do you suck *smilax* down your throat?" said Mary Kath.

"Looka that, looka hey. She walks she talks she might could force a rime sometime, or nine. Summat off beam bout smilax?"

"Never got past the thorns myself but — are you male or female, tell me first."

"Drogyne, you straightmouth thing you," the smoky midget grinned. "Neither fish nor fowl nor good red herring but *with* a thorough grounding in the classics."

"Have you never met an drogyne before this day, Mary Katharine?" said Dulse, sweeping her years round her like a gown-train. "Rimehouse is a haven for them. *Born that way*," she whispered, "*can't help it, poor things.*"

Mary Kath closed her eyes. Dulse Geratty was clean out of her mind, and that was looking at it charitable. Dreaming over a puppet she's tricked up and named Daniel M'Cool has caused her brains to ooze straight out her piehole. She whispers like this small person lacks ears. "Was you indeed born so?" Mary Kath asked Rimshot.

"The Burning made a many changes," said Rimshot.

"The granmams have sucked eggs," said Mary Kath.

"The shoe of my uncle lacks soles," said Rimshot.

"The soul of my uncle was shooed," said Mary Kath.

"Shod," said Dulse, the something in her face as could turn to laughter sticking its nose out its den, quivering.

"*Language*," said Rimshot.

"What I'm on," said Mary Kath.

"Give us a tab of it," the red turban in great danger of unspooling to its original form, "so's I can have such pupils as you."

"Novice has no pupils yet."

"Nor will pupils come to school with such small fish."

"Shutter up," hissed Dulse. "Goodwin's scrapping at the door."

"Been at a great feast of language —" said Mary Kath.

"And stole the scraps," Rimshot finished underbreath.

Goodwin entered their refuge with all sails set, rigged out in pale green with shoulder-cape and train. "Ah, good my bairns," she said, and, "Freeze them where they stand," she said, slurring the traditional greeting as she glanced at Rimshot, who'd an arm thrown to its eyes so to shade them.

"Oh my stars," said Mary Kath to Rimshot.

"Oh my gorry underdrawers," the drogyne responded.

"Oh good morrow," said Dulse. "How be's the proud vocation?"

Mary Kath and Rimshot exchanged looks. Goodwin inclined her neck so they swam into her field of vision. "Ah, Mary Katharine. So glad to have this opportunity to again welcome you to The Rimehouse, as we familiars call it. Has Dulse shown you all our treasures — which treasures indeed they are — has she shown you all?"

"Yes'm," said Mary Kath. "Most instructive she's been altogether."

"Good," said the old woman. "So glad." She trailed her green robes cross the stones, her grey hairs swoffing up round her head as she moved. "This window is a perfect half-oval. From the noon courtyard all receivéd light fills that grassy bowl from these half-ovals. I was forty-three last week," she told them over her shoulder.

"Ah. Ah well. Many happy returns," said Dulse. The other two could no get a civil breath in their mouths. That she'd own to her antiquity!

Mary Kath got her sense back — this was Goodwin, after all, who plucked her from tween the vats and named her Anathematizer — and allowed as her mam always said the finest perry was the longest aged. Good-

win sighed and thanked her. Was there something maybe in the Rimehouse air? Rimers could no get their breath thout sighing? Did she hear
one more whoof of patient endurance she'd start doing front-flips; anything to shake the air different.

"You can't know how invisible is an older woman," said Goodwin,
stroking the skin neath her neckscarf. "We are considered useless by one
and all. Yet we could be correctives, vital gyroscopes; we could be yeast! We
hold the race's moral history in our bosoms! Our perspective is past price!
While our men dally round Gessel's shop, polloping their folderol, we
women could commune, weaving bonds that could ne'er be broken. Instead
we languish, leaking power day by day."

"Sure you're right ma'am," said Mary Kath. As if Cider Mother leaked.
As if Bedelia Coldhand'd let a single drop start off her frame.

"How my own power is absorbed in compassion for you young girls.
Below, in Charnholm, a girl is hori or she is naught! Yet your countenances
betray no *tinge* of disappointment. You wave a hand at your more fortunate
sisters, trudge up stones here to Rimehouse, and plunge into Anathematizer
lore as though it were your chosen sea. Oh youth oh supple youth. Oh you
dolphins! So brave, so very brave."

Rimshot's eyes was rolled near back in their sockets. Dulse did a fine
imitation of a dead fish. Mary Kath shuffled foot long as she could hold
back fury. Then she let fly: "It's said you've a fine mind on you, ma'am,
which I seen myself since you plucked me off the vat floor, but you left it
home today, mayhap. How's all this supple youth we got on us less of a
mass to cart round than your years and your position? Your tears is so lack-
salt we could drink them. Think the horii fortune's chosen? Horii are nobbut spag on two sticks; they'd be first to tell you so. Hot the flame and short
the burning, that's what horii sing."

"Shutter your gob, pert lackmanner spawn," Goodwin's green robes
snapped as she spun.

"*There's* the way," Rimshot snorted.

"Oh what is sharper than a serpent's tooth but an ungrateful child,"
said Goodwin, one hand to her brow as she climbed steady back inside her
iambic carapace.

"Am I to nobbut serve up yeah and amen here? You've verse-chaunters enough for that roaming these halls, scribing the walls with yesterday's gruel scooped from their backsides. I am Mary Katharine M'Cool and my rimes turn their backs never."

Goodwin was blanched near white as a skin robe. Dulse said, "Stow your gab, Mary Kath. You're Queen of the May, Star of the Sea, Laughing Princess Onna Stick, soever you like, so you be it on the quiet. Want to learn the Rimehouse? Or would it choke you to stuff one more scrap of learning down your glutted maw?"

Mary Kath looked down at her boots. Her face gleamed back at her from their copper toes. Cider Mother swapped a gudgeon of her three-year perry for those boots. She was a rimer and what could she do else? Haul till her back bent, scrub till her knees swole, hang round the docks with her mouth wide till some fishman tossed her a bite? Making anathema songs out of her own head got her clothed and fed and a *position*. The dentical wantings for which she just now chided Goodwin. "My tongue goes off quick and rough without me," she said to the old woman. "There's a dunnamany ways I could said that more seemly." She swallowed. "Hope you'll overlook it ma'am," she said.

"Most salutary comments, Mary Katharine," said Goodwin. "When you've my years," and if by the first rat's hind foot she did no *sigh* and sniff in a one breath, "you'll see how hastiest judgments go oft awry."

Mary Kath muttered something that could been agreement was you that way minded, an you was determined to keep your vision high and on the bright side. Goodwin tilted her head one handswidth, gracious, permitting the girls to swim from out her high bright field of vision. "Let us freeze them where they stand," she said, and swept the roomdust out the door atail her green robes.

Soon as latch clacked behind her, Dulse turned on Mary Kath. "Have you no more sense nor a soup plate? Druther sit at gaze in your mam's house till dusty death steamrolls you? Lumpenbrain! Hollowhead! This is the *Rime*house! You be luckier nor a legless rat to have a place here."

Gulls scream round masts when the catch is in. Sailors pay them no mind. "Yeah," said Mary Kath, "now that's done, what's next on tour?"

Rimshot wound the pokeberry red diaper round and round its head. "Thought you was goner that time sure. But sithee, while there's scores of tales 'bout Goodwin's turrble lashings, I never seen her give a one. You, Dulse?"

"No; yet there's no smoke thout fire. They'd no talk of her lashings less there was lashings to speak of. Must be in your M'Cool blood," she mused, "Dan one time rared his teeth at a passel of blockading scutmen; my bones rattle yet off that." She sighed.

Mary Kath and Rimshot swapped shrug. Keep a civil tongue, keep a civil tongue, keep a civil tongue, Finn said. Right aright. Mary Kath bent at knee and sing-songed, "Then show what's left to show / and so we'll both us go." Mayhap there'd be less of the somber swaddle, now, less of why dregs should crouch long every waking moment.

Dulse sighed. "I'll get the keys to the Lydian workshops and the new annex. You and Rimshot stay right here; since Goodwin's mensal bleeding's quit, she gets kerwicketty fits, cleaves to every word of rulebook's writ. Novice walkround is *only* with a Rimer made; do you stand here in the shade." One sigh, and Dulse slid out the room.

Mary Kath gave up a great sigh her own self. She walked to the windows that looked over courtyard. "There's no window to the street or docks, why so?" she said.

"Maybe 'truders, maybe scapes. It's Gov Don fixed up this place, mind, a rare deep file, he is."

"Gov Don's nobbut a galanty show, his seeming shape blown large by hot light."

The red turban shook vigorous.

"Come now, the man's a launching, a skyfool, a pocket of flat stones."

The turban shook again.

"You're no of my opinion?"

"I said naught."

"No but —"

"Mark me, he's the model of an intricate artifact. He plays fine the fool, but I been on puppet krewe, I pulled the marionette strings, nobbut one twitch sets them going."

"My sister, Mary Patricia, she's Lady Mandra's parlogal. Mary Pat says Gov Don's a cipher in his own compound."

"Which she'd know from her position. Ha! Parlogal! Fine double of bezoms she got on her, yeah?" Rimshot pushed its skinny chestflesh towards its heart. "Bends good? Does a low low curtsy? Parlogal." The drogyne spat out of window. They watched the gob shine through the air to the soot-dark stones below.

"She's no flightsome at bottom," said Mary Kath.

"So it's her bezoms only?"

Mary Kath bit her lip and went on. "She's the clear sight on her." Rimshot's turban tilted to one side. "She sees through this time to the next. Unclear, sithee. She'll see scutmen coming round, sure, but the when of it? no. She slacks working on it. When my friend Rose-Marie give us exercises for her, Mary Pat nobbut yawned and said why waste her delectable years; time enough to plump her talents when her flesh sags."

"I never had that trouble." Rimshot gestured down its body. "I'm a thinking reed."

"So what twitches your fork? T'other drogynes here in Rimehouse? A girl a boy a —"

Rimshot leapt up from the window, sprung forward onto its hands, brought pointed feet overhead in a half-circle arch, and backflipped to land in its starting place. "Ta-daaa!"

"Right," said Mary Kath, slow, blinking. "That was *flight*, that was. Best I ever seen."

The drogyne wiped a sleeve cross its nose. "Why they keep me on, I dessay."

Dulse flitted through the door, ruffling her indigo robes. "Like I need to hear once more how careful we're to be in the annex. *Laaa-deees! The annex is un-der con-struc-shun! You will beee cay-air-fullll!*" Mary Kath gave her a short laugh. It was hard to tell who had Dulse's loyalty at a given time. "Come long fore they decide I've forgot the layout again already."

Dulse hiked her robes and strode out, tossed a hand at the instrument-makers room, the solfedge studio, the robers bent over their tables; she sped them past the tumble room where dancers adored their own thin bendiness and tumblers agitated the air, past felt-clad doors that muffled blatting horns and squeering viols, and there was still whole hallways they passed on the half-run.

Dulse brought them to a full stop at a set of board-and-batten gates. "The new annex," she said.

Mary Kath stepped through the opening into a barrel vault room, every rib showing. "This is metal from a scraper," she said. Her throat was tight. Now, why was that? "They pieced it together to skeleton the room." She dipped a finger in one of the troughs down the room's center. "Ground sand and shell. Plaster," she announced. "They'll add seawater and plaster the walls with the mix."

Dulse said, "Is it no a lovely hall? Gov Don built us this so's we know in every bone how vital we are."

"In the vitals it where it strikes me," said Mary Kath. "All this for the gorry rimers? No drap of jam for buboed dregs as they fall to dusty death? A dunnamany scutmen lash dreg backs so they'll plunge into the shallow inlets as boil the skin off you. Right. From these shallows the dregs mine shells. They walk round and round a capstan as grinds them to lime. They lug the lime up here, it etching grooves in their flesh the while. Right. All for a plaster'd room we're to dance in, singing *oh the lovely lovely oh*, while dockside dregs moil dark to dark for a bowl of ryeberry stew. All so the rimers get a pretty room to play for pretty richards in."

Mary Kath was stopped by the wail as pierced the ears. From the bones of the room came Nora's fret and cough and long thin screech; from the bones of the room came the previous-born Seamus, choking on all he wanted but could frame no word of; the bones of the room gave the just-born's cry as grabs a woman's spine and twists it, wailing as shakes the ear-bones and cracks the gushy heart in the wail that rends ten thousand days of careful weaving, topples ten thousand days of laying block on careful block, smashes a lifetime's store of ollas built coil on coil of rivermud, freezes the voice that links effect to cause; that plants us in time's whirl, wails as stars explode, wails as lava springs high, wails as earth cracks in a dry streambed, wails the wide-eyed flat-nosed soft-crowned wail of those who've tunneled out tween a woman's legs, fresh-come to air, dust, want, cold, pain; the room's bones wailed its death coming, its lungs emptied and its eyes come out from its head and its starfish hands stiffened and its limbs jerked; its eyes twitched wider and then wider and then glazed. And then cold. And then flat.

Mary Kath turned, and again turned, to find the mouth as wailed so. But in all that vast space open to the eye, there was no spawn nor nowhere spawn could tuck away in. She was twirling still when it stopped, stopped altogether, cold and flat, like it never sounded. Mary Kath looked for the other two. Rimshot was in crouch neath the window. Dulse was flung gainst the gate. Her eyes was fixed on the roof-ribs. "You seen your fill of the new annex, Mary Katharine," said Dulse, flat. "Look sharp now. We're to be in Great Hall for your singing-in."

"What," whispered Mary Kath. "What —"

"The singing-in's meant to be a surprise so best look surprised. We sing in all the novices straight after their walkround. Come long now, there's but so much thrill to a building site."

Mary Kath's feet followed Dulse out the gates and down the hall. At the turning, she grabbed her elbow: "Is it in the walls?"

Dulse stared straight before her. "Lovely the echoes in the new annex, hmmm? You sha' see it next when plaster's laid. Now come long while the feast's still hot."

Mary Kath stood firm. "Did you no hear —"

"The winds do sing in the roofbeams, times. Gov Don says it's nobbut a trick of the wind. Those who say other likely want to dodge their needful work. That's what Gov Don says."

Mary Kath's hand fell from Dulse's elbow.

"That's the way, Mary Katharine. Come long to Great Hall now."

The two girls walked through shafts of plum light alternating with shafts of stone darkness, long the hallway and down the stairs and round the corner to the Great Hall, which hummed already with voices who knew that, later, there would be cake.

# Masks and That

"GOV DON STOPPED HIS PALANKEEN at my door today," the comper told the sembled scutmen. Both shifts filled the benches of Scutage Hall. "Ah ah! Did he put his lady toes on your stoop?"

Back rows of the scutage hall was prime muck for that kind of heckle. Comper scowled the heckler down. "Course he did no get *out* the palankeen. With the piscines as drain my street? Hah! They'd eaten the boots right off him." Even the back rows laughed and leaned forward on their elbows so they was with him again; leastwise they'd slaver quiet till meat was served. He went on, "Gov Don said we got to tell the smiths to quit off their gatherings." The comper was an old dreg, pushing fifty, still with those big hauler arms on him from a lifetime of going down into wreckage and laying hawser round great stone-chunks and skimmying, foot on careful foot, back topside, then giving his crew the word. A lifetime of taking the first shock of the haul on his own arms and back, so despite his years and his hair nobbut tufts on his scalp, the comper did no look a fool complete when he intoned: "These gibbous gatherings got to go." There was a bit of pushing and harrumph in the back rows when he said it, but no more nor he could quell with a look. They come back to him in ragged chorus, "*Got to go.*" Couple of voices right in the back hooted, *Sots will mow,* but he knew them by name and no man echoed them. "Right," said the comper. "When smiths meet, they got to meet open. They got to let us come in on them. Me and Gov Don decided it this very morning." He looked down on his notes. "A har-mo-nee-us society must be open to all its cit ... its citi ... to everybody as is in it." Dead silence answered him. "Look now," he said, leaning over the table, his weight on his hands, "we can no have a passel of carenaught dregs running round the hills mouthing off bout the great lame smith. Or whatever it is they do up there. For their own good and the good of the spawn as is to come, these smiths got to lend their hands to the work before them. They're nobbut dregs like we was, tired like we are, who sit round a fire making chant in masks. Think they'll get back their young spunk so." He leaned farther forward. "But we've no least notion *what* they're up to, have we? Could be planning to deep-six the deeplade docks. Or tumble the tumbling krewe." Some in the scutage hall was a bit slow laughing at that one; the comper noted their names. "The smiths could be whuffing ... *tarponesse* ... up the caves, weakening their manly spirits." He pounded one fist on his palm: "We got (*pock*) to know (*pock*) just what (*pock*) they do (*pock*)." The blows wranked his spine. He eased his back flat to the wall, flexed his hands as they hung to his sides. "Tonight's a gibbous moon as marks their meetings. Find out what it is they do up there." There was some stir mong the men. "Do it!" he bellowed.

The scutmen formed up into patrols slankly, with much adjusting of hats. "How's this frame?" said Mottle.

"Cock it right ... up in front ... okay. Did you get all that he said about harm-on-us society?" said Spink.

"Naah. You been on this lay so long as me, you learn any comper loves to hear his own throat twang. We'll keep eyes to the cliffs but we'll see naught; half-dozen empty bellies crawling the bluffs plucking basket-grass from Lady Mandra's most darling adorable picnic site, maybe; that's all the molehill they aim to build a mountain out of."

Crump and Bannon was younger to scutage work. "The richards say the smiths sit round *sage* they burn on firecircle," said Bannon.

"Oh pretty pretty," Crump agreed.

"Burn sage over chant and mask and greasestick," said Bannon.

Crump was still mazed at his luck. Scutman! Meat and more meat! Allotment of potable! A perfect match, him and the scut patrol. "I hear they call up some lame smith from times before." Bannon grunted in answer.

"M'Donal got it straight off Lady Mandra's swizzle; how this lame smith can make a sword as'll shave richards down to nobbut scrapy bones."

"Pretty to think so," said Bannon.

"Well, M'Donal, he's Gov Don's headgroom. He should know what's what. There's troublefluffers leading on the simpler dregs. Got to winkle them out."

"Maybe so," said Bannon. They joined the patrol as it streamed out the vault.

"Keep your eyes to the cavemouths!" the comper hollered after them.

Through the night, the cold gibbous moon glanced off the tin hats of every scutman in Charnholm. They stood long the jetty dense as reedgrass, necks crooked to stem-break, ears stretched, eyes fixed on one cave mong the dunnamany cave-mouths in the sandstone bluffs above the harbor. Did a crumb of sand dribble from a cave-mouth, some scutman leapt to source it; did a leaf of sea-bramble rustle in the land breeze, some scutman marked it.

⟜

It's a marvel surely that a scutman can find his own ass with his two hands, for who'd dig nobbut one entry to a cave? The smiths come a quick-step crouch through tall grass to back entries, holes sunk in the beetling cliffs; they clamber down shaft rung on rung; they vanish down the caves, dust off their eyes, and walk forward to the sentry.

"He was thrown to the sea," challenged nose of bone, scalp of dust, hunchspine, eyes twitching far back in their sockets.

"He rose lame yet walks," answered flat face, wide-grin, eyes looking past the day's dross to the sea-edge where sails wink out. Every mam says, *look away far and your eyes will freeze so*; here's how that looks when it comes true.

"Pass, brother." Dust flakes drifted from his scalp; snotballs jigged in his nostrils.

Flat face took his own mask off the wall and drew his blanket round him, a patchwork of woolfray trimmed with ratfur. His long gaze glared over collar as he shuffled his blisters through crumble dust, mong cobbles (the cave's gums are rotten weak), down the glottis to a full wide cavity dug perishing long ago from the sandstone cliffs above the harbor.

Flat-face Quix hunched over his ratfur collar and shuffled his blisters through firelight shadows round the perimeter neath the low, jagged ceiling. They had no started yet, only ten or a dozen sat round the fire, well short of the 26 dregs of manly persuasion as made a mennan. "Manly persuasion" was a neat round-the-neck the framers penned to let in all the drogynes and uncertains; so long as they had bore no spawn they was counted in the mennans. Course there was some ruckus from dregs who *had* passed spawn from out tween they legs and since come over, but these was so few the smiths sent it to committee and in committee it remained.

Quix folded himself, creak on creak, tween Drosh the spagchandler and Innsmort the netmender, who gave him time to settle and regain his wind fore they spoke. They was equal old and achy, all round their sixth Seventh. "How's trade, old carp?" said Drosh, clapping him light on the knee.

Quix grunted, his flat face smoothed out over its bones. "Wafters is more trouble than ratbuggers. Did Orion Shipwright himself come down from the stars, he could no satisfy their wild demands. Want the whole convoy fit with slidey bails, and it please you."

"Those are no good soever," said Innsmort. "They'll open of themselves, come a squall or a rightabout."

"Do I know it." Quix pulled a flask from his inner pocket and took a deep slug. He wiped the top fore handing it round. "One wafter fits out his scout-junk with a single slidey port so his aged dap can feel sap in his bones standing soldier at the viewport, and every other wafter got to have the same. Come a sharp wind and the bail slides open, will they blame their bad idea? No and again no. It's me they'll hunt with a bodkin."

"Patrons," said Drosh. "They want the goods thout the bad of paying."

They shifted where they sat. They had twelve decades mong them by the meanest calculation. It was no wonder they ached so always. Innsmort, Drosh, and Quix. Innsmort fined down to near naught, wrists a swelling in his etiolate arms. Drosh with some flesh on him yet, though it hung rucked on him, flaccid bags round all his organs, his skin itself a sack of done-in lymph.

The firelight cast, betimes, a kindly light on their faces as soaked years off them. They sat quiet for a space while restless smiths fardeled round looking for their place to stand and roar their wantings.

"How now, old trout," said Innsmort. "How be's the lamby work?"

"Did I no tell you of it just now?" said Quix. (A smith who'd found his stand roared, "Give me back my good left shoulder.")

Innsmort stuck two fingers down his maw to the hangflap back in his throat, and as gravely slid them out again, spittled and brown-flecked. "Can

no just charge my memry with it, Cappen. May be you had a dream on it."
(A smith roared, "Take the fresh spawn and you must, leave my Rose here.")

"No dream soever," said Drosh. Bubbles come to his lipcorners as he spoke; weak-skin, yellow bubbles. "Quix is as bound to us as we to him in work given and work taken."

"Ease on, my starty-up. Nobbut a question, there, nobbut that." (A smith roared, "Let him learn to spike them clean and I'll cart rye every night this month.")

Innsmort steepled his ague-wranked fingers. "Though you can no deny there's been precious little work sput out by the dockyard this tenmonth and more." He cracked his long swole knuckles neath the clamor of the night's boss Smith hammering the rimrock. The twenty-sixth was past the guard. "Mennan's made," he said, with his talent for stating the known.

"Co' up, co' up," the Boss cried, and the din of his hammers filled the cave.

The smiths sat round the fire. They covered their seamed faces in masks. They sat up straight as they could, laid their hands palm-up on their knees, snorted up their nostrils the dark lungclot ropes coiled in each man's chest that'd one day kink as they uncoiled and so stopper a smith's last in-breath. Each palm-up hand twitched with the strain of being empty and open and still. Each white-clay mask glowed red.

"He was thrown from a high place," said that night's boss.

"Weak and sickly born," answered the mennan.

"He rose up lame from the sea."

"Though his legs are broken, his hands are canny."

"His hands remake the world."

"As makers forge every day this world."

"Hail Smith!" called the Boss.

"Hail Smiths!" they echoed. There was beating on tin and whistling through teeth. The smiths rose, creak on creak, and stompled, bent and honking, three times round the fire, then sank where they'd stopped. Chests wheezed. Wind whistled. Flames crackled.

"Any scutmen find the back ways?" said the Boss.

A snapple of headshakes.

"Right then," he said. The boss tamped a short iron rod on the stones at his feet. "Another good befooling in our pockets. I want to thank Berk, Quix, and Lando for the scutmen's new tin hats. Can see a scutman three shiplengths off in those." Laughter. "Also thanks to Pomchalder, whose brother spools a tale as pretty as he swizzles Lady Mandra, first froth of the brew to you and him both!" Cheering. He stood and stretched. "One of the M'Cools brought a dozen carboys of scrumpy and a new pup he vouches for. What's the name, Finn?"

"My name is Palan."

They looked him over, head so high as Finn's shoulders. "Take off the black cap," said Berk, All Goods Laded Safe and Sure. Palan revealed his yellow crown. "Well, you're a washed-out son of a —"

"You're Fergus spawn," said Innsmort, and spat on a winking coal.

Palan bowed. "I have that dismal honor." Finn looked at him sharp.

"Fergus crawls up here all times with his *tarponesse*," another lungclot to the coals, "well and fine when you want to sidestep this life for a few hours —"

"Call it a few days, Innsmort, there's few has your *restraint*," said Pomchalder, on the broad grin, clacking his knuckles gainst his firlot of scrumpy.

Innsmort stared purse-mouth at the spattered coals while some smiths hooted and honked their praise of tarponesse. When they was done, he said, "Tarponesse is well and fine — for a few hours. Fergus is clever at its distillation but Fergus stinks of rotflesh. Now here's his rotflesh spawn mong us making his richard bows —"

"Less of it," said Quix. He turned his white mask to Finn. "M'Cool brought the pup, no?"

"Speak up for yourself, Palan," said Drosh. An easy man on his prentices, Drosh.

Palan stood next the Boss, the way all the smiths could see him. "My dap he's evil and clever, both. As Innsmort says. For his evil I've made amend so far as —"

"I'll speak to that," and Finn told the mennan how Palan went up gainst Ambrose for him in the barracks.

The smiths nodded and the Boss shouted "Co'op, co'op."

Palan continued. "His clever, I got in my blood. I come up cave with Finn to tell you of that."

"So," said Drosh. "Go on and tell."

"How I'm clever is my hands. Show me a problem and my hands elucidate it."

"Lucy-ate. That'd be what when it's at home?" snarled Innsmort.

"Puzzle it out, see? Gov Don called me in off the Hunt. Finn and me was in barracks together, I went on to be Hunt Boy."

"We know all that," said Quix. Finn looked straight soldier at the grizzling coals. "There's some framed wrong for Hunt Boy. No blame to them."

"No blame," the smiths echoed, some more vigorous than others.

"Sure," said Palan, "I know it come hard to me. Anyhow. Gov Don come through and saw how I fixed tubes to the portholes, the way we could bring light inside, or twist them to darken the barracks entirely."

"Saw those," said Berk. "That was no bad work."

Palan thanked him with a bow and went on. "Gov Don said, I see you made some clever changes in the barracks. He said the richards in their compounds adore the Rat Hunts, yet fear the air the smell the noise on their timpani the smuts on their flesh. So he asked what could I do. So I made pipes for them, you see?"

"Pipes?" said Drosh.

"Yeah. View pipes. The way the richards can lounge happy-safe in their shelter caves to watch the Rat Hunt as it passes, need never expose themselves to the rude and blood and stench of a Rat Hunt, see it through the pipes, you see."

The mennan was silent still and silent all. "View pipes," Innsmort said.

"Yeah. Pipes as bring down sound and sight. See the Hunt clear from two-three fathoms down. I figured it and I drew them the plans and Gov Don's pipes is *in* now. I got talking with Finn and his —"

"Decision was, we should take it to the smiths," said Finn.

"So no richards in the stands when Rat Hunt passes," said Innsmort.

"They'll be snug down-cave fore the first beater hikes his tunic," Finn confirmed.

"How do they work?" Berk asked.

Palan crouched to draw in the sand — "nobbut a sketch, mind" — the polished metal — "like corvisers, see?" — that bounced the visible from above to below. The smiths gathered round asking, "How'd you figure that angle?" and "What's that made of?" while Palan sketched and answered.

"How'd you get round their fans and filters?" said Quix.

"I was bound to be mute —" Palan looked up, his gold hair all in his grey eyes.

Quix snapped, "And your loyalty to richards is forged of what?"

Palan sat back on his heels. Then he nodded in Quix's direction, bent again to draw more details of the pipes.

Quix crouched next him. "Can sounds come up from them?"

"Come up?"

"Co'up, co'up!" said Innsmort and Drosh, waving their firlots.

Quix paid them no heed. "Can you get sounds as come *up* from below the pipes? Are they that way baffled?"

"I dunno," said Palan. "Could, I suppose." He sketched a pipemouth baffle.

Quix leaned in. "So strange sounds could pass through those pipes."

"Strange sounds?" Palan grinned. "What, like richards in intimate converse? A bit of slap and tickle, grunt and hoo?"

"No. Like a justborn wailing."

"I do no see just how they ..."

"For strange sounds been heard," said Quix.

No slouch, tonight's Boss. Creak on creak, he stood to his impressive ell and a half, "Tell the mennan what it is you speak of."

Innsmort grumbled, "Yeah, and tell us in regular speak."

When Quix stood, he topped the boss by a full handspan. "What gorry use are these mennans?" he said.

"Always room for one less," said the Boss, bit of a grim on him.

"Shutter up," said Quix. "I been up the compounds a goodly while. Richards, you know; an one has iron trellis, all want iron trellis. This past moon, I been hearing a justborn wailing from out the stones. Thought my ears bespelled. Cause who can hear through stone? Comes Palan to tell us, any man who walks past one of these pipes can." Quix paused a couple beats till the muttering died down. "Richards prisoned a justborn down one of these tubes. So I ask you, and I Will Stand Here till one on you can answer — sha' we trace those wails?" The muttering rose again; Quix spoke over it: "We got to. We maun. Else what gorry use are these mennans? Supposed to spread the word, no? Supposed to scheme how we'll get the gorry richards off our back, no? Here's evidence; here's proof; here's why we got to rise up to depose these care-naught richards as has killed off a justborn and laid it in the stones for to make the walls more stout." Quix took breath. "The crapul richards say they're nobbut poor weak things crawling twixt heaven and earth—"

"Nobbut scrape *long* with our philtres and our shelter caves till we fall to dusty tombs," said Finn in a mancy voice.

Quix said, "Ayuh. Richards say, *You dregs sha' be the lucky ones* — every jack of you knows they say this, for fact — *once recovery's complete* — which, when will *that* day dawn, I ask you? — *you dregs sha' be lords of all this demesne, for we can no breed* — oh how they spit it sad tween their square-cut teeth — *which off that sha' come an end to us. Our labor's but to ready you strong and fertile dregs gainst that glorious day.* So they say."

Quix took breath. He opened his mouth to roar and closed it again and looked down at Palan's sketches in the sand. He said, quiet, "Yet they live on and on and now there's babes mewling down the shelter caves, my brave boyos. I have heard them wail."

Berk was no grand image like Quix, being a full two handspans shorter and crooked withal, his right shoulder twisted in, hands as ague-wranked as a bindle of locust twigs though he was three years short of his fourth Seventh. He said, "You know I'm a ryeman come in off the fields as novice. As Hunt Boy, I made point first time out the box. Three years a spearman, two years on the oven, and one year harum guard." He ignored the inevitable hooting, *Oh hard labor that*, and *Some stiff work there*, etc. "I known Quix a good few years, and isn't Quix all times hearing sounds none else hears? Fore this mennan goes straight up in air over this news, has any other man heard a justborn wailing?"

"True, true," said Innsmort, draining his third firlot. "Did you go by Quix ears, there's a rat in every arras."

Finn spoke up. "My sister heard it. Mary Katharine. She's down the Rimehouse, the new compound, where she heard wailing on wailing. New compound's nobbut frame, nowheres to hide a justborn. Still it wailed. From the stones, like, she said."

Pomchalder said he'd heard of it being heard, which drew hoots as a plaguey rat draws fleas so the cave roared with it. Neath the roar, Palan whispered in Finn's ear. "Why'd you no tell them what Mary Pat said? Of the leathern purse?"

"Tell them what Mary *Pat* said? They ready to disbelieve old Quix, a man as foursquare as they come. Mary Kath they credit only since she went for rimer. Think they'd give ear to Mary *Pat?*"

"So they'd no give ear to Dan?"

"Shutter up," said Finn. "Shutter your gorry gob and fast. They'll no hear Dan's *name*, even. Keep your ear on them. They're roaring fine now. When they quiet, that's our time."

They stood well back from the fire while the smiths roared, roared less, went quiet. Then the whole of the mennan huddled in till they was near touching the coals. "We need to break this up," said Quix. "We got to head down the new Compound right now."

"Best do it by sunlight," said Finn, and for a stunner, even the oldest smiths heeded his words. "Do it by night and scutmen'll rise up quick as cock in harum. Daylight, now, what's to wonder at in a passel of dregs breaking for tiffin? Naught. Say we meet for nuncheon down by the lookout."

"We'll picnic," said Innsmort, pretty far gone by now.

"Pastoral repast!" said Drosh with some difficulty, spitting the last froth of scrumpy. "I've no been on picnic since I was courting. Picnic!"

"That's no the worst idea ever," said the Boss. "Who'd spicion us round a spread cloth? Tell any asking richard it's one of our hols days."

"They'll swallow that, true enough," said Berk slowly.

It was so decided and so resolved: next midday they'd break out the cider ("More cider!" cried Innsmort) and rye kibbosh and smoked carp and the smiths would have themselves a picnic ("Picnic!" cried Drosh) in admiration of the new compound as so many had put in a few licks on.

With considerable shushing from the heaviest topers, the smiths hung their masks on their hooks, some needing two or a few tries at that delicate operation, climbed one by one the ladder, slunk halfcrouch through the grasses, and so to home.

"Lawks!" said the warm lump in Innsmort's pallet. "Was there a drap of cider left in dockside when you'd done?" Innsmort mumbled that there was terrible chatty pallets these days, these fearful last days, and she smoothed him with her cool hands.

# Rat Hunts As Was

"THEY USED HAD PIPERS," August Inkwhistle grumbled into his scrumpy. "What's 'at? What's 'at? Speak up, Augie, you old pike," said Bedelia Coldhand from her tanglenest of yellowgreen curls.

August Inkwhistle cleared his throat. Dust strangulated them considerable, these days. Dust used to lay more thin. "They'd pipers to the Hunts, one piper to lead the rats, lure them, and all us dockside boys followed after with great thwacking sticks." He took a slug of scrumpy and coughed. Dust was worst nor ever this year. "Frolicsome, it was. Of a fine afternoon we'd sing and thwack in step behind a piper. Slaying rats, that's duty, seeing as they carry the blue lumps in their fleas. We made game from needful slaughter. Now," he downed another mort of scrumpy, "since the richards come up mong us, they gussied the Hunts to a fare-thee-well with their rimers and their musicians and that. A larky fellow can no get a look-in on what Rat Hunts they got now."

Bedelia shook her yellowgreen nest at him. "You got to own it's some spectacle we got now."

"Spectacle! Spectacle, to be sure, it's some kind of spectacle," said Augie Inkwhistle, his lungs wheezing the sounds over the jaggedy scrim of his teeth. "Swell it may be." He nodded. "Ours it is no."

They drank to that — they'd've drunk to aught by then — and Bedelia filled their empty mugs out the carboy tween them.

"May be. For my part, I look forward to the new krewes they planning," she said. "Will make it the more swell, and the rats is getting big and careless, too, down the docks."

"Swell it may be," he said, his lips fumbling at the mug rim, "ours it'll no be."

"Well, ours or theirs or the Lord of Misrule's, I wish they'd run the Hunts closer by," said Bedelia. "Hunts has gone blurry in these putra times.

Dust's thicker. Back when there was less of this dust I could see them clear. Sure, in those days I could see ships as they fell off the edge of the world."

Augie raised his firlot to her, "You was the far-seeingest hip-swinginest hori ever was, Dele. Your cold hands put life into a dunnamany Hunts, they did for true." He cackled. "Scunt passels of boys near *up* t'pole, tha cold hands did."

"Made lively of them, didna? Think now, I had even Ambrose tween these hands; oh what I could done with him and I'd seen to what he'd come."

"Come he did!"

"Quit off tha cacking, old pike old rambottom old sniggermaw," thwacking him feroce with her limp bonnet. "I got some re*gard*, those times. Yeah, and when I was cordwainer, platting my fingers to bone, I got still some regard. Every ship in this fleet did scrape and speak me soft so to wheedle coils off me, from mercer-thread to hawser cable who'd they call? Bedelia Coldhand." She tilted her firlot and smacked her frothy lips. "Up till ague latched its jaws round my knuckles, I was stringing them long. Fine string. Fine plait. Fine work I did. I done."

Bedelia Coldhand moved restless in her chair. She picked at the blanket stitch on her laprobe. Her two youngest worked it for her round their second Seventh. Dab hands at it, they was. She taught them bawdy song while they stitched, while they giggled back of their hands; ready fruits they was, fourteen and twelve, nubbing out their blouses fine. Having made it so far, they'd likely live to make old bones, no? No. One morning they said their bones felt wrong in their arms and then their mouths went dry and then frothed and then they stiffened and there was an end to it. It come quick, was a comfort. In the usual way they'd years enough on them to eat the fat off of while the fever raged. But her spawn had no come neath the rule of usual. They came neath another rule; the law of gravity, the which none can appeal.

Bedelia Coldhand teased the blanket-stitch on the lap-robe. "This room needs redding up," she said.

"Leave off fussing and fluffing," said Augie Inkwhistle. "You'll nobbut raise fleas, so. The dead come back to us never, though we fluff their pallets never so high. Leave off, I tell you."

Bedelia Coldhand ground one palm gainst the other, like milling rye. "Time was, remember? shades of the dead was so thick we had to push 'em aside on waking? Remember? We'd crawl from our earths and greet each other of a morning, 'Who's left?' we'd say. 'Who's left?' Was I to ask that now they'd their quaintance brows strangle and look strange. I do, times, grit my teeth over how lucky the spawn have it these days. How smooth they do come up."

Augie struggled upright from the many poufs on Bedelia's settee. "Spawn these days think they got a heavy load when their dead count's three or four in a year. Think they reached their uttermost strength when they slave a twelve-hour."

"Think barracks or harum rose up of their own."

"Praunt their corvisers up jetty and down."

"Swing their slick hips like such was never seen fore."

"Got their beaters and long pikes — out of course they spike near every rat they get their eyes on. Be different was they close in like we was."

"Fancy oils perfumed by richards's store, small the wonder they raise any Hunt Boy's eyelids sharp."

"It's no their eyelids they raise, Delia."

"Shutter up, August Inkwhistle," Bedelia said. "I think I got a decent knowledge of what raises on a Hunt Boy."

"You do, you do indeed," he said, pacific.

Bedelia settled herself mong her strawticks. "But you're in the right, much as I hate to swell your head by saying so. Back then, our bones sang with how lucky we was to wake each day."

"To them born since, why it's nobbut a tale told by a idiot." Augie reached for the carboy slow and easy, the way it'd no disrupt Bedelia.

"Right enough. Spawn these days is humpback and frisky, little care for their olders. *Was* you to keep yourself to less than half a dozen pots of scrumpy in the day —" here a pointed squinch of her eyes from out their yellowgreen nest — "you could reckon forward from those signs." Bedelia drained her own pot of scrumpy, precautionary gainst Augie's creeping fingers. The man was main good at snaking round her potgrip and upending its contents, rapid, and slap it down again, and wipe dry his mouth and look up with his odd blue elsewhere eyes and say, "Oh, now, was that one yours?" and make never a motion to get up off his rump, open the spigot, and fill her empty pot, no never once.

Augie tipped his firlot. Why'd he always forget to bring a carboy when he was headed to Bedelia's? True, was no a *plan*, ever, to walk through her velveteen curtains and settle on her pouf bench. It was nobbut a thing as happened. That it happened most days of the week soon as he sold out of doves; that there was fewer doves each week to sell; that his custom rarely chaffered over price nor fresh these days: Augie *noticed* these things, sure, but they was transitory, nobbut clouds passing over, a temprary condition as'd right itself when the rains come and laid this pestiferous dust.

Augie licked the last foamdrop off his pot. Bedelia was still giving him the fixed eye. "This Galanty Hunt, now," he said. There, that turned her stare off him. Follow up, follow up. "This Galanty Hunt it has *tumbling krewes*," he spat. "What need of tumbling krewes? Them's for hols days, when richards spike caged rats. Lady Mandra and her ilk laid on these tumblers, surely, for only an aged female'd take pleasure in watching flexish roll-about, stead of lusty Boys scouring Charnholm of its rats."

Bedelia smoothed her yellowgreen curls. They sprang back from her touch like long-wound wire. "Aged females got their place in Charnholm well as aged males, August Inkwhistle. Mayhap we're weary of watching aged males slay off young ones, hmmm? So's they can recline and swill scrumpy off the *aged females*."

Augie's scrumpy was down to the last froth. "Ease off, Delia. No blame to our years that we can no longer spike them like we once could." His shoulders dropped and his neck bent and his right hand eased the empty firlot toward her.

Bedelia Coldhand topped him up. Augie was easy to read as a Boy in rut. "It's how changes come by the cartload these days. No word gainst tumblers, mind, but with the changes coming so fast, our days now are cut off entire from days past. Am I right, or am I no wrong?"

"They're dustier, that's for gorry certain." Augie coughed long and spat a couple lungclots out of window. "Sorry," he said, creaking back mong the poufs.

"You're a slackspine creakjoint elder," said Bedelia, thout heat. "Dustier, sure. That's no the root of it." She leaned forward to drive her words down Augie's ears. "Used to be we scraped and patched most every waking hour. Then come the richards up from their shelter caves with their greens their philtres their potable. Out of course we was glad to see them. Did they no give us time and health? It's what we swapped for that, see."

"Well it's hard to slamp a finger on just what," he said.

"You call it hard because you can no remember what's hard. When your bendy noodle stiffened yet, you knew then what hard means. It's no so gorry hard to lay a digit on how these days is different. Soon as I'm over this bout of milk leg, I'll plait you a hawser made of the every thread of how it's different these days."

"Mmm," said Augie. Delia'd been homefast with milk leg whensoever it was convenient for the best part of two years now. She could scaump round her rooms but little more. Though when she felt like it she walked well enough with a stick or a firm fist neath her elbow. He coughed, short, down his sleeve. "Since the richards popped up from their caves, we done what most amuses richards," he offered.

"True enough, but can you blame them? After all them years neath dirt, sure they want to drink some life, it's—"

"Blame I can, and blame I do," he said. "Are we born to make sport for richards? We are no. Our sweat is more than fountains as play for their refreshment."

Bedelia Coldhand sat bolt upright. "August Inkwhistle! Fifty years I known you—"

"Call it sixty and you'll still be shy of the mark, I mind when —"

"Fifty-some years I known you, an you *will* have it, and you stound me yet. To make sport for them. There's the difference, Augie, clear as blood. Time was, we hunted for our own sport —"

"It was needful."

"Needful, yeah, but for sport as well. For our own sport."

"Have I no been telling you and telling you that dentical thing? I —"

"Whereas now we hunt on *their* say-so. At *their* times. In the way as'll please best *their* fine palates."

"True for that," he said, slump mong the poufs, "does it no wear you to think on?"

Bedelia Coldhand shook her head. "Huh-uh. It's like after the old shell cracks wide, fore the new one toughs up."

"Was you thinking on putting that into dayspeech, now?" Augie stood up and stamped first his left foot and next his right foot. "Ss-ss-ss-ss-ss," he hissed tween his teeth. "Your settee's like to lamed me, sure."

"*After the old shell cracks, the new shell hardens slow.* That's what the draioch, Matia, said when she quit her stall by the deeplade dock." Bedelia hauled herself to her feet, thrust her nose tween August's eyes. "Matia said," Bedelia closed her eyes with remembering, "She said Charnholm was every which way cracked, said we was about to break up altogether. Said swords'd flame in the sky and slash it to thimbrels; south winds'd rise and plait the thimbrel clouds to ropes as'd trail their fresseled tips gainst the jetty stones. Then should come a gold-hair born at sea, Matia said. He'd come in a cloak of music to lead a May dance of flexish spawn, none past their third Seventh, who'd grab hold the fressel ends and circle round the gold-hair — like the gold-hair was the pole they danced round; a skweering viol'd music their feet, said Matia, circling and plaiting till the cortened ropes yorked them off their soles; they plaiting still, as they come closer and closer to the pole. Ah. Think on a strand of *that* heft. Now thicken it. Then see them haul on it. They'd haul, horns'd blant — *ba-ba-ba*-BOM, *ba-ba-ba*-BOOM — and they'd haul till sweat ran so down them their toes'd slip in it and still they'd haul." She looked away from the dove-seller, and the room he sat in, away off from the dockside altogether, plaiting that hawser tight.

Augie cleared his throat. "Right aright. So there they are, our nubile dregs, glistening as they haul. AND THEN WHAT?" he boomed. "Sounds a fine pole dance. Sounds fine sport for richards, it does."

"No," said Bedelia Coldhand, still looking afar off, her bent fingers picking at the blanket-stitch on her lap. "No, they'll haul, cords of their necks and arms and backs'll stretch, pop, they'll haul on. Till at the last they sha' bring it down." She looked straight down August Inkwhistle's eyes. "Which *what* they sha' bring down, I've no least notion." She whomped the poufs with a good round fist.

Augie shuffled his feet. "There's a fine crystallabration, Dele, ought take that straight to the richards; they'd listen to you sure. Chance to lend ear to common dusty dregs? Wouldna richards count their lucky stars for the chance. Suck at your tales till their lips was swole, they would."

"Shutter up, Augie Bumwhistle, you dove's delight, you rawskull squint-eye brown-nose. The Rat Hunts swallow every bit of gumption us dregs might could have, setting up these Hunts how they do, all sword and flame and horns ablare, think that's for sport alone? Or on account of it murtlicates our brains to gruel?"

Augie shouldered his way into her first pause. "Might be they want to give us some dazzle and spark, hmm? same as you said filled you with admire, hmmm?"

Bedelia Coldhand's outbreath whistled as she leaned back on the poufs. "Was you launched me on this and now you gone lackwind, dory in a whirlpool, any breeze as blows'll find Augie Come-at-whistle flat down neath it. Dazzle and spark! Sure there's times I see I lived too long. Spark and dazzle! What's that but to blind us? Next you'll smear pap on my lips and say, *Lick up now babby.*"

August Inkwhistle slapped his knees. "A fishman'd net you any time he pushed craft out from dock, Dele, so easy do you rise. Out of *course* richards siphon the blood courage right out of our veins. Out of *course.* Try getting one of these spawn to see it so, hah." He spat, pocking the dust. "When I was young myself, when horii stroked oil all down me, you could no wake me lest my own mam was drowning." He rubbed his hands together.

"But how an the horii had some other chance."

"Horii? All the Hunt Boys you can stuff tween your legs, all the food and potable you can guzzle, after — where'd they find any chance so good as that?"

"Well now who sets them to wanting that, hmm? Is it no the richards dangling all that before them?"

"Ah by the last nose, Delia, it's no off richards dangling. Show me a young one who'd no want that, richards or no richards. Was any put off in the palaces of fucking? Was no. All dregs has itchy forks."

"Yeah and it'd be *main* hard for richards did they no." Bedelia Cold-hand folded her laprobe. "Another firlot of my scrumpy, say? I seen your bones rustling dry this half hour and more."

August Inkwhistle reached out his firlot. "I'll no turn it away, Bedelia. You'd do well taking my advice on this matter; natheless, I wish you a fair wind for it."

Bedelia Coldhand snorted. "As you say, Augie. It's all times edifying to talk over trouble with you. Here's how!" They clinked firlots and drank a long sweet draught.

# A Wail in Stone

Finn m'cool and palan fergusson bade farewell to Daniel M'Cool — so much as they could while they three helped ready *Hail Janus* for her departure, so much as they could with Captain Ettore pulling his beard over his crew's sluggish progress. Tween haul and lash and the Captain roaring *Hump yourselves you dirty sods* and *Leave off now sure are you deaf*, they rolled flagons upramp, swept back the lovesick and idle-eyed, and totted up the lading bills for the Captain who read no word but could compare their scratch marks to the swayed-up cargo with one eye while with the other he scored some hapless dreg's liver: *May gulls pluck your fool eyes, you swayed one cask up ship's side when you could easy run up two.*

As Dan stomped his hobnails upramp, seasack on his shoulder, Finn and Palan hollered, "Doan hump too many mermaids you stiffrod," and "Remember 'left' and 'port' has equal letters," and "We'll take care of all the girls you left behind."

Dan turned round at that last and shouted down, "Would need the both of you," the least grin on him, and was gone. A real crackface I am, he told the ladder as he descended to the sleeproom, the grin gone off his mouth and it again a stiff flat line; I'm a crackface as could coax laughs from eelgrass, he told his downstepping boots; I'm the boyo makes the crowd slap their every knee, he told his seasack as he slung it through the narrow sleeproom door, dodging hammocks and strewn duffels and a last flexish girl planting red smacks on her seaman; oh uproarious glee's my middle name, he told his cracked tin chest by the starboard porthole; could I get this gorry frissome voice out my ears I could sail easy and easy take my rest; should that day ever dawn 'twould be the maddest gladdest day of all the glad new year, by blood of the last rat it would. He sat on his tin chest and sunk his ears in his hands. It did no good, never had, the voice even sounded the clearer, so, but it was somewise restful.

Gold chains and gold circlets and one gold ear-ring swirled round the crowsnest lazy in the hot updraft. Touch them and they'd stamp your hand scarlet with their heat. Pages and scraps and empty covers swooled round each other in country-dance, 'Face your partner, round you go, to the next one, curtsy, bow,' all the words writ in water at the last. The city convulsed and groaned and screeched and wailed as eruptions of scorch and roar spat frottage out to sea, where sea-winds minced it well, till the leavings swam round the crowsnest before they lazy swanned down and down and wrapped the decktars' ankles where they stood weeping. The wave sway sifted the detritus now to bow and now to stern, in heaps like gathered leaves on a bright fall morning they fluttered and clumped and lost their bright colors and at last they clogged the scuppers as the ship's pitch raked the limp brown leavings down its swale and so to seabed.

Daniel M'Cool sat on his tin chest, hands on his ears, till the bosun roared down the hatch that any who chose to take their richard ease while the ship come about and picked its way through harbor thick with wantwit craft would be flayed and gladly; he the bosun wanted no such slackwaist dullhand mong his tars. Dan fumbled blind at his seasack. The motion of his hands gentled his mind back to its working groove. He scrambled into his oilcloths in two shakes, clambered upladder while he secured his hat, and was chest out and eyes straight next the bosun before that good boomer had well begun his second hooroar.

⌐⟋

Finn and Palan heard the bosun roaring from the pilings they was slumped gainst, flapping their tunics to air their sweaty trunks. They saw Dan's frame snap on deck to report for duty. Fog lay heavy on the cold harbor; the light came from no one source but rolled in neath the fog's lifted skirts, shone off the matte grey water. They lost sight of *Hail Janus* fore Dan was halfway up the rigging to the crowsnest.

"That's our Daniel sorted, that is," said Finn.

Palan made no direct answer. No point getting twixt brothers. "Figure they'll be back in the month they plan?" he said.

"Sooner, later, no telling. They'll head back when they got enough dried cuttle on board to satisfy Ettore's mad cravings. He steers by nose, see, quivers his long stem this way and that till he snuffs a piscatory pool."

"Ayuh," said Palan.

"Fact, plain and simple," said Finn. He shoved off from the piling and began to coil rope. This leavetaking reft him somehow, though sure he and Palan together could spread the word mong those dregs with ears to hear and eyes to see; sure they two could do it without Dan, and when Dan came back, which out of course he would, he'd find the word spread and the weight off him, the way he'd stand straight again. It'd happen so. "Might be back in three days or as many months. We knew right long we could no count on Dan in making the stirabout."

"Ayuh."

Finn coiled the last rope. "Mary Kath says that, up the Rimehouse, she heard a justborn in full voice, down the new annex. Nobbut stones and the wail in the room. I tell you?"

"Ayuh," said Palan.

"Max says it's that justborn as wails out his viol in Hunt Wagon prow. Max says the wail comes out the strings on its own, like. We ought start the stirabout with him."

"Well, I'll come on search of him with you, but as for making sense of him, that's over to you."

They scunted down the deeplade dock, turning cartwheels to beguile the empty length of it.

                        ⌒

Max stood by his bedroom window, locust leaves flickering above, his head arced back, his eyes closed, his viol tucked neath his chin. His bow flashed over the strings as sparlets swam through the locust, flutting their short wings, peeping their shrill songs. The viol sang back to them and they chirped the louder till it went so far past them they could nobbut gawp at Max as he played their air till it swooled out into clusters that made new concentric rings that widened, oh now widened ...

"Aaay-eeee-yerp!" shouted Finn.

"Eee-uhh-yerrrrrp!" hollered Palan.

The viol gave a great squeak. Max leaned out of window. "Finn M'Cool," he said, "Palan."

"Aaay-eee-yup!" they said.

"Yes?" he said.

"Want us to give our news to all, Max? Or sha't let us in?"

Max nodded and disappeared from the window. He rubbed his eyes with the heels of his hands. They'd want to draw him in. They all, always, wanted to draw him in. His playing stounded them and their eyes opened new on a new world and the first thing they wanted to do in this new world was take he who made the music and draw him in. When they first smelled sage flowering they did no think it'd make a stornry latrine paper, but when they heard him play the viol they wanted it to smooth their ears or hail their entry or call night-scattered spawn to bed. Max stilled a half-born sigh, for Goodwin had sighed enough sighs to last a lifetime, and did he want to mimic his poussilating mam? No. Max slid downstairs.

"We come to see you, Max," chanted Finn by way of greeting.

"Oh ah," he replied.

"Could no take another breath till we seen you," said Palan.

"How about that," he said. "What news can there be as you two dare no shout from rooftop? Who has schooled you in comely speech?"

"Sit you down and rest you," said Finn. Max struck a middle tween stay and go; he leaned gainst the locust tree, one eye to the splat-heavy spar-lets popping mong its branches. Finn snapped a twig and stuck it in a corner of his mouth. "Listen. You know you said one time you nobbut played what you heard?"

"Yeah," Max said. "Hold it." He raised his finger while two sparlets sang together, then flew up the trunk in spiral and blossomed from its top. "Yeah, I said that. Why?"

"Ever hear wailing come from stone?" said Finn.

"Yeah, I do. Look, I got to practice. What's your gist?"

Palan said, "Ah by the rat's last tooth. Quit your shim-shammering. Is it a justborn's wails you hear, Max?"

"Yeah." The locust tree, empty of sparlets, rushed its leaves gainst each other; *whish, ta-ta-ta; whish, ta-ta-ta.*

"Where do you hear it from?" Palan tried to grab Max by his eyes but there, you could as easy grab air in your fist as catch Max's flit-flittering eyes. "Anywheres particular, Max?"

"Tongues in trees, books in the running brooks, sermons in stones," said Max.

Palan and Finn listened for more. They kept on listening. Max listened to wind thrumming last year's locust pods gainst each other.

At last Palan said, gentle as dust settling, "Max?" who turned his head in their general direction, "Max? From where do you hear the wailing? That you play?"

"Oh, the wailing? Comes from stones. I said that."

Finn said, easy as knifing froth off a mug, "Max, we clean forgot. Tell us again, an it please you."

"A justborn wails from the stones of Rimehouse annex. Pull the bones out your body with its grief, it would. Hear it clearest just by annex, but once you open your ears to its resonations, you hear it everywheres. It travels long the stones and carries cross the water; those high thin notes reach far, you know, it's their nature; where your low tone sinks down in amongst you, your high tone — now this is interesting — you hear *better* when you're watching it. I've a dunnamany times said this to Bran, how different pitches travel, but so long as there's *song* and *story* and *what the people want*" — Max spat — "sound could be made of rye or eelgrass, it's all one to dear Bran. Tools!" Max spread his hands wide, "Bran thinks music nobbut a set of tools." He shook his head. "I've spoke to him and spoke to him, does no good in the world." He knelt in the dust round the locust. "Look. Your low strings vibrate so." He drew a line with long loops spiralling round it. "Where your high strings vibrate more like waves in a fresh north wind," and he drew a line with many short sharp peaks and valleys. "Do you see?" He looked up at the two open-mouths before him: "Matter of length and thickness."

Palan started in on how length and thickness was ofttimes a great matter, but Finn jumped over him. "That's wild interesting, Max, but could you tell us a bit more of the wailing?" said Finn.

"No more to tell," Max dusted off his knees. "From out the stones of Rimehouse annex comes a wail which the viol joys to play. No more to it nor that." He stood up and turned towards the door. Mid-turn he paused: "Do you no hear it?"

"Mary Kath hears it," said Palan, though Finn's elbow was sharp in his ribs. "Mary Kath heard it t'other day when Goodwin was by."

"Oh, well, Goodwin could no hear it for a lifetime of potable. Her ears is made of spag. Mary Kath, now, she'd hear it, sure." He swung towards the housedoor. "Well, I need to practice. Go well, and —"

"Max! How can there be a justborn inside of stone?" Finn drove his fist into his palm.

Max shrugged. "Those stones been wailing long as I remember. Mostly places do make their own sound, right? Take Dead Horse Moraine, now; there's a scatter-cluster of plink-plonk comes from Dead Horse any time the wind blows east. The deeplade dock sings 'Dome – dome – dome' but you can hear it only when tide's at neaps; any water at all in harbor drowns those big full bell tones. Now, harum puts out a sound as tessels your balls, can stiff you up or jump you back depending on how flat your hairs lie. Barracks, now —"

"Look at the time," said Palan, gripping Finn's shoulder, "sun's near to top of her climb and here's we palavering with you still. We maun tear ourseln awee, as the song goes, though it brakks our hay-arts in twee," turning Finn to go. "Good seeing you, Max," he said over his shoulder. "Have a good practice!"

"Yeah," said Finn, "see you come Hunt Day."

⌒

"Well," said Finn, as they walked long the jetty, "An we want examples of how the Hunts suck out our juice, we've nobbut to hoist Max high and bid him speak." He nodded to August Inkwhistle who doddered by, his tongue flicking the poll of a white dove clamped to his chest.

Palan laughed till he bent. "May rat-teeth cleave my septum an I ever saw a dreg so light-freighted as Max. Does he reckon aught, ever, cepting music? Think you he remembers we was there?"

"Sure, sure," Finn practiced leaping from jetty to walltop in a bound. "Probably worked us by now into a tune, long with they sparlets." Both boys stood soldier, eyes downcast, as Ambrose sailed by arm-in-arm with Matron.

When they'd passed, Palan flexed his knees and alakazam, he was atop the wall. "Prowling for a new passel of novices, those two."

Finn nodded. "Poor sods," he said, and jumped at the walltop again. "Anyhow. Did we get aught useful from that?"

"Course we did." Palan tapped his heels gainst the jetty stones. "Try a full stride fore you launch," he advised Finn. "*There* you are. Now that was main fine."

"Bit of a stagger on landing," said Finn.

"But you swayed up from it smooth. So here's what we learned." Palan counted off on his fingers. "One, Mary Kath's no lone in hearing the wails; two, she's right and the wails do come from stones; three, we know Max unladed his whole cargo of knowledge on the subject this day."

"A fair haul, a decent haul," said Finn, judicious, stroking his chin like there was enough hairs on it to slow a falling cobweb. "But whence comes the wailing?"

"Max has the right of it, mayhap; the wailing's nobbut another sound." The *Mam Can Cook* was tied fast to the end of shallow dock for a week or two now. The lashings was sunbleached and the portholes thick with dust. That was curious. No tarponesse this past week and more, so what in tarnation was Fergus about? "Mayhap a mort of places *do* make sound as only some can hear. Mayhap there's naught to fret on."

"Mary Kath does no fright easy." Finn leapt down and back again. "Ha! Right aright, let's think on the wailing later, maybe when we get so we can hear it. For now we got to rearrange these Boy heads so they're ready to quit off Hunt life. Huh. Fine trick that'll be."

"Give up the lovely horii," said Palan.

"Oiling."

"Oiling. Yeah. And sliding."

"Sliding down pole, down all those slick sleek breasts."

"Their soft hands gainst your—" Palan broke off short. "May kingrats bite my rump, here's scutman Dingle his own self. Shutter up. Hear? You think simple face means simpleton; it doesna. Mind your words round Dingle; I'll give you the whyfore later. Hoy Dingle!"

# Sport Mong the Bowly Boys

"**H**OY DINGLE!" PALAN SHOUTED. "Hoy Pal!" shouted the square brown dreg stuggering up jetty, one hand to the bankmen wall so to keep his passage more nor less even.

"Palan," said the goldhair, but only in mutter. In overvoice he said, "Dingle you old rapsal, what's toward? You all kitted up for scutman; must be some maskyrade *ball* you've but this minute stepped out from." They two clapped ass and butted chest, which knocked Dingle somewhat off his perpendicular, he being in his altitudes.

"Nah, nah, me I'm scutman for true. Got the ear of Sganal, no less." Dingle draped his arm round Palan's shoulder for steadying. "Who's the buck?" tossing his red eyes at Finn.

"Finn M'Cool. You'd ken him fine, Dingle, an your brain was firmsocket the now. He was up barracks with we."

"M'Cool, M'Cool." Dingle shook his head, wushing his nappy copper plaits over his puffed cheeks. "I can no just charge my memry." He straightened a hairsbreadth. "Wait now — was you no with us on our first free Hunt? You're he who melted into weep first time we hunted on our own with no proved Hunt Boys to protect your tender flanks. Was you as come all over salt when come time to stick your first rat! Yeah that was you right aright. That was you. I ken it like was yesterday. What a moil you was! Ha, ha" — he laughed it that way in syllable — "Ha gorry ha. And so now you're beater, am I right? Nobbut a beater now, right?"

"I am Finn M'Cool," he said, "and last I saw you, Dingle Leadkeel, was up the cloacal roof. It was you as told Bourke he could fly. With a hard hand tween his shoulder blades, it was you as told him."

Palan said, "Now, you canna wish such boyish malfease served you on a plate, eh Dingle? What with Bourke's dap still asking why his boy flew off that roof to his death. Me and Finn been mute till now, but it'd be a rare kindness to ease that old man's wondering." Though, truth to tell, Bourke's dap barely noticed his second-eldest's passing, and *had* the old sot noticed, he'd thought only there was one less maw to stuff; Dingle was nob-but one of the crowd as clamped Bourke and gripped him the tighter the more he shivered and grew pale; these facts Palan put aside. Since Dingle had to be broke quick, twere well it were done quick; the sputty cod was too far gone in drink to feel a soft hand on the reins.

Dingle leaned gainst the jetty's stones, shore side of which was all times clammy as day-dead gills. His plaits hung all in his eyes. "I'm scutman now. Can no mar scutman. We take no stain."

"Oh by the last rat spiked —" Finn came forward a step.

"That's right," said Palan, shouldering tween them. "No living dreg can harm you evermore, so long as you *be* scutman, Dingle."

Dingle wiped his sleeve down his face. "I stepped out from the lay-by tween rounds of bowly to get the boyos more scrumpy. I'm so mizzled the world lumps round me. What's it you two want?"

"Want?" said Palan sweet as jam on a cracked tooth. "Want? What should we want, Dingle, but to play at bowly-ball? We'll wait you by the iron rings. Go on now. Go on."

Dingle grinned. "You'll wait me. It's my coming you'll wait on. Right aright. By the iron rings in a brace of shakes then." He strode off with a lot of stumble to it.

"That murthrin corf. That pusdrip coldeye murthrin corf. Bane his mawkbit, I'd dree his woolard farth and joy to." Finn opened his set jaw long enough to spit on the stones where Dingle'd been and then snapped it shut gainst all comers.

"Finn," said Palan, quiet. "Finn, we need Dingle. Dingle's our wedge."

Finn stalked round him in ever-tightening circles, like the leash tween them shortened by one Palan with each circuit. "I'd unseam him stem to stern, stuff his maw with his cocknoodle then choke him on his own en-trails; I'd puke him down the salt-rime barge, let the swole-gut rats have their fill of him; I'd—"

"Finn," said Palan. "Now Finn."

"Leave be, Palan. I'll smooth down by and by."

Palan curled himself in the jetty shade. Finn riled up quick off being a beater. *Nobbut a beater,* he'd moan after a second firlot of perry. Like it weighed so much as a dustspeck. Rat Hunts was sport for richards, no more nor less, as Finn knew well as he. Richards joyed to move dregs round so's they'd a fresh back neath their whips. They both knew it up one side and down t'other, but Finn was all times likely to spout wild. Palan shrugged. Well, Cider Mother was the onliest as lacked all crook, crank, nobby bits. "Finn," he said as he uncoiled, "we've to have speech with some old Boys, eh? Which those turned scutmen will give us best replies, no? Come now, make yourself into a steady flame on this."

Finn somersaulted off the jetty wall and landed on his feet, no stutter. "Right aright," he said, and shook himself. *Nobbut a beater* – that had no fretted him for some while. Likely it was the tale of a justborn immured as set him back. "Right aright. Let's go play some bowly-ball."

Finn and Palan swung long the jetty, no more footering, all fixed intent. Finn chewed the inside of his mouth; Palan tapped his thigh with his fist. "Scutmen," Finn spat. "I tell you Mary Kath had kindly speech with Bedelia Coldhand?"

"Hmm?" Now whyever did the *Mam Can Cook* sway choppy in a calm sea? "Mary Kath and Bedelia?"

"She's why we're doing this."

"Who, Delia Coldhand?" The junk was riding easy again now.

"It was her said it was dregs used to run the Hunts. Horii, barracks, krewes, all that come later, did you know?"

They passed neath the crumble arch. Palan flicked a spall through one of the iron rings two fathoms overhead. He hefted a second flint, "All that come later, did it now? Do tell, Dingle," one eye on the next ring, other on the jumblekarp stacked in the wall's lee, its bulgy sacks, tubs, water filters of dusty sailcloth; one of the jumblekarps as harbored such unco' fat, sleek, smug rats that Hunt novices trained in them. When richards on the gawp required certain sport, they was taken to a jumblekarp, where even a blind spawn with one arm lashed could scare up a fat rat passel as'd drag their swole bellies from their karp dens out to light, torch, shout, spike. Palan tossed the flint through a second iron ring. "Do the ladies think we should beshrew the Hunts? Let rats live and grow in numbers to their natural tenure? Fondle our buboes and give thanks fasting?"

"Palan, by the first flea —" Finn took himself in hand. You slide no new thought down any ears, even Palan's, an you load it on a red-hot spoon. He began again. "Look. No dreg thinks the rats is anyhow our friends. Yet they and we feed off despised scraps, nest in corners from which we can be any moment chivied. We make with our hands and see a few years forward, is all the different tween us and the rats. It's the richards keep us quivering in burrows. Throw us sops, fablish Hunts and so on, all to keep us quiet. So say Bedelia and Mary Kath." He stopped neath three black, hoary iron rings, each thicker nor his forearm, at the end of the high wall. He leaned gainst a coign of the bankmen, from which vantage he could see Dingle coming, or any other.

"Yeah yeah," Palan folded his arms cross his chest, "and sun rises in the east, what of it?"

Finn bent to a clump of stunted wormwood mong the rubble. He crushed a sprig in his hand. The sharp sour of it. "It's the justborn, Palan," he said slow. "It's the wail has us on the jitter. Most times I care that," he snapped his fingers, "an I'm beater or no. Today I started spleeching like I was still in boyo clanch."

Palan grunted in answer. Finn'd call a different tune if he'd made Pike, stead of being knocked back to nobbut beater; he'd be singing swole chest and shoulders back, was he a Hunt Boy now. Once they sorcelled you in brass and velvet, once Ambrose handed you your pike, that was riches and to spare. You strode through Charnholm better honored nor the richards. "Doubtless," said Palan.

"Who's most to fear mong us? Hunt Boys. For they've least to lose? No. Who mong us dregs has aught to lose but life? Palan, lend me your ears on this. From your second Seventh to your third, any male bristles up quick and to bristle is to bite and to bite's to draw blood. Which the richards know well. To suck the froth off these furied boys, they found what best beguiles them — a host of paint and show and trumpet and horii with their oil-smooth hands, bright corvisers and well-stroked cocks — Palan, you know this well as I."

"Yeah." Palan spoke short. Paint and trumpet and oiled horii hands on his cock; he'd have these still had Gov Don no pulled him out to make their spyscopes. Still he'd never gone wrong yet listening to Finn. "It does soothe the fury," he said.

"Considerable," Finn agreed.

"Be a wrench for Hunt Boys to give it up. Mayhap when they see how richards been wiggling them in their hands like toys they'll come round."

"Sure to. Right aright, here's Dingle, some sobered — we'll do so much as we can, Palan. Remember we got to talk them clear and gentle."

Two boys squatted on their hams, tossing pebbles at a lion head as roared silent from out its smashed mouth, above a half-round basin choked with rubble. The guards stood up so lithe it was easy to miss how quick: "Who goes?" said one.

Dingle come out of shadows to roar out their names, an arm round Finn and Palan all comrade-like.

"Trail round with *beaters* now, Dingle?" said the second guard.

"Do beaters no bleed, Lebone?"

"Yeah and it's grand fun to make 'em," said Lebone, popping a fist in his palm.

Finn slid from Dingle's hug. "Me and Palan come to have a small chat with you. You can hear us or you can die crampshot and wailing, choice is yours." He crooked his first and little fingers, so, at Lebone's padded cock. "Now, would you take it so kind to lead us in."

"Unspell me, M'Cool, or I'll pluck your gullet. You know I can," Lebone's legs and voice was tremble.

"I will an you bring us in."

Palan stared at Finn as the guards swung them through "Was that what you meant by talking clear and gentle?" he asked.

"Course," said Finn, striding tall. "Did you think they'd come to us at whistle?"

"No," said Palan. "No, but I —"

"Hail Finn M'Cool! Hail Palan Fergusson! Welcome to Bowly-Ball by the Sea!" Thursgood bellowed from a reed mat island in the low marsh, propped on a railing of verdigris tridents. Fiddler crabs ticked their long legs over Thursgood's boots, pausing to feel the air with their waving front claws, then scuttled to better feeding on his far side. Thursgood paid them no mind till they tickled an ankle. Then he stomped them to ooze and shards.

"Yeah we come to play a few rounds of a different game, Thurs. Sit up and ope your ears," Finn raised his voice, "and all your fellows likewise. I am Finn M'Cool, brother to Daniel, who taught me considerable. You can hear me now or I can give you a taste of what agony's to come. Yours the choice, mine the power: ask Lebone, here, an you doubt me."

The sembled eyes turned on Lebone as one. He nodded; they turned back to Finn and gave him wide-eyed attention, hands over their codpads.

Finn said: "The Rat Hunts suck the juice out of the dregs. We must leave off!"

And every eye glazed over.

"What Finn means," began Palan. He told them what Finn said of the bristling and the biting and the blood as rises easy tween a male's second and third Seventh; he spoke of how the richards wiggled them as toys where in old times the dregs ran the Hunts their own selves, which raised considerable murmur. He spoke well and feelingful and all eyes was steady on him while he spoke.

When he was done, a boy stood and grasped his bowly bat. "You come here to ask us to give up the Hunts? You was Hunt Boy, Palan. Do you no remember? We may fall to scutmen, after, but for now we're kings; slathered in blood or cockspurt we rule Charnholm for now."

"Say it, Jabez," the crowd muttered.

Another said, "Give up the Hunt's to give up the horii. Have your wits steamed to vapor? Horii's the only where we young males win out over the old ones."

"The onliest," agreed Jabez.

Palan said, "But the horii lasts so little time."

Finn said, "My own sister was a hori —"

"And good value she!" cried a voice.

"So I've a special feeling here. Being hori uses them up so quick."

"Well, so are we used up quick," said the batsman Jabez. "Look at us here gathered: our occupation's gone. We're nobbut keeping close to the jumblekarp they'll toss us on, and any of us could toss a spall from today to our third Seventh. An we was in overkrewe," he glanced at Lebone, Dingle, a few others, "we'd a likely chance to be picked for scutmen. Was we pikemen, might come lucky by some guild work, weaving or forging or shipwright. Was we beaters —"

"You'd work hauling and be glad of it," ended Finn, a grin cracking out of him. "Right aright."

"Glad of it," echoed Jabez. "After the third Seventh, the only choice is mong unlucky chances. So why should any give up what they got for the few short years it's on offer? Think it'd better our lives did we run the Hunts our own selves?"

Lebone squared up to Finn and Palan, "Hunt's our natural place. Our strength springs from the earth. We drink what water springs from the earth and eat food drenched by that water. We'd be soft as richards did we drink nobbut potable, eat only clean-raised and clean-caught. Us dregs come *through* thout all that soft-making round us. On *account* of lacking it."

The sembled agreed to that in shout. "Uh-huh!" "Tell it!"

"As Gov Don all times tells us," said Finn, "and he sipping potable from a china cup the while."

"Look," said Palan, while they was still working that one out. "We're no asking you to leave off the Hunt. We're asking you to leave off letting the richards manage it. Horii are nobbut bait. Can we no forswear them for a time?" When he paused, a voice called, "It's they can no still their itchy forks!" Palan wiped the back of his hand cross a smile, and went on with the script. "Well, there's sense to that," he said, and another voice called, "Barely stand up, they can, off the itching!" Palan spoke from the bottom of his chest in his Galanty Show voice: "Boys here sembled! Can we no form our own strong krewes?"

"Yeah!" shouted several still-drunk boys.

Palan continued, "Out of course we can."

"What comes after?" shouted a boy.

Palan opened his mouth but naught scaped his teeth's barrier.

Finn stepped up to that one. "What comes after? We've no least no-tion soever. There's the beauty of it. When richards run the Hunts, the harum, and the barracks; when richards dole out the potable, we know well what comes after — you heard what Jabez and Lebone said. Throw off the richards and we sha' drift at sea, time and tide taking us where they list."

There was no positive avalanche of glee at the prospect.

Finn said, "Look. Every boy here was novice up the barracks. We *know* what all we was taught about speaking up or out of turn." They all laughed short, remembering Ambrose in bellow: *Shutter up and shutter sharp. Did I want to hear a bunch of doves pluckering, I'd go up the cloaca and grab some off the roof. An you had one word worth the saying, think they'd thrown you here?* Finn said, "But we're outside that now. What've you to say?"

"Want answer now, Finn M'Cool?" Lebone and Dingle and a brace of boys closed in circle round Finn and Palan.

"I would, yeah," said Finn, mild as once-brewed tea.

Lebone and Dingle shook their heads in chorus. "No."

"No, is it?"

"No, and again no, and a thousand times no, thank you kindly," Lebone and Dingle taking it in turns to bow their noses near to their feet.

"Right aright," said Finn. He and Palan did the polite and walked from the lay-by scatheless, holding their breath the while. "We'd a few takers, think?" said Palan, once they was clear of the arch.

"There was none, Palan. There was less than one, there was zero."

"Yeah, could been more. Give them time to mull. They'll come round."

"Maybe." Finn looked back at two guards who again squatted in the archway, again tossing stones at the lion's mouth. He walked some dozen strides fore he said, "Mary Kath and Mary Pat going to have to try the horii. Boys'll maybe listen to horii where they'd no listen to us."

"Maybe," said Palan, "Maybe so."

"If there was no horii, would you gone for Hunt Boy?"

"Maybe no." After a time, he added, "Yeah, I would." After still more time, "Well, no harm trying," said Palan.

"No harm. Right aright," said Finn. He and Palan walked silent a good long while.

# Fergus Goes His Rounds

A PASSEL OF SMITHS watched Gessel saw their locust boards: Brast, Cancho, Innsmort, Drosh, arms cross their chests. "Those four need to be three gov long, Gessel," said Brast, companionable. Only fools gave the sawyer a *command*; he'd throw down saw, block, and locust, all, quick as ratleap.

"Mind they're long as Gov's arm was fore he burnt his fingers dabbling in what does no concern him," said Cancho. Scutmen had snatched his nephew right from Cancho's house, three days since, and smashed the table needless, after. "This Galanty Hunt, now, where's the sense in it? Boys could easy die off all the close-in he's running. Does Gov think on that? He does no." The other dregs was silent. "Maybe none of you has Boys in the Galanty? Or none whose fate you care on?"

No dreg took up the pike where Cancho laid it down. Gessel liked it quiet. You had to sleep and eat raised off the floor, the way you'd a chance to swot life out of a thieving rat as it ran up table-leg, bench-leg, bedstead. Gessel had the saws and Gessel liked it quiet. Gessel got the saws off his grandap, who wandered mad after the Great Burning; like so many thought himself the last man alive; stumbled forward through the rubble, wife gone boys gone girls gone brothers sisters parents workshop home gone gone gone, stumbled through dust; it all had turned to dust, no bones no flesh no sweet mementoes, all gone to dust. As he pushed dusty soles gainst dusty stones, a long saw wedged tween two stones twanged at his passage. Gessel's grandap levered the saw gentle from its slot, tucked it underarm, and dusted forth to find more saws, prowled the rubble till he'd a dozen saws neath his arms. Why should the last man living need them? Gessel's grandap could no said. His feet took him long dusty lanes and through dusty rubble where he groveled mong paper scraps, they the only moving thing in all that landscape but himself, chewing dust for days fore he saw another pair of living eyes. Gessel's grandap passed the knack and the saws to his son, who in turn passed them on to his nephew Gessel, a man with two living spawn and a third (spill perry on the earth lest you rouse the sky's ire) on the way. Gessel's saws was all the whole saws there was now; one cooper's saw lost a half-dozen teeth when it bore down on a metal rod in a locust trunk; drove through by the Burning's winds; no blame to any, a terrible shame natheless. A scutman broke a miter saw to shards gainst a stone cistern's hatch. A hacksaw was melted down accidental by a young Gessel in help of his unca, and so forth.

So the smiths waited for Gessel to saw their locust to planks, shifting from foot to foot, muttering "Sha hafta go na bit" and "Howsda grabe horii ban?" tween tight chapped lips in sounds as made sense enough mong these long-knowns, rubbing jointaches or past-torn muscles. Each had finished supper, pushed back his bench, said, "Be home fore scut patrol," and come out to Gessel's.

"Gan t' Galanty Hunt, Gessel?"

He paused, kerf steady in the cut, "Glanny Hun? I see mysel," snorted Gessel, and back to sawing.

"I got two boys in this Hunt," said Innsmort, "if they this time let 'em off the bench." He nudged Drosh in the ribs. What ailed the fellow? standing down the jetty all on his lonesome that night when Innsmort tocketed by, his soles tapping out *WASTEnoTime WASTEnoTime WASTEno...* He'd asked Drosh if he was keeping the ships afloat by the force of his two eyes purely, and when the smith did no reply, dragged him dreaming long to Gessel's. On the way, Drosh stumbled at flat places, halted some few times at common sights like they was spanking new: couple of leatherfoot spawn hauling spag buckets up hill, gaggle of horii spilling down dale to the musky perruker, old Inkwhistle dragging his empty dovesack behind him. If Innsmort said *"Come long, Drosh,"* once he'd said it a dozen times. Now here he stood, no word out of him, no light in his eyes; what ailed the man?

Gessel stopped sawing just shy of the cut's bottom. "Like t'see those Fergusson viewtubes," he allowed, grudging, like desire chafed him. "Sound canny." He flipped the timber and finished the cut from the other side.

"Greater lauds be there none," hissed Innsmort down Drosh's ear. "Gessel's afire, hey?"

Drosh nodded. He was took out of himself, but how he was took or why, he could no told for all the rye in Charnholm. Coming down jetty that morning his feet lifted of their own like he was a young pikeman once more. Like he was under sail. All that day since, as he walked here and there, as he held speech with this one and that, his muscles sang like wind in the halyards, the weight of him swam through the air. After promenade was over, his feet took him down jetty. Likely they knew why they scuffed dust to the bankmen. The susurrant evening air opened his eyes further yet, as a new mam licks her justborn's belly till it breathes on its own, and he stood in amaze. How light spangled the waves as they slurred shoreward. How the ships tugged graceful at their lines. Innsmort surprised him, so. Innsmort come down jetty, his boots ringing *WATCHforDeath WATCHforDeath WATCHfor* — he let the man lead him where he would but there was such sights long the way. A brace of waist-high spawn with 17 ribs each, patient of their breath, hauling uphill two slagbuckets heavy as themselves, past making game of how stretched they was. Next a bevy of horii laughing with the perfect sleek of themselves in a twilit offtime as they went down, down, sag away from this apex they went down. Third the wide-awake eyes of August Inkwhistle sparking at his own as the old dreg lugged a sack chockfull of doves as once was, remembered doves, Inkwhistle's old eyes flaring up as Drosh passed him. The stars was numberless in their courses and the cold wind lifted his spinehairs and the *choof choof* of Innsmort was strange aside him, sprung from a known bow and aimed at a known mark, and all the while Drosh's own breath launched his blood again and again on its courses. He started when Innsmort whispered down his ear. He owed Innsmort a reply. "Hah," he grunted.

Innsmort was still looking sideglance at Drosh when Fergus come up singing.

*Turn every young girl upside down / Upend them every one*
*Turn each girl till her holes do drip / Pucker lips, sweetly sip*
*Charge, charge, retreat in form / No matter if she's done*
*What's her pleasure? / Do no measure / Pull out when you list.*

Fergus was lean, even for a dreg, his elbows thicker than his forearms, his legs thrown out anyhow with each step, some piece of his foot come down by continuous happenchance. He skritched his chin, wiped his nose on a wristrag, and pushed his black curls back off his sweaty face. "How now, how now, my bully boys? What news on the Embarco? Brast, you owe me yet a hogshead from when I last was here; Cancho, you're my creditor to the tune of sniff-and-sniff-again, so here's your powder; and Gessel, good Gessel, hard at work as ever, a man who sees as far as his own nose is a bright light in a naughty world, equal praisable for seeing clear and for fore-seeing where sight should stop, for that man whose nose sniffs constantly in every man's knowing knows more than he can carry; it bears him down, forbear, your bear's a fearsome enemy, and so an end to it. Innsmort and Drosh, Innsmort and Drosh, good day to you; may your grim features soon break into smile on smile as a pool is rippled by a thrown stone; depose the statues who now rule your faces and set up ring on laughing ring in their stead. Take you a whiff of this. Who else for cheer? Who'd halt his woes?" Fergus's pupils was so wide swole that his grey irises was but their coronas; his legs jigged constant, and his long fingers waved this way that way all round the houses.

"Looking at you's like running a choppy sea," said Brast, "gives the same queer stir to the mid-section."

"Well Brast, well Brast, let's go down your hovel in a bit and I'll provide you sure certain remedy, I will indeedy." Fergus's eyes roamed the crowd, every man's eyes on his and each with a spark in it, cepting Gessel fixed on his saw thrusts; well Gessel was a close-grain clutchfist. But eye-spark by its lone emptied no purses. Young hots grew old, grew cold; once they'd some firlots of scrumpy down their gullets, later, up the caves, coin'd melt right out of them. "Where's t'young bucks, hmm? Where be the Hunt Boys as is and as was and as sha' be scutmen? Like to keep up with young dregs, I do; my own Palan would have me leave him; he's a mind to make his own way so, 'Well,' says I, 'you've made your mind now you must lie in it;' all on us tries to tell our spawn which end's up but who can melt spag out their ears? Likely where Hunt Boys gather, there sha' Palan be, can any mong you tell me where?" Fergus danced from foot to foot with impatient; he was ripe for a snort but could no show his flask here without he shared it round, which'd leave no friendly drap to help him after. "Down the fire hollow, mayhap?"

Innsmort said, "Down the fire hollow, right enough."

Drosh said, "Down the rings is where you'll find them. Innsmort keeps too close to his net-mending; it's horii as meet in fire hollow these days."

Fergus looked round the cold-drawn faces. Gessel spat *prppp, prppp.* "Rings," said Brast. "Down the rings," echoed Cancho. They was a close-hauled passel, right aright.

"Well," said Fergus, "I sha' see you up the caves some evening soon," and slap-happed down the stones singing: *Turn every young girl upside down / Upend them every one...*

"There's Fergus for you," said Brast, and Cancho shrugged in answer.

"Your planks," said Gessel. He handed Brast his locust, and spat. "Beveled," he said, and in a burst of loquace added, "Never lack for breeze so long as we've Fergus by."

Down by the iron rings, the Boys quit off their bowly games to greet Fergus with many a glad cry and hearty clap. Lips hollered "Where you been?" while ears paid no heed soever to his answers. They did no care, and Fergus would only answer, anyhow, in glister bubbles, soon popped. All was shine as the sniff passed round and firlots raised in toast to *Trepid Fergus!* and *Glanny Hun!* The Boys sang him a dunnamany choruses of *Tip your horii / Tip 'em high / Loose your codpiece / Watch 'em fly*, which Fergus called a song past price, a marvel, a testament to the singers.

"Tesamenn?" said Dingle, who lay at half-mast cross Thursgood's legs.

"Testament," Fergus nodded. "All is rotten in Charnholm! The richards suck your sap! Use you and toss you. You are the ones to destroy the old order." He was charmed by how he could keep the pot a-bilin'. "In smashing and breaking we spend our days," said Fergus. "How can the new be born without the old is tore straight down?" He passed round the tar-ponesse flask and every Boy took giant sniffs. Fergus watched their dosage careful; once they got the taste of it they'd shell out all they had for the kegs belowdecks on the *Mam Can Cook*. Meantime he'd but to keep them stirred. Simple enough after so much sniff. "Every object has its use: the pot keeps the stew above the flame; the horii keep your cocks from wasting away neath your rough hands; the richards keep you from smashing the very stones you stand on. But the richards, mark me," Fergus leaned forward till his chest scraped the ground, neck bent back long his spine, his mouth drinking moonrays, "has gone way past what's needful. Way past! The very stones you walk on cover the dead; they tip neath your feet off the dead rot understone. Tear up the stones! You've the power in your blood to make a new Charnholm once its old rotten stones is smashed for all time."

"But them stones is roads!" said Kellock, a beakface shamble with too much leg on him, his skin in boil, his black hair in lanks. "How sha' we get round once the roadstones is smashed? Kneedeep in mud we'd be, come the rains. Who sha' build the roads?"

"By the spitted rat, what matter?" Lebone took a hearty sniff from Fergus's outstretch hand. "I'm to be scutman and scutman houses is built on good stone. It's the plague-ridden shacks of the dregs as we ought smash. And burn." That was the one word too many, even Clarch was squirm; these shallowgut hidebounds feared burning in their bones, so Lebone spoke quick, "We'll smash every rotten in Charnholm! This town's built on rotten like Fergus says. We got to tear down so to build up again."

"But who's to build up, Lebone?" said Kellock. "The old dregs is too weary and the richards too finical. Dregs has but crept under any roof going, into what two-ups and scrapers as was left by the Burning. Think there's fine building stone neath the rubble? There is no. And who sha' haul and make once we unhouse the dregs?"

There was quiet round the coals at that. Fergus and Lebone leapt to smash the thoughtful quiet: Fergus offered all another sniff and Lebone jerked his chin at Clarch.

Clarch nodded and turned on Kellock. "What gorry difference if we tear down or no? Time has its prybar in the chinks; sure as we speak here this town's moldering. *We're the dregs as survived.* Got that in your billybag? Did we survive on account of we had nancy shelter caves or serried gudgeons of potable? No," and the other boys shook their heads in time and mouthed *No* with Clarch, "our grandaps come through on account of they was tough. They drank the green water and they ate the black food; nibbled rat leavings and woke hale the next morning. Talk your talk, Kellock, then ask your ask: whose forebears'd be here this dental minute had they prissed round wishing for *roofs* and *nice roads?*" Clarch spat and latched noses with Kellock, who shrunk up on himself, "Nah, they'd be spag like the rest of them if they hadna been tough, and we come from them. Roofs," Clarch laughed in his throat and knocked Kellock's skull back. "Roads," he snarled and stood. "We've their blood in them yet, no?" The boys hollered *Yeah.* "We've no need for prancy *roofs* or roadstones silk neath my lady's slipper, no?" And the boys hollered *Yeah.* "We're the sharp pike of the dregs." *Yeah.* "We're needful as any pike spits ratflesh." *Yeah.* "Choose we to smash what's rotten?" *Yeah.* "Choose we to smash?" *Yeah.* "Choose we to smash?" *Yeah.*

"But first," said Fergus, "a little matter of business."

Once the pot boils, a good cook banks the fire so it turns to the steady business of sucking marrow from bones.

Fergus passed round his flask. "Let this last drap tune you boys to a fare-thee-well. Who's for more? Who's for the drop that cheers? Get enough in your gullet and you'll have it in you to smash whatsever you will; take heart off bounty of the sea, distilled by a dreg who's proud to be a worthy son of dregs tough as whitlow; sniff this and you sniff a man!"

They set it to meet him down his junk in an hour's time, when he'd have for each his exact desired quantity, and when their pockets was emptied, Fergus stood to leave. He looked tall as a crowsnest to the addled Boys. He said, "Clarch here knows what's what. We've sinews strong and backs broad; we stride the earth and sail the seas; we are colossuses, Charnholm's pride. There's sly-snouts as whisper we could have softer lives, easier: they speak in whispers so's we true dregs can no hear how they plan to make us weak; their eyes is envy-green and all their spite knows to do is pull us down to the self-same mud they mire in. Close your ears to them! An they've aught to say gainst Gov Don's kindly rule, let them stand up like men and speak it loud! You boys is made of what's needful; what smash you do is needful smash! Boyos, a toast to the strong, the brave, survivors all: the Rat Hunt Boys!"

The boys hollered *Yeah* and Fergus slipped away. Thursgood and Dingle tossed flints long as their arms through the iron rings set two fathom high in the stone wall round them. Clarch and Lebone wrestled foot to foot, forearm to forearm. Four boys squatted round Bannock as he showed them how to knot a dove-snare.

Kellock shifted easy towards Stampel, who was cleaning his hobnails, "Was that no Gov Don's speech last Reap Day as Fergus just give?" Stampel nodded. Kellock gathered courage. "Why give any heed to what Gov Don says? Out of course he likes things how they are." Stampel nodded. Kellock grew bolder. "Why should we smash the stones we stand on? What good to tear the roofs from off our shacks? How—"

Stampel knocked one boot gainst the other to loose the crumbs. "Tell you," he said. "I'm bone weary with being this man's, that man's puppet to shake in his jaws. Did I never hear another word about a great plan as ought guide our every act, it'd be too soon."

"Ah," said Kellock, and sat back on his heels.

"This Galanty Hunt, now, grand affair for which the richards brung in all manner of newfangle krewes, well what of it? I got a mood to smash it up, what of it? One wave in the sea never takes a mind to sport different so's to lead its fellows in a newfangle pour. Do we smash or pass by, the waves as break over our heads will change no drop. All the rest's the tarponesse talking." Stampel nodded short and strode towards the crumble arch. "Coming?" he said over his shoulder to Kellock.

"Yeah," said Kellock, "And another thing —"

"Shutter up," said Stampel, and they walked quiet, shoulder by shoulder, toward the jetty.

# Uncork and Pour

THE BEATERS HAD SWABBED THE HUNT WAGON down to its last red rat hair and was spit-polishing its crimpled trim. The novae and the once-was had mopped every oiling couch free of spag and smegma and kelp oil, and they was edging toward the Wagon when in come Matron, hair in a boil, hipflesh swinging. She pigeontoed straight to her errant fangles, swung round on them on one heel and said, "Girls, you're brim with zeal! Dedca-tion! Self-sacafice!" and, suiting act to word, she incanted, *"I do applaud / your wondrous zeal / but now you must abate / for tasks await / you scupper'd keels / which never shall be bawds!"* She set her hands into her hips: "Who wrote it? Name him!" The girls was silent. "Him as wrote it! Now!"

Dorween Once-Was raised a wrinkle hand. "Keeley, ma'am?"

"Yessss. Ver good, vare good," said Matron. She took her hands off her hips. "Some point there's been to all your years of schooling. Keeley it was indeed. Sky-High Keeley, we called him when I was a lissome girl. How he could turn a word or phrase, how he could adorn 'em! If I know aught of sing-song, was Keeley taught me how, oh! Keeley was —"

"Indeed the author of that grapcious slum," said Ambrose, his beaters crouching neath his voice. "*Move* your hincty fordums," he barked at them. "You note," he waved to Matron and her fangles, "that I keep my hellions' feet to the fire but never be it said I grind their eyes with Keeley. You girls best keep off Keeley, I tell you straight; he'll rot your thoughts if you've any left after all these hours rubbing drippings off the couches."

Matron shook her pinna at her charges. "I'd like to know what the lot of you is gawping at? Has none of you learned her simples? Or has the charm of *Ambrose, Lord of the Hunt* blanked what clever you got? There's no need of you to help his Boys; sure and there's plenty to do. Look on these couches! Here's a speck ... and here," sniffing her cloth-wrap finger, dainty, "is oilstain." Her voice, all times rasp, sunk to peatmuck, "Which how can there be when you my best girls has cleaned these couches? No, no, these eyes must lie. Ayuh, there's the way of it. Poor frail Matron's done too much," tusks gleaming tween her lips, "sees oilstain where none can be; gone round the bend, poor Matron, and why?" her yellow fangs bared, "on account of you slackwaist traphead muffisheye shelks, you passel of tainted gramaveers with twists dry as sand, you wattled —"

"Right aright," said Ambrose. He ordered his beaters to scut off to barracks, which they did backasswards, tugging their forelocks as they crabbled off. He gave Matron's hanghead girls his long slow smile — '*O he was wounded sore by some carelack girl,*' sighed Dorween to Mornich — and Ambrose smiled again and said, "Lash off these gentle maids and give me ear, I've a rare bone to pluck with you."

Matron's distaste for taking orders stippled her skin in goosepamps, redded her face till — '*You could warm your hands on her cheeks,*' Mornich told Dorween — Matron stertorated, "Girls, about face / Turn and unlace / Stand with grace / At bathing place — Go!" her arm an arrow, the gates the ratseye.

When the last hori cleared the gates, Ambrose offered Matron a handker. "Thought we'd have to play a few more acts of that one," he said, "and me wrung out by these past few days. Galanty Hunt!" he snorted, "Canna tell me why the richards got to fashion themselves a new hunt." He pulled a gold flask from neath his tunic. "Bit of perry, Matron? Grease ourselves a truce thereby?"

Matron grinned back at him. "Well. So's it's for the truce only, I'm agreed."

They sat side by side on their usual bench in the carriageway tween pool and courtyard, cool gainst the great stones in that barrel vault. "Double cleaning today," said Matron, and took a healthy swig of perry.

"Polishing, me," agreed Ambrose. "For the *Galanty* Hunt," the thick black syllables treacling from his lips.

They was silent for a time, passing the perry in a thrillip of tiltbacks; Matron drank sip-sip-a-sip then patted her lips with her hand's back; Ambrose drank gulp-a-gulp then spuffed *whaugh* and hunched his shoulders like to cage the raw spirit. Ambrose broke first. "Car-lot-ta. Sure, they've no least notion how well we play it, and out of course by the last rat it's needful, but with all I got to think on these days, it's main tiring to remember you and me is mortal foes."

Matron sniffed. "Tiring for you, how tiring's that? You're male, no?" She burped, genteel, back of her empty hand flutted quick to her lips, "Comes natural to act like you've too much stick up you for a reasonable dreg to bear."

"Well you did no bear, did you," said Ambrose quiet.

"Shutter up on that," she said. "Them few as could, did. No blame to the barren. Rimers say it, Gov Don says it, and I say it. You can shift your cheeks or shut your piehole, one." Matron snatched the perry from his hand.

Ambrose put his elbows on his knees and his chin in his hands. So braced, he let time pass till the walls quit revolulating so rapid. Most days he could lade perry till his keel was full and still wear ship, but this night he was ready to lay out every dreg who'd take him on, he was that fed to the backteeth with the prep for the Galanty Hunt. Carlotta'd never notice he was anywise different; walked in a hall of mirrors wherever she went, did Lotte. No matter. Ambrose was ready. Last time he was this battle-ready was the long-since Reap Day when he and Olympia danced the half-hawser. How he arced to the crescent moon she made of herself; how their hands slid into each other as he caught her from the air and twirled her; how the rope sang neath their weight as they slid its length *en jetty,* he with daub of spag on his nose from Olympia's two high-held torches; how the crowd cheered their leap and their landing; how they roared. His chin slipped off his hands. That was then. Now Olympia brewed cider and he fermented Hunt Boys. They two'd ended up in the same line of work. Lotte was chuntering on of her own young days. No matter.

By time they was on their third or sixth slug of Matron's own perry, he could no get his elbows to stay on his knees, and Lotte still on about her past: "I could make a skull's eyes leap out its sockets and bid the *waves* halt in their crests; I coaxed cold cocks coffin-bound —"

"Yeah, you was prime right aright. Hand me that flask. What gorry difference does it make now? No speck nor grain. Once we'd the necessary which now we lack. Hand me that flask, I say. Once we wet their forks," he hoisted the flask in Lotte's direction, "or stiffed their rods and now it's otherwise." He tucked the flask tween his scrabby lips. "So now. Wheening will no roll back years, so here's a question from this time we're in. Your hellion charges gone uppity this past month? Raise their snouts? Roll their eyes? My novices been asking questions. Even after they was taught a couple flight lessons from the barracks roof, they keep on asking. No lesson teaches them. They've no sense of history, like mayhap the sea sha' taste sweet on their tongues tomorrow. Yours changed?" Ambrose wiped the flask mouth, polite, fore he pocked it in her waiting hands.

Matron braced her heels on the floor and took a long drink. "Could be! First time for everything! That's what they say. I tell them and tell them how to mind me; mayhap one word in ten goes down their ears. Even when buboes come tween they legs they keep on doing the same thing over and over and —"

"Got it," said Ambrose, rubbing his stiff knees. "Over and over. Go on, Lotte."

Matron wiped sweat off her soft moustache, her cracked lips tight over her yellow fangs so her words come through on the whisper. "Even when the pus turns blue-black they nobbut look down, *oh, I've a little friend here*, and keep on grabbing for what they want. Full well they know they got to feel themselves nightly, but they say, *oh I sha' stay sleek and tight forever and ever, with what tricks I got*. Too few years on them to see how these tricks work for a short time only ..."

Matron's voice droned on but Ambrose went away from there. Tricks. *Treeks*, Akrim would said. *Theez gawpers wan' you should take dive*, Akrim said, *they no here for watch you easy to walk it the rope*. It was nobbut a trick to juggle stone and rope and firlot, mayhap, but *theez gawpers they no interest when they think they can do same. Deefecul you must to make it look*. Sides, there's no thrill like looking down throat of your own death. Olympia used to say, *What dreams may come when we have shuffed this mortal give us pause*; Olympia hightoney then as now. Tricks. They was only tricks an you counted it *tricks* to fuddle their eye-lids open to this fact: *Heartbreak to the wise as we walk surface for a short time only*, which Olympe'd said a hundred times. "Real heartbreak," Ambrose said now, the words lost in Lotte's mouthwind as she chuntered on of brainlack spawn as did the same things over and over. Could he but do the same things over and over. No trouble there cepting it was impossible. "Like repetetto'd put a spoke in time's wheel," he said.

"*Just* what I'm saying." Matron sat up straight. "No *idea!* An it works for a time, these fools think it works for all time. They got no per*spec*tive, know what I mean?" She dug her bony elbow in Ambrose's ribs, who nob-but huffed and stared straight on. None of his male tribe could hold their spirits any. Give them a few decent tots and they went stone on you. She wrested the flask from his gone-stone hands and kept herself company with that.

Ambrose roused after three flask-gurgles. "So's your flock uppity these days? Like they hear no word you say?"

Matron zamined the notion. That's to say, the notion climbed the shelves in her skull, peering at cellarage records, clay queenlets, spare whip-plaits, shell-crust boxes, borrow-dangles, stockings, mateless ear rings. "Well, as to uppity. They gipper and japper of the Galanty Hunt. Old timey, they call it, and every last one of them thinks she'll get the old-timey treatment. Course they no magine they'll be set to clamber uphill to dig for sweetwater, the old-timey way; in boils and eructations scratching a scant flask of muddy potable from out the earth. I tell them and tell them there was nobbut a handful of proper horii back then, *and* no oils *nor* no depilation — all they hear's they'd be rare. The crowds wild for least touch of their flesh."

"Was no crowds," Ambrose clapped a *ta-ta-ta-rum*. "Was nobbut us back then when the richards was yet down their holes."

"Right aright," said Matron. "Glorus glorus time, yeah. Can you turn back time in its passing? You can no." She nodded, her irises sloshing back and fro. "What do these novae think they sha' find better nor what they got now?"

Ambrose shrugged. "Naught. There's naught to find. Lean too far out and fall overboard, they would, and take us with them. If our novices —"

"Or novae—"

"If they fall off the boat fore they turn Hunt Boys —"

"Or horii —"

"Right, if we've no new passel of *nitiates* to show Gov Don, he'll find others to put in our place. Very hot for new blood, is Gov Don, when he thinks old blood's cooled."

"I say we come down on them sharp."

"I say rap their knuckles and do it by the book."

Matron narrowed her slitty eyes in their pouches. "Rap them, is it? Rap them's a pleasure *and you know it*. So long's it's for their good, I'll rap them."

"Oh it's certain for their good, though they've too few years in their kick to know that."

"We maun teach them and guide them."

"Guide them and ride them!"

"*Ride them till your juices pour / Ride them till they can no more / Ride them guide them till they tire / Then heave them ho them in the fire!*"

Through this exchange they hitched their chairs closer and closer together till by its end their nosetips touched. Each laid thumbs athwart the other's windpipe. They locked eyes. They kept the pressure light but steady on their nosetips, on their thumbs. Each waited for the other to break. They was waiting still when the jetty broke into cry.

"You broke first," said Ambrose, as they jostled to window. "Like you done every time since we was puling spawn."

"You broke first. Speak first, break first. *Everybody* knows that." She leaned out of window. "That's Bedelia Coldhand screeching," she said. "Nobody else got a yellowgreen nest top they head, eh Ambrose?" But the warm air he'd stood in was empty and Fergus stood flat gainst the wall below her.

From halfway down tunnel, Ambrose said "I got to get back to barracks," and waggled a hand. "Thanks for your hospitable," he said.

"Oh my," said Matron. Fergus took cover neath the window sill. She stretched like loneness was her all in all. "My!" she said, tossing the empty flask in her basket, swishing her skirts past the mute peeping Fergus, "An it is no time for depilaten muster!" She strolled down tunnel, pausing at every porthole to hum, tween which she talked to the air in clear, ringing tones. "My, sporting with Ambrose I forgot the time," and suchlike till she ended shouting by poolside. "You lackbrain slackwaist lumps! You dim-thinks! Every one on you stinks foul of crotchdrip: dive and give me twenty laps! Now!!"

While her horii floundered in the pool, Matron settled herself on a ladder step. They was still clamoring down jetty. Max was bowing a new kreel, one with considerable go to it. Matron's feet tapped the tune on the poolside tiles. She jumped down from ladder and looked out of window. Fergus's black curls dove for cover. Bedelia was screeching still from jetty. She'd good scope on her lungs. Matron shouted over her shoulder: "Twen-n-ty laps you miserable spalp! Fourteen's no twenty! Keep it up, now!" She craned out of window once more. One clump of elderbushes quivered. "Few pleasures in this life great as pulling the grass over Ambrose eyes," she said, like to the empty air. One black curl waved in the breeze. Bedelia Cold-hand was wailing in a corolla of dregs on Galendock. Six Hunt Boys shoul-dered through neath a withy palankeen. They was *massing*, what it was. Massing.

Matron left off taunting Fergus. Massing, now, that needed seeing to. She went in search of Sganal, who commanded many, many eyes.

# Out to the Sea in Ships

BLAY INNSMORT WON HIMSELF A WARRIOR DEATH. His frame was carted from the sanator three days after the Hunt in which he got his mortal, in the hour when buboes lumped neath his jaw and his eyes went rusty. Six of his fellow Rat Hunt Boys shouldered a withy palankeen from the lazarhouse through a mass of keening dregs, Bedelia Coldhand screeching loudest, straight down promenade to Galendock, where they laid him easy in a waiting skiff. Blay tightened his bald eyelids gainst the light, twitched a finger in farewell, no more; a Hunt Boy is all times straightback and close-mouth. The remaining Boys lined the pier, straightback, closemouth, while an oarsman rowed Blay's hot flesh past the breakers, till the body was safe laded on the white barge that lay at anchor there.

Only then did their backs slump; only then did their mouths unclamp. One said, "Mayhap he'll come back hale in a week's time or so."

Another snorted. "Lebone, you've spag tween your ears. Ever seen one come back from the white barge?"

"No."

"None ever has," Kortch said. He cuffed the smaller boy. "Time for Innsmort's. I heard the tables groaning as we come. Jennels, our duty's to those platters." Five pair eyes stayed on the returning skiff as it met a breaker sideways, as it recovered, as it bellied out of the trough. "We're wanted to give comfort, which there's a brace of swole-breast pullets kin to Blay I'm first to offer bricious comfort."

A pair of Boys clopped down the pier with Kortch on that, kicking stones over the coping, shoving each other up the ramp, forcing a barrow to the promenade's verge, all the while singing an old catch: *The rat came out of its burrow / The rat came out of its burrow / The rat came out of its bu-ur-row* (Kortch took the next line solo in a fine rising tenor) / *With death upon its teeth* (all three harmonizing for the next) / *With death on every tooth /*

*With death on every tooth* / (shouting the capstone line like any toddling spawn) / *The rat come out of its bu-ur-row* / *With death* ...Their voices died off as they turned sharp through a narrow passage in the stone bulwark.

The three left on the pier watched the oarsman tacking home gainst the rising land breeze. Lebone said, "He's no brought back the palankeen."

"It's nobbut reeds as'll sink with Blay, come time." The speaker scratched his dark hair. His long Roman nose flared. "Smells a rich feast they've laid on," he said. Hands in pockets, he rocked on his heels in time to the waves breaking on the bankmen two score yards away.

Lebone came close and lowered his voice, "Here's thirteen Boys gone to barge since spring."

"Thirteen," Finn agreed, still rocking easy on his heels, time his servant.

"That's more Boys nor we lost any year since I remember," said Lebone.

"That's so," said Finn.

"How'd we come to lose so many?"

At this, the third boy broke silence. "Makes a better show," he said, and stuffed his gold hair neath a black knit cap.

Lebone's eyes squinted as he tried to make aught of this.

"What Palan means," said Finn, rolling a splinter tween his palms, "is Ambrose has set his Boys to cornering rats fore they spit 'em."

"Yeah!" said Lebone. "The close-in! It's how warriors of yore did it. Gives you a chance to show what you're made of."

"Gives you a chance to show the seabed that," said Palan. "Down to your last innard."

"Is there no all times that chance," said Lebone.

"Right good one an you poke a cornered rat." Palan nudged a flailing beetle right-side-up. "Richards wants Hunts as raise their bloodless cocks. Ratbite stiffs them fine. Fewer the boys, more the horii and, breeding chances being what —"

"Skiff's near," said Finn.

All three turned to watch it steer up to the dock. Finn caught the aft rope and wound it to a piling. He sent Lebone down pier to tell Innsmorts they was coming. Soon as the dust rose from the boy's spurt through the bulwark arch, Finn turned on Palan. "What are you about, spilling the gaff? Does your life so pinch you maun offer it to any comer? Make a hols day gift of it?"

Palan shrugged. "Think Lebone's matter enough tween his ears to hold what I said?"

"His lips are wide as a hori's legs, though. He'll spread them as easy, and you're a dentical fool, Palan."

The oarsman now come hand over hand up the moor rope. His eyes was darker blue than most dregs and set deeper, like cavemouth guards. The sun, falling lazy down its summer arc, lit him from behind, and "Could hear you from halfway back. Pair of you is dentical fools," said Dan, and walked off to the *Hail Janus*.

Down the bankmen, two girls bronze as their brother Finn watched him wave his arms at Palan. They pushed their headwraps off their brows and leaned their wiry arms on the cool stones. While Dan battened the skiff, Mary Patricia said, "At tiffin up Lady Mandra's yesterday, the ladies was atwitter bout the Galanty Hunt."

Mary Katharine roused from a new scheme to make chorus of the novice Rimers. "Galanty Hunt? What's to remark? Grant you, the new drummer can no pop skins like Thirk did, but he does *Whisker Freeze* with a backthrum I never heard the like of, the sway it set on us all —"

"An you shutter your trap, I'll tell you." Mary Kath swung herself onto bankmen and pointed at her clamped lips. Mary Pat went on, "Other night, Lady Mandra was in pillow talk with Gov Don —"

"Our gracious Gov." Few can curtsy well from a sit, natheless Mary Kath give it a try.

Mary Pat said, "A fool you do look," thout heat. "Anyhow. Lady M and Gov Don was on the husks and she says as how none of them wants to go down the bleachers no more cause they seen the Hunts *and* seen 'em till they know them backwards. So Gov Don he splains how they going to change up, see, get the richard hearts slamming again by moving Hunt Boys closer in, and Lady M asks him how close is close. Mary Kath, he says they can be nose to nose an it please her. So long as it stirs her right way round, what he means. She gives him some honey out her fork, and next day he skips off all smile to Ambrose."

"Ambrose."

"Gorry Ambrose." They both spat in the dust. "So Ambrose sets up new training for the Hunt Boys." Mary Pat looked round. The boys was up the dock yet, and no dreg strolled the jetty; even so early, the heat was squamish thick. Still she spoke low, "Training them for close-in." Mary Kath nodded. "Close-in on *cornered* rats," said Mary Pat in whisper.

Mary Kath shrugged. "Rats make a one leap strike for the eyes. Tricky, but a canny spikeman knows how to parry. What's so hush in that?"

"Ambrose tells them — and this the Boys swallow whole — they'll best show manly dare an they assail thout no anath'matizers soever to soften the rats fore they spike."

Mary Kath come down off the bankmen quick enough at that. "Oh Ambrose he's a wily one, a scout rat to his fingers ends. Thinks he, these rimers come at too high price; says he, Hunt Boy burying's cheaper nor ours and so he'd lop rimers from our lotted —"

"What he lops off is Hunt Boy lives, Mary Katharine."

Mary Kath nudged dust into a pyramid with her toe. "Sure I was coming to that."

Mary Pat looked at her sidewise. Did it no wear out the back, carrying so much fury round? "Thirteen Hunt Boys gone over the breakers since spring. Now Blay gone, and he so canny a spikeman as ever was. Hunt Boys'll go where Ambrose points them so long as they've horii by, and sufficient potable —"

"And the choice viands —"

"And Hunt Wagon musicians playing their every lunge and strike —"

"And the richards cheering them from lofty bleachers —"

Mary Pat clapped her hands to make an end. "The richards kill off the Hunt Boys so to make better sport."

"Richards kill off Hunt Boys for sport?" Mary Kath's eyes was wide.

"Ope your orbs a bit, Mary Kath. Course they would. Do. Over tiffin yesterday they said the close-in 'raised artistic tension through the roof,' they said."

Mary Kath nudged her shoulder. "For sport they never would. Kill them off by plan's what they'd do."

Any day in their lives fore this, Mary Pat would said, 'Mary Katharine M'Cool, you'd see conspiration in a smooth pool.' Now she said, "That's likely so."

⌣⟶

On the pier, Palan lifted a finger to show Fergus coming round the point, making for harbor.

Finn said, "There'll be stir mong the bowly boys this night an he's hauling tarponesse."

"He'd no make harbor was he no hauling."

Finn give him a short punch on the upper arm. "None blames you carrying his blood. Fergus been hawking that slum since before you was thought on." Palan neither moved nor spoke, only his shoulders come down a notch. "Come long," Finn said, "they'll be looking for us up to Innsmort's."

"Think it's what Innsmort wants best? Couple dozen boys walking round hale while his own's nobbut smoke in a stiff breeze?"

"Likely that is what he'd want. The going on of it, see. Come long. Mary Kath and Mary Pat's waiting by jetty wall," and with such sharp nips at Palan's heels Finn herded him off the pier.

"Innsmort's," said Palan. "We've but this hour sent Blay to the end of the world, each of us being all the world to himself, and you feel no craving for quiet, after?"

"Quiet enough in here," said Finn, knuckling his skull. Palan rapped him back, and they scuffled till they come up on the two girls sitting chin in hand on bankmen wall.

"What's towards?" cried Finn.

"Mary Kath and I been nobbut luffing here, talking change of weather," said Mary Pat, quiet and comfortable.

"Ha!" said Mary Kath.

They argued through the bulwark arch, past Mr Inkwhistle selling doves from an empty sack, past the alleys full of *hssst* where fools laid down their dosh for a flagon of *'leaf drip, morning leaf drip,'* past the harum's open windows full of splash and thrash ('training them to open up neath water,' said Mary Pat, knowledgeable), past the long gallery whose every alcove held some splayfoot crookneck armgone nonose pasthope gumming his beggar's cry, past Dead Horse Moraine's rubble and bogeymen, past the municipal cloaca (mumchance, remembering all the spag they mined there), past a row of crumblebricks leaning on each other's roofs like smiths coming home from cavemeet, past the cordwainers and Bedelia's terrace snug in their midst, and sharp right to Innsmort's gate, still arguing.

First off, they argued, what act of theirs could anyways turn richard currents awry or, as Palan said, do aught but give us a fine white barge send-off of our own. None quarreled with the notion that richards could, would, and meant to slay dregs for sport. And they was of one mind that dregs had an imperative to action. ('Mary Kath gone all Rimehouse on us,' whispered Finn to Mary Pat.) The white barge, though, now that quieted them. They walked quiet to Innsmort's doorstoop.

Where Mary Kath took it up again. "This is the prime casion to rouse up every blinkless dreg as this day lost so likely a male as we have. By the last rat! Will they no be so deep in fury as we are."

Palan shook his gold head. "Gutwrenched is what they'll be. We could find no worse time."

"Right aright," said Mary Pat. "*Let time pass, it is better than much thinking.* Richards is killing off the strongest young males with this close-in. Now, an the richards keep it up, who sha' we have left to breed with?"

"Who'll be left?" said Palan. "Are we who keep our skins whole, our blood and spume safe within, no worth to breed with? Flash-crazed you are to harp on Boys with muscle everywheres, seeing how it's thickest tween their ears. We're who'll be left."

Mary Pat repeated "We'll be left," and was still turning that round when Innsmort opened wide the door. "Who's bereft? That would be myself, thank you for asking. My only living son has gone off on the white barge from which no traveller's ears return. So. Come in and drink a glass to his fine memry." Innsmort was a strong stone dreg like always, cepting the salt beads on his face. Cepting that. His eyes come alive a twitch as Mary

Kath passed by: "Give us a chant as'll honor my Blay. These rimers here has pulled nobbut mold from their sacks." Innsmort's nose was pulled down all into his clampshut mouth and his irises rolled lax in their whites. The hand he put out to them quivered slightest.

They followed him down a short hall lined with crayons of ships and towers, rats pouring out every porthole, pursued by gold Hunt Boys near tall as the highest spire, wielding spikes longer than themselves. "Spawn work," whispered Finn to Mary Pat; "Young Blay," said Innsmort thout slacking his pace.

The hall let onto the back court, which was pissoirs, plain and simple in most dreg shacks. Innsmort's was gravel paths curlicue round islands of locust and veg beds thick with greens. Where he got potable for veg was a open question — Innsmort said only as he was fortnate. Dozens of dregs gathered to the bakemeat table, slice of this and glass of that in hand, muttering their condoles to any Innsmort as drifted past, keeping their voices low on account of scutmen these days was very down on dregs gathering; though they'd likely pass by a wake like this one, you could nowise be certain. The muttering dregs greeted the M'Cools and Palan and their host Innsmort in speech low as wind in the locust trees: *Yor. Yor. Yor.* And dipped their noses back in their ciders.

Mary Kath went off to honor Blay in chant. She gave them, *End the artache and the thous natural shocks*, to which all the company lent quiet ear, cepting the Innsmorts. They went in and out making sure all comers had what to drink and eat, trays in their hands all times, for weighted hands did no rise of themselves to cover damp eyes; busy back and fro kept the ache off. Bedelia Coldhand plaited reeds, a bucket of brine at her feet; Berk 'All Goods Laded Safe and Sure' balanced on his shaky pins mong his krewe; Lando and Pomchalder danced a quiet reel with Cirk and Thilben tween the veg beds; a tight passel of once-was horii linked arms in circle, looking round at the male forks on view and chortling; Quix and Drosh, shoulder to shoulder neath a yellowgreen locust, remarked to Palan and Finn what fine weather it was for picnics.

When Mary Kath come up sweating, Mary Pat told her Palan was right: Innsmorts was gutwrenched. "So drear of him," Mary Kath agreed.

Whenever Innsmorts wasn't being condoled at, whenever they was no required for that, their heads turned to where the white barge lalluped on the ebb tide. Mary Kath shook her head. Every one of them struck to sadness. No one of them angered. How should they few reverse that? Like turning cider to apples. What power could roust their timrous hearts and place there carelack valor? They few? Finn was lascivating down some wilted hori's ear. Palan was watching light play in the locusts. Mary Pat was doing the polite to Lando's dap.

"Sure," said Mary Pat, "it's a tearing shame and all. The close-in's every time a danger." Old Lando wheezed over his grey moustache. "Did no use to be all this close-in, a gorry shame I calls it." Mary Pat drew back, her palms in flutter. "No? Do tell." Out of course old Lando was more than ready to spatiate on how much better it was done in his young days. He'd ramble to any open ear how *new ways bring new deaths*. Mary Pat, like always, was doing right, what they'd agreed to, slow and careful, where Mary Kath wanted to leap up, wrench the present to a better shape, like main force could do that. Dreg force. Huh. Dregs lacked armo, filters, shelter caves, and full bellies, all what richards sat on comfortable. Dregs could no match the richards so.

Mary Kath wanted to challenge richards to single combat or summat. Mary Pat said no. Swift, silent, up from below was how they'd bring them down. Guile guile guile. From her lips fell a few distillate drops in old Lando's brew as brought it quick to froth. Frothing, he mandered through the crowd while Mary Pat sat lids downcast in her corner, smooth as spagmelt. Any dreg who spoke with her come away with the notion, whole and entire, that the close-in was killing off Hunt Boys so quick, so often, so *needless*, that Gov Don would soon levy a new tax so to build a new white barge; no, a *fleet* of white barges. Which was more to the point than raging.

Finn lifted one eyebrow as his lips nuzzled the wilted hori's cordy ear. Over a dozen smiths pulled their left earlobes in response. What's to remark when a rucked-skin down-mouth once-was grabs a male, even an he's nobbut a beater, and offers herself to his fresh hot breath? Palan pulled his left earlobe at Finn and strolled out to the bankmen. He stuck a toe tween two stones and took his place mong the dockhands, yawl crews, trashed scutmen, and lookouts all watching the ships rock on the harbor. Dan stood at prow of the *Hail Janus*, a sail line held to his lips, making ready to cast off. His deep blue eyes and Palan's clear grey eyes followed Fergus's junk as its bloodrust sails closed on the pier. Palan kicked a small stone down the bankmen, down the ramp, and long the pier like any ambler. He and Dan chatted a few minutes of the fine weather expected the next day, how the smiths said it'd bring out picnics up the lookout, specially round midday. Dan nodded short. As Palan strolled back to Innsmort's, an idler by name of Tallat swept his scutman moustache off his thin lips with a thin finger: "Got a whole headshake off Dan, you did. A wonder all that loquace did no sweep you off your ankles." Palan allowed as Dan was unsociable; would no even join Innsmort's bakemeat tables; and walked slow through the crowd of idlers. As he walked, Palan dropped a word here and a word there of the thirteen skiffs as'd sailed to the white barge since the dark of the year, all so the richards could joy in watching Hunt Boys dance the close-in, Palan said. Most nodded, and returned to watching the ships rock in the steam the late sun boiled off the shallow harbor water. Tallat kept his droop eyes on him till he was well away to Innsmort's. Then he scampered off to Sganal's lair, his mouth full of notice.

# Banked Embers

"HOLS DAY HOLS DAY HOLS DAY," the smiths chanted, jingle strips bobbing from their hatbrims, as they stompled up the path stones to the lookout. "Pinic pinic," hollered the sprats as had tagged long, spite of their mams' nay-say. Spawn lugged reed hampers and carboys slung from poles; olders leaned on beribboned staffs; the whole procession climbed in a cloud of song. *Merrily merrily sha' I live now*, they sang; other light chanteys and catches they sang as they skirted Dead Horse Moraine and rose in easy zig-zags to the lookout, a flat bowl on the north side of Short Point.

Governor Donal watched them skelter from the tower of his compound. He turned to the conclave, but none other remarked them, or perhaps none found them worthy of remark. He shrugged: dregs making merry, well let them; there were matters of greater pith and moment to discuss. Still, it was unusual. Gov Don quietly instructed a footman to keep his eyes on the frolic. That done, he strode to the high table and addressed the benches. "With all the effort we have spent to date —"

"Enough to keep a thousand dregs in cider for a year," the numbers totter, one Marcus Narquist, interrupted.

"As Mr Narquist puts it. With this mighty effort we have raised the walls of The House Of the Teaching Company of Anathematizers. The House will systematize and purify rimer teachings. We provided ample store for crumble books in workshops for their preservation. The House contains luthier ateliers, tumbling rooms, music chambers lined with thick pallets to muffle sound. Are we to toss these efforts in the harbor?"

"Nay, nay," Blane Plory galumphed to his feet and shook his red moustache at the conclave. "Naught keeps the dregs so quiet as a bit of Hotcha."

"Old dolt," whispered young Kev from a back bench, a muscly sprat of forty years, invited to represent Youth.

"Lard brain," agreed his cavemate Bri.

Noble Willeford raised his voice the merest trifle. "Our goal is more than keeping dregs quiet, which we might achieve by less civilized means. Our responsibility is to raise up the dregs, that they might one day attain our level of culture."

"One day!" mumbled young Kev.

"Better late nor soon," Bri pointed out.

Gov Don spoke. "Thank you, Willeford, for your elucidation. The House of the Teaching Company of the Anathematizers must be completed for it is meant to be built. We secure the future by adapting the past to the present."

The gathering murmured as it worked that one out.

Gov Don glanced at the skeltering smiths as they rounded away out of sight around Short Point. What hols day had the smiths been granted? His brow furrowed in search of the answer. But the benches were watching; to the benches he had obligations: "After the unfortunate incident last week, all construction on the House of the Teaching Company of Anathematizers halted for three days. Three days, gentlemen. Three days that we can never recover. This must not recur, and the only safeguard against its never recurring is to come down *slap and harsh*, as my coachman would say. Effective action is immediate action. I put it to you, gentlemen all, that we must and shall continue building. For is it not meant? Are you with me or against me? Let all in favor say, *Aye.*"

"Aye, aye, ay-yaye," stertorated the crowd.

"Then let those walls *rise*, gentlemen. Let them *rise!*"

The benches rose to their feet as one (excepting young Kev and his mate Bri, who swayed on their bench, smiling sweet at their olders). *Rise rise rise!* they cried.

Gov Don thanked them, and asked them to go about their business. "I've received your mandate, the which I shall faithfully discharge." The benches rose and draggled off. A few remained behind in uffish chat.

"The wall is built of blocks. Might they not create a cylinder of air, sufficient to sustain some small life?" said Blane Plory.

"If the child is meant to get out, it will find a way," said Noble Willeford. "That's if there is a child," he added hastily.

"We are not here to change the stream of history," Marcus Narquist agreed.

"Exactly," Gov Don purred up behind them. "While its wailing is a present irritant, that will cease once it chooses its next step along the path of life. Should it choose to stop wailing, it will have leisure enough, and, one hopes, sufficient intelligence, to extricate itself from its predicament. That is, after all, the glory of our kind, that we so readily adapt to circumstances." Gov Don moved off to join his particular supporters.

"Smiths taken a hols day," said Janno in idle greeting. He was more interested in the roof of his own compound a dozen fathoms off. Thassy was directing footmen to hang tiffin flags. She was always up to the knocker, was Thassy. Lady Mandra thought herself all the crack; she was a puff of wind compared to his Thassy. Not that he'd say so to Donal. Poor stick.

"The dregs have been uppity lately," said Ross. "Have you noticed?"

Janno shook his head. "Wouldn't allow it. Keep them up to the mark, sharp, that's best for them. Backchat's their ticket home. Now this hols day, who permitted it? Idle hands breed idle thoughts."

"Well, a bit of sport airs their muscles," said Roger, tolerant. "They're capable of good work as long as you stand over them. Taken delivery of that lacquer-piece yet, Janno?" Janno waggled both his chins. "Good, good. Chantal's looking forward to viewing that come the big tiffin," Roger assured him.

Ross was looking past all Charnholm at the deeplade dock. "Oh, yes, Gaby's eager to view it too," he said. "See the *Mam Can Cook*'s in port. Has he sent word?"

Gov Don shook his head. "Comes when he chooses."

Roger turned his back to the view. "Lot of chaff at this conclave, Donal. What've you in hand?" Gov Don promised he'd see come Galanty Hunt; "You mustn't grudge me the occasional surprise, Roger." Who shrugged, turned, descended with Ross, leisurely, chatting of snuffboxes the while.

Janno and Gov Don, left above, watched them out of the compound. "What's the hols day, Donal?" Gov Don shrugged. "Well, so long as they can turn a hand to work on the morrow," said Janno, and took his leave.

Gov Don remained in solitary possession of the ramparts. None of them ready to do a hand's turn of work themselves. Leave Donal to govern; oh, times the burden of it did lie heavy on his shoulders. Felt they no obligation to levitate the dregs? To pass on their refined culture? With great power comes great responsibility. Including the responsibility to protect dregs from their baser nature, their foolish sentimentality, their continual focus on the trivial. Well. Mandra might be done twirling by now. He looked forward to discussing the conclave with her over stuffed filet and flowering rye.

⌒

"Hols Day Hols Day Hols Day." The young ones danced round the lookout while the smiths unpacked hampers and uncorked carboys. "Easier to carry it down in your maw than on your back," said Quix to Drosh.

"Best speak up quick, fore they're too deep in those carboys," said Finn to Palan.

Palan did his manful best, Finn told him later; those smiths was just too thirsty. Palan told the glut-maw smiths how richards mated his dam and sire. "They'd both good hands, so richards put them together to —"

A smith interrupted: "Down a shelter cave!"

"They *bred* them," Palan repeated.

"Sun rises fra' the east, boyos!" "Sea has tides to it!" "Right aright, they give them the dreg treatment, go on with your tale."

Palan took a deep breath and obeyed. "Any road, they was together long enough to make me." "Palan Goldhead!" "Palan Fergusson!" with much hoisting of firlots. Palan told them how he was so clever with his hands that Gov Don took him off Hunt Boys — "Yen for your pretty hands, had he?" — and put him to mechanic work — "Naught mechanic to it soever!" "Comes from deep down inside!" — crafting viewtubes for the Galanty Hunt.

At that, a few smiths tried to gather their floozled wits about them. Had the goldhead no drawn such tubes? in the dust? up the cave? "Pipes he was calling them then," said Drosh to Quix; "Them then then them," said Quix to Drosh. Palan told the smiths how he'd put tubes down a few shelter caves, but there was nobbut one tube completed — "Pipes he then them, hem?" — and it in Gov Don's compound. That all the richards would be down Gov Don's shelter cave come the Galanty Hunt, special to watch it through that one completed tube.

The smiths was rolloping on the yarrow turf, a few playing leap-back, others on their knees intent on knockstone, flicking their chosen pebble all avid. Finn cupped his hands round his mouth and stertorated at them. "An all the richards is down below at one moment, and we knowing that moment, can we no some plan devise?" said Finn, drawing it out in hopes some stray smith would lend an ear, but no. "Some plan as'd pluck the wailing justborn from its immure?" A pair of smiths lifted their firlots and groaned, "Mure more mure more," and no response else. "Hopeless entire," said Finn to Palan, "they've but the one notion in their skulls." "There was no drink up the cave," said Palan. "Yeah," Finn agreed, surveying the fallen, "best plan, that."

Bedelia Coldhand come moiling up the hill, followed by a haul dreg bent neath a carrypole. "Carboys on that pole," said Palan, "think they're full of potable?" Finn shook his head. "Nor I," said Palan. They sat shoulder to shoulder and waited for the females to arrive.

⌒

Bedelia Coldhand said, "Never known a haul dreg so uppish. Get your legs neath that weight, fool, and breathe a bit more steady like."

"Easy enough to say when you've nobbut a handker to lug," said Mary Katharine. "Whyever'd I complain of the whiteskin robe," she muttered, "these sailcloths bring a finer sweat, yeah and quicker, too."

"What's that? What's that? Speak up, now, *keep* those carboys balanced, *lay* that pole cross your shoulders, these is smiths we're on the route to, mind." Bedelia Coldhand stumpered uphill on two sticks fashed to her elbows, grunting at every step. "Why they could no meet down the jetty I sha' never know."

"So's to avoid comment."

"I *know* that — *mind* that left carboy slipping near over the tunk — tunks stayed steady at pole-ends when I was a sprat, call this Gessel-work? I think no — but was there no place lower, flatter, more commodacious altogether than the lookout? Males is scampish, no two ways bout it, can no slay a rat, even, thout they dress it up and slap in pipers. Hunt Wagons. Was no Hunt

Wagons in my day; fore the richards come there was no Wagons soever; any time a justborn lost a chunk off its cheek, we sent out pikemen to stab, flood, burn, anywise make the neighbor rats unwelcome."

"You said that, Bedelia. Said it time and again. I'd no be bentback up these stones an you'd no said it and said it."

"Stands saying again."

"No," said Mary Kath, and she'd a sackfull of words to go on with but Bedelia Coldhand swung one huge leg round a spall in the path. Mary Kath shut her lips and followed after. The leathern purse swung tween her breasts; the damp should no harm it enough to matter fore she handed it off to Finn and was done with it. The last of the seaward breeze puffed downslope, wrapping Bedelia in a fine cloud. A stone skishered downslope back of Mary Kath. She turned sharp, but caught nobbut a black cap vanishing in a thornbrake.

Thassy watched the females and their carrypole round Short Point. Dregs. They might do a decent day's work if you stood over them every minute. Othergates, they scampered off to roll in dirt right up to the forks, by the smell of them. She turned back to the important task at hand. *That* was exactly what dregs could not would not learn: Focus. Perseverance. "If you were to lash the flag *to* the pole, why that would *keep* it there," she instructed her footmen. "Brock! Doole! *Try* to be a bit less fumble-fingered!" They flapped their hands in assent. Mandra once took her to task for shouting, and at her own footmen no less. Really. "Considering that their arms are no longer than my foot," Mandra had said, "surely you grant them a bit of leeway?" But they'd strength enough in those arms to lift Thassy's provender to their mouths, so they could just *use* that strength to do her bidding. Mandra would see. When she came to the next tiffin, her jaw would drop in pure green envy over what Thassy had achieved by all her labors, so she would. "Brock! Doole! Lash the flag so it stands *up* to the wind, don't merely loop it!" The day's last breeze slid past her cheeks, tilting her sunhat. She'd be dark as a dreg if she had to stay up here much longer with these slack-handed ... "Brock! Doole! Stir your stumps! Tiffin's but a day away!"

# What You Whirl On

GREAT BIG MALGO saw them coming downstones, he did, he saw them tripping lightfoot to stir trouble with their easy mouths. "Did you ... yeah I ... he took ... saw him? ... put the purse in his hands, yeah ... said? ... naught ... naught? ... but listen ... Bedelia Cold ... said ... then let's ..." Great Big Malgo waited for them. Malgo shifted his bulk on the three-leg stool Gov Don give him, Gov Don give it him for his own cause Malgo was harum gardeen, cause Malgo was no threat to horii on account of he was born smoothed out — Malgo'd clubs for feet and bumps for dangle, nobbut piss slit and shit hole tween his legs. Malgo was found smoothed out on Barracks doorstep. Gov Don found Malgo and took him in. Gov Don was full of brain he was. Gov Don made Great Big Malgo harum gardeen, Protector of Horii; on his stool Great Big Malgo made sure no dreg harmed horii, on his stool Malgo tucked dove pie down his gullet chased with scrumpy scrumpy scrumpy was good. These lightskirt dregs coming downstones lugged a firkin tween them. They was laughing. Probble laughing at him. Scrumpy was good but lightskirts was bad. Malgo spread his vast thighs so to block path. "What you do here?" he roared. Great Big Malgo liked to roar. "Great Big Malgo!"

Their mouths oped and shut, pretty teeth but no bite to them. On and on. They give him the firkin to protect cause he was safest he was strongest. Spitter spitter on till Great Big Malgo's ears ached. He protected horii. These once was horii. So he protected. He said, ayuh, he'd test the scrumpy for them and, ayuh, let them within and, ayuh, let Gov Don know they gifted the perruker with a whole firkin of year-old scrumpy. He laughed up his sleeve as they passed through. *Course* he'd no fret Gov Don over one firkin of scrumpy. Great Big Malgo was a perfect vault for secrets. Lady Mandra told him so her own self, and Malgo run those words over and over his tongue till they come out right every time.

Mary Katharine and Mary Patricia would laughed at him in ordinary — as if Malgo could keep a firkin stoppled! — but they was too tight in the throat for it now. Getting in the perruker was no sail fore a fair wind. Out of course there was Great Big Malgo, who'd easy pull out the brains of any paul-pry dreg, but the stench of valerian in the depilation spag clamped the throat and locked the breath; it was the valerian as truly kept prying eyes out of the perruker. Mary Kath and Mary Pat staggered gainst each other there in the darkness framed of cracked smokeblack columns twined with ivy and grey clay webbed with grey fungal as the rotten sweet of mold and valerian clutched their gullets hard. They retched till there was nobbut yellow strings to bring up as they fumbled in their pockets for the flops of sphagnum moss to lay gainst their noses. A few breaths later they could stand on their legs. They cracked the portal door one eyewidth.

The perruker roof was held up by white stone trunks veined in rose and black, with gaps where columns fell long since, and laid higgledy-piggledy since they fell neath a thick crust of earth as had sifted over them, grain by grain. There was two portals to the entry hall of the perruker. Mary Pat squeezed Mary Kath's elbow, and they tightened the moss close over nose and mouth and strode in through the second portal.

At the first full stride, hot steamclouds gulfed them, damp with orris and sweet rush as stung clean the nose-bridge. Two steps inside the mist, every pore was open. The third stride brought them to the mist's thin edge; Mary Pat tugged Mary Kath back of a fallen column where a fungal mat gave cover. They raised their eyes careful to holes in the mat-mesh. Every hori in the perruker was bound wrist and ankle. Pressers held horii to the floorstones by vinegar poultices jammed tween their jaws so the waxers could work easy. Waxers brushed hot spag on flushed hori skin, and laid long cloths in the hot spag, and pushed the cloths in the spag till it cooled, when the waxers ripped the cooled stiff cloths away, stippled with short dark hairs. Few horii could keep from gasping then, half-drowning the murmur of the pluckers at the next station. Pluckers fondled goosepamped fresh-waxed horii flesh as they murmured *turn*, and *lift*, as they snabbed remnant hairs out the horii's bound flesh with their ragged yellow talons.

The horii stood arms raised and legs spread by ropes bound to column stumps, their backs cold gainst cold stone as the pluckers turned them in their ropes, as they murmured, *all to close your pores,* as their chapped hands pulled hori limbs this way and that as they susurrated *only feeling for last loose hairs* as they gave the horii a lick occasional and a tongue twirl to raise their nipples, followed by long slow laps at the tender neath their arms, then slow short overlapping tongue and palm and tongue strokes upslope their breasts to again the nipples, now well raised, the horii turning in their bonds and sighing, *aaah* from out the corners of their poultice gags, their shoulders straining back to push their breasts forward that the pluckers might suck them with full mouth, pressing them forward to mouths as come down on them with only softest tongue in small laps in circle on circle on circle as rippled out till *aaah* the horii sighed and *oooh* they groaned and arched their backs gainst the stones warmed with their straining but the pluckers did no would no ope their mouths they would no suck them in; they nobbut pulled short brushes from behind their ears and flicked the nipples harder till the horii's muscles was cords as they strained gainst the ropes, whereat the soft brushes stroked up and down in long straight lines from throathollow to a handspan below navel, no further, *aah,* the horii dripping now, each rolling her cheeks gainst a column to open herself to rub the smooth hot stone, as the pluckers laughed short as they grasped a long hair here and there tween their teeth and pulled, then put tongue tip to the plucked spot, holding the horii steady gainst the column by the tops of their thighs, licking in longer and longer strokes till again the horii sighed and writhed and their last lips opened. It was then a plucker crouched and spread the ankle ropes to open that hori to the wide. For the final.

For the final, one wielded the brush and one plucked the lips opened to it. *Hold still,* said the pluckers, till the last stray hair was teased out limp and drenched. Then, with a quick movement, brusher and plucker together turned their hori round in her ropes till her sweating front was pressed to the column. From nape to heels they brushed and plucked their hori who was by now so flushed the hairs slid from her skin.

Pullules, dregs of dregs, hustled through the steam in crouch to bring fresh spag to waxers, who threw the shaggy cold stiff cloths at their heads:

*Away! Gormless fackle, haul this away out of here* at when the pullules staggered off, their empty gullets rumbling.

Mary Pat tugged Mary Kath's sleeve. They scuttled round the hall to an alcove where three columns had fallen beam-end out, their tops leaning cross the hall to meet a scalloped ledge. They crouched by the alcove's mouth. Mary Pat looked over her shoulder to be sure the mist shrouded them entire, pulled aside a filthy cloth, and scuttled within. Mary Kath followed on the crouch down a narrow tunnel to a dark low space.

The space, lit by one dark lantern, was full of gasp and horii. Horii bucked gainst each other on the mucky dirt, their hands still bound behind them their mouths still half-gagged they rubbed each other, length to length and all entangled, straining their bound fingers in wriggle tween naked thighs licked and stroked past bearing; the least firm touch convulsed them; rubbing each other's legs, wrists, a big toe enough to set them quivering and still they sighed and shivered.

Mary Pat pulled from her beltpack two applewood lengths sanded smooth as a justborn's cheeks. She nudged one into Mary Kath's hands. They crawled mong the writhing bodies and whispered in the first-found ear; *woodcocks* whispered round the cavern as hori after hori arched gainst them begging soft *please*, Mary Pat and Mary Kath laid them down in the dirt, one by one, and slid the woodcocks up into them and pulled them back in long slow pulses till each hori raised up on her bound fists and thrust furious again and again and bit her tongue tween her teeth and arced high ... and laid soft in the soft dirt. The M'Cools dried each woodcock on their tunics and up again and took another.

When the last hori was done and her sweat had dried in rusty tracks on her, Mary Pat and Mary Kath sat up and brushed the hair away from their faces.

The perruker hall filled with scream. A pullule'd tipped hot spag onto a waxer's ungloved hand and all her fellow perrukers was cursing the poor creature in roar. Neath the ruckus, a hori spoke soft to the M'Cools.

"Many thanks. By the last nail in the last paw, we was near done for."

"Last Hunt was two weeks ago *and* some."

"They joy to set on us when we ache for it."

Daccordo chorus come up at that. "They do so joy!" "Absolute!"

"Still, who'd work the perruker?"

"Onliest thrill they got's setting on us."

The horii yawned and stretched.

"May rats die at your feet, you come timely," said a fresh voice in slur.

"*They* did no come," answered another, sharp.

"Shutter up, Galyse," drawled Chrysta. "I'm grateful if you are no."

"Grateful and then some," said Galyse. "You do get accustom to the stretch within," she said, and yawned.

"Interior *friction*."

"You get used to it."

"Get used to aught, even hanging."

"Look," Mary Pat said low — the pullules was weeping so loud in the perruker hall as to cover her voice — "one good turn deserves another. Am I right?" Chrysta assented for them all. "Look, we want to talk to you about the Galanty Hunt."

"The big one?"

"The one two se'ennights hence?"

"Shutter up," Galyse hissed. "We're no to speak of it. You want to be sent down here? Eat gruel twice daily, sleep on husks?"

Mary Kath spoke in low vibrato ratquell. What worked on rats should work on horii. "There's a big surprise coming at Galanty Hunt. You want to get it or give it? The choice is yours."

The perruker hall without was quiet now, nobbut huff, huff as the last batch of horii was fitted with their vinegar gags. The horii in the cavern had gone quieter still. Mary Pat judged they'd a few minutes left to speak in. "Galanty's your last hurrah. Richards figured how to disband the harum." She spoke over the resultant whoorl of *ssss* through the teeth. "Richards got a plan to do away with the lot of you from Galanty Hunt forward forevermore."

The whoorl of *ssss* grew stronger. "They'll no get rid of *horii*."

"Our Boys must have their hots thrice daily."

"Else they can no stride forth."

"Their corvisers'll rust right on em."

"They'd cramp up like ratjaws was on em."

Mary Kath closed her eyes. There they was, the fine silt drying on them, their forks leaking slow on the dirt. Cram the gullet and you lost the mind, Cider Mother said; one good clysm tween their legs and these blinking fools thought the sky a parasol held over their heads by a grateful hand. Every column will hold its place, every fish will leap to net, and the horii'd reign ever and a night till the cellulite come, when they'd go forth to receive the grateful plaudits of a grateful Charnholm. She repeated Mary Pat's words, "Richards got it figured to do away with horii altogether," she said. No reply. As well spit forward from a prow.

Mary Pat undid her ear from the doorcloth. "The perruker's giving this last batch their final. We got to slide from here while they're on that. Look. Richards got new tricks you never heard on up their sleeves. You want to hear about it, come talk to us tomorrow night. That's it and that's all. You'll be remembered as winter is come summer; no least trace sha' linger. We been talking with our Finn and Palan —"

"Aaah, Palan."

"The goldhead Boy."

"First rank, he is."

"Mmm, and the thighs on him."

"Hush yourselves!" Mary Kath spoke in ratquell, and they shushed. "Palan and Finn, yeah," she said. "They've a fine plan to fix the richards. Get our own back. We'd tell it you but we've no time now. Come down the blood shacks tomorrow noon, whether you're on the rags or no; down the sour crags we'll spiel you every last word. We would now an—"

"An we could," Mary Pat gathered her stained tunic round her. "But we can no. Come tomorrow noon," she hissed over her shoulder as she and Mary Kath parted the doorcloth — the lastbatch horii was squealing to split themselves now — and skirted the hall, scuttle freeze scuttle, and then gone. They slid out the portal with nary a dust mote to mark their passing.

"Great Big Malgo!" Malgo tipped the scrumpy at them. Lightskirts was gone. Malgo was guardeen. Scrumpy was good.

Mary Kath shook her head when they was out of his sight. "That was main better nor how we did up to Innsmort's. You've good foresight on you, Mary Pat. Springs to catch woodcocks when the blood burns." Her sister gave her the long look she'd been giving her for a lifetime. "We'll see how it goes down the sour crags tomorrow. I got to be up the compound for tiffin tomorrow by four," said Mary Pat, and they agreed to meet by tower end of the jetty at half before noon the next day. "That'll get us to the sour crags by noon, Mary Pat, on the bawdy prick of noon an you must have it." Mary Pat rolled her eyes. "Go off and rime, would tha? Wit so honed as yours could slice an ear off." "Known, honed, known," said Mary Kath, bowing as she trotted off backwards.

# Down the Sour Crags

PAST NORTH END OF CHARNHOLM JETTY, neath the lidless arches of the stone tower atop North Point, at the back of the Point's steep cliffs, a marsh of reed and cattail gasped its sulfur breaths, choked with flotsam of the neap tides, hemmed by sharp-point stones as jutted from the brackish water. Neath the cliff's overhang, their backs to the Point, stood a half-dozen shacks of driftwood and canvas, spalls stretching to the water from their feet. Mary Katharine and Mary Patricia come down the steep path at the neck of North Point toward the shacks. "Out of course," said Mary Kath.

Mary Pat shook her head. "Maybe so."

"Are they no dregs, same as we?" said Mary Kath.

"No. I mean, yeah. But no."

"Oh you're clear as Reap Day potable," said Mary Kath, pulling her twisted ankle from a crack in the path stones.

"They're dregs, right aright. But."

"But what? Are there no a dunnamany horii down the bloodshacks at this dentical moment? Did I no summon them? Think they come to tell us they've no wish to fix the richards?"

Mary Pat slid round a shattered step like a gull gliding. "Yeah. I mean, no. Well."

They threaded careful mong the spalls till their boots touched peat of the saltgrass meadow tween the crags and the cliffs. There all the female dregs as were on their time sat crossleg and quiet mong the rushes, some cramped, some drained, some alert after their monthly days of rest, joined by the perruker horii who lounged dry on reed pads; any horii past her first week could lounge anywheres, could lounge in a dungeon, which is in fact where Matron trained them. "Why on this knight do we recline?" she asked on the first day of dungeon training. "Because the gorry dungeon's carved full of them," Mary Kath answered in her time, which told Matron that this nova was going nowheres fast, but the dam Olympe was so fine a rope-dancer it'd seemed impossible her spawn could be so gawkish as she proved. Neither crossleg nor lounging females leapt up when the M'Cools reached the saltgrass meadow. Time ran slow down the sour crags. Mary Kath and Mary Pat unrolled reedmats and laid them on the marshgrass and sat on them till someone spoke.

"Fiddler crabs and kelp and no crumb else, by the first rat," said Galyse after a bit.

"No blue-eyes?" said Mary Pat.

"Could be. None of us thought to carry hook nor line," said Raincats, a fetchandcarry dreg they'd seen round since they was spawn. This was the first time they'd held speech with her. She was no on their cycle. Seemed her shackmates was the gap-tooth thickwaists round her, all nodding on her nod.

Mary Kath leaned back on her hands. The old monthly blood smell was highest now, dry season, low tide, sour on the back teeth mong grasses drizzled with clots of rusty rags; their rank scent lofted to the nostrils each time the peat exhaled its sulphur. The smell was naught when your skin was soaked in its own bloodsmell. Mary Pat was blathering on about how gorry nice it was to meet new faces here where they could let down their hair — yeah and all else — Mary Pat making sweet like she was wont. Mary Kath gave her half an ear. Fiddler crabs scuttled from their burrows in the tidal guts and waved their feelers at the bloodsmell, drawn to it as rats were, but the sour crags was too often flooded to draw rats. Whic was why they was there, think on. Mary Kath stirred a palm-sized pool by her knee till the water turned pale red. Mary Pat was telling them of Finn and Palan's schemes for the Galanty Hunt. Mary Kath bit her tongue. She'd sworn to let Mary Pat tell it thout no interruptions soever. Chrysta and Galyse, practiced show-naughts, was zamining their nails; Raincats and her fetchand-carry coven had their eyes turned in Mary Pat's general direction, so maybe their flat faces was listening; Naila was plaiting cattails, thoughtful; Dorween was pursing her lips; Bonaveel and Tarlish was fixed in adoring pose, which meant zackly naught, same look they'd deal a Hunt Captain or a beater or even Ambrose; any eyes could see they'd nobbut the trick of the gaze, no more; and some springy fish of a girl who sat on her heels plaiting long reed strips while Mary Pat sketched the raid on the Galanty Hunt. Mary Kath tucked her tongue back of her teeth's barrier. The horii was all, *Oh who'd rock the boat; I'd no* and the crossleg females was *No affair of mine soever* and Mary Pat carried on talking sense — taking over the potable works? now there was rare sense — so dregs could lift their eyes from time to time to what was round them, stead of slaving in change for potable.

When a couple novae dusted their asses at Mary Pat's face and strolled down shore, Mary Kath's lips come unglued of themselves and her legs uncoiled and she was hands on hips anathematizing them fore she knew it:

"Harlekkin sposhfrays! Grabchance twitchbottoms! Snapspined dampwit shortsight cut and come agains." That opened their ears for fair. "Draping lounging licking shitholes smiling. Richards could flay your nearest to bone while you was at it with a noily Hunt Boy and you'd nobbut pump the faster off the thrill of the new, you mold heart —"

"Oh give it a rest, M'Cool," drawled Galyse.

Mary Kath spoke even-keeled as she could. That was no so very even. "What life have you, Galyse? Or any hori? Bow scrape truckle all day *and all night for scraps and potable*," the fetchandcarry coven hummed *Potable* at her back, "by luck of the draw. You done naught to get what you got, yet you flaunt round like honest work reaps its rewards. *You done naught*," though *"Screech nobbut stirs the rats,"* said Goodwin in her ear. Mary Kath carried on regardless, *"naught soever* to get what you got." She steadied her voice. "The Galanty Hunt's the time you can do summat. Galanty's *the* Rat Hunt, Hunt of Hunts, when we dregs sha' hunt these rats down their holes and get their filters, their silks, their down, their silver. Who are they to keep such stuffs to their own selves? Hunt down the rats! the richards spur us. We sha' and all. Hunt them right down their holes we sha' hunt them. Catch the rats in their burrows, lounging on their downfill chairs, patting their fat bellies."

Mary Kath paced a small circle. "If you're in, speak now. If no, we sha' pick our way easy over the clinkers and we wish you the very best of gloamings." She sat down abrupt. Her eyes was all full of soggy tears. *"That's wet that is,"* James A would say, *"Stiff up your spine, Mary Katharine,"* he would said. Yet here she was, dripping away in front of a gaggle she'd harangued top to bottom.

"Good thing they made you rimer, Mary Katharine," said Naila, dry.

Chrysta and Galyse slapped palms to the old knockstone chant, "*Sour grapes all in your teeth / Sour grape juice on your lips / Do you want it? / Yes you do / Can you have it? / So you say / I want it no / The grapes are / The grapes are / The Grapes Are Sour.*" A few joined in till Chrysta, bored, plopped down on reeds again. "Sheeiminy cripes," she said. "Why should we help break up Galanty Hunt?"

"So you'd be free," said Mary Kath, weary plucking dust out her eye.

"Free? *Free?* Free like some hairy roundface, skin dry as ash," Galyse keeping her eyes, polite, off the crosslegs, "the kind as'll spread it for smith or haul dreg even. No technique soever. Yeah they may *come*, may spurt topfroth but what amachoor draws their last drop? Begging your pardon but you know it's true," this last to the crosslegs shifting on their reedpads.

Dorween nodded serious, "Yeah, cause does so much as a drop remain, it'd run round their systems till it clogs the heart."

All the horii nodded. The others looked at each other sidewise. "We never had one die on us," said Hevo, a dump twurf next to Raincats, her pudding face in pout.

"Well you maybe never got the quality we get," Bonaveel explained.

"Hunt Boys is picked for can they bear the strain," Tarlish agreed.

Hevo shook her head. "Males I been with haul daylight to dusk, same as me, and are they no strong?"

All the horii jumped in at this. "Hunt Boys got to leap." "Spear." "Lunge." "Get right up into the flames." "Face *down* the rats." "Steady drudge does no strain the heart like Hunt does."

Raincats and Hevo and the coven nodded amen. Mary Kath bit her lip. Old known fury come barrelling up her chest. Once force open their eyes, surely they'd come round and thankful too. "Tomfools!" she began.

Mary Pat spoke cross her, calm and quiet. "Look. I was hori and I was good."

There was some muttering but after all Mary Pat was picked by *five* Hunt Captains. The horii settled down. "Go on," said Chrysta.

"No female walking can match horii at drawing the last drops of jism and that's flat." Cheers. "Is that our all and only?" No cheers. Mary Pat looked straight tween two crags at a high stone wall drip with blood. She rubbed her eyes and went on. "When I left harum I was quiver as you are off being free. Think that does no please the richards? Hah! Soon as we think we got all that freedom on us is when they got you locked in place, sure as ratteeth grow."

A nova skritched her new-shorn skull and said, "I heard you was a fine hori, but maybe the air up Gov Don's compound has ate your liver. Think we horii exist to please the *richards*? We're here to fan Hunt Boy courage. Hunt Boys. Our only stay gainst the rats as bring death and disfigure. Hunt Boys brave rat-teeth and rat-leap, withstand bubonic splatter. We're here to honor Hunt Boys. Put heart in them. Was we to open our hearts to them or scauper off free, either, spears'd go lax in they hands." All the novae and many of the others echoed yeah and amen to that.

It was Chrysta, of all of them, who shook her head.

Chrysta ranged her feet-tops on her hip folds, straightened her back, and laid the backs of her hands on her knees. They all settled in for story. "You maybe think," said Chrysta, "I say this to stave off the cellulite shadow hanging close over my head. No. There's no better times than being hori. Best of the food and potable sufficient to *bathe* in —" Here, some gasped, haul dregs and novae as'd never heard on such stravagant waste. Chrysta plowed forward natheless, "but we're nobbut part of the show. Hunt Boys'd charge out there and shine for the crowds even an every one on us walked off North Point cliffs this dentical minute. Take the males as never make Novice, even." Nods. "They cockstand three-four times a day, whether mining or net-hauling out to sea where there's no female to be found, am I right?" Nods from all. Vigorous nods from the crosslegs. "They'll come on mud, down a knothole, in a pipe, am I right?" Universal shrugs of agreement. "So by the flaming rat what heart do we put in them? What flame do horii fan?" Confusion.

The incoming tide scuttled the fiddler crabs to their holes, rinsed blood and sulfur from the marsh, lapped thighs. The sembled nostrils widened at the fresh salt air.

At Chrysta's side, Galyse opened her arms to claim their eyes. Mary Kath started to speak; Mary Pat laid a hand on her wrist: "Best it come from them," she said low.

Galyse said, "I used to believe the pap you novae spout. True, horii satisfy Hunt Boys more nor any roundface could. I'm good as they come," cheers, "and I tell you we do no more nor that. Hunt Boys need no fanning nor honor; was we to give them our hearts they'd likely set them down somewheres and forget where they was next minute." Laughter. "We'd no *drain* them did we ope our hearts to them. It's us as'd get drained."

"You never let such words scape your teeth's barrier fore this," the shave-skull nova objected.

"Give my head over to Matron for washing? Never was *need* to say it. Why spit in the wind? What'd I get off it? What'd we get off this freedom?" Galyse folded herself and waited for the horii storm. Which rose, right enough.

"Freedom to eat roots."

"Drink scum- and saltwater."

"Sprout a fine thick pelt."

"Free to sleep on verminiferous husks."

"Free to haul and sweep for richards."

"As I do now," said Mary Pat. There was a short silence, then they broke out fresh.

"Stead of a daily swim in the scented pool, we'd scoop a few handfulls of harborwater on ourselves."

"Any time we'd a yen to drip kelp and scum."

"What is it, by the run rat's thin whiskers, you think you'll be doing when cellulite comes?" said Mary Kath, quiet as a street of shuttered windows. "What then?" There was a minute of quell, then the storm broke.

"So why rush on it. It'll happen when it does."

Mary Pat said, "It'll happen when it does."

"In the meantime, we—"

Mary Pat said, "Ayuh. In the meantime."

"We got picked for horii; we got lifted out for a few years and then it's straight back to it. Come on. Every dreg breathing knows that."

"What do you think'll come to you when Matron boots you?" Mary Kath said.

Darnelle stretched and yawned. "Sha' couple with a big rude Hunt Boy gone for scutman, likely," looking out the corners of her eyes to see if that stirred sufficient mischief.

"Scutman? You'd go with a scutman?" couple dozen voices screeched.

"Scutman's a dreg same as me," said Darnelle, sturdy. "Cept he's a cellarful of provender and potable. *And* a steady slave. *And* stands first with the richards when goods're doled." They did no look so convinced as might be. Darnelle tossed her head. "I should worry, I should care. My mam dravelled over four spawn after me, one with hands coming out of its shoulders and its twin that its ears was nobbut holes, and two as come out in buboes fore their first Seventh ... My spawn sha' drink potable, an they come, and good store of perry for my own gullet when they die. Free free free. Womb to tomb we dangle over-cliff. What's this freedom of yours cept freedom to fall? What's up comes down. How sha' you change that law?"

Those as was on their time got up here and went down shore. The splashing of them rinsing their forks in the rising tide mixed with the soughing reeds.

Mary Pat stood up. "Thank you all for returning the favor we done you in the perruker by coming cross the water to hear us out. Any of you want to join the raid gainst the Galanty Hunt, I'm up the promenade every gloaming."

"But –" said Mary Kath.

Mary Pat overtalked her. "As you say, Darnelle, there's every chance we'd drop and drown was we to let go. We're taking the chance we might swim. A deadeye who dassen open to this chance willna get another."

Naila roused up off her elbow. "Never took chance while you was hori, Mary Pat. You was best of trucklers till you went for parlogal. Why the change, cept it's now you can no pluck you a Hunt Boy off the bush?"

Mary Pat was sinking in peat as tide rose round her ankles. She let it. "Maybe it's sour grapes like you say. I tell you, the shape's clear once you're outside it. Once richards no longer use you for sport, you can no magine how light you step."

Into the considering silence, out of course Mary Kath spoke up. "Richards suck your juice to keep Hunt Boys in line," she said. "*That's* what drains the Boys, is the way richards got it set up. *The richards set up the Hunts like they are so to keep the dregs down.* Who'd ever say them nay? The Boys. You nor no one can enchant the Boys more nor their cocks do; it's their cocks as lift them, which the richards know full well. Have our Boys spunk enough to say no to richards? Negatory. And why? Cause they've horii as titillate and befuddle them, one, and scutmen to knock them sidewise an they step wrong, two. We dregs have number sufficient to take on the scut-men was the Boys clearhead, am I wrong? You're the only ones can make them so. You've power to alter the life of every dreg in Charnholm. How? By backing out of the setup. You only got to—"

Darnelle rose and wiped her damp hands down her robe. "Yeah. All we got to do is what you say stead of what Matron says. What we get off listening to Matron is clean and fed and all the flou we can wear. What do we get off you?"

"Fair point," said Mary Kath. She kept her voice steady as cliffstone. "Stead of kissass and stepfetchit after cellulite comes; stead of that, what? *I've no least notion.* I know it could be better; how could it be worse? The richards spent all those years in their shelter caves figuring the setup we got now, so going gainst the setup maun improve our lot, no?"

Mary Kath stood up at Mary Pat's nudge. She bowed a farewell. Mary Pat said, "We've sore necessity on us, else we'd stay. Up the promenade every gloaming," and waved farewell. She was many fathoms away and going strong fore Mary Kath caught up her wits and followed after.

Darnelle was a pace behind. "We know it well as the nose on your face, Mary Katharine M'Cool," she spat. "Get it out your head you're the only as knows which end's up in all Charnholm, hear? We sha' figure how to upend the Boys, see an we fail. Go long with your hightone rimer ways; set all the other dregs in their proper way to go; sit yourself in a high chair and a lonely one while we loll in rosewater thinking on you all lone with your crumble books and your scour-verse." Mary Kath walked straightback over the spalls away from this screer, though on it went and on, "All lone you'll be. Memry *that*, Rim'us Goosestep! Stuff *that* down your earholes and set it to sweet sweet lirks, hear? Do you hear? Rim'us Bimus big fat Himus! Was I a rat, I'd flee you certain —"

Other voices joined Darnelle's, now Mary Kath was in the tall reeds. "Just the smell off you'd do it!"

"Just one look on your hairs!"

"Just one blooger out your nose'd scutter them better nor any beater living!"

Their sweet faint voices pursued Mary Kath through the reeds and tween the crags and over the spalls and round the point till she come to the outskirt shacks of Charnholm, enshroud in dust born of dust born of ash, till she caught up Mary Pat on the broad path. "We'll take our ease till we go up the orchard tomorrow," said Mary Pat, and kept the air stirred with what foods they'd bring and what clothes they'd wear, till Mary Kath got her voice enough settled to answer clear. "Yeah," she said.

"None so deaf as they who can no hear," said Mary Pat with a strange smile on her.

"Do you know aught?" Mary Kath said.

Mary Pat nobbut smiled the more. "Could a wall drip in blood be anywise a glad sight?" she asked. When Mary Kath shook her head, "I thought it could no," said Mary Pat.

They walked a ways in silence. "You done well," Mary Kath said.

"Right aright," said Mary Pat.

They was well past age to hold hands but they walked close-gripped natheless.

# Tiffin in Great Hall

MARY PATRICIA COME HOTFOOT up the zigzag path to Treesa's compound at harbor end of South Point. Treesa — Thassy to her intmates — required all serving dregs to arrive at tiffin by third bell, which rang while Mary Pat was still scrabbling through fresh rockfall some twenty foot above the bankmen in a cloud of red dust. Red dust in her hair, her eyes, her pores, her clothes; red dust mingled with the rust brown of the bloodshacks as coated her tongue. Dry horii lips chittering gainst their dry teeth rang in her ears yet, *Oh Mary Pat, mayhap richards is killing off Hunt Boys with their close-in, but that nobbut strengthens our blood — did you no hear Gov Don last Reap Day?* dry horii lips shaping sing-song like Gov Don on the dais, *The flower of our young males sha' bloom the stronger when these weak weeds be plucked from round them*, their voices grainy tween her teeth. She spat out the sounds of them through salt-cracked lips. *Five six*, Mary Pat climbed faster, *thirty-one thirty-two*, she could no lose her slave now, *fifty-eight fifty-nine*, now when she'd her amanensis perch in Gov Don's compound, *ninety-six ninety-seven*, round the last curve to Treesa's watchshack.

Mary Pat lost more time while the shackman played he'd no least notion, no none, as she was wanted within. He sent a footman to Lady Mandra, which footman returned rapido with Gov Don's lady's demand that her amanensis be produced and forthwith, "So soon as you be presentable," said the hangface footman, while the shackman leered: "Could scrub you down with these hands, an you liked." Mary Pat tossed her copper hair; the lank tresses slapped her cheeks with the smell of blood and dust and marsh sulfur. No word scaping her teeth's barrier, she strode head high to the lady courtyard.

The sandstone bath trough in the lady courtyard was fresh with Treesa's own scent of rose and clove. Mary Pat dunked her crown three times till the water turned rust-color, and stood, rust rings at her knees, to wring her hair in her two hands. One of Treesa's hand dregs, Mally, come up on the double hustle with a clean strigil and a mouthfull of cluck over the water's state. "No use to any now," Mally said as she strigiled Mary Pat's curves. When she was done, Mary Pat stepped out the trough and said, "Do you pour it on Thassy's *flower beds*. Save her using potable like she mostly does," which shut Mally's ryehole for her, but good.

Mary Pat bound her hair in a clean cloth. She slid the grey amanensis robe out of her tumpsack and over her head, clasped the cestus round her hips, laid a hand on the lumps in its placket formed by pad and stilo, and scurried off to the portal, still tucking hooks into eyes. When she come in sight of the trumpery krewe standing legspread, she slowed to saunter. Their brass horns dangled from their hands, though course they'd no blow accola for a mere dreg, let alone ope the great studded doors they flanked. Still, Mary Pat could never resist teasing them. Once she got a young one to play the first *trillalil* fore he saw she was nobbut a dreg. This time, no. A footman in linsey-woolsey livery tapped his clog on the stones by a side entry; Mary Pat followed his onion smell up the stairs out into the airy vast of Treesa's Great Hall.

The tallest ship in Charnholm could sailed into the Hall thout stepping its mast. There was stars set in its dark blue ceiling like those over the harbor on winter nights. Mary Pat walked click clack over tesserate floors of stone chips laid in fans, click clack she walked over chips of gryphons leaping at a spikeman, click clack over a band of light-draped females laying red fruits in a withy basket in a bright green grove, click clack over ships coming in to harbor laden to the scuppers with cask and sack and chest and such, the topman blowing a trump as long as he.

Click clack cross the tesserae to the prow of all this lofty, where the tiffin ladies gathered round a low brazier, their wide skirts circling their pouffes. Mint steamed from the kettle on the coals; sugar spewed from the mouths of the ladies:

Oh it's definitely art. / One does the best one can. / Remarkable workmanship, considering. / Not what you'd see back in the days gone. / Well what is. / Treesa says Janno oversaw each step. / No dreg unaided could have essayed it. / Nary a one, my dear Thassy. Nary a one.

The last speaker, Lady Mandra, leaned back from Treesa's eyes and tapped her cheroot's long ash to the tesserate floor. She raised her long lashes to acknowledge Mary Pat: "Ah, Mayry Patriza. My tardy amanuensis."

Mary Pat ducked her head. She'd be blooded an she did more. Chantal's amanensis drubbed her nose in the dust did her lady vouchsafe her a word stead of a finger snap — blow that! "There was fresh rockfall on the path, my lady." She'd give her a 'my lady,' so much and no more. "It hindered my progress." Roll that one up and smoke it.

"Hindered your progress, Mayry? D'you hear, ladies? Proper training, a systematic application of reward and punishment, and some of these dregs can become quite useful. Mayry Patriza, here, adds literation to her excellent memory, removing much of that burden from my own shoulders," shrugging them in all their salt whiteness near out from her bodice.

"Freeing you to continue your mission of uplift," said Mary Pat, a quick slant of her eyes at Lady Mandra's droopy breasts.

Lady Mandra, no least disconcert, adjusted her chest bands. "As you say, uplift. So kind of you to remind me. But do be seated. You have caught us mid-discussion of Thassy's newest addition to her charming collection of artwork." A nod to their hostess, who raised her lens hoop by its jewel handle to her eye, and peered at this dreg who was to be seated among them. "What are your impressions of the work, Mayry Patriza?"

In the west bay of the room was a copper-gold fountain, a scallop edged with trees, the branches flexish as a dancer's limbs. Each copper leaf was crenellate in gold, the trunks stippled gold and copper that seeming danced neath the play of water in a mirrored pool on which floated pink and gold water-lilies copied from a crumble book open on a rack nearby. Mary Pat stepped closer to compare the one to the other. At center of the ring of dancing trees, a bronze boulder. On the boulder sat a copper justborn, its round legs upthrust in game, flinging water from its fingertips. Its left index finger pointed to a flock of gold ibis who sat wingspread and widebeak on the lowest branches. Pale Nora matched this one line for line when she'd four months of life, when all of them snugged their belts a notch for her till her omphal stuck out and her chin doubled. The copper justborn could been pale Nora, whose skin was copper, smooth as melted spag. Mary Pat turned round, her mouth gape, eyes wide — Lady Mandra bent one finger to the charlerie mong the ladies:

*It was* Charnholm *smiths? / No they could never / such detail to the face, a body'd think it could speak / had they* painted *the skin on the babe? or dipped? and was that* potable?

"Thrilled you like it," said Treesa, the jewelled handle wafting past her chin. "Our coulees brought us the centerpiece. They'd some notion that we should give it a proper burning." She laughed. Her laugh was a series of coos and trills, a dream dove flutting mong treetops. She patted the corners of her dark red lips with a silk handker. She pinced a cup of tea tween two long nails, trained in curve on curve by cord webs every night. She lifted her cup in salute. "Darling Janno was all for tossing it in Dead Horse Moraine but I saw its possibilities on the instant. 'This is *art*,' I told him. With a little taxidermy — isn't the smile *marvellous?* — and a coating … well. *For*tunately, we've excellent smiths who carried out my orders." Treesa's thin lips spread in the smile that makes least wrinkle. "They coated the thing in some *marvellous* — isn't it marvellous? — skin. Seamless, whatever the material, and the shine to it! Mmmm." She sipped her plum-color drink and smacked her new-darked lips. "There was a delay when some fools in their midst swore up one side and down the other they heard it wailing as its new skin set. Janno had to sit them down and explain that wailing was simply impossible, but no, they *claimed* they were too shaken to continue." She smoothed one eyebrow with a knuckle. "Of course they were simply trying it on. I mean, this is *art*. One simply can't judge it by outmoded standards."

"Excellent composition," said Mary Pat, and Lady Mandra gave her a small nod as she folded herself inside her grey amanensis robe by her pouffe.

"How did you get round them, Thassy?" asked Lady Mandra, a stilling hand on Mary Pat's knee, like she laid it there in accident.

"Doubled their wage. *That* set their principles to rest." Treesa laughed again.

"No question it's a lovely thing," said Chantal from her lounge of rose and sage. "The expression on its face." She waved a languid hand at the fountain. Her talons were not quite as long as Treesa's, but they grew round seed pearls. Chantal one time told Lady Mandra, while Mary Pat was ragging dust off the mantel, "You run the nubs up and down the vein, you know, the blue vein beneath. Yes. They'll go on their *knees* for it."

Chantal chuntered on about the workmanship while Mary Pat sat froze neath Lady Mandra's long fingers. *They heard it wailing. Some notion that we should give it a proper burning.* Chantal leaned back gainst her herb pillows. *They coated the thing in some marvellous.* Mary Pat swallowed and swallowed again. Chantal waved her seedpearl talons. Treesa waved her spirals. Their movements stirred the ratgland they dabbed on pulse points. Mary Pat swallowed hard.

How was she to keep it down. Near this strosity of a fountain, her bile rose at the curdled stench of the justborn's breath now prisoned in some airproof skin. She kept it down, though. She kept it down. While the ladies went on over the workmanship, she swallowed it down.

The tiffin ladies circled the thing, touched its copper skin with their free hands, sipped their drinks, pressed their cheeks to its shrunk cock. Mary Pat kept it down. They vied in mewing the justborn wails the smiths claimed they heard. Out of course they made hash of their mimicry. Few richards heard such cries, and they seldom. Richards was too weak to kindle since the Burning. A pity. Mary Pat knew she ought pity them, knew it clear as her feet knew her doorstone. Still. When they chortled and mewed, she snapped. She stood up, twitched her skint grey robe away from her legs —

Lady Mandra said, "Do you need the fluvia, Mayry Patriza," all level in the eye.

Mary Pat looked at the older woman, whose skin hung rucked at wrist and neck, whose chin slumped mong her swole chins, whose lobes sagged off her ears, creases round her nose, creases where her cheeks drooped. Mary Pat twitched her grey robe and said ... naught. She could no walk away from her slave as Lady Mandra's amanensis. Walk from a perch inside richard compounds with Galanty Hunt so close? No. Taste she never so much the withered copper casing of the justborn in the fountain, no. She would, by the first rat as ever was she would, she'd tell Finn soon as she saw him: she would be eyes and ears inside the compounds; so far as in her lay, she'd pull the richards from their burrows by their stinking necks while they shat themselves green in squeaking terror, may the rat bite with long rust teeth did she fail. "What's that, milady? The fluvia? Dropped my stilo, is all." She showed it in her fist. Lady Mandra looked at her narrow, but two heartbeats later she was back gazing on the new fountain tween satisfied looks at her own fingernails painted in moonphase, a waggle of her hand flicking from new moon, to gibbous, to full moon.

While this revolt rampaged in Mary Pat's gullet, the sun continued its placid fall down the sky and the tiffin ladies strolled mong the pouffes, chat crawling on them like so many fleas. Lady Mandra waggled a hand — waxing gibbous, waning gibbous — at Mary Pat, who swallowed again and set stilo to notepad. The tiffin ladies was readying for Galanty Hunt.

"Ross insists we see this one through Gov Don's viewscope. He's spent weeks with that new dreg, that Palan, who's installing it. Just an excuse to tinker. Ross says we'll see the whole hunt from the comfort of a plush settee. I said, what's the point of that?"

"Just so. Give me my cushion, my flask, a good view from bleachers —"

"You've *always* a good view, Gaby; your husband's coulees put *up* the bleachers."

"Notwithstanding. You know. There can be accidents when one has to sit where one can." She gave a sharp look at Cinna, who'd sat "By accident, as I live" in the seats clear marked for Gaby two Hunts past. "Yes, Ross was insistent that we see it through the viewscope, so my new gown hangs on its rack till I don't know when."

"Can you not wear it to the Hunt Breakfast?" asked Lady Mandra, unfurling a carmine fan.

"I *could*, I suppose, but it simply breaks the Hunt Day to smithereens. After the Hunt we *always* go down the cave to doff our bloody muddy garb and *that's* when ... well, when Ross takes advantage of the moment." The ladies tittuped. Mary Pat held her stilo so tight it creaked. Gaby sat back, a smile tugging her lip corners for a bit till she remembered what made wrinkles and reposed her features.

Treesa sat apart from her guests on a quilted jonquil pouffe, backed by her two flipper-handed footmen, their thumbs level with their nipples.

Her head leaned gainst their thighs. "That's when he enters your right little tight little world, is it?" she offered, and relaxed into two livery codpieces. The two footmen, Brock and Doole, stood still for it. Her massy hair was spiked to her crown with long pointed sticks as'd spear their sensitives was they to move.

"Oh Thassy!" said Chantal, and Mary Pat's stilo creaked louder. "How *else* does one occupy the time between Hunt and Hunt Breakfast?"

Treesa stretched her neck back and fro. The two footmen sucked themselves in. "Janno and I analyze the Hunt. We parse it in greatest detail." There was silence and lookaway in Great Hall. "Janno is passionate about spikemen, you know. The new shafts are all his design." The silence deepened. Kettles tipped into cups. "Often he brings the most expert Boys over for a private demonstration." Treesa looked out of window, the footmen turning as her head turned.

"Proper shaft design is most important," Lady Mandra agreed. "I know Donal has every confidence in Janno's judgment. Now," replacing her cup on its saucer, selecting an iced cake from a passing tray, "who else plans to use the new view-scope? Shall we have any among us to fill the bleachers?"

Every male on South Point had seeming laid it down that, this time at least, their females company them to watch the Galanty through Palan's new scope.

"You know how they are," Larga shrugged, raising her nipples to her neckline, so. "Must try out their new."

"Of course," said Lady Mandra, and flicked a crumb from her lower lip. "Then we'll focus on the Hunt Breakfast. We are, all, still planning to attend that? Mmm?"

Of course. What would they wear? They was, straight, nipple-deep in ruche and flounce, gore and bias. "My diligent amanuensis has her work cut out for her," said Lady Mandra, waggling two fingers — full moon, waning gibbous — at Mary Pat scribbling like fury.

Mary Pat watched the tiffin ladies as she took down their words. The vomit was well down in her. She watched Treesa most. The woman rolled her head gentle back and fro gainst her footmen's codpieces till they stiffed up. Brock and Doole was beaters fore they was turned out on the wide world; Mary Pat danced at their third Seventh a month fore she went for hori. They'd no choice but to stiffen, poor slaves; their cocks rose at pouches, keyholes, cups, caves, let alone this slow side to side gainst the thin codpieces Treesa dressed them in. The ladies sketched their newest decolletage in the air while that massy bronze swept up and down, Treesa patting a little yawn like she was nobbut stretching a tired neck, Brock and Doole rising on their toes, their mouths falling open, their nipples stiffing clear on their bare chests. Treesa leaned lazy and pulled slow the spikes that bound her hair, back of her hand brushing the footmen where they lived. The spikes dropped to the floor tween a tesserate lion's white tesserate teeth. Treesa laid her head full back and rolled it in wider circles, wider, soft and easy. Sweat glowed on the bare chests and their breaths came quick, but what other slave could they get an they flouted Treesa? Sitations was no so thick on the ground for the flipper-handed. Brock and Doole was helpless rigid, the soft mass teasing them in slow ovals now. Treesa yawned again and stretched her arms up over her head, her hands falling pat on their cocks. She stroked up and down with her open palms, they swinging to keep her head on their hips, their cocks juddering neath her long slow fingers, drops oozing from their tips. Treesa's fingers kneaded light. Brock and Doole's eyes was gone to nobbut slits. Their chests heaved. Treesa's palms pressed up, circled each cocktip, stroked up, and down, in circles, softer, harder, the cocks dark purple at their tips, pulsing ... Lady Mandra said, "And what do you plan to wear, Thassy?" at which Treesa's hands glided forward to sketch the simple bias cut with jagged scallop hem that Treesa's dresser had fashioned.

Brock and Doole stood soldier back of Treesa as she gestured, only their knees on the least tremble. "Quit fidgeting, you two," said Treesa over her shoulder. The tremble left their knees slow and they was stone again cept their eyes twitched again and again, a tic that stilled slow as a landed fish drowning in air.

Mary Pat and Lena, Chantal's amanensis, noted tremble and twitch and their die-down. Doubtless the tiffin ladies noted it as as well, but it lacked novelty; their eyes followed Treesa's sketching hands. Brock and Doole's mitts being only a foot past their shoulders, they could no stroke themselves quiet till they was off duty when each could favor the other. The ladies granted them the occasional flick of an eye, same as they'd watch a dropped coulee, flush with heatstroke, to judge how long the palanquin might be delayed.

"Good sunfall tonight," said Larga, idle.

"The sun spreads its gold and crimson fans over the coupling of firmament and wave," said Deirdre. The tiffin ladies smirked back of their fans. Deirdre was their youngest, their sport; the only born since they went down the shelter caves. Her aunt Mandra took her on when her mam Clare withered and dried to dust blown off the palm. Deirdre come up thin, flexish, dry-eyed, among olders who taught her to read and stuck her in corners with some handy book while they went about their dozy lives. Small wonder, the tiffin ladies whispered, that the girl was strange, all times blithering of light and such.

Mary Pat and Lena wrote down Deirdre's words. After, Mary Pat rolled her eyes at Lena, a gorky dreg made of long leg and arm with a tiny head popped on her neck, like her maker reached down the wrong size and stuck it on anyhow in the press of business. Lena gave her a small muddy smile. The ladies was still gogging the sunfall. Lena turned her pad so Mary Pat could read: *eve star*. Mary Pat raised a brow. Lena twitched her pinky floorward. Mary Pat closed her eyes for a breath.

"What's all this?" said Chantal. "Thassy, the drink's gone cool." Treesa shook her ankle bells for a serving dreg. Chantal kept her nose to the scent, going so far as to lean close to her amanensis. "What's this, what's this?" she said, in rare animate, "Helena? Have you two secrets?"

"Got a bit low in my feelings, milady, seeing the dark come on," said Lena. "Gloomy, like. Lucky I am you taught me writing so's I could show that to another thout disturb in you." Chantal nodded, satisfied.

Mary Pat could nobbut admire.

Treesa's dregs lit spag in sconces round the walls to push the dark away, their spag-lit hands turning the copper and gold of the fountain. A few cakes staled on the trays. Treesa lofted the full kettle, "Stirrup cup!" she announced. The tiffin ladies downed their potions mid pools of light as widened with every sconce lit.

The fountain gleamed in the new light. The potable splashed from the babe's outflung hands, rivvled down the leaves, and rose, to vanish as mist. The strosity's smile was wide and glad as sail entering harbor.

"Night, and the cares of day are doffed," said Deirdre.

⌒

Lena and Mary Pat was sent down to rouse their ladies' coulees. They walked down stairs head high, nodded to the side door footman, and strolled cross the courtyard to the gateshack, where the shackman patted down their every inch.

Once they was clear of him and the compound they stopped at the viewing platform. The quarter-moon lay low on its back overharbor. A few spag lights guttered below in Charnholm, most dregs having turned in and shuttered up.

"Gessel's working late," said Lena.

"You did great on Chantal."

"Ah, well, that one swallows what she's served."

"You've the trick of it, certain."

Lena nodded. "Lady Mandra's more a handful, no?"

"She is that."

They two stood on the dusty platform in friendly quiet, the flush lush laughs of night-time richards muffled by spearthick walls. They spoke of small matters: of the moon on the water, of how long a smith could linger at Gessel's shop, of the scents the wind brought. They smelled each other.

The evening star was dimming when Lena vanished into Chantal's compound. Mary Pat made west for Gov Don's stone walls, bluewhite at that hour, the scutmen in their towers nobbut lifting a slumbrous hand as she passed. She lay on her pallet in her closet neath the roof, revolving the day.

Lena said she was Deirdre's nurse from birth to past her second Seventh. They'd moved from Gov Don's compound to give Lady Mandra more room for her twirling. No gainsaying, a dreg like Lena, one who knew the compounds inside outside, would surely be a staunch help come the Galanty.

An they could trust her.

Could they trust her? Who could she ask when asking, of its own, stirred talk? She'd put it to Finn, Mary Kath, and Palan on the coming night, up the apple orchard.

The moon was falling fast. Mary Pat rolled to her left side and laid her face on the inside of her elbow. One of them swore that piece of her was soft as her cunt. Nash? Bonner? Martin? Whatever the name, he begged her rub him with that piece of her. Mary Pat slid a finger up inside till she brought come, rolled to her right side, yawned. She sucked come off her fingers; anodyne for many ills said Matron; the door to sleep.

Cider Mother held the four-month in its copper skin to her thin breast. The four-month flung lye from its upthrust hands, and smiled wide and glad as Chantal stroked her seedpearls down the blue veins of James A's cock while Treesa weeded maggots off its copper skull and popped them in her mouth. The floorboards dropped out from under and they sank. Waves filled James A's mouth. Mary Pat dared no scream lest the waters fill her own mouth and stood helpless by as James A sank down to shelter cave. All the mouths opened then and soughed, whished, sang, dried to salt on her tongue.

# Up the Orchard III

THE QUARTER MOON HAD GONE FROM GOLD TO SILVER by time Cider Mother joined them up the orchard. "Scutmen is lackbrain foolguts," she announced herself as she distangled brambles from her tunic. "How full of briers is this work world!"

Fergus, crouched in the thorny hedge, wrapped in spagcloth and tarponesse, was proof gainst berry thorns. Well, guard one portal with all your might, you may be pierced through another; Fergus had no shield on his affection. Nor ever needed one fore this. He was by her entry rapt: *Oh she do teach the torches to burn / Beauty too rich for us or earth, dear;* oh silvered figure aswim mong leafhung trees, lift up lift up your red ripe fruits for me. She spoke. *Oh speak gain, bright ange, for thou art glorus to this being o my head,* whispered Fergus.

"I've but so much clout in Charnholm," said Cider Mother, extracting a last blackberry cluster, "enough to ward off a single spy, but battalions? Think scutmen blind? All these years they been turning the blind eye till this night when they was *bliged* to notice the passel of you thoughtless sprats stompling up the orchard path. Forced to see it, they was."

Fergus's heart slammed his ribs. *Course* they was bliged to notice this woman. She scunned through the clearing with all sail set; her barge burned on the water; her eyes gold mid the darkness; her hips a harbor most desirable. There was others round the fiery furnace — stones, mischief on a stick, a tall creakfinger whose eyes looked out from twin caves, an invisible longbeak whose invisible hands pressed gainst his invisible ears to still an inaudible voice — mong all these shadows, oh how she gleamed. Her gold eyes gleamed and silver gleamed in her hair and her palms shone at her sides. Fergus dipped up another sniff. I have you my beauty, all in a closefold frame, your hairs of flame, your skin of hammered copper, *in moving how press and admirable.* Her lips parted once again in speech.

"Since fore you was born, scutmen verted their eyes from the orchard, all for the skill in these hands, and now you lot might as well lit bonfires saying, 'Here we are! Come and take us!' "

The coals shone full on her face. Fergus fell back mong the thorns. *Oh blessed blessed night.* The moon silvered the fruit-tree tops. He closed his eyes gainst so much lovely. In sleep, he drifted off to the *Mam Can Cook*, made beautus by this gold-eye figure at the helm as gleamed and proffered fine old perry. He tucked his nose down her bosom and dreamed off.

The passel round the brazier was quiet. A few feet shuffed in the cushy grasses. Palan Fergusson hung his head and watched the moon move cross the blades tween his feet. Once Fergus was snoring regular, Palan spoke in usual voice: "Thunder might wake him now. Naught else." Mary Patricia motioned the two guests out of the thorny hedge.

Chrysta settled by the brazier in one supple twist. Raincats angled gawky aside her. Their ambergris mingled with the sour of the coals, and snoring Fergus's tarponesse stench, and the white clay sweat of the smiths. Finn cleared his throat. "So. Let's keep off the perry till we've done meeting. Here's what it is: Every richard plans to be down Gov Don's shelter cave for Galanty Hunt. That's why the Boys is doing so much close-in now. For practice, like. Blay Innsmort's no the first to die off the close-in. There's been a dunnamany Boys gone over harbor to the white barge of late."

"Since Palan brought in the fernal viewtubes!" shouted Innsmort.

Palan stirred, and Finn stroked the air tween them. "It's no Palan as ordered Ambrose to thrill up the Hunts. It's no Palan as set the Boys to all this close-in with no dirk nor poniard training soever. It's no Palan as thinks us dregs is nobbut fodder for richard sport."

Quix stirred and spoke for the first time: "That's so." Drosh nodded slow agreement. After a few nods, Innsmort joined them to the extent of a headjerk.

Finn closed one eye halfway at Quix and continued: "Think on, the richards sha' all be in a one place for Galanty Hunt."

There was silence while they thought on that, into which silence Mary Katharine spoke cold as seafloor: "We've years of training in killing rats in their nests," she said.

Silence widened in the wake of her speech till the whole semblage come up boiling like August cod, snapping their jaws for a gasp of air. They spoke atop each other:

"Lay them head to toe in their own blood!"

"Do it slow!"

"Depilate them!"

"Give them the full perruker!"

"Then put cold steel down them."

This last from Drosh's slow lips. Silence dropped on them again. Cider Mother laid a few handfulls of dry grass on the brazier. "There's death enough and to spare without us adding to it," she said.

"My hands is too frail to hold all that blood," said August Inkwhistle.

Finn stood up. Smoke billowed round him; his lashes cast shadows gainst his lids. "Us dregs, we're landed fish, for fair. So then, what's the hook through our lips?" A few said it was scutmen. Palan grunted *hummmp* at top of his throat, and Finn gestured him quiet. "Scutmen are but shadows in Galanty Show. What's back of the screen?"

"Richards," said Cider Mother and Drosh, on one beat.

"They've potable running out their ears," said Quix.

"Potable," sighed Chrysta. "There's the hook we dangle on."

The pause was shorter than Mary Pat or Mary Kath expected. A hori spoke good sense and none but they marvelled long at it. Which was by itself a kind of marvel.

"An we'd potable enough, we'd have time and strength enough to gather fish and rye and kelp enough. Was we no slaving all hours to get potable off the richards," said Mary Kath. She kept her backteeth slammed, after, lest she break into ratquell. That might set their feet on the path, yet they'd wake by and by from it, and so lose the name of action.

Innsmort muttered, "Lot of slum talked of potable. My dap lived a year past his seventh Seventh, and *he* drunk whatever was put before him."

Now, had she spoke in ratquell, he'd never walked off-path.

"What do you drink?" said Raincats.

"Hom, hum, now, aaah," Innsmort havered.

Mary Kath followed up quick, despite she was stunned. Raincats! Who'd thought a haul dreg could — "Potable?" said Mary Kath.

"Well, hom, hum, a certain amount."

"An you drunk aught else, cepting my brew, since you come off your mam's dugs, I'll fill your courtyard with perry breast-high," Cider Mother come in for the kill. Innsmort maundered how his small courtyard could no, any road, which — "Right aright," said Cider Mother.

Bedelia Coldhand plaited up the loose threads. "There was some few, before, as drank pools and pissoirs, and they come through. They was few, though. Powerful few. The most of us, now, we're made from potable. Right aright, an potable's the hook through our lips, how sha' we unhook?"

"Raid the potable works and seize their infernal machinations!" said Raincats.

Mary Kath pinched the soft skin at her armcrook. She did no dream; she was waking and haul dregs was talking large. She looked round in case Fergus walked from the berry hedge with crumble books made whole. But the night had more in its purse.

Mary Pat spoke slow, looking past and through them. "Dregs sha' make their own potable, and none sha' truckle to any richard, once the babe is pulled from the wall."

"Now Mary Patricia," said Palan.

"Palan and I been up the annex, Mary Pat; we walked round, knocked, oped our ears wide, and there's no justborn wailing," said Finn.

"Likely a trick of the wind with those new-laid stones," said Mary Kath.

Mary Pat said, "You —" but they three looked at her steady; wiped their eyes in big sweeps like the smoke was thick in them. Mary Pat leaned back and swept her own eyes gainst the smoke. She said, "You do well to pull me up. Since I been parlogal, I get fancies in my mind, like."

"Trick of the wind, then?" said Mary Kath.

"Trick of the wind," agreed Mary Pat.

"Right aright," said Finn. "So the richards have us firm hooked with potable. We can die slow, same as we been doing, or we can raid the potable works and make our own potable from that day forward."

A curious gasp comes from dead lungs when pressed. A similar curious gasp comes from living lungs when they first throw off an old pressure. Such a gasp the semblage now gave.

Mary Kath said, "As the Galanty Hunt nears Gov Don's shelter cave, the richards'll crowd round the viewscope to watch the derring-do. The close-in'll lure them. While they're rapt, we here sha' nip up to the works, load the machinations on our backs, and haul them downhill."

There was silence. "When you said you'd drop it on them easy, this was what you meant?" said Mary Pat in her sister's ear.

The semblage dropped their eyes. "Hashel who romped me lovely, he's gone to the white barge off the close-in," said Raincats to her knees. "They'd slay every last supernumry, playful, an we let them," said August Inkwhistle, cracking his long dry fingers. "They'll slay the strongest and leave us naught to breed with," said Chrysta to her breasts. Mary Pat said naught.

Mary Kath was calm as August noon now she was talking action. "I'll lead rimers to the viewports. When I say the richards want us there, Bran and Goodwin'll quimple up and urge us on fastest. Our cloaks'll block their eyes; Finn'll lead the beaters in racket round us to drown the heeltaps of those going through to potable works. The onliest is, how sha' they get through those gates? They're no wattle and cord, the works gates, but solid stuff. From the scrapers, mayhap."

Palan stood, the way they could all get their eyes on him. His wrists and ankles was grown out of his sleeves, his flesh chasing his bones as they grew. "I was scouting round with Gov Don. Making certain the viewtube showed the Galanty whole and clear, ah. Those gates are thick, but each depends from two pivots only. Pair of smiths can lift and topple one." He sat down again quick as a stool folds gainst a wall.

Drosh scratched his wiry beard. "Sure and we can lift them off, an it's only the two points. But how's it so much of this plan lays on the shoulders of Palan, son of Fergus?" Quix and Innsmort grunted, mayhap in agreement, or uncertainty, or on account of they drunk their perry too quick.

Whatever the cause, Finn rose to Palan's defense, Mary Kath and Mary Pat come in chorus behind, and the old dregs added their portion till the smiths allowed as yes, true enough, howsoever, yet, what about —.

Daniel crouched and bit his fingers, his back flat gainst his Seventh-day apple tree. When a crowd surrounded him, the voice pierced his ears in jaggy shards, a word from one mouth, a phrase from another, and behind it all a far keening from a pinched throat, *Ship's hit a trough and great jaws open in it*, the voice so clear he could drawn its every crest and curl. Few spoke on ship once they learned their duties. On ship, the voice was nobbut wind in the shrouds, line rattling through pulleys, nets running out, fish flopping in last gasp. On land, mong seagrass mats of dregs, the shrouds flapped, the voice rose. Dan dug his shoulders deeper gainst the tree. That quieted the voice some.

Round the brazier, Finn said, "So we can raid the potable or let time pass while richards kill us off." He spread his palms wide. "I'm for the raid."

Drosh lumbered to his feet, his brows a roof over his nose. "Will they no slay us as we grab the potable works? Scutmen have stuck dregs till the life run out of them for less. What should stay their hands?"

Finn said, "An they know of it, they would. Was any of us to inform richards of this plan, surely, scutmen'd lay their pikes in our hearts." he said, and sat straightback in his place.

Mary Kath launched on reasons why richards could no would no spy them. First off, cause they'd be down cave. Dregs would take the potable works so quiet, no teacup'd rattle in its saucer. The raid was needful, be the risk no larger nor it were, to keep the lively spawn from the bent limbs and crooked joints as was now an old dreg's portion. More, to keep every neck out from neath the richard yoke. She spoke well and overlong. By time she was done, Chrysta was filing her nails; the smiths was shaking sand out their ears; the moon had climbed the sky and rolled lazy on its back.

Quix shook his head like to drive off flies. "It was asked before and answered, but how's it certain we need potable? We lived a dunnamany years with never no potable till the richards come up with it," rattling clinkers in his pockets. "Can we no drink down whatever we find? Are we no customed?"

Innsmort was quick to sail fore any strong wind. "Gov Don says we sha' grow weak as richards, did we come customary to potable and other delicati." He looked round to make sure his jib was full of breeze.

Mary Kath started in fury, and stopped, and spoke in best ratquell. "So says Gov Don. For love of dregs, think you? Richards want us content with our lot. They say so with every breath they spare us. Who'd turn their wheels, dig their mines, haul their fish and salt them; who'd stitch their days together cepting dregs? Turn it on its head, Innsmort. Would you be weak as a richard? raising your hand for dregs to come here, go there, while you sat cush on your divan?"

Innsmort considered. "I take no pleasure in sitting round, Mary Katharine."

Cider Mother spoke quiet, the coallight turning her white hairs burnt orange. The berry hedge gave out a pale snore. She spoke the softer: "None do. Potable makes life. Do you no want all of that you can have?"

Quix nudged the considering Innsmort in the ribs, "Out of course. Who'd no?"

"Any on us excepting your Innsmort here," said Mary Kath. "Which is why we sha' raid the potable works six days hence," holding up three fingers wide.

"Hence?" said Mary Pat.

"Six days from this day," said Mary Kath showing her three outspread fingers to the sembled eyes.

"Hence," Mary Pat snorted. "Rimer-bound is what you are." Mary Kath shrugged. Mary Pat said, "Say we set on the richards with pikes spears daggers poniards all. What's our good end? Richards use dregs for their own ends, true enough. There's the sharp on the knife. Now, an we walk their road, sha' we come to some other end? Sha' we no become soft cruel richards our own selves?"

Mary Kath said, "A knife lances pus from a boil, a knife pulls life from a heart. Is knife in common knife the same? It's all in how you use it. You go on and hear the future whisper down your shelly ear; as for me I'm fixed in the present where I'm cold at night and hungry by day, less I want to swallow whitescar one-eye greenflesh blister-gills found floating on the sea. Dregs as came before us had no choice else." She rocked forward, elbows on her knees, tense hands packing air into a ball tween her and Mary Pat. "Do you see? We could do like we done, sure, but we've a choice now, Mary

Patricia," raising her voice so all round the brazier heard her clear, "There's more spawn living to breeding age; think the richards have no marked all the second Sevenths?"

"Course they mark them," said Chrysta, honing a thumbnail's curve.

"Is that so?" said Raincats. "More now than when?"

"Than before," said Finn, short. "Since we been drinking the potable." He tried to speak kindly to her through the racket of Nora's hacks, wheezes, coughs in his ears; Nora's coughs coming to an end; Cider Mother coming up from cellar lugging an armfull of silence; the kiln roaring below; the stench of burning flesh.

"Since the potable," Cider Mother agreed.

Bedelia Coldhand left off playing pit-a-pat with August Inkwhistle. "Richards figure more healthy spawn's more Hunt Boys. More fetch and carry dregs, likewise." Pit-a-pat, pit-a-pat, baker's man.

"More horii to stroke them up, too," said Chrysta, and stretched, and watched through half-lid eyes as one male after another sat up, crossed his legs, and threw his chest out. She smiled on them easy.

"Yeah, well, horii'll be doing that till fish drown in the sea," said Finn, willing his cock to stand down. "Horii'll never rise up gainst the richards."

"Horii nor Hunt Boys neither. You'd no luck sparking the bowly boys," Chrysta arched her back and twisted side to side. That got him up again.

Palan left off staring at the line where greenblue harbor met pale blue sea. His soft cock nuzzled his right thigh. "Small luck the M'Cools had on that with your lot as well."

"So you say," drawled Chrysta, "yet here we are."

"Two on you."

"Two more than none."

They looked at each other and bust out laughing. The berry hedge rustled. Mary Pat mouthed down Chrysta's ear, "Why *are* you here? Was it cellulite? Need some new harbor therefrom?"

Chrysta tucked up crossleg, her back pole-straight. "No," quiet as kelp in a tidepool, "I listened to what you said down the sour crags. That and no more." Mary Pat rolled her hands palm open in apology; out loud she said, "Well, Palan, he's a hard one to get to," jerking a thumb at the rustling hedge in answer to Palan's quizzical look, "but he'll likely see you different now he's seen you close to."

Raincats said, "Sides, what could horii do to sway the Boys? I kept myself back from a dunnamany haulers. Never budged a one of them one hair off their path."

The dregs round the brazier looked everywheres but at Raincats's slump round face and swole stump legs. Chrysta brushed her shining hair aside and spoke in clear, ringing tones as reached the berry hedge easy, "Hunt Boys'll never rise up so long as any clamor for them. Horii could disappear like smoke and Hunt Boys'd still be out there for the clamatory hoorahs. Now, an the richards go down cave, there'll be no cheers no clamor. Hunt Boys care *that*," snapping her fingers, "for oohs and aahs they can no hear. Let them prance through one silent Hunt and they'll lend you an ear, certain." The hedge rustled like a live thing. Chrysta looked round, pleased with herself, her back in ready arch. Mary Kath whispered to Mary Pat, who nodded, took Chrysta by hand and led her to where the hedge rustled. There they oohed and aahed like woodcocks was upon them.

Neath cover of their groans, the remaining dregs drew close round the brazier. August Inkwhistle pulled his hands from Bedelia's and cleared his throat. "There's sense to waiting. Raid them after lack of cheering softens the Boys." He looked past Palan to Finn for answer.

But it was Palan as answered. "I'd say no. For Galanty Hunt and this one only, richards are stoppered up where we can sneak up on them. They're planning viewtubes in another half-dozen shelter caves. There is a tide in the fairs of men which, take at the flood, leads on to fortune."

Quix clapped his hands. "Right aright," he said. While Mary Pat and Chrysta groaned by the quiver in the hedge, the dregs talked the moon down out of the sky with planning. Each received some part to play; at the last, they agreed on forelock tugs for cognize and shrill whistles for urgent.

When Chrysta arched her back to get a rise out of the males in the semblage, Dan eased himself upright and walked off neath the trees. The leaves rattled gainst each other in the cold nightwind. Below his boots, below the moonsilver grass, a web of sweet water lapped the roots.

When richards first come surface, they set miners to digging wells down to the sweetwater web. Five-six dregs died off the bad air fore they come to water, said James A. When at last they hit water, three-four dregs died off drowning. "Was that no strange?" said James A, "So deep in the ground to die of water?" The water gushed out the hole for a half-day then went bone-dry altogether, the way skin seals over a wound.

Dan walked neath the trees, lost tween wind and water, tween his first work in the orchard and his last walk on *Hail Janus* deck.

Starting when he was kneehigh spawn, every spring he climbed the trees, sticking his nose in every flower he could reach till he got so heavy he snapped branches. He went off to to sea the spring when Mary Kath started climbing.

Had the water lasted, dregs'd been digging still, but even richards could no milk the sweetwater web. The orchard did that. Trees was fashed for that. "That's when they set up the Potable Works," said James A. "Built fence round a great swath of land on South Point. Then the richards come down mong us," said James A. "They picked sturdy and they picked sensible, favored those as had spawn, summat to lose." Here James A had spat and drained a perry flagon. "Richards said it was job of a lifetime, which right they was. No dreg come back ever to Charnholm from behind the fine fence."

When Dan first went off to sea, the voice come to him in puffs, quiet and seldom, whispered down his ear; he could put the voice out of mind when he chose. Every time he set foot on land the voice come louder. Dan bit his fingers as he walked tween leaves above and water below. The voices round the brazier drowned out the voice James A'd handed down to him, for a wonder. Palan was telling them to take it at the flood. He'd the gold head the voice nattered of but Palan's crown had no passed through no Charnholm dreg's fork. Palan was Fergus spawn. Fergus. Cider Mother said she'd sconce his reckoning. The sembled dregs was moving off now, their farewells hanging in air like smoke; the coals muffled neath sand. The voices were going away, and then gone.

Dan whirled round, hands pressed to his temples, the voice shouting the scrapers out the ground, scraper windows popping like so many boils, trees somersaulting over their roots, flames rushing from gapes punched in walls in faces rushing their hairs crackling out their heads flames dancing on the rainbow water that rose and rose again till it slipped through every crack till it flooded every bed but its own and then the cries cracks hisses screams puling soft as cotton the fallen with their bones ready broken landing like exhales, *hoough, hoough,* the voice's screams torn from it by seawinds high above the ship in the rigging high above the screams blown to tatters by the wind the city a torchlit march mid green-edge darkness billowing and the voice cried without cease as the flames leapt as rocks leapt and split mid flames and salt settled in every split. Then the quiet. Smoke drifted off, the ground sighed as it turned its old bones to bear new weights, the voice a whisper only by time it reached the city from where it cried so far, too far, out to sea.

Dan stepped forward as best he could towards the damped coals' acrid smoke, feeling his way from trunk to trunk. A hand reached up for him and he took it grateful, and grateful laid his ringing head on her shoulder. "Ssh, ssh," said Chrysta. They was all gone while time folded on him as it liked to do, they was all gone but Chrysta who held him while the tintinabulate faded from his ears. "Lay you down and rest you," she said, sweet oil on her skin, and he slid down her breast to silence.

# Shuffle in Gloaming

COME DAYBREAK, dregs as can rise from their pallets go about their work, fetch and carry, haul and fashion till at last day's threads are wound on its charred spool. Till the gloaming shines.

Mary Katharine leaned square gainst the stone jetty tween two hangs of grey-green slime, the sun burnt-orange overharbor. When she complained that it was hotter nor dustgrains in a charred skull's teeth, Mary Patricia, leaning next her in sequence of graceful ovals, nodded, which out of course she did graceful, "It'll cool down soon enough." When Mary Kath said she was right, Mary Pat shielded her eyes with one gullwing hand, "Am I? That's rare enough."

Mary Kath sing-songed in Matron voice, "Petulance strips hori lips of perk and pucker," and drilled the jetty with a spike of mica, idle. Mary Pat took it from her to buff her nails. Dregs promenaded neath the hot orange sun, downjetty to the salt-glisten barge, and turned, and upjetty to North Point light, and turned, and arm in arm laced they shuffled long the cobbles. A few smiths was singing, *Snug my pallet / in the gloaming / come and feel it / if you list,* they sang, shouting *Come And Feel It!* when any hori sashayed past. A brace of plump hips as slowed, swaying like a bumboat in a crosswind, sent them snuffing and whooling away off in their wake.

Mary Kath pocketed her mica spike, ripping the pocket's mouth in her push; no matter, they was only clothes. A pair of horii, now, was mayhap important. "They any use to us?" she asked.

Mary Pat shook her head. "Rub sots, all times thinking on the next stiff poke."

"Drosh is coming. Look sharp," and Mary Pat pushed off the wall, graceful, and glided toward the lumbering smith.

Mary Kath strode after, humming. Drosh was constructed for teasing. "Drosh drills dinghys down by Don-Don's dock."

Drosh gave her a lipcorner tweak of a smile, a drap or two of affection in it but large part get-off-my-back-now. He widened the smile for Mary Pat, never no trouble to no-one, as he answered Mary Kath, "Hey, young sand up the nose, best go off and stonish some sprat with your rimer drills, they're nobbut buzz in my ears."

"Good to see you, too, Drosh," said Mary Kath. "Who's here? Let the infiltrating begin!"

Drosh swept his arm wide. "Innsmort has a scutman as did no make patrol. Quix found himself a passel of miners so green and round-eye you'd swear they sweat mold."

Mary Pat spun, beads on her tunic hem krattling gainst each other. "Well, mining's careful work. Mayhap they'll work out."

Drosh shrugged. "I'm no just easy in my mind. Quix's solid, I'd vouch my neck to a rat's last squeal on that, but he's a taste for burrowers. Where Innsmort's plain as spilled salt, Quix, now, he attracts twisty." Drosh shook his head.

Mary Kath turned her back so to keep her smile from Drosh's eyes. When the smith shook his head, you could hear the careful worked-up thoughts bonging gainst each other. The burnt-orange disk had fallen behind the white barge, and in three heartbeats the sky had gone that blue you can no hold in your hand, blue as frames every locust tree like it was the one and only, the last. "Gloaming's come," she breathed.

"Right," said Mary Pat. Mary Kath'd faint over a mere trick of the light, was she no brought up sharp. "We'll arm in arm to North Point, easy as she goes. Who knows," the voice on her coated in oil like she was soothing Hunt novices fore she shaved them, "what we'll maybe find that way?"

Drosh snorted. "Mystery on mystery till the wayfarer could drown in it. May I be gnawed by three-legged rats an you've no fashed a dunnamany meets, accidental like, for this night's promenade."

Mary Pat gave him a small smile at one corner only. "Is it no remarkable how often you find just the dregs you want of an evening's stroll?" She pulled Mary Kath away from her gape-mouth contemplate, tucked Drosh's slab of muscle neath her right elbow, and led them off.

Finn stared at the white barge as gloaming blue washed over it. "Stare at the sun long enough, it'll get trapped in your head," warned Palan. No reply. "Then it'll glow out your hairs, as it did my own, then you too maun roam on two long stones a burning crown up promenade and down, a quaver in your bones —" Finn passed him a thick slice of rye from his carrysack. "Now we've nobbut to work on but the terrible parch I got on me." Finn laughed and handed over the flask, still straight-gaze on the white barge. Palan swallowed first the bread and then the potable and when Finn would no turn round to watch him clog a few merry steps, he swallowed that too. "Come long," Palan said, tugging Finn's coat, "time's come. I'm in search of a miner dreg, a thin little wan little creature, him as we lowered down shelter cave to reckon viewtube depth. He's maybe on promenade tonight."

Finn stood fixed as any jetty stone till the deep blue that hides at the bottom of the bowl had emptied over the sky. Then he yielded to Palan's grip, and rubbed his eyes, and walked next him down promenade towards the saltglisten baulk. They clove south like bowsprits through north-flowing dreg streams, their heavy boots *clatter-clomp* on the stones, their kelp sweat wafting as they parted for Palan and Finn.

In a jetty alcove where the dark stones stayed warm longest, Bedelia Coldhand and August Inkwhistle leaned back, passing the time of day, their oldbones sucking warmth from the stones. They watched a passel of scutmen catch up to Finn and Palan.

"Peace of the evening to you, spitlick beaters," said Mottle.

"Cotentment to your nosehairs, flem of miner throats," said Spink.

"Strength to your walk, flatcrotch do-naughts," said Crump, one eye to the olders for sure he was hitting the mark.

"Does your mam know you're out all lone?" said Bannon, never quite on step with the fine points, a tin ear for badinage but a thick fist as evened the scales.

Finn and Palan bade them good even, the words sliding down their noses. Crump gave Finn the elbow to the ribs that was barracks greeting, with more gouge and grind nor usual. Finn smiled. Dregs gathered round the passel, keeping their distance, nobbut happening by.

Gov Don looked down on the stubborn clot in the promenade through his spyglass. He tromped the lookout deck; from every coign of vantage, the clot remained discrete, indissoluble. "Take it how you like, there's a clot in the promenade," said Gov Don.

Blane Plory jumped out of his way for the fifteenth time. "Yassss," he said. Gov Don strode and Blane Plory ducked and, "Gov Don, you *told* scutmen to ring the two in quarrel, no?"

Gov Don stopped mid-stride. "Are you daft? Are you fevered? Would I tell scutmen how to conduct patrols? Orders crush initiative. It best becomes a man to choose his own path."

"Ah," said Blane Plory.

"Now here some few scutmen have *taken* initiative to quarantine a pair of snip-nose stir-ups who are out to soil the Rat Hunt Boys with their buboed tongues. A few proud scutmen have *chosen*, on their own initiative, to protect the public health from such infection by slicing an abscess off its work-toughened skin," here flinging wide his arms to embrace an invisible, adoring crowd, "for which I do laud them, honor them, salute them."

"Ah," said Blane Plory, and shifted his lumpen mass from Gov Don's tromp for the nineteenth time. He sighed so quiet it was nobbut a ripple down his buttons. That morning, Norinda said to him for the thousandth time that Gov Don was the onliest key to them getting out of their two-shack-and-a-washline compound and into a larger compound, one as could hold a few spawn, did he no want spawn? and when Blane Plory reminded her once more how often they'd tried and tried and failed and failed, Norinda threw the teapot out of window and turned away and wept. There was no spawn but Deirdre mong the richards; natheless Norinda was certain spawn would come had they but rooms for them. He leapt out of Gov Don's tromp again.

Gov Don lifted the spyglass to his eye again. "Sulking," he said to Blane Plory, "may the last rat bite my last finger if they're no sulking."

"May the rats stay ever far from your gracious."

As Gov Don waved the polite reply aside, the spyglass slipped from his sweaty hands and clonked his breastbone. Gov Don rubbed the place, and parted his shirt to inspect the wound, and rubbed it again, and began to invite Blane Plory to inspect it too, but Plory had no skill in healing. Plory said yes, absolutely, when Gov Don said yes, but of no use when Gov Don's breastbone throbbed and, yes, *pulled* when he lifted his right arm; oh this needed Mandra's eye on it, yes; soon as he dealt with these sulkers he'd show her where the knurled eyepiece gouged him; Mandra'd lay cool poultice on it, he could trust Mandra;, she was every way different from Blane Plory here who lacked real compassion, standing off from him, head ducked, likely he was smiling back of that, no doubt; Blane Plory was unable to fully submerse himself in the great plan Gov Don served; Blane Plory had yet to shed his self, self, self like so many clothes and leap from the bank and dive, dive into the sparkling water. Till he did, there'd be tears. And they'd no be Gov Don's tears. Dive, dive into the sparkling water and swim in Gov Don's wake, that's what Blane Plory had to do. He must make it clear to all Charnholm's denizens that if all swam together in synchro- nized formation, they'd make the great plan happen; yes, soon as he chas- tised these sulkers, Blane Plory would be his mouthpiece to command the formation that should effect the plan, yes. Gov Don shook himself. "Sulk- ing. I disallow it. Once they begin sulking they dredge up a gyle-tun of trou- ble for themselves. Am I their guardian or not? Stir the pot and pop the skin. I mean, mash the apple and out squirt seeds." Blane Plory was giving him a look. He'd no right to give him looks. Who was Blane Plory? No more than kelp on a rock or weed on a keel. Gov Don stiffed his spine and slapped his gloved words over Blane Plory's features, "The dregs are mine to guard. It is I who tenderly care for their welfare. Potable I grant them, the ocean deeps I make them free of, the vasty sandlands are theirs to har- vest, and any unclaimed arable spot is theirs to plant rye in. What more? Cider and perry I give unto them that they may make merry and merry they are indeed. Would they sing by day and by night if they were unmerry? What more?" Gov Don spread his hands wide. "I give unto them the Rat Hunts. The grandest spectacle ever was, and a valve invaluable to their tem- pest-tossed spirits." Gov Don was proud of how well he'd navigated the treacherous reefs of alliteration. He resumed his tromping and Blane Plory resumed his leaping out of the way. "They've no foresight is the thing," burst from Gov Don after one roof-long tromp. "Theirs is to see the day, mine to see all the days. My outstretched hand shelters them. Ungrates! Plotters! Sulky, cross-grain flench! I'll show them the end of their plots plans schemes. At the Galanty Hunt I'll show them."

Blane Plory nodded, which seemed safe as houses, while Gov Don stalked the lookout deck, pulling sparse hairs from his dumple chins.

Cider Mother pulled the skimmer from the frothy vat. She sang as she skimmed: "*The rats come up / the rats come out / they clamber over the richard's house / The rats come up / the rats come out / they bite their way into richard's house / The rats come up / the rats come out / their bellies swole with the richard's mouth / The rats come up / the rats come out / they scamper over the richard's foul / The rats come up / the rats come out* ... Drab and furgan!" said Cider Mother as the skimmer fell to the floor tween vats. "Oh furgan and drab the gorry blanse," she said. She hooked the scumfroth bucket's bail over her arm and backed downladder. Skimmer'd need boiling fore she could finish off this vat. While the kettle heated, she reached a dusty vial from a high shelf. Nose and mouth swathed in pomace cloths, she climbed the ladder and emptied the vial into the frothy vat. It spittered and coiled in spiral. She took one careful sniff and yes, certain, it stank of the perruker, right enough. Cider Mother watched the vat till every spiral drowned, till a pale red mist rose from the vat, till she could see clear to the bottom. Then she tended to boiling the skimmer, singing the while: "*The rats come up / the rats come out / they gnaw and nibble the richard's house / Loola loola loola loola baby / Go to sleep, my baby / The rats come up / the rats come out / they gorge on flesh till the sun falls south.*"

Lena arched her back gainst the jetty some fathoms north of the salt-glisten baulk. The gloaming breeze pressed her dress round her form. She tapped her left sole on the stones and then stopped; though he was late and late was usual these days, they still did no like to see you fretted. What they did no like they kept off from. When they was first meeting, he was all times early; back then it was *his* foot as tapped. How'd the balance tip? How'd it come to be that she was the one as waited while he strolled up here and down there, hands in pockets, sniffing the air while she whirled down jetty to meet him sharp to their pointed time. Her left sole tapped again. Lena shifted her weight on it. Be quelled, she said, be belled be delled be felled befell befall be still and still she waited still. Feet padded down jetty from South Point. Lena looked north with a little hum hmm, no notion soever that he was late, late? he? they'd a pointed time? Sure she was nobbut reclining in the gloaming after a long day's slaving. Lena batted a small yawn with the back of a hand and arched the back she'd all day bent over whipstitch mong my lady's farfallrie. Pad, pad, the steps prowled closer. Her breath shallowed. Pad, pad, some blurry shadow inclined its head in passing; yet another dreg who was no him. This evening wind did sting the eyes main fierce.

Sure there was naught in Lena to tire of. She was taut and supple as any nova, though her third Seventh was a few summers past. Who was Lena what was she that any swain would leave her? She tossed her head in the fresh breeze and looked seaward where Fergus's junk, the *Mam Can Cook*, sloughed its furled red sails at anchor. A star hung in the moon's thick claw. Only a slackwaist dripcunt hori let herself go soft over a armourer with a mouth full of promises. Click clack, she slapped her soles and stiffed her droopy spine. You'd no find Mary Patricia M'Cool waiting so. She was likely on promenade this evening. Lena gave her rogue left foot the office to clap slap on the stones and start her going north; as good a direction as any. Her right foot swung in reply to her left foot's slap and they two carried her north long the jetty wall.

⟲⟶

A thin little wan little dreg by name of Lalom wandered up jetty and down. He nodded at an old female who arched her back gainst the jetty stones, her left foot tap-tapping, as he nodded at all who passed. Few returned his nod; none greeted him by name, for those as knew his name was gone, left behind him in the ragmine camp. From fore he could remember till his second Seventh, all times small for his years, they lowered him down deep holes to filch rags. The jokesters up above twitched the rope, warned him it was giving way, rats was gnawing it, and suchlike japes and pranks; well, he was used to it, he paid them no mind. He'd ease a rag from the pile, easy so the pile'd no collapse, tuck it in his beltsack, and again, and again till the japesters hollered, "Ho Lalom the rope's pulling out our hands!" when they hauled him up all anyhow till he landed gasping on surface. He caught what breath he could while they emptied his beltsack and then they lowered him again, "Hi Lalom what you been gorging makes you so all-fired weighty!" and so on till the daylight failed. Then it was broth and porridge and sleep in a pile of dusty rags. Come dawn they shook him, got another bowl of porridge down him, lowered him again, and again, and so on. A week since (though he could no make that reckoning on his own), a great-gut man come hi-ho over the hills on a table held by six dreg shoulders, a squint behind him holding his hat. The great-gut man plucked Lalom out the rags and brought him to Charnholm for fortune in the shape of a fine husk pallet and rare provender and potable four times daily. All he'd to do was go down a hole so narrow even Lalom's shoulders brushed its edges, lowered by a gold-head dreg, a gold-head as spoke him fair, "There, now, Lalom, there's a broth of a boy, that's fine guiding," he'd say as Lalom came down toe first in the middle of such gawpy splendor he'd no words for it (few words he had for aught, indeed, but for the gold and silver glitter he found at the hole's bottom he'd no words soever, could waved his hands in the air all day long and still come up with no way to tell it), and there in the light at the bottom of the earth he placed weights on the guide line and gave a least tug, once twice three times (so far he could reckon) then up the gold-head hauled him, clapped his shoulder, tipped sweet drink down his gullet. For three nights he was lowered to light and raised to dark, then the gold-head stuffed Lalom's beltsack with rye bread and apples and a flagon of good cider and wished him well. Lalom had wandered Charnholm since then in a daze past magining. The stones, the sea, the ships, the people so various, the light — he'd no seen light come and go over a day's whole face in all his short life. Lalom wandered up jetty and down, hoping to see the gold-head, hoping for more sweet drink and sweet words.

But he'd ill fortune, had Lalom.

Stead of the gold-head dreg, he found Sganal, the squint as held the great-gut's hat for him. The squint's face tightened when he spied waifish Lalom. He reached out his hands to Lalom's shoulders. Lalom grinned, closed his eyes, opened his mouth for the sweet drink to pour down his gullet. Sganal's hands tightened on Lalom's shoulders. That was matey. The hands tightened and lifted and swung the light weight out over the jetty wall and onto the rocks below where the tide boiled. The boiling tide covered the snap of Lalom's neck, washed away the little blood, sucked the light weight down its maw. The squint dusted his hands careful on a clean rag, tossed the rag over the jetty onto the boiling rocks, walked stiffspine down jetty toward North Point light.

⌒

Chrysta watched the squint toss the rag over jetty. Only scutmen or richards'd waste what was mined with such effort. This one with the squint, now, she knew him someway. "Galyse," she said, "who's that yonder with the winchet eye?" Galyse was busy swaying her hips bumboat. It took a time fore Chrysta got her attention. "Him?" Galyse said at last, "he's Gov Don's hissy pissy hat-holder; no point turning your wiles on him, my dear, his heart's belonged to Gov Don since they played tosscock at their first Seventh. So Matron says. Sganal's never had no eyes for no one else never."

"He takes it from behind?"

"He takes it no way. What's tween his legs is so much sack to him, likely he'll no touch it even to guide the spray. So Matron says. He's blood and bone a richard tool." Galyse looked south away from the squint, a man no manner of good to her. "There's Dingle," she said. "He chose me these last three times. Good value, Dingle. Goes gong to gong."

"Keeps it up all that time?" Chrysta was impressed gainst her druthers.

"Mm-hmm," Galyse said. "He's shoulder-clap with Thursgood and Lebone. You done Thursgood, no? He any good?"

"Nah. His balls is swole to size of his fists, which they drained off his cock, seeming, for it shrinks limp tween them. And *was* Thursgood fashed to give a hori pleasure, he would no. He's the kind as joys to stick his raspy fingers up you till you're scraped raw. He'll jam up both holes at once if Matron's eyes is elsewhere. When he kills, he likes to break their backs first so to watch them twitch in the dirt, mewing. The boyo's green meat, Galyse, he'd knot your innards did you taste him."

"Bit of a challenge, eh?" At Chrysta's look, Galyse tucked an arm in hers, sing-sang, "*Roll me bowl me hold me tight / I was wrong so let's no fight.*"

Chrysta rolled her eyes. "An ever you have sprats, I shiver to think what slum'll pass their lips. That verse, it's the worse."

Galyse grinned. "There's reason I'm no Rimer."

"Could fill a mash-tun with the reasons," Chrysta agreed.

"Mm-hmm. Listen, this is your gallivaunt, right aright, but are we no supposed to goose up any Hunt Boys we run cross tonight? Suade them to break ranks come Galanty Hunt?"

"Infiltration, they call it. Of these three, Thursgood's out; do you take Dingle — I did him time or two but we never sparked. I'll lamp onto Lebone, he's a great bully cept his tongue gets tangled by horii. You ever done him?" Galyse shook her head. "Who has?" Galyse shook her head. "*Somebody* must done him *sometime*." Galyse shrugged. "Rat got your tongue?" Galyse nodded. "Willa take na' Dingle?" Galyse nodded vigorous. They advanced in undulous tandem on the three hapless Hunt Boys.

From the south, Darnelle and Raincats hustled so fast toward the Hunt Boys that their toes scuffed. "No need for rush," said Darnelle. "I know you haul dregs has small luck with Hunt Boys. And this clanch is little worth, any road," but Raincats matched Darnelle step for step, her round face flushed, her spaggish nose drip with sweat.

When they was all seven joined, a clot in the dreg stream that parted weary round them, they flipped their hairs back off their heads, thrust their pelvises forward, leaned in close. Thursgood stuck his elbow into the clot. When that roused no ripple, he turned to Raincats, hoping for something angry or unlucky off her round face, her stumpy legs. "What's that round your neck?" he said. She ducked her head. "Naught," she said. He plucked the dark blue pierced stone from its nest tween her teats. The warm bread smell of her skin rose from the stone and smoothed the crease tween his eyes. A real surprise to himself, that. Thursgood fell into step with her as their clot dissolved and moved south toward the salt-glisten baulk. "Have I no seen you hauling?" he said. Raincats nodded. "Are you on the Galanty Hunt?" she said in a thread of a voice. Thursgood leaned in the closer to hear her, to breathe in her scent.

Chrysta and Dingle walked a handsbreadth apart behind them. "Thursgood?" she said. "He's his points," said Dingle. "Mmm, maybe so," said Chrysta, "but you've more." "I'm with you entire," grinned Dingle. "Shutter up," she shoved him away. He bounced back a handswidth closer. She asked what position they'd give him for Galanty Hunt, and he told her.

Darnelle and Galyse was left to sandwich Lebone, who'd no objection soever. They was good oilers the both of them. When they begged him to tell all, all of the Galanty Hunt, he let every last known detail slide right off his lips.

⟨⟩

Bedelia Coldhand stumped north long the jetty with August Inkwhistle and Gessel the joiner. Was they holding kindly chat? No. Strange notions Augie did take, dragging a lockjaw like Gessel round, a man so jealous of speech as any justborn of its apple-butter tit; a man as mute as boiled kelp. She dragged her feet back of the silent pair till Gessel was held fast by a hauler needing a new bench. While Gessel spoke actual words, in plural, Delia hissed to Augie: "How's strolling with this two-legged silence further our work on Galanty Hunt?" she said. Augie nobbut smiled. Times you did want to haul off and clop a male. Augie said Gessel was going to help. She put hands to hips and asked him how.

"Hark at him, Delia, saying he's too much work as it is. I saw with these eyes his workshop bare as barracks on Reap Day. Gessel's naught in hand yet he just now put the hauler off till next week."

"Oh," said Bedelia Coldhand, "that's aright, then," and snapped her eyes round for more dregs to pat into shape.

⟨⟩

Finn and Palan had the worst of it in their bout with scutmen. Crump and Bannon held them while Spink and Mottle took it in turn to whomp them. Well, even had they the great lame Smith at their backs, no two dregs could best a passel of scutmen. They was all one bruise and groan while Mary Pat and Mary Kath disladed their harvest of news at their feet. Chrysta and Darnelle braced them some, though whether it was their news or their slithring body rubs was a question.

Lena waited in the shadows till Mary Pat set off up the zig-zag compound path, like it was by chance, and step by step she threw wide her heart to Mary Pat, and believed that Mary Pat had oped her own in return.

On the far side of the jetty wall, a thin little wan little sack of bones rolled up shingle and down again, up shingle and down.

# Moon Comes More Nearer

"ONCE UP ON TIME, long fore you or I was born or thought of, the draioch Matia fell pole-axe to her knees babbling prophetry. She said Charnholm was on the cusp of smithereen. Said swords'd flame and slash the sky to fimbrels; south winds'd blow and range the fimbrel ropes to trail their fressons long the jetty. There'd come then a gold-hair born at sea to lead a Maypole of flexish dregs who'd grab the fressel ends and dance round him. A skweering viol'd play as they circled, each revolution closer to the pole as their plaited fimbrels shortened till they was cheek to cheek round the pole. Then as one they'd haul that thick rope and bring down the heavens, and all who dwelt therein."

"Ayuh," said Max, chewing rye and saltfish, "Fine tale, that. I'm the skweering viol, is it?"

Palan nodded. "Which I'd be, out of course, the gold-hair born at sea."

Max laughed. "No need to look so glum over it. Where'd you delve up this folderol?"

"May the last rat devour my thickness an it's no the solemn truth."

"Ayuh." Max swallowed. "Foolery aside, where'd you get it?"

Palan sat down next him neath the locust tree. "You've a snug harbor here. You lived here your life long?"

Max nodded, blew a blade of grass tween his thumbs. "Any time you feel to get on with it, Palan, I'm agreeable."

Palan leaned back on his palms. The locust fritted in the stale breeze, dappling his gold hairs. "First I remember we was at sea, Fergus and I, my mam left ashore. Winds was shredding the topsail and Fergus was below-deck crooning to his tarponesse while I was stuck partway down a scupper. I yowled my head off. Fergus nobbut crooned the louder."

"How about that now." Max plucked a second grassblade. "My own mam and dap, fine crooners both. Their spawn fore me, a likely boy name of Cranoch, went for Hunt Boy round the time Bran and Goodwin was put in charge of Rimehouse by Gov Don his own self. Cranoch was one of the first Boys practiced the close-in, I believe. Mm-hmm," whistling down the new grassblade, "mm-hmm."

Palan turned his hands palm-up. "So?"

"Tale's short enough. Cranoch charged close-in, holding pike two-hand over his head, like the painted Hunt Boy outside barracks. Rats come in neath the pike, tore his eye from socket. They say it took a long time fore the life ebbed from him altogether."

"So your mam and dap have their own grief with Gov Don."

"Have you nobbut kelp neath those gold hairs? Bran and Goodwin closed themselves in house for three days, at the end of which they'd composed a glorus ode dedicate to Gov Don the resolute. *Boldly strike / where least the blow's / expected. / Raise the pike / on rat so close / and strike dead. / Fearless Boys / all dregs hail you / prostrate before you.* Etcetera etcetera."

"But I've heard that," said Palan.

"Course you have. Beaters chant it; rimers sing it; popular tune it is. Richards say the Hunt Wagon did ought to perform it." He spat. "Which they will no so long as I'm on prow. Bran and Goodwin say all grief's fodder for tunes. *Rimers.*" He spat and rinsed his mouth from a flagon of potable and again spat. He looked up from the speckled dust and asked, "So. You want me to play the skweering viol. When, where, for how much? What do I get? We're talking one performance, are we no?"

"Ayuh," said Palan.

"Galanty Hunt, right?"

"Ayuh," said Palan.

"You'll no tell me where you heard Matia's babbling?"

"Bedelia Coldhand," said Palan.

"Right aright," said Max. "An I've to carry that slum tween my ears, backed only by Delia Coldhand's puling words, that plumps your cost considerable."

⌣⟋

Quix and Innsmort stood in a clot of smiths outside the forge gabbling over the new lading swing. "Cordwainers greet it with a glad cry, doubtless.

More work for them and steady, too," said Berk, "but for safe lade and fair weight, give me wafters every time."

Pomchalder nodded, and nodded, and nodded. Lando slipped an arm neath his elbow, hissed in his ear, "On the vertical, boypup, else scutmen'll swing you there." Pomchalder staggered gainst the jetty and grinned wide. "Let scutmen come and welcome, for Lando wills it so." Lando urged him, quiet, to shutter his mouth and ope his eyes to the clanch of scutmen legswinging up from the north. Pomchalder nodded. "Merry scutmen sha' play skittles with our noggins. Trust scutmen to find value in what lies tween our ears. Skittles! Who's for it?"

The smiths drifted off, leaving Pomchalder nodding in Lando's care. In the slack days before a big Hunt, scutmen was likely to apply all and each of Gov Don's dunnamany ukases, including those they mostly turned a blind eye to. Galanty Hunt was the grandest Hunt ever and scutmen was irritable in proportion; might could trot out the punishment for ill-wishing scutmen, even. As they drifted, Quix said, "This new lading swing, how'll that further aught?"

"Make no difference soever," said Berk, "nobbut a new toy for large craft. Any road, these swings is *ready-forged*," and every smith spat on the jetty stones at the phrase.

"Ready-forged," said Quix, "there's a fool notion."

Innsmort's head near bobbed off his neck with agreeing. "They'll fit the Hunt Boy to the pike, next."

"Your lading swing needs to fit your ship like your Hunt armor fits your body." The smiths nodded at Quix's words. "Likely the richards can no see how a ready-forged corviser scrapes and gapes," he said, "likely they can see it the less from their newfangle *view tube*." All nodded grave assent.

Innsmort followed up immediate; once you spike your rat, you maun follow with your pike immediate, "What'll they see of the Hunts from cozy down the shelter caves? Thrust and flash, no more. You know Ambrose been working the Boys on the close-in." He stopped mid-speech as Blay come up in memry, peckish and rascally, all braggadoce with his close-in prowess. He come up sudden, as the dead are wont to slide sudden through the most ordinary chinks of the most ordinary moments.

Quix jumped in, "Viewtubes and lading swings. May the last rat bite my last toe, richards got no sense of what's fit these days. The Boys, now, they're working the close-in wearing corvisers as shield them no more nor horii oil, greaves as gape off their calves, armed with nobbut these ready-forged pikes—" Quix stopped short off a swole throat, "I steered Blay Innsmort's first toddle round the courtyard. A free-striding sprat he was, always ready, curious—" and stopped altogether, and turned away.

The *Hail Janus* was rounding North Point. She'd more sail set than most craft could handle in the point's cross-winds. Daniel M'Cool was atop the rigging in the lookout, a hand shielding his eyes. That boyo was always on the watch; where Blay was leapish, too quick mayhap, Dan'd ponder and cogitate till the sun fell from the sky.

All this in a moment. Quix blinked and spun round quick as Blay would done. "Off respect for Innsmort's loss, we maun remind richards what's fit. Let us rattle their cages a bit come Galanty Hunt." Quix waited for his words to spiral down their ears and lodge within. He sketched the raid for them once and again and a third time, circling back on his words till they'd zamined it close and from every vantage; till they saw that Galanty Hunt was the one time for smiths to rise up. That it'd proceed as richards planned, did smiths stand idle by. Quix was scratch-throat and dull with repet repet repet ition when at last the smiths began asking where when how, how when where, when where how. Gessel told them. Every smith listened to Gessel. He spoke so rare, they was customed to stamping his every word in their recall. None asked who and none asked why. Who was plain as water in harbor; why as familiar as their warped and aching frames.

Ambrose was briefing the scutage hall in the lee of North Point. "Comper's resting tonight" — comper was thin-heart by nature, else he'd been more nor hauler by time Gov Don named him to the top spot — "so you've to put up with me for this night's briefing." There was a brief stir in the back rows but Ambrose had no wrangled novices for a dunnamany years thout learning to quash troublefluffers. One long look and they shut their ryeholes. "There's plans afoot to break up Galanty Hunt," he said. "No point asking how I know. Take it as spoke. Some dregs so love trouble they'll fash it from mud and sticks an they have naught else to hand. Well, they'll find we've sticks our own selves." Cheering. Fool thwackers. Naught so joyed them as lifting a bludgen and setting it down with a swing on some dreg crown. Wished they was Hunt Boys still with pike in hand. A rare jape, that, seeing as few of them ever made it past novice; no, this was a crowd of beaters at best. No matter. They was here and they'd scatter from hence at his bidding. "You're all familiar with Galanty Hunt, am I right?" Every head up and down till you'd think they'd upchuck off the rough tossing seas. "Richards are to stay down shelter cave and watch the Hunt through a newfangle viewtube. Any on you seen them?" No head nodded, though he knew for certain that comper'd told the most of them. Was they half so clever as they magined, they'd still be wantwits. "Dregs plan to sneak up on the richards while the Galanty Hunt's fore the viewtube and commit unspeakables." The murmur started from the back rows. Ambrose spoke on and over, "We sha' set patrols round Gov Don's shelter cave come the day. That's where first blow sha' fall."

"Why?" from the back rows.

"Why? Why?" give himself time to build answers, "Why? During Galanty Hunt? When all eyes sha' be on the Hunt? Why d'you *think*?" Turn it over to them, always a sure ploy. Whispering mong the benches; now they was getting it, they was getting it sure, and *now*, now was the time to loose the gaskets from the furled sails, *now*, "You can whimper *whyyy* — or you can stand up soldier like scutmen. Who's to bear the brunt but you? On whose shoulders does Charnholm's future rest but yours?" They was swallowing Gov Don's customary spiel like it was best perry. *Now* rove the gantline through the block and up sails for the open sea, "We've need of you. Each of you has proven worth" — oh that his tongue did no drop black from his mouth for that — "and each of you's a link in the chain as anchors Charnholm gainst such storms." Swing round the jib and tack away quick fore they saw how shallow lay the water there. "Prove yourselves come the night and you sha' no find us ingrates." Mawkish slackeyes. By the last rat's singed whiskers, he could do with a jolt of perry now. "Go out. Flap your ears. Dregs chunter up promenade and down. Stow their words in your pockets, purses, sacks, your cuffs." They sat on gape-mouth. Drizzard slugs.

Ambrose took on full cargo of air and spoke from his plexus: "Go now. Report back when promenade's over. When the moon falls over North Point. Go." When the last was gone, he upended his flagon.

Lady Mandra and Deirdre sat upon silk cushions in the bay window above Gov Don's front gates. "How goodly are their dwellings from this vantage," said Deirdre.

Lady Mandra snorted. Charnholm shacks were lovely if you compared them to a pile of stones. They protected the inhabitants from most weather and vermin; should any want ventilation, they had but to step outside. She lacked the vigor necessary to contradict Deirdre's rosy point of view; bring the girl face to face with facts and you'd spend half the day reassembling her, her big eyes looking at you sorrowfully meanwhile. The girl sprang from Clare's womb, certainly, but she'd none of Clare's spark, no flicker of the young Clare who swam out past the raft, built sandmen with cocks erect, led the twirling dance along the waves. Deirdre had betimes a look of Clare about her but it was muffled, like making love through a sheet. Mandra fidgeted with her broidery hoop. Donal wanted her to keep Deirdre close until the Galanty Hunt. Since asking why would prompt one of his rambling discourses, metallic sweat pumping from his pores with its rank accompanying stench, Mandra refrained from asking why. There were but a few days of Deirdre's company to endure. She dredged up a response to the girl's admiration for Charnholm's hovels: "Distance lends cohesion to any composition." There. Let her twirl on *that*.

Deirdre rhapsodized over the ocean's putrid hue, imagined the terrors faced by mariners, la la la la la. Oh, and how she looked forward to Galanty Hunt. It transpired that the girl had never seen one. "My father thinks it would excite me unduly, and of course I have complied."

"Thinks seeing it from down the shelter cave'll be safe enough in that respect, does he?" said Mandra. By the first plaguey ratbite, their life together down that hole must be old cold porridge; a lumpenlife. Deirdre nodded. "Where's that dreg of yours gone, that Lena?"

"She is collecting blackberry leaves. I have read that such a poultice tones and tempers the blood."

"Is your blood so hot, then?"

Deirdre nodded. "I fear it is lamentably hot. My father oft deplores my lack of philosophic temper."

That was the truth and no mistake; heat such as hers would freeze the touch. Mandra was stuck like hideglue to Clare's washed-out spawn till the falling sun struck the northwest windows. Hours. And she with a new footman who'd a topspin on his twirl. She shifted in her seat just thinking of it. What a waste entirely. Her thighs burned. Twirling toned the system. Was she to court illness merely to guard a gaumless girl? No and again no. She made some hasty whyfore to cover her going and slippered from the room.

Alone in the bay window, Deirdre plaited her pale copper hair. Locust leaves shissled in the breeze, last year's pods dark among them. She watched — idle, vacant — the life of the compound below her, her pale green eyes roving over courtyard and Charnholm and the sea beyond. A sweatsoak lanky dreg toiled up the hill to rest below Deirdre's window, staining the stonework as she panted there in grampus breaths. Gracious Deirdre leaned over the stone sill. She proffered a silk purse of well-considered largesse in her long slim hands. "This is for thee, poor sprite," she said. Softvoice, she added, "Hold fast to it, Lena, till we meet later. Mandra searches my clothes, you know." Lena nodded, panted a few more grampus, and bent, and plucked the thin purse from the dust, and bowed low, and shuffled off. "Thanks to you m'lady," she wheened over her shoulder.

⌒

Mary Katharine M'Cool stalked in fury on her lone. The richards was on to them; it covered the scutmen's smug faces like pox, *I know summat you do no*, the spawn's hopping jingle, *I know summat more nor you*; may the rat king gnaw their bones if they'd no found some way to protect the Galanty Hunt. Small use to go mong the scutmen; was she sly coy flirtish they'd refuse her; did she come on straight hail-fellow they'd refuse her still. Mary Kath stalked the jetty with no company but her fury. All these years of buds pinched off to force more leaves from the stalks so richards could lounge in leafy comfort — pssst! rat scat to that! She closed her eyes and visioned pools of hot blood leaking from their spawnknots, there where they was cut off and tied off — even richards was born, think on — hot blood spooling out their spawnknots as they lay mong their silks and downs, white circles forming from the hot blood, white circles hardening to pustules in the hot blood pooled on their lazish guts, their limbs made lead by the hot blood's foul effluvia — "Mary Kath!" — stalk she would straight past these simper dregs as'd lay their tunics over puddles so richard soles might pass unsmirched. Sure the Rimehouse was packed with folderol, but leastwise they was no passel of tomfools as'd extend a hand for the chop and whimper their thanks that the richards had no took the both of them. Rimers'd talk the ears off any richard as dared to — "Mary Kath!" — they'd be snort asleep by time a rimer quit off talking. So, for now, who could get in mong the scutmen since she could no? For all that, who could go mong the richards and loose their chary tongues? Darnelle. From down the sour crags. She'd a longing for scutmen. Mary Kath nodded short, satisfied. There was one, then, Darnelle to the scutmen. But in and out mong the richards, who? Lena. Mary Pat said *maybe* when she spoke of Lena; *maybe* Lena'd be their ears there. How could she — "Mary Kath!" — talk to Lena? Up the richard compounds she'd stick out like a rat in a spawn crib. Who then. Who but Mary Pat? Right aright. Find Mary Pat, find Darnelle, they was bound to be on promenade, then head to Rimehouse and —

"Mary Kath! Have you no heard me calling? What's towards?"

Dan was gnawing his fingers and staring bloodshot out to sea, craning his bony head this way and that on his long neck, his pockets stuffed with artifact and shell, knife and string, his feet twitching on the cobblestones. "You always look the same, Dan," she said with great affection, "I was nob-but dreaming long. And you?"

∽

Dan bit his fingers. What was Mary Kath about, saying he looked all times the same; what did she wear thwart her nose, blinders? every second as washed over him changed how he looked; he was Daniel M'Cool whom voices shredded and taunted, nobbut a stick hung with shreds; so how'd she cheek enough to ask him how he did? To speak of her dreams? Like his dreams was easy as hers, like her bookays of easy blooms was anywise like his. His dreams raged. He was a field and his dreams was so many boots trompling it. He held his head tween his palms, he did his possible to hear her words but the boots stamped up one side and down the other in his skull; they bellowed, *how it burns how it leaps in burning while we stand out to sea with naught in our power to save them*. How the glass leaps from its frames. How the scrapers cartwheel. How the trees shoot from the earth. How the smokeclouds mirror the gaping mouths of the burning. The reek of it (he dropped to his knees, raised his hands to smother his nose, ears abandoned to the voice that cried *mercy, mercy*; like that'd close the spigot) could he but get the reek of it out of his nostrils; he'd pulled every stinking nose hair out by its roots yet the mucal flesh held the stench; he'd scraped bare the tissues and still.

What drove him screaming to his knees every time any where was the high whine of thick glass shivering in its frame. The voice saw it the voice heard it though he never. The glass hung there, whining high, crazed and mazed and yet intact and yet in place and yet and still it pulled roots of his balls up his spine with fine strong threads ...

And then silence.

He pulled himself upright by aid of the jetty and strove for air like any landed fish. "Cider Mother's asking for you," he said.

Mary Kath was saying she'd a few tasks first, then she'd to go up Rime-house. He scratched the words inside his skull with his bloody nails. "I'll pass it on," said Dan.

⌒

Deirdre and Lena walked the privy courtyard of Treesa's compound. *Night soil pavilions* Treesa named it; privy courtyard what it was. There was no lower toil than to empty the cullners every morning by dawn; the Keep made those sorry dregs eat from the cullners to be certain sure they was cleaned to Treesa's satisfaction. The compound was used to seeing Deirdre and her lady-dreg together, Lena poking for rats neath the platforms while Deirdre overstood her lest she scant. Lady Mandra asked how Deirdre could bear to keep ward on her dreg all down among the privies (Lady Mandra called a fecal a fecal) but Deirdre said Lena needed the chastise task, she being a dentical flissome dreg as thought her tongue was her own to rasp with; what a pity that no other dressed Deirdre's hair so well; what a pity that only the privy pokings put any proper fear into the fool.

Behind the reed huts, tween the platforms and the reed screens, a grove of head-high oaks flourished. Deirdre caressed each soft limb, "the marvel of it, Lena," who nodded as she poured sweet water over their roots. "Some day these shall cover the earth once more, Lena. From these saplings shall spring forest on forest from the mountains to the sea, and in their shade we'll find respite from the wind's bite and the sun's burn; damp and fragrant shall be the soil held in rich place by deep roots, and birds shall sing once more in leafy branches."

"Uh-huh," said Lena. "That'll be a treat to be sure. In the years till then, we're slavishing this near-potable on what can no be eaten. Might as well pour it in the sea."

"Lena!" Deirdre laid one long delicate hand on her breast. She widened her eyes. "How can you say such things?"

"Oh may privy rats nibble my toes, lay off wasting our short time here with your histronicals, willa?" She braced her lower back with her hand as she rose. "That's done, then. I tell you straight, could I grab a sprat off the promenade and steal her back and knees off her, I'd do it quicker nor a corner rat could spring. Why the years got to go direct to your bendy parts when they could busy themselves elsewhere ..."

Deirdre took the empty pour-can. "I'd slake their thirst myself, but they'd stare and quiz to see a richard work while a dreg stood easy by." She laid a slender hand on the nearest sapling. "They stare a mort enough as it is. *"There's Clare's fair one / Bloodless and good,"* they say. None of them from here as I am. Know-naughts." She filled the can from a cask labeled *Non-potable! Danger!* "I wonder who Treesa thinks this label hoodwinks. Take this, there's no eyes about," she slung the can to Lena. "Once these trees set down their roots, they'll have no need of watering. They'll spread wide roots and branches to make havens for dregs and richards alike. We are as they, able to snatch life from this earth's bones. Dregs shall draw strength from the earth while richards make food from light — is that no the way of it, Lena?"

"This can's done. Rat in a hole but my back slays me," Lena straightened as she spoke. "Did richards make aught that they'll give the dregs free gratis for nothing, may my back be ratgnawed from this day forward forevermore. Let alone food from light. What have richards to do with light? Great stone halls to hold the dark's more their style."

"That's as may be." Deirdre took the empty can from Lena and stashed it neath the nearest privy platform. She dusted her hands and tidied her dress. "Lena, you look a fright," smoothing her hair, rubbing her shoulders.

"What's all this?" Treesa stomping bout in a pair of bell and glitter slip-slops. "Deirdre Claresdotter will you have the goodness to tell me what, in the name of all that's luxe calmay voluptay, is going on here?"

Lena trembled neath Deirdre's hands, who kept rubbing, working her thumbs along the knotted muscles, "Ah, Aunt Treesa, I am glad of your coming. Lacking your years of experience, I can not explain to this chaff how to rub my shoulders and am reduced to showing her." She finished with a series of gentle circles at the back of the head where the cords disappear into the bones, "That will be all, Lena. Run up and prepare my evening clothes." Lena ducked a courtesy and hustled off smooth. "Now Aunt Treesa," shaking out her skirts as she walked back into the courtyard, the older woman constrained to follow did she mean to continue clacking, "how kind in you to involve yourself in my enterprises, with all the other pressing demands you have on you." So was Treesa diverted and the trees lived another day in the privy courtyard.

Which, as it befell, was all that was needful.

# Boola Boola Weerna Roola

BY TIME MARY KATHARINE WAS SURE Daniel'd memrized the message *and* member to pass it on, she was past late for her meet at the Rimehouse. She rushed, panting, to no purpose surely: Rimers was never timely.

So out of course every last one of them was sitting round the table hands folded. As Mary Kath entered panting, they twisted their faces to her, as one, then twisted as one to the east window where the sun was three points above the sandstone bluffs. "Belated," she said, and slid to her seat.

From head of table, Bran announced what every rimer knew; that Mary Katharine M'Cool would range the rimers for Galanty Hunt as her journey-piece. Those who'd helped her to this gave a small grin at their hands, and those whose obstructs she'd greased with tokens of esteem grinned wide.

Rimshot was on her right hand, just where she wanted the drogyne, and Dulse on her left where she could screen Goodwin's quashing presence. Mary Kath greeted both as she ranged her papers and her thoughts. She asked after Goodwin's health and told Bran how well his vest became him. On Rimshot's right, arms akimbo to mark his territory, the blind anathematizer Thorn, instructor in rodomontade and repet-ti-tition, an able alliterator and scatologist sublime. There was a full complement of versifiers and syntacticians, mechanics of rhyme scheme and word use. Every one on them had the long stare of those who look past what's in front of them, be it never so delicious; every one on them could split a hair ninety-seven times fore breakfast and still have stomach for a donnybrook or heroic ode on the nature of each hair-fraction.

Mary Kath swallowed a mouthful of potable and clapped the meet open. She clapped in trochaic trimeter, DAH dum DAH dum DAH dum, SHALL we COME to ORder. Rimshot gave her a squint wink and an iambic response — or SHOULD we PISS our PANTS? — their old rowdy back-bench clap. Rimshot held that trochees was distress signals pure and simple, *Ne'ver ne'ver ne'ver ne'ver*; any rat'd know itself safe off a trochee. Dregs as chanted trochaic, said Rimshot, had brackwater blood; the salt so thinned in them they'd barely hold a pike, let alone use one on a rat. Rimshot sang in iambs when it wanted to be let in on whatever was going, which now was the latest Galanty news. Mary Kath had no more to tell. Rimshot knew sufficient, for one who could no more keep from flaunting secrets than a cresting wave could keep from breaking. Rimshot purely lived to spin plates in the air. Yet these rimers were Mary Kath's tools. They were the ones who'd showed up. Put down your bucket where you are, Cider Mother said. Mary Kath slapped her bucket to the tabletop, took breath, and began:

"**Boola Boola Weerna Roola!**" The rimers chorused hearty, thwomping the table, loudinating with each repet-ti-tition. She took heart, breath, and pen. "That's my journey-piece's name and chorus. As you know, Governor Donal's planned a fine Galanty Hunt to celebrate the viewtube Palan Goldhead slotted down the Gov's shelter cave, and Gov Don's charged the Rimehouse, special, to anathematize the rats with hummable tunes."

"Hummable! Balderdash!" said Thorn.

"Would you care to expand on that?" said Mary Kath, polite. Always be polite. Burn no bridges.

"Think rats'll jump to *hummable*? A naught thought, that is," harrumphed Thorn.

"House of the Teaching Company of Anathematizers was no created to make the rats to *jump*, Don Thorn," said Goodwin, placid, "but to stavage them, to plump their eyes out their sockets, to turn their blood gelid, to raise their each particular hair," she said, hands folded, eyes downcast. "As well you know, Don Thorn, it's beaters who make the rats to jump; a crude crowd-pleaser for tickling the richard ladies. It is we Anathematizers who paraly-size the rats." Thorn muttered into his beard that he knew that well as sea knew to yield to tides. Goodwin sailed on, "Governor Donal is wrong to demand hummable tunes of us, true and noted. Natheless, we sha' gratefully supply the Governor with tunes as any dull — ah, with tunes as any richard can blither through pursed lips, and we sha' supply them timely, that is to say two days hence."

"We're to create, transcribe, *and* rehearse in two days?" said an arthritic jongleur at the table's far end. Goodwin nodded, pool of calm, into which Rimshot leapt with both flat feet. Mary Kath flattened her hands on table. It did no shutter that heedless voice.

"Hummable scummable, whatever makes those thick skirts twirl," said the drogyne. "Ninnit our grateful rimer duty to bow shuffle scrape fore our munif'cent ben'factor, hail him, our Gov Don — *eaarrrp! eaarrrp!* — fashonk, alas, he's deaf to our hails — *eaarrrppp!* no, those ears of his're choke full of schemes to welfare every last dreg as can shuffle down jetty and tug a grateful forelock. Grateful. There's a rare one for you. Thanks to Gov Don, there's a double handful of dregs — out of all the dregs in Charnholm town — pacing and chanting the Rimehouse halls who give grateful thanks many thanks to his tootle tootle tutelage, but times they need reminding, like any dreg, that they're na here for blaze o' glory joy o' making oh for the love of the last rat's tail tip no. Rimers are the Gov's own creatures, and like all his creatures we're made fine by beating." Rimshot chanted, badaba badaba BUM BUM, badaba badaba BUM BUM, as it swayed, snapped fingers, kunched shoulders, rolled its eyes.

Mary Kath snuck in fore Goodwin could spit more twice-chewed pap down the table: "Many thanks, Rimshot; your improvisatory powers are all times a marvel. But by the newest justborn's eyes, I charge you, every one, to pull a hummable tune from out your talents. To satisfy the Gov we most times need only a catchy refrain, like glor'us Rimshot's *badaba badaba* BUM BUM. For the Galanty Hunt, our tunes maun draw wails from stones."

"Richard ears is flexish as stones," snorted Thorn.

"Well, true enough that richards judge our anathematizing tunes by their effect only; so long as a song seizes rat sinews, richards think it fine. We must comply with Gov Don's order, but let us put verberations in our songs at pitches that lie outside a richard's audible range. Give richards song they can jongle and hum. Meanwhile, our verberant tunings sha' wail babes out the stones." Mary Kath sat back, main pleased with her succinct.

The rimers was all alive on the moment to the chance of that. To do what none else can. To do it well. There's the respect that stiffs the spine of rimers, smiths, horii, Hunt Boys, all. To be of use. Desuetude rusts motive power quicker than any salt, lipidizes flesh till it's spag to the touch. To do what any can do is a blow; to be replaceable a blow; and all day every day such blows rain on the dreg plexus. Rimers, like any living, love what most engages them, what uses every faculty. The table hummed with their gears ratcheting up to take the extra strain and glad of it. To be of use. To be used. The best within them used in full.

The prospect of using all its powers drove Rimshot spawncurl neath the table, its nape a sweet target, cormigant with glad fear. Terrors tumbled in its head like fish in a haul-net. On the body alone, there was sores as did no heal, purple blood clotty in the pubes, and a stab in the left armpit that betimes shot down the arm. Beyond its skin, beyond Rimehouse doors, there was the heads as snapped on necks and the mouths that hooted *'Ware riot, drogyne's nigh!* as Rimshot passed. Beyond Rimshot's own circle of fear and trembling lay greater horrors. Take a one of them. Richards slaughtered many a woman soon as she'd pushed the fetus from her womb; one quick bloodless stab fore the justborn wailed so it'd imprint on some richard lady. Rimshot saw them on the backs of its eyes. They inserted the blade with concentrate technical hands. They tossed the corpus in the sea fore it was cool. Rimshot's knees knocked its ribs as it cramped the closer so to blur the pictures. So then. Since we must die, we sha' die on our feet, stead of on our knees.

Mary Kath could feel Rimshot through the table — its tremors pustullated the air — but Galanty Hunt, now, was paramount. She laid one palm on the pokeberry turban while she kept the talk flowing. She appealed to Bran and Goodwin to help fashion hummable tunes, brought potable to those who flagged, took notes on a small pad on her left thigh, leaning down to sotto voice at Rimshot to hold on, hold on.

"Sithee," Rimshot hissed back, "I sha' stay cramped in madness a while yet. When this busy chatter's done, I've a flagon of perry in my beltpouch."

Mary Kath nudged the drogyne with her toe. She placed the jongleurs smack front of the viewslots where they'd both distract and block. Course richards'd druther see gore, but they'd say so, after, and after'd be too late. Mary Kath put drummers here, tumblers there; assigned massing areas and krewe runners, all the while Mary Patricia's words put heart in her:

As they'd scrambled down the sour crags, Mary Pat'd said, far-off look in her eye, slow as poured pitch: "Yes. Your plan sha' succeed." Natural enough, Mary Kath was glad to hear that; natural, too, that Mary Pat had more on her tongue. "Yes. Your plan sha' succeed. An you take the long view." She'd no more to say, right then when more would been a powerful help; that was the way of it with Mary Pat's foreseeing. No matter, and so Mary Kath'd told her: "Well if that's all you have then we sha' go on. We're done crawling. An we win long view or short, we're up off our knees."

Mary Kath took a deep breath of those words and went on with managing: "Rimers! Slunch your gorry yaps! Bring best of your hummables to Annex at sunfall, and we'll choose mong them." On the quiet, she told Rimshot they'd meet next door after the rest was gone, for its tunes as'd pull wails from stones. Mary Kath sliced through resulting hum: "Bran, Goodwin, you best know which tunes'll best please richards, so would you kindly take your station in the solfedge at sunfall to judge the tunes. My thanks to you. Meanwhile, remember: **Boola Boola, Weerna Roola!!**" The rimers roared that chorus three-four times, maffick off what tunes they'd make. Mary Kath tapped twice the pokeberry turban, stood up, sang her four-note signature — B-flat *zwhoo zwhoo* G-flat *woo* D-flat *whoo* — and glided off. "I can glide an I want to," she told Rimshot next door, "I glide lovely, no?"

"Mm-hmm," the pokeberry turban nodded. "You're a gliding fool, you are." Rimshot lit a smilax tube at the handiest light eternal, burning neath a crusticated render of some rimer past. "So many rimers dead and gone," said Rimshot. "This one now, all times asking: 'Are I Stophanes?' Yes you are, coodle-woodlums," chucking the geezer's fallen chin. "So what was all that folderol round the rimer table, Marekat? Clunch of gobbledrab staps a jongleur's quizzik and shutters Goodwin's eyes, but what plan you got? We're to compose hummable tunes as draw wails from stones; what kind of grade-A fishguts are you passing off as stew? Firstly, and to start off with, what gorry bubo-doll of this House ever wrote a tune as'd draw such wails? Secondly, and next, should you hear such wails, do they craze your skin like lightning? Set the brains boiling in your skullpan? Race round your feet so quick you'll blink three times and whisshle! you're enmoated? Do the wails from stones take tea of a morning? Third and lastly, have you aught of provender about you? Fishcake? Crumbs mayhap? A nice red apple?" Rimshot elbowed Mary Kath in the ribs, who handed over a few pieces of jerky, then walked off to look out of window, no word to say. Rimshot used that extra air. "Some smoke and mirrors, huh?" Rimshot said as it snapped the head off a smokefish, "What's the actual plan, Marekat? You've the rimers nice foozled but come Galanty Hunt there's all times some who'll chant what's prettiest, whatsoever gets most clap. There's nobbut a handfull of rimers as can turn ratblood gelid and those few hardly never come to Rimehouse meets, remain up off in towers, chanting in whish, eyes wide-glaze, skin twitching neath weight of its hairs. Your joebee, comely, where's-me-muffin rimers care no scrap nor skittle for your transform transcend your immanent ineluctable change; they're in it for the guzzle and the glory, Marekat; give them a fine slow pace to measure longside a pack of whiteskin pacers and they're sate, replete, full up, cock-a-whoop — "

"Known and honed." Mary Kath swung round. "What else sha' we do? Refuse this chance? This is the tide in men that we take at flood. Richards all down one shelter cave, Hunt Boys above. It willna matter if the rimers think they're plucking daisies on the verge or jousting with scythemen, so long as they keep out the way. And who knows? Could be they'll come up with summat immanent, ineluctable. Could be they'll rise to the need."

Rimshot folded itself into a corgi knot. "Right, then. I'll see if I can mayhap come up with a tune or so as may no totally fail. Smack of perry?" it offered. They drank, and wiped their mouths, and paced in mutter by the Rimehouse windows. *Boola boola weerna roola* came from round the House. *Draw wails from stones*, they muttered in answer. "Got to sink commands in these as'll shiver up their spines," said Rimshot at one point, and at another, "Rimers roll belly-up to ratquell same as any fourleg, snapped orders jerk their limbs all 'bedient. No matter what they *think* they're doing."

The sun burned through overharbor haze and smacked the windows full. Mary Kath roused. "I'm off. Dan hailed me special to say how Cider Mother'd need of me. Rimshot, your tunes is fair decent. Craft a handfull more of these — you've the better talent for paraly-sizic panic, anyhow — I'll return soon as I can. By nightfall, surely. Galanty Hunt's two nights from tonight. We'll need to rehearse them tomorrow night, d'you hear?"

"For the hummable?"

Mary Kath waved that away. "The hummable, sure, Bran and Goodwin can spiel that out with both ears stoppered." "Likely do," said Rimshot. "And likely do," Mary Kath agreed. "No, it's the tunes as draw wail from stones that we maun slide down them, tomorrow moonrise, soon as promenade's done."

"Till then, my flower," said Rimshot, spitting a few threads of smilax out the side of its mouth.

⟶

Cider Mother crept neath the smaller vat. "Ugh," she grunted as she inched a thick-wrapped package out from under. She was backing out careful when a sharp crack sounded. "Mary Katharine M'Cool," said Cider Mother, still half neath the vat. "Have Rimers no yet taught you to walk in graceful quiet? To mind the beam at cellar door?"

Mary Kath rubbed her brow. "Dan said you'd need of me."

Cider Mother dusted her pinna. Unwrapped the package with a single tug. Tipped half its sweet contents into the frothy vat. "Right aright," she said brisk. "Here's the makings. Sweet tea for richards come the Galanty."

Mary Kath took a long sniff. "What's in this?"

"Such stuff as dreams are made on."

She gave her mam a long look from which their shared blood leapt out. "Right aright. How much for each?"

Cider Mother waved one airy hand. "Be generous, Mary Katharine. You've enough for one richard amphor there. Ladle with an open hand. Be sure every richard flagon's full."

"They'll drain it to the lees."

"That's certain," Cider Mother agreed. "Put it on to steep. Give them *Boldly strike / Where least the blow's / expected.*"

"With all the choruses."

"Ayuh."

"Serve when done."

"Ayuh."

"Good night sweet prince?"

"Ayuh."

Mary Kath grinned.

⟜

Down the bankmen, dregs swooled round unco' thick and leapish. Palan spoke in undervoice, "Willa do it for six carboys of potable and a gudgeon of perry?"

Max let a clanch of horii pass. "Throw in two oilings and I'm your skweering viol as sha' draw wails from the very stones," he said.

A passel of clenchtooth smiths come clockning by, knuckles tapping jawbones, *ka-klonk, ka-ka-klonk-ka.* "What type hori is your druther?" said Palan, when he could hear his own voice again.

Max bowed to a straggler knocking his only fist gainst the side of his head, clubfooting fast as he could in the wake of the clockning smiths. "Soft-handed. Gentle on my own hands. Can loosen my knotted left shoulder. Other than that, they're all much of a muchness."

"Done." Palan spit on his palm and they shook on the deal.

"Boola boola weerna roola," said Max.

Palan spread his hands. "Fortunate we are to have Rimers as can come up with catchy jangles like that one."

They said it soft together: "Boola boola weerna roola!" and fortunate they was, for with all the scutmen in full swool long the bankmen, none marked them sunk to the stones off laughing.

⟜

Finn hollered his brother's name from the dock longside the *Hail Janus.* Her reefed sails waffled in the gusts, anchor chain squealed in its runhole. Dan twitched to the taffrail. His dry lips stuck to his teeth as he said, "What's towards?"

Finn took a swig of potable. "Dry work, hollering you out the depths," he said.

"What's towards, that you disturb those done naught to fret you?"

"Charnholm has need of you, Daniel. Come down and talk awhile with me."

"No. I'm none of Charnholm, but of the *Hail Janus*. An she goes down, I sha' be of some other ship."

"Sha' no drown?"

"No. Born to be hanged."

"Why then all the more. Come ashore. I've an end to your troubles."

"It's all trouble ashore. Which is why I'm all times at sea."

"Troubles leap from land to ship and back again, Dan. As you're my brother, come down." Dan shook his head. "Are you no my brother? Come down, I need your counsel."

"I am no —" said Daniel, and the wind took the rest of his words.

"You're no coming down?" said Finn. His voice on Dan's ears dulled the roaring, blotted out the dark red stains and charring, coaxed the glass silent in its frames; listen hard as he might there was naught in Finn's words but Finn himself, and, "I sha' be down directly," said Dan. Finn gave a little hop on the dock there, same as he might twelve years previous when young Dan let sprat-Finn tag long of him on ventures mong the fishsmacks.

They paced the dock's length, Finn painting the raid gainst the Galanty in grand strokes with his words and arms while Dan stalked long of him same as he nightwatched on board; twelve even paces to bowsprit, and turn, and twelve paces to stern, and turn, and so till the watch bells sounded, hands clasped over his spine's base, smelling the air, listening close. Still there was naught in Finn's words but Finn's own voice.

Into this grateful sound Dan said, "Ever know a dreg name of Lalom?"

Finn said he never run cross the fellow, and plunged back into the sea of schemes and stratagems cooked up for Galanty. Oh smiths and rimers and Gessel was in on it, even horii was up to summat, even Bedelia Coldhand and August Inkwhistle had their places, near all the dregs was in on it, haulers too, and there was more coming all the time.

Like it'd anywise tip the balance.

Palan was mainspring. Palan was no Charnholm-born.

"Palan's a trusty body," Dan agreed, "ever hear him speak on a dreg name of Lalom?" No, said Finn, he never had; but what did Dan think of the flanking sweep they planned for a dozen smiths with ironlump flails? "*That's* fine threshing for you," said Finn, his chest so swole at the plan's beauty he could no see his boots. Mary Pat was bringing in a compound dreg name of Lena and her cave-born richard, Deirdre. Cave-born, yeah. Yeah, Deirdre. No, that was all Finn knew; a richard born down the shelter caves by name of Deirdre, so less than three Sevenths on her. Well, an Dan was so all-fired eager to know more, he ought shoof off up South Point and lay his eyes on her.

"An you're so keen on my counsel, stopper your gab," said Dan. He walked longside Finn, pulling any loose threads on the plan, one by one, to see how they'd mayhap ravel. So long as Finn named each thread, so long as he kept their sounds in the air, the voice kept its distance, the way Dan could compare one thing to another. So long as the voice was quiet. They walked up deck and down, up bankmen and down. As the ships swung gentle at anchor in Charnholm Harbor, they wove a net as'd enmesh the Galanty, and thereby the richards.

Was they no prepared? It's no any gloaming stroll to scavenge through rubble of fallen blocks and beams. Nor is spag-diving a walk on low-tide sands. They was ready. Even here long the stone bankmen they put each foot down careful, for the world we walk upon can burst at any moment; at the least touch or at none it may fall away from us. A dreg knew how to walk the shifting sands. Knew, as well, that all that mastery would no deflect capricious blows. Their world could toss them off tween one heartbeat and the next. Jaunty with it, laughing, Finn and Dan plotted the next double handfull of moves.

# Book Four

# Galanty Hunt Day

Phoebus Apollo drives his chariot across the skies, drawn by two horses, Abraxas and Therbeeo, intelligence and passion, skeptos and eros, and only he can hold that team steady as they mount to free the earth from darkness, as they career across the south horizon, as they slowly descend into the west. It takes a firm hand and a light one to keep the horses pulling together. A driver less experienced may soar too close to the sun, or dive into the sea, or otherwise miscarry, for be the horses never so willing, they depend on the hands that hold the reins to direct the tender mouths.

In night's still center we fall back, to wake refreshed for the struggle. In the abysses of sleep what dreams do rise; with what ease we then weave the ragged daylight threads into a sailing carpet. In these hours we glide above the grunt and sweat we're heir to.

# Devilled Down

*It was full dark in Charnholm. In the town, the blackness of back-coves and cellars rolled over, spilled out, stained the sky a deeper black. Over the harbor, the blackness was roiled by the wavecrests that threw silver glints against the low, matte sky. The stones wept cold, and the air above the stones was cold, and dregs in their shacks fitted themselves to their bedmates, close, or rolled deeper into lonely bedcovers. The streets held only blackness; scutmen dozed over stoves, coulees burrowed in their straw, richards laid hands on their full bellies and snorted in their featherbeds. When the night was darkest, the air coldest, the first of those who had work to do for Galanty Hunt woke cold from their pallets.*

The Rat Hunt Boys woke into their dark. On their pallets, hands behind their heads, they counted.

Hashel lost to the close-in.

Blay lost to the close-in.

Lebone's nose near gone to the close-in.

They laid these accounts in the dark's keeping.

There was a Hunt in three hours.

There was a final close-in drill in thirty minutes.

In the courtyard, Morsnal crouched over his cage of rats, one for each letter of the alphabet, twenty-six rats in all. He crooned their names in order as he picked them up in order, stroked their bellies in order; fair's fair said Morsnal. He'd gave them special training per Ambrose's express command till they could leap into air and twist a double somersault in time it'd take your average rat to prick up his ears. Ambrose had the Boys training for the close-in on these special rats. They trained with reed fascines tipped with kelpjuice. Every green-brown splash on their fur counted for a hit. Ambrose said, Morsnal had a gift for training. Ambrose said, Morsnal'd receive special consideration when come time to choose the new Wrangler, who lived in barracks on three squares daily, clean tunic and trous weekly, a carboy of potable all to his own self, and all he'd to do for this was train the rats to train the Boys. Who'd go off then and kill the bad rats as slept in foul and carried buboes neath their tongues, which bad rats was as like his rats as seep water to potable. A carboy of potable and another of cider every week, and Ambrose said Gov Don said there'd be perry by the firkin for the right candidate. Food coming regular with him stirring no stump about it. Morsnal crooned *"Firkins and carboys and bolls of rye, firkins and carboys and bolls of rye,"* to G and P, his brightest quickest charges. But the other boys was stirring, so Morsnal quit off whispering to his favorites.

Lebone lay on his pallet like a spag clump like he'd done since he lost his nose to a rat's long snout; a tug, a snap, and then nobbut air lying heavy on his face. His hands twitched at his sides. He lay still as cold spag while the other Boys was up and hustling one-arm into double drab tunics and, fasten tapes flapping, out the door and down pier to where Ambrose hollered fit to ring the barrack stones, "Get those clobber lumps out your mouths you graffish thubs else I'll—" as the first Boys crossed the threshold. Lebone stayed lumpish on his pallet.

Ambrose he kept on spouting.

"The close-in, you muddlesome clothheads, is the seen car none of the Rat Hunt Boy. This technique, vanquished for age on age, has been re-erected in this our glorus age by our own glorus Governor Don, who could no be on hand for this your final training — sit up STRAIGHT you whore-son slipthumb or I'll give you summat to bend for — and is the summation of all your spearence. Yay amen, the beaters stir up the rats from their nests. True enough, the stirred rats is froze by the anathematizers. But it's you Hunt Boys as puts the spear to fear, as routs in bouts the plaguey prey; it's you Hunt Boys as have the liver to lean in and knife their lifeblood even while they bestare you — stare them down! slice their innards! dim their black black eyes! Hold them fast and stick them deep with nobbut your own feroce blasting out your eyes."

"What of Blay?"

"What of Hashel?"

From the back of the crowd the royster words fell thin.

Ambrose squared up to them, hands on his hips. "Is there a one mong you as came for Hunt Boy thinking it'd be days of perry and lavanda? That hunting rats was sport as any weakknee could joy in?" Tides of silence flooded in. "When I tell you close-in's the valor way, you can believe me yay or nay; stand soldier mong us or skillivate off to rub your noses gainst another malcontento's. Mayhap you'll make fire, so. You boys are the onliest I ever trained as could do the close-in. Proud of you, I am. Swole pride. If now at the eleventh hour you gone rumble-belly, I sha' swallow that same pride down the downly, call off the Hunt, pull off my boots, and send the lot of you back to your fine deep-pantry homes to loll on silky cush, where you may guzzle perry till you rot. The choice is your own." Ambrose turned his back on them, selected pikes with great care till he'd a fine bokay; till they gave him the *Oyez Hola* and the left foot forward. He laid down the pikes and turned round to the Boys again, face flat as stone, voice even as brackpond. "Now then," he said, "sha' we commence on the close-in? It lacks nobbut two hours to the Hunt. Time you waste here is time you'll no have mong the horii, mind." They doubled in laugh like he'd expected and, they still laughing, he placed them in their two lines with Morsnal's cage at their head, twenty-six rats jostling for place nearest the opening. "Leap!" he commanded, and slid open the the cage door.

They leapt fine.

They was well trained for leaping.

Morsnal, on his toes to watch them over Bannon's shoulders, pumped his fist in the air to celebrate their fine leaping. They learned from each other how to leap; the blind kits felt their elders leaping in the cage till the intervals, the height, the supple feints, all, shaggled up their milkwet paws and ah now the *next* generation, mind, would be some kind of acrobatic. Yes.

Cepting, it seemed, the next generation was to be a small one.

Hunt Boys was stabbing Morsnal's rats.

With long thin blades they was slitting their throats.

Well that was a mistake, sure, that they'd real pikes in their hands, stead of reeds tipped with kelp-juice. They'd no kill them all. Maybe blood a few. Till they realized. Course they could no get them all. Course they'd no. Mayhap the few edged tools'd damage N through Z, mayhap, but the early letters was powerful smarter, been under his training for months now —

They was killing them all.

Ambrose had the Boys practicing the close-in with real weapons.

C lay in a corner pawing at Fraser's garotte tight round its neck. E leapt valiant at the spot three inches off Tomal's nose, squeaking *zee-zee-zee* to let Morsnal know he was ready for the treat he'd get, after; and was cut in two, neat as neat, for his pains. G and J did their pair dance, twining in and out of Doyle's ankles. This was some of Morsnal's master work, and he looked to Ambrose by habit to see his eyes widen in approval. In this way he missed the first slam of Doyle's pike-butt on little G's skull. As J nosed his mate's oozing eyes; they none of them having seen blood till now; as Morsnal opened his throat in gasp, Doyle thumped J's brains out tween his ears. A and B was his first pair. They liked to ride Morsnal's shoulders, exhorting their fellows from that lofty perch. He gave them their special whistle and they streaked out of the ring and climbed him, squeaking, so high as his ears. They licked his lobes and snugged inside his tunic collar. D and F was spiked like kabobs as they raced in to tap Bannon's toes with their paws. Bannon slid them off the spike with a grunt and crouched forward to dispatch another couple. Morsnal stepped forward; F was done for but the spike had nobbut pierced the loose flesh above D's neck. He scooped him up and wrapped his neck with a strip of his tunic.

One by one they slew them, letter by letter.

A and B crawled deep inside Morsnal's tunic, shivering. Morsnal himself stood soldier throughout.

It come to an end as all things do. Ambrose took Morsnal aside. "Fine work," he said. "A good job of training and I'll no forget it."

"You said you was nobbut going to use the reed fascines on my rats," said Morsnal.

Ambrose took a big sigh and delivered the speech Sganal the squint-eye worked up for just this. They'd need of Morsnal, despite him being the soppiest handker in the drawer. Keep him calm and keep him training, Gov Don said; Ambrose sighed again and gave it his best shot. "Well, sure we used the fascines every time till now. Think, Morsnal. This is the Galanty

Hunt. This is the big one. I got to know the Boys can carry out the close-in fore I send them out where Gov and all the richards can see them. The viewtube is but so big — if the Boys kill the rats at spearlength, no eye down the shelter cave'll see how fine the Boys are. Barracks, armor, food, potable — they none of them come by wishing, Morsnal. The richards give them us. They give them us so we'll rid Charnholm of the rats that carry plague. I've no need to spell this out for you of all people, Morsnal." Oil. You could no pour on too much oil. "An there's viewtubes, there's got to be close-in. An there's close-in, we got to be the ones doing it. An we're doing it, by the last rat's last whisker we'll do it perfecto supremo." The boy's face had all the expression of the jetty wall, less maybe if you thought of how the kelp drapes moved in the breeze. "I'm so glad you helped us out," said Ambrose. Sganal, that slip-clay whisper, had drilled that phrase into him, and Ambrose moved his shoulders now he'd got it off them. Gov Don was in the right of it: only Ambrose could deliver those words so the wet reed Morsnal'd believe them. "So glad you helped us out," he said again.

"They're every one dead," said Morsnal.

"Yeah, well, we done that," said Ambrose, going off script some, but in the range, sure, in the range.

"I trained them from kits so's the Boys could learn the close-in," said Morsnal.

"Uh-huh, and a fine job you done. You —"

"Months I trained them. I fed them up on a cloth damped in cider-water till they was of a size to bite carp."

"Yeah and good work you done; when I tell Gov Don, he'll doubtless slap a medal on that tunic."

"I trained them month on month so you could have the Boys cut them up into so much fatspock stew."

"Can't make a mulligan thout you slice the meat for it," said Ambrose.

"You could told me," said Morsnal.

The script flew away. "You could oped your eyes, Morsnal." Bluff, bluff, bluff and misdirect. And always call them by name. "D'you think we cared more for your scabby rats than we care for our proud young Hunt Boys? Their safety," back on script again, "must e'er be our primary concern."

"Bowel spat," said Morsnal.

Ambrose turned on Morsnal quick as ratleap. "What's that by your neck, Morsnal? You got a boil there? What's this? A rat!" and he grabbed B by the tail and dashed his skull gainst the stones in the time it takes to read of it. "These're rats, Morsnal," Ambrose hissed. "Nobbut rats. Get a good hold on your spit-leaky self and report to me in an hour's time. No oiling for you, Morsnal; you sha' go out mong the richards like dry mold."

Morsnal looked at B curled on himself. The silly kit would squeak up to any pair of hands and lick them, no sense of self-preserve soever. Where the other kits slept curled in a heap, B had always preferred Morsnal's neck, his tiny nails skritching the nape as he dreamed, his belly pressed gainst Morsnal's long pulse. He slept that way now, cepting now his neck ended in a sack of whey.

The Boys ran round the hall pumping fists in the air high in glorus triumphal. Morsnal stepped forward. He picked up B's body. It was heavier than it had been. "Right aright. Best dispose of this one fore it breeds foul," he told Ambrose. "I'll join you shortly." He walked away from the hullabal, A flat gainst his belly, breathing fast, D in his tunic pocket leaking blood, snuffling for his customary treat.

There was good rats and bad rats.

Bad rats slept in foul. They spat buboes.

Good rats slept in snug piles and frisked round Morsnal's ankles, their warm hearts skippering when he whistled high and fast, G-G-G-E-flat. When they was kits, they pinched him with their needle teeth by accident sometimes.

The bad rats, spear fodder, had no names.

The good rats had names and ran up to Morsnal when he called them.

The bad rats was living yet.

The good rats was dead.

They'd come to Morsnal as a scrabble pile of mewing kits, their eyes gummed shut. They pressed their small pink toes gainst Morsnal's chest as he gave them suck off a clean handker dipped in ciderwater.

The bad rats lived anyhow, helter-skelter, cock-a-leekie, bubotic.

The good rats lived a clean life in a clean cage and died trusting.

Morsnal walked out the hall along the line of this knowledge, careful of his balance.

"If he's that carelack on a passel of tame rats, what'll he do to the Boys?" thought Daniel M'Cool as he sponged D's lacerations, who licked his hand, grateful, the while. Dan said out loud, "Steady there, else dock-salt'll get in your cut."

Morsnal said, "Can you keep life in him?"

Dan snorted. "Certain as tides."

"I've a mate for him," Morsnal confided.

"Have you now," Dan busy with kelpjuice. "Lay you still," he told D, "this'll sting considerable." D closed his eyes and whimpered soft as the kelp dripped on his innards. He flattened his belly gainst the rail as Dan swaddled his throat in folds of clean handker, "lest he scratch or bite it accidental-like," Dan told Morsnal.

"I've a mate for him," Morsnal repeated, like that'd make it real. B was A's mate, yet B was dead and whey, his tongue stiff in his mouth; B was what was, and there's an end to it. Morsnal pulled A from his waist and gave his two-note whistle, *Tzee-tzwhoo*. A was born to charm. She run up the taffrail to Dan and triple somersaulted, ending with a bow at his busy hands.

Dan rubbed A back of the ears and crooned over her. A laid flat on her belly, her eyes half-closed, her nose gainst D's. The *Hail Janus* rocked gentle in the wake of a passing boat. Dan said, "There's Galanty Hunt today, Morsnal." Who nodded, his eyes on his rats. Dan repeated himself, "Galanty Hunt oils in a half-hour, Morsnal." Who nodded again. Dan shook the dreaming boyscrap. "Best get you gone, Morsnal. Think Ambrose'll let you slip out from this Hunt? He will no." He shook his head as the voice hammered his temples. He raised his own voice to drown it, fair shouted at Morsnal: "Get gone. If your own skin's no matter to you, think of these two here, and of my own skin. Will Ambrose send scutmen for you? Ayuh. Will they find you? Ayuh. Will they greet you with a glad cry and a backslap, carry you through Charnholm streets in palankeen? They will no. Pick up those stone feet of yours and —"

"I'm gone," said Morsnal. "You'll guard them gainst my return, no?"

Dan pressed the heels of his hands gainst his temples. "Course, course, did I no say so? Get on with you, you carenaught lackbrain."

Thus lapped with Dan's assurances, Morsnal slid down ramp and glided down pier and round the bollard waygate to barracks. Dan looked down on the ratpair panting on the taffrail. A many sailors had rats as pets but none was fullfed and fluffcoat. He whistled tuneless "Sss-ss-ss-ss," tween his teeth as he painted them with flecks of tar and shipdross so to look like every rat as ever peered from out a sailor's vest. "A and D. Those are barracks names. Best have free names now. Alpha and Delta. Sss-ss-ss-ss."

*The great stone scrapers fell roof on floor on roof on floor on squeaking kit and rheumy snout alike. The live brown towers that spunked green at their tips come rootfirst out our tunnels our caves our storehouses our meethalls our shitcoves, all, to dust crumbled as the roots croppled, our paws scrabbling in dust on dust that lay heavy on the dark lively eyes of our nestmates our kits our hobbled king in his thrash of tails –*

Of tails? Of tunnels? Our paws, kings, kits, shitcoves?

*And in that dust we thrashed in that dust we choked, stung with a thousand bites and stuffed with a thousand grains we writhed and leapt gainless as dust fell and fell as the tunnel walls shook neath the stones falling and the live brown towers crashing rootlast and the skrales of bipeds, aves and anthros, the first wingfurled falling, the second skincurled burning, all burning above us. We who lived on –*

Aves? Winged creatures? The gulls heard skweering in the far mists? The singing flights of crumble books?

*who lived on huddled nose by nose neath the outmost vents –*

What?

*only a fool tunnels underground with but one outhatch – we huddled neath the outmost vents as twoleg after twoleg was licked to bone by the flames, we grinned as they crumbled, truth to tell. Were not they our sworn foes? Was not their every tooth gainst us?*

Dan's bones tingled over his ear. What of the wave?

*The wave?*

When the harbor water drew back to the edge of sight and then come back mighty.

*Ah. The ocean scours our tunnels when it lists. We swim with its rise and land with its fall. We scrabbled through the outmost vents and ran up and out and all away. From even the sandstone bluffs a two-clam run from the stone jetty, from even there we could hear the wails skrales keens screams of those who live surface while we bit the tips off the good salt grasses in the lee of the sandstone bluffs and raised our snouts to smell the carrion.*

"Ahoy *Janus!*" from a chockfull dory waddling through the harbor, "has every man jack of you gone gormless to their sleep?"

Dan leaned out, letting his tunic drop so to screen Alpha and Delta from view. He shaded his eyes with his left hand while his right hushed the two warm bodies. "Ahoy there, Fergus. What news on the embarco?"

# Oil on These Waters

*Thin fog lay over Charnholm. The sky was grey and absent, riffled with a small, cool breeze that drew shawls over shoulders, rubbed hands together. When the sun pushed its shoulders against the horizon, making tatters of the grey mist, the last sluggards of those who were to work the Galanty Hunt woke to the faint steam that hissed from the stones.*

A HUNT BOY COME IN THE HALL whistling G-G-G-E-flat, no care in the world. None turned a hair at the sound. Ambrose hailed him, standing from his crouch in the thick of a boypack: "What's towards, Morsnal?"

"The close-in done, we shuffle off to harum," Morsnal answered, whistling soft as he stood at ease fore the Barracks Master. "What else in all the world should we do?" He nudged a mat of bloody hair aside with his toe.

"Shuffle off we sha'," a Boy yelped.

"Oiling oiling oiling," the Boys chanted.

Fraser, Tomal, Doyle, Bannon.

"Oil for these Boys!" said Fraser.

"Soft hands bestride me," said Tomal.

"No rat in *this* town sha' find purchase on *my* skin," said Doyle.

"Float like a kelpbulb, spike like a sneert," said Bannon.

"What the gorry ratsnout's a sneert?" said Morsnal.

They was silent. The Boys stayed squatting, their balls brushing the cold stones, craning their necks up at Ambrose. "Well well," he said, "we are no *Rimers*, are we?"

"Nay!"

"We are no *Beaters*, are we?

"Nay!"

"We're Hunt Boys, are we no?"

"Yay!"

"We sha' conker every rat the beaters flush this day, sha' we no?"

"Yay!"

"Spike every rat the rimers freeze this day, sha' we no?"

"Yay!"

Ambrose clomped the stones as he waded through Boys to the slack-armed Morsnal. "Got it, boykin? Got a *wimper* in your belly where your guts ought to be?" The Boys snickered *hanxh hanxh*. "When we go out there, it's each for himself and the Hunt above all; can you keep that in your weaky leaky brainpans?" Ambrose caught himself up as his questions brought squint-eye Sganal's questions hissing down his ear: *Wouldst scuttle a boat for nobbut you slipped on its deck? Hast so many tools you can toss any downpit? Careless careless, Ambrose; as you love your cushy berth, I bid you take care.* Ambrose moved closer to Morsnal. The rat-trainer's washed-blue eyes was dark grey. His copper skin was pale, stretched over his cheekbones like a drumskin. Ambrose spoke quiet in Morsnal's ear: "You know how these louts are, I can no keep them in line thout they tremble." He put an arm over the Boy's shoulder, and turned him, and steered him towards the harum gate. "Do you ride prow till we reach South Point, ayuh? Be my eyes in the air. Help me keep these scaff-raffs in formation, right aright?"

Morsnal swung round. "In the prow? With Max?"

Ambrose clapped him on the back as he pushed him through the gate. "There you have it. We could no done this Hunt without you trained those rats. You got a eye, Morsnal, you got you a real eye. Me and Gov Don been talking about how best to compense you for it. For now, off with you, tell Matron you're to be oiled for prow."

"For prow," Morsnal repeated, like he'd no grasped it.

"Ayuh, for prow," Ambrose said. He looked over his shoulder; a few Boys had rose from squat and was warming their froze balls tween their hands. Next they'd be gangling out the harum gate all anyhow, yarrowping and leapish; they'd divagate away to naught was he no there to shape them. "For prow, right aright. Give Matron this," sliding a hoop of metal off his finger, "and tell her you're to be oiled for prow. Got it?" Morsnal nodded, twisting the hoop round his own finger. Ambrose's gut queezed at the sight, but all the Boys was up now, larruping their cocktips, Bannon waving a flask of perry — "Go on;" he gave Morsnal a great clout tween the shoulder blades. Morsnal staggered forward to the harum gate.

"How now, Fergus," said Daniel M'Cool, his left arm holding summat to his body, making no move to unhook the rampchains. "What can I do you for?"

Fergus grinned, showing all fourteen of his teeth, "Well Danny. Well now. Is it no a matter of what *I* can do for *you?*"

Dan seemed to consider this. Then he said, "No, Fergus."

Fergus spread his hands wide and his lips wider. "Now Danny, now Danny. My Palan says you're troubled with voices hammering from inside your head."

Dan stepped back from the taffrail. A hit, a palp'ble hit. "Palan told you that?"

"Well now, well ... Who'd tell me, else?" Fergus spread his hands wide from his body; nothing up his sleeve, no threat soever, his weatherproof grin fixed in place. "Now Danny, be reasonable. A few drops of tarponesse'd quiet those voices down to nobbut hum. Now what sensible man'd turn it away? Has suffering some virtue? Does it speed the crops, grind the meal, net the fish, clean the water? Has shape so lovely you maun keep it by you?"

Tarponesse'd still the voice. Well, that was true enough. M'Cool he'd yield. Out of course. He reached a long arm to unhook the rampchains. Fergus's toes twitched; oh that about Palan was a master stroke; M'Cool was kerfuddled entire; his fingers was on the hasp — and then he drew back. "I thank you," said Daniel M'Cool, "for your kindly thought, but I've no need of it."

Fergus bowed and pulled a flask from deep inside his clothes. "As you like. I tilt my wares down no throat. Still and all, take this with my compliments on this holsday. Finest perry in all Charnholm, it'll dull the voices in your skull, though it won't still them entire like tarponesse. Catch, now."

Daniel leaned gainst the taffrail as he readied to catch the perry flask, at which his left side shuddered, independent-like, and back he drew. "I thank you, but we've good store aboard. No call to rob you of your stock."

Fergus tilted the flask's contents down his own throat. "Refuse to drink with Fergus, is it? What's Fergus done to you, Danny, that you spurn him with your foot? What has Danny M'Cool done, eh? Tell me that. What has he done that he's latitude to puff up and mortificate a working dreg as never done naught to no one. Tell me that. Up Charnholm and down there's dregs as *bones* ache. A pinch of tarponesse and they can outdance a tumble krewe. Where's the harm?"

Fergus had played this music well for a dunnamany years, yet M'Cool sliced him off with a gesture. "Enough, have done," he said. "I thank you for your cozening but I've work needs doing. Do you give a hearty clap to Palan when next you see him," and Fergus stood gapemouth while M'Cool slipped into pilotshack and was gone.

⟨⟩

Alpha lay next to Delta in Dan's kit bag. She licked Delta's neck with her long tongue, over and over. Sometimes she paused and looked up at the dreg. Sometimes he looked back at her. *First a yellow fog rises behind the ears; after the fog comes, come the buboes. On first sighting, we drive the befogged onto Charnholm verges, and there we leave them with sufficient store of carrion and gutterspill to last them till a Hunt comes.*

Why do you no bite their necks through?

*Sink our teeth in the buboes? Drink the pus? No. How else could we despatch them? No. Dreg hands hold spikes that bring death quick, all the gift we can make the dying; a quick death with a full belly.*

Wait. You can see a fog as brings the buboes?

Alpha licked Delta's neck with long strokes, her eyes closed in deep concentrate.

⟨⟩

The horii was ranged sloppy round the harum pool, on the broad yawn. Matron stifled a yawn of her own and stertorated: "Pull the spine long, gerruls; perk the ass *up* by a long *pull* from the *crown* — and *left* hip, *right* hip, *left* hip, *right* — now shimmulate, all together, shimmulate — Galyse, Chrysta, you know better nor to chat now; get in corner and drop and give me twenty — shimmulate, shimmulate; Hunt Boy heart relies on your art so *move* those asses tick-tick-tock, move them *round* the oiled cock ..."

Galyse and Chrysta slippered off to the corner and dutiful chose two fascines with which they whipped the wide-spread backsides of the other horii round the pool, flicking their forks methodic to Matron's rules.

"Three," said Galyse, "this willow's lost its flex, so it has."

"Seven," said Chrysta, "I gave Thursgood a bout of willing last night."

"Eleven. Gerruls as go off harum comes to a sticky end, I hear."

"Thirteen. That's plain foolery. All come's sticky."

"Seventeen. Did the willing please him?"

"Nineteen. Made him speak, Galyse. Thursgood. Can you feature it? A wordspout, he was. Softer nor what you said, too."

"And that's twenty!" Matron shouted. "Gerruls, come on back and get some get-go in you. And *swivel* and slide down, and *swivel* and slide down — we're short on woodcocks this morning; share and share about, now; share and share about."

"What'd he say?" said Galyse.

"He rambled on of —"

Naila hissed at the both of them.

Matron loomed up. "What did I say?"

"They was schooling me in flutter, Matron," said Naila straightface.

Matron squinted at them. "Flutter, is it? I'll give you flutter do you open your traps again. Now: *pump* and sigh and *pump* and swivel ..."

Goodwin's hands trembled as she paced back and fro on the courtyard dais. "She's ofttimes frettish," said a jongleur to a cantatrice, who carried on *do-re-mi-fa-sol-la-ti-do*. The jongleur told a tumbler, "Even the smallest Kit Hunt sends Goodwin staccato," but the tumbler nodded, only, stretching his hamstrings in the early morning cold. "Damp the air off harbor today, is it no?" the jongleur asked a cloaked form pushing up on his left, who drew back its white hood a handwidth and stuck out its tongue at him:

"Slunch your yap," said the whiteskin, "you'll look nohow an you miss one turn or twirl of this layout." It pulled the hood forward over its long thin beak and shouldered through the crowd toward the massed rimers.

Goodwin searched for Bran mong the semblage. He was somewheres out there gathering the prentice mutes — jongleurs, tumblers, rope-walkers and such — the outflanks of the rimer wedge. Bran should been the one whiteskin mong a swool of dark cloaks, easy to spot — and there was the whiteskin. Goodwin pulled her left ear at him. She planted herself on the omphal of the dais and took breath for the incants.

⌒

Cept the whiteskin mong the dark-cloaked mutes was no Bran. While the dark still lay thick on Charnholm town, Bran lay on his back, three piers over, knocking back perry with Finn M'Cool. "My good good friend," Bran called him, and slapped at his back, and missed, and drank again. Finn smiled on him when he'd drained the flask. "Down to the dregs!" said Bran. "*Dregs is up and richards out / All for lack of a sharp rat snout*," gibbering spocks of drool down his whiteskin cloak, his plump cheeks flushed, "for I'm gone to be for rimer fore e'er morning comes," Bran nodded wide-eye at Finn, "when the dark dark passes, the light light rises," pushing himself up on one elbow when the quiet coil of Finn made no move, "see if I'm no there, ah, umm-phmm," tilting the empty flask down his pout, "for I sha' be, right enough, come the light light morn you'll see Bran mong the dark dark mutes in rimer semblage, you'll see him, ummm," his right hand falling lax to his side, his fat lips puffing bubbles as he snored.

Palan come up to Finn at that sound. Together, in silence, they eased the snorting Bran of his whiteskin cloak. Mary Pat laid a hand gainst his breast — "warm enough," she whispered, and Finn and Palan slipped off with the cloak, while she glided through the bushes to the beaters. She laid her body gainst the tallest of them from behind and spoke over his shoulder to the rest as she swiveled her hipbones round his asscheeks: "This is the dull part, the waiting," said Mary Pat, "yet it'll raise you every one from beater, this day. Make like you're running drills till you hear Finn and Palan come whistling over the wall. An your courage fails you, head up the look-out to help the semaphores." She stroked the tallest down his body and flowed away over the rubble.

The tallest beater followed her to the foot of the wall. "Sha' you come back when they come whistling?"

Mary Pat laid a palm on his chest. "If I'm no back by then, may I be rived by longtooths." The dark was thinning over the bluffs. She stroked his throat. "Give me a jump, willa?" She was over the wall and away fore he'd his hands back to his sides.

⌒

Mary Kath stood in fury by the salt baulk. Lena was late. Mary Pat was late. Finn was late. Matron'd be readying the horii for the Galanty Hunt. Mary Kath ran through her own chant, chanted it quiet as the grey lightened over harbor:

*Hear now you rats of Charnholm*
*You noisome clanch of vapors*
*Remorseless, treacherous,*
*Lecherous, kindless scum.*

*Old, cold, loathed enemy!*
*Enemy inveterate!*
*You herd of boils and plagues,*
*You wild and wanton herd.*

*Baseness unconfinable!*
*Loathed issue of despised loins!*
*Your name blisters our tongues*
*Most foul rats of Charnholm.*

Neath the dome of the Rimehouse, the musicians was tuning up. A stringbass pushed away a flagon with his elbow. "Ale I have in plenty," he said, "You've the ears of a mudwrump. I said, Give me an A." Two viols wrapped gut lengths round their waists gainst possible broken strings mid-Hunt. The drummers stood cocky by the windows, their ass cheeks on the beat, tightening and loosening, one-TWO-three-FOUR, one-TWO-three-FOUR. Max tucked his viol tween his left shoulder and his chin, the scroll supported in his left palm. He played long bowstrokes on the open E string just above the bridge, and took it off his shoulder to turn the tuning pegs till the pitch was right. He played long bowstrokes on the second string, and fiddled with the tuning pegs till A was A. The catgut keened E-A, E-A, the drummers twirled their sticks and rolled one-TWO-three-FOUR, the horns blatted A-E, A-E, the cymbals clashed, the locust beans rattled inside macaraca gourds, the stringbass pulsed G-D-A-E bum-ba-bum-bum, G-D-A-E bum-ba-bum-bum.

Into this welter come Morsnal. Two cymbals rang gainst each other to mark his dazed entry. "Max?" he said. A drummer rattled a roll on his drum-rim, tossed a stick up to catch it mid-spin, and pointed the butt end at the viol-player bent over his tuning. Morsnal whistled G-G-G-E-flat. Max snapped his eyes Morsnal-ward and drank in the mingy upright frame. Max lowered his bow. His left hand plucked the unbowed strings, E-A, E-A; he raised his brows. "I've come from Matron," said Morsnal in answer. "I'm to be oiled for the prow."

"Ah," said Max.

"She said you'd know where and all."

"Ah."

"Ambrose give me this ring in token, but Matron she'd no take it from me," holding out the hoop to Max.

Max fingered the strings, D-G, D-G, as he eyed the hoop. "This'll get you inside compound," he said. "Maybe more nor that."

Morsnal shook his head. "I could give a barnacled fillip for that. Do you show me how to wrank that Ambrose off his perch, is all I ask. You see this?" He opened his tunic to show B lying stiff and curlpaw gainst his side. Max flinched, swallowed hard. You did no want to startle a dreg with a dead rat at his waist. Best to let him tell it.

Morsnal said, "Couple hours past this was my clever B. You should ought seen him. Dance on his hind legs, he could, train a ratkit to tumble quicker nor you could say 'keep your tail up.' He was a one, was B. Ambrose slew him." Best to say naught of A and D till he'd sussed this Max in full. "Ambrose slew them all," he said. "Promised and promised he'd lay spike to none of them. I trained them from ratpups at his command, trained them special for the close-in. This morning thout no word, none, he set the Hunt Boys to let the life out of them all. I want his own blood let, the way the wild rats sha' feast on him. The wild rats they're the bad ones. They're the ones to kill. My two dozen and two was no his to kill. I'll do what all it takes to let the blood out of Ambrose slow; I want him wranked with ague; may he boil."

Max said a curious thing. "Do you know Mary Katharine M'Cool?"

Morsnal folded the tunic round B's stiff body. "Seen her round. Why?"

"No reason," Max shrugged. Blind fury spilling all over the place. Its potency'd turn to vapor was it no bottled. "Come out to stables. I'll show you Hunt Wagon prow. Mind, you're to keep out the way of my bow arm all times."

"I'll mind. You'll aid me gainst the Barrack Master?"

"I'll do you better. Come along of me. This is a great Hunt, the Galanty."

The drums rolled one-TWO-three-FOUR, the horns blatted A-E, A-E; cymbals clashed; locust beans rattled inside macaraca gourds; the string-bass pulsed G-D-A-E bum-ba-bum-bum, G-D-A-E bum-ba-bum-bum, as the cold dark lightened.

M'Donal spat out a ryestraw and whistled high, high and low, chirrup.

Six dregs square and true rustled from out the nearest stall. "Rations rations rations," they growled.

"Get your double rations come Hunt Breakfast," growled M'Donal in return. "Shazzle up the Hunt Wagon till it shines! Roll her out to yard!" The coulees disappeared into the stable. Song and scrub issued from within. M'Donal went on speaking, but softer, like his cork was popped, his words spilled out willa nilla. "Safe enough you'll be, no matter what all you do. Every scutman born of woman is round the shelter caves on the fret that dregs is up to summat." His wizened mouth worked in and out a few times till he'd enough sliva to spit on the clean stones. "Like to see summat, I should. What's more likely nor a passel of starveling dregs knocking the richards off their thrones? Next the sun sha' tumble backwards, and the waves crest downwards, and Ambrose hand out sweeties to every spawn in the bleachers. Ha!" M'Donal's lips worked in and out over his long white-spattered tongue. He spat again. "Talking to the empty air like a gorry richard. Hump." He moved closer to the stable's pillars and raised his voice: "So, Max, hast come to check prow?"

Max stepped out from pillar shade. "Always a treat to hear you spattle your inmost thoughts, M'Donal. This is Morsnal, pointed by Ambrose to share prow with me today; we're here to view Hunt Wagon." Max was breath to breath with the halfcrouch dreg, his shoulder gainst the rheumy, red-veined nose. He looked down into the head groom's bloodshot, yellow eyes. "Come to check prow, M'Donal, sir," he said.

M'Donal shuffled his feet in their leathern shucks. He gave a huge bass whistle. Morsnal jumped; Max nobbut lounged gainst a pillar. The six dregs square and true come trompling and boistering and stinking of scrumpy, hauling the Hunt Wagon into the courtyard.

"Ah hey, it's nobbut Max."

"Thought by a's shadow 'twas Gov Don."

"But it's our Max walking s' tall —"

"Sheering hither all t' tell M'Donal —"

"He's here —"

"Glory the day!"

"Here to check prow."

"Who's this doesna trust our work unchecked?" The coulees come at the young dregs in a body, shoulder gainst shoulder, their great neck cords flexing. Morsnal stepped back but needless, they'd come for Max. They bent their cider-thick mouths to Max's nose and sniffed, loud and all to-gether. "Yeah, nobbut our Max," said one, scraping his stubble gainst the smooth viol-player's cheek. "Gi' us a tune, our Max."

"None of yez clever rat ratspit, neither."

"Summat as'll tap the toes."

"Put a bit of jig in a body."

Max gave them a tune, right aright, one made of cider mash and sweet peelings, an 'if only, if only,' they'd heard a dunnamany times, a harkback to the times when every gut was full and death took the aged only, a hark-back to times as never were. "That'd pull the heart out your body." "So it could." "So it has," stubble-thick pushing a tear from his eye with a great thumb. They stood slackarm round Max, their leerish eyes wranked in sor-row, till the tune ended and the air was still. M'Donal whistled bass, at when the coulees clapped their hands together and set to work, polishing the Hunt Wagon to a high gloss, hissing tween their teeth *ssshhh-sssshh*, like to calm a frettish justborn.

"Call this a polish?"

"Better nor what you could do with your own mam's spit."

"My mam she's dry of spit after mocking how you carry on."

M'Donal motioned Max up the Wagon ladder. The coulees rubbed on as Morsnal trailed after.

"Spot here needs vinegar."

"Vinegar's no good for that; here's double-distill perry."

"Ah now that I'll put where it'll do most good."

"And I."

"Yeah and I."

As the hot sun rose red over harbor, the coulees rubbed doubletime to give it a fine red Wagon to glint off. Max and Morsnal was forgotten at the prow. There the first rays found them, looking away off south to the richard compounds, where the Hunt Day stir was just beginning.

"*Now* we head off for oiling," said Max.

# The Slippery Slope

*The hot red sun seared the fog. The sky's charred edges shriveled back from its advance. When the last sliver of the disk had cleared the horizon, every leaf on every tree in Charnholm turned transparent in one breath. Those who woke only to watch the Galanty Hunt woke to rosecolor on their eyelids.*

*In the dregshacks, sleepcrusts were pushed from eyes, ryetoasts arranged as prettily as might be on tin salvers, potable was sipped by chapped lips, shoulders braced to haul and carry. In the richard compounds, eyes fluttered and lips parted in sighs to acknowledge parlogals bringing the new day on trays that held tea and applebread and m'lady's facewash bowl, white porcelain that steamed with potable and chamomile flowers. In m'lord's room, the parlogals had less to carry but more to bear. The day came smooth and sure in the richard compounds. While the parlogals did their duty, the footmen lounged and smoked round the front door; afternoons were their time, when lords was on the stroll and ladies damp from their baths.*

O N THE PARAPET ROUND THE RICHARD COMPOUNDS, the fogwet stones steamed. Deirdre said, "You see, where there's room to stand up, a body stands up."

"Yeah and where there's water all round, a body gets wet." Lena looked at the sun, just clear of the horizon, and at the walls round them. "Nobbut the shadiest corners is still anyhows damp," she said. "Hunt'll be massing soon."

The pale hand waved that aside. "Listen to me. Will you listen?"

"Out of course. Are you no my mistress? Am I no your dreg? Ask me to listen, what other sha' I do? My ears are flapping wide as hori legs."

Deirdre's hands fell to her sides. "That's unfair."

"Unfair, is it?"

"Yes, it is. I've always treated you as my friend, not my servant. Our lives have appointed us to these positions. It's life itself that is unfair."

"This life's unfair, is it? Well ope my eyes and call me Nancy." Lena pulled her canvas smock away from her throat like it choked her. "I've my own death here in my pocket, and here's you wanting to make sure everybody gets the same slice of cake; Deirdre the Gentle Richard'll compassionate the unfortunate that much." Lena did no spit, for Deirdre's mouth was pursed to weep. Lena said, gentle, "What you know of dregs is what you learned off me, only. You walk the parapet with me and hear my tales, but a body takes nobbut so much harm through its ears. You look on the coulees and your heart hammers fast, but *your* shoulder was never tore, *your* knees never splintered. You look on us dregs and your soft eyes drip," shaking a handker in Deirdre's gone-closed face, "think you're a princess in a crumble book, you do, come to save the pitiful. *We are no pitiful!*" Lena gripped the parapet rim. "This Galanty Hunt that's to you a grand diversion is life and breath to us."

Deirdre's lips may been pursed to weep, but she did no weep. The sun clambered its way up the sky. "Yes," she said, dreaming-like, "so I must go among the dregs this morning."

"Go mong the dregs? This morning of all mornings? There's fearsome business afoot this morning, Deirdre, it's no time for scamp and frolic."

"Give me the death in your pocket, Lena. See then if I'm all foam and no force. I will place it in the proper hands in your stead."

"Canst no," Lena breathed, one fist to her plexus.

"Yeah I can. Canna talk dreg for all the world as tha can? Canna smutch my face to look dreg as tha'art?"

"Canst no," she repeated, lackforce.

"I can, then. Give me t' vial. What's death to you's nobbut a slap on wrist to me," said Deirdre.

Slow as a rat leaves its den in a rainstorm, the dreg's copper hand stole from her pocket and laid the cloth-wrapped tube in the other's pale fingers. Her eyes steady on the blanched face, Lena said, "Cider Mother laid this in my hands."

"Uh-huh." Deirdre Claresdotter wrapped the cloth in her own handker with her initials stitched in one corner.

"When you give it, you got to come pat with the words, Deirdre."

"Uh-huh. *Boola Boola Weerna Roola.* Fool saying, an you ask me. Right aright." She tucked the clumsy bundle into the tiny broidered reticule that swung from her wrist. "See you in Potable Works," she said, and with a flip of her pale hand was gone.

"Boola boola," said Lena.

At the Rimehouse, the whiteskin mong the mutes bent low its cowl in response to Goodwin's nod. She raised her arms on the dais; all the rimers circled round raised their arms. Goodwin reminded them that this was their final rehearsal, then began the incants in a low, sonorous voice:

> Hear now you rats of Charnholm!
> You noisome clanch of vapors!
> Remorseless, treacherous,
> Lecherous, kindless scum.                    *Ulla!*

The jongleurs danced three times slowpace round the Anathematizers, shaking their long, belled poles, and ended by knuckling their brows to the whiteskins who now in ratquell voice repeated Goodwin's every line:

> Old, cold, loathed enemy!
> Enemy inveterate!
> You herd of boils and plagues,
> You wild and wanton herd.                   *Ulla!*

> Baseness unconfinable!
> Loathed issue of despised loins!
> Your name blisters our tongues,
> Most foul rats of Charnholm.                 *Ulla!*

> You sha' have thirst but no drink
> When your throat fries in the drouth
> Salt the flame be in your mouth
> Thirst but no drink for the rats of Charnholm.

Mutes and whiteskins, all, held the final *Ulla!* with a long breath. Goodwin cut the air horizontal to end the singers. The cowled whiteskin mong the mutes brushed its crown in reply with one long finger. Goodwin took heart from Bran's presence, though he did look a bit hunched; well, they was all on the fret with this Galanty. She eased her shoulders in their sockets. She clapped three times, took a long breath, and began the final incants:

> Choking sha' come on you
> Convulsions sha' strike you
> Put poisonous pain in you          *Ulla!*
> Evil, death, short life to you          *Ulla!*
> Death and smothering on you          *Ulla!*
> In your grave fester
> You rats of Charnholm.          *Ulla!*
> Out upon you!
> Blasts and fogs upon you!
> Pestilence on you!          *Ulla!*

"Rimers, louder on that last line, PESTILENCE — and pause — and drop it a fifth — ON YOU. Again, please."

> Your forms, muddy vestures of decay,
> Sha' moulder by the end of day.
> Your bones, marrowless;
> Flesh, bloodless.          *Ulla!*

> Blight skull, and ear, and skin,
> And hearing, and voice, and sight,
> Ulla! before the day be out,
> Blight, rot, burn, melt, blight.          *Ulla!*

"And all together on this one, keep the words clear while you bring the volume UP—"

BLIGHT ROT BURN MELT BLIGHT.

"Remember, wait for the crowd to give you your *Ulla*. Break for ten minutes — and let's keep it to twenty minutes," Goodwin's voice rose over the scrum of chat as the rimers untied their whiteskins, rubbed their feet, rolled their necks, stretched their limbs, bent at the waist, scratched their noses: "We've but a short time fore the Hunt, Rimers," as she strode from the dais. "There you are," she hailed the cowled whiteskin, "glass of cider?"

"Certain," putting back the cowl, "draw it mild and keep it coming."

"Rimshot!"

"Easy now, you'll go to spill the cider. Waste makes want, Goodwin."

"Where's Bran, Rimshot?"

"Last I heard, Bran was down the salt baulk, making a proper vessel of hisself."

"What?"

"There's but so much perry in the tuns; take heart, he maun drink it sometime up."

"Drinking?"

"Drinking? I'll take another, thank you kindly — the man was sucking it up his pores, to hear tell." Rimshot drained its second glass. "So I grabbed his whiteskin and took his semblance. Rimers might gone kittle-kattle had they no seen his cowl." The drogyne clapped hand on the old woman's shoulder. "He's the habit of it; naught new in Bran drinking."

"I must — but the rehearsal — we're to hit our marks in a half hour's time — you say he's drinking heavily — what, on Galanty Hunt? — who else can — no, it must be I — it's but five minutes walk — but what if —"

"Goodwin, tha' scansion's gone piscine. Calm tha'sen. Go and see to Bran an you list. Me and Mary Katharine can range them in their places gainst your return."

"Well — it's — he's no gift for drinking — you know he never —"

"Go, Goodwin. Me and Mary Kath'll see to all."

"Well — if you're sure — I'll return in a quarter hour — such an important occasion — make sure they tie their cloaks to the throat — and —" her voice fading away to naught as she trappered off to the matted verge where the beaters sembled.

"Right aright," said Rimshot when Goodwin had faded entire. "*Now we sha' hear some nathematize.*"

Chrysta slid an elbow down Galyse's hips, who ass-cheeked Naila, who shoved the next girl in line off her toes. "Gerruls, gerruls!" Matron put hands to hips and whistled shrill. "Wipe one oildrop off your skin and it's great trouble you'll be in." Her hips shook off the power of her whistling. "Are you pole-climbers or are you no? The Hunt Boys is goosing the musicians' asses; the musicians is more nor ready to slide pole; *and* you've the shaving and plucking and oiling all to do fore Hunt can weigh out the doors. Chrysta, Galyse, leave off jangling. Naila, spit out whatever's tween your jaws. We've nobbut a few minutes to make ready. To the pole, gerruls, to the pole!" Matron's hips shook neath her as she swung arm. "First passel — climb to high tier! And easy! And *through* the cuffs ... and link ... and hold! Second passel — climb to middle tier! And easy! Naila, less of the frissome snather — with breastflesh of your own enough, you've no need to bite Dorween's. And link ... Tarlish, slide your cuffed arm *through* Bonaveel's; there you are my flossies ... and hold! Third passel — and *stroll* and bump and *stroll* and grind — remember, you'll bear the brunt of them — and easy! Chrysta, hast ever done this fore now? Canna count tha' limbs? One through Galyse — through her arm, her *arm!* — mind the oil, mind the *oil!* — and one through Darnelle — and link — eyes *front*, gerruls — and hold!" Matron circled the pole, her eyes flicking every which way out their sacs. "Darnelle, weight equal on your feet, thank you very much. Naila, dig your talons in Dorween again and I'll send you to beaters, by the rat's last snarl I sha', could slide a nova in tha' slot easy as spike a dead rat. Chrysta, Galyse, shutter up *now* or you'll have a special session with Hunt Captain."

"Who's Hunt Captain?" said Bonaveel, idle burnishing her left toes gainst the rough stone pole.

"She's as'ing," said Galyse through her teeth, her lips fixed in Mona Lisa.

"Ooket 'Atron, she's 'ike-uh ex'lode," answered Chrysta likewise.

All Matron's gracious fell off her in a one-beat. "Ooze Un Cappen? Ooze un cappen? Izzis wunna *my* gerruls az-gin? Wunna my gerruls azgin ooze un cappen? Oodya think? Oodya think's a cappen?"

"Steam out 'er ears, 'ust a'out," said Chrysta.

"Ayuh. Otch er ow." Galyse oped her lips and raised her voice. "Matron, 'mission to speak?"

"Hooo-duh thought wunna *my* gerruls woood —" Matron shubbered to a halt. She took a long breath, her flesh bubbling in its rolls. "Speak, then, Galyse, go on."

"It's Thursgood, Matron. It's Thursgood as is Hunt Captain this day."

"S'ag'd stay cool in tha' 'outh," whispered Chrysta in miration.

"That is correct. Gerruls, ope tha' lips and say after me, 'Thursgood is Hunt Captain this day.' Louder! Every one on you! Naila, an I have to lift my tongue to you once more this day ... right. Right aright. Thursgood's Hunt Captain, and he's chose Morsnal for prow," every breath was intook — Morsnal! — "and Chrysta for hori. Good heaving, Chrysta. Finn he'll be Beatest — and do I see a gerrul of mine making up to Finn M'Cool you sha' *wish* you'd nobbut cellulite on you; Beaters is no our beat, hear?" The horii hung their heads, but Matron walked steady round the third passel, squeezing each and every thigh where it met a hori's plucked fork. "Right aright," she said. "Now let's see ripple ... second tier ... Bonaveel, it's your *belly* you're to ripple, no your shoulders ... first tier ... think I can no see you from down here? I said *ripple* ... there you are ... third tier, you're flissome .. aright. Now. Musicians are a minute hence. Check your limbs in their cuffs. Any chafing?" Even the newest-made hori knew to shake her head. "Right aright then. Deep breath in ... and out ... in ... all the way down to your forks, gerruls ... and in ... out ... and —"

The holecover atop the pole groaned as it was pushed aside. A few rust flakes fell in the topmost tier's hair. A hand reached down and soft brushed the flakes away. Two hands wrapped round the pole. A creak as the guide rope was unsnapped. The horii sturdied gainst the pole as the soft rope-end flicked their skin as it was played out to the toes of the lowest tier. A grunt from Matron as she bent to snap the rope to its anchor. A creak as the rope was run up taut. The swing ropes rattled as they was run through their pulleys. Two pale soles fumbled for the footloops in the swing ropes. One bronze hand and then another reached for the loops, and then with a flenk rush come the whole weight of Morsnal, his cock so stiff it twanged gainst a top tier skull. "Play her out easy," Ambrose shouted from the floor above them. "Keep him on the dawdle." Morsnal's oiled chest slid down the topmost tier. "*Pull* that guide rope in, it's no his nipples he's here to rub." Matron swayed the guide, stuffing Morsnal's cocktip down a hori ear — "Eyes *front*, gerruls," said Matron — and swayed it, drawing a wavy line in jism on the breasts and bellies of the second tier, the swing ropes jerking as Morsnal's hips spasmed, and swayed it again, drawing the pulsing cock down Bonaveel's inner thigh, who moaned till Morsnal's hips was stilled, when she quit off moaning and resumed polishing her toes gainst the stone pole. "*Play* it out," shouted Ambrose. "This one's done." The swing ropes let him down, his cock slapping Darnelle's toes, dribbling down Chrysta's neck, laying its last few drops tween a third hori's breasts. "*Set* him down," shouted Ambrose. "*Get* your feet *out* the loops, Morsnal. Think you're only Boy as slides this morning?" Morsnal staggered downramp till his feet touched pooltile, just sufficient self-preserve left to push off with his toes as his head carried his body into the water. He splashed, he sank, his mouth filled with water as he fountained out through his teeth. He floated, his arms and legs splayed full long. His limp cock bobbed gainst his thigh.

"Next!" Ambrose shouted.

The next one came. And the next. Max was the last musician down pole.

"Waiting for a footman's invite?" said Ambrose.

Max took him in from toe to crown. The Barrack Master was rank with sweat, his hair falling limp in his grey eyes, his round nose sunk tween his flaccid cheeks. There was no fat on him; he was dreg for all he'd his hand deep in richard pockets, but the skin hung from his bones in loose folds at armpit, waist, jowls. His eyes whirled in their sacs. Max fingered the extra viol string he kept round his own firm column of a neck. "Waiting for naught," he said, and slipped down rope one-hand, his soles to the pole, the viol held armlength out, touching no hori, tasting no oil, landing firm on the poolside tiles. "My thanks," he said, and strolled off.

Ambrose knelt at the hole-rim. The gold hoop on Morsnal's left hand sparkled. Max strolled to a dry couch gainst the wall, the viol string round his neck glinting. No time to say or do aught with Hunt Boys massed thick at his back, each primed for the slide. Ambrose shook his head. Those two'd keep. He turned to his Hunt Boys: "Now the Musicians got them warmed up for you. Who lacks cockstand, come here by me. Thursgood, you're Hunt Captain, you send them down." Ambrose walked to his low stool while Thursgood above and Matron below guided one Boy after another down pole. They come on, and they come on, and they come. Ambrose pulled on his oiled mitts as he sat to tend a couple flaccid members, Boys as had already spurted in the press of bodies. Ambrose stroked the shaft of the last overready fool; the drop was going smooth, nobbut a couple Boys jostling each other as they waited for swing rope. The last fool Boy was stiffing up nice under the oiled mitts when Ambrose heard the wailing. Through the joints of the stone wall, the wail of a justborn choking for breath, its soft nails scrabbling at the grout. "Get down with you," he slapped the tomfool's ass, and walked slow as he could muster to the hole-rim. The wailing rose, and the horii shook; the wailing skreeled, and the Boys went limp. The wailing sailed above hearing, and every bone rattled in its socket. "What the —" Ambrose breathed.

Max lifted his bow from the viol's strings. The wailing ceased. In the silence after, the tomfool last Boy swung from the untended guide rope, slupped gainst Chrysta, and bounced, and rasped the stone pole, and bounced, and rubbed long Galyse, caught short there, his feet three handspans off the floor. Matron lay sprawled anyhow, her mouth agape, her eyes so wide they stretched their fleshy caves. Ambrose played out the swing ropes till the tomfool was on his feet, whereon he stumbled to bathe his scoured, halfmast cock in the pool's chill water. Max set the viol on his knees. The hall was silent but for the splash of water from the last Boy's plunge. "Musicians to the Wagon," Max said into the silence.

⌐

Cider Mother shifted on her stool as the wails died to silence. In shifting, a small leathern case fell from her pocket. She traced the two words writ on it in gold: "Aqua Pura." There was more. She turned it this way and that to catch the light. "Aqua pura," said Cider Mother, and sat in the weak morning light. Suellen cried, "Mam, Mam," and Cider Mother set the spawn on her knees. "Aqua pura," she told Suellen, who was playing, content, with her tunic hem. "Means aught to you?" Suellen smiled. Cider Mother stroked the child's hair. "Oh may a ratnest romp on my heap of wheat if — August Inkwhistle," she told Suellen, who nodded. "As ever I live. Inkwhistle. Stay here on this stool for one minute and you sha' have ryebread and apple butter." Suellen bounced on the seat while Cider Mother raked out the coals neath the vats. "There," she said, tying a kercher over her head, shoving flasks and casks in her carrysack, "we can be gone the whole day if need be and no harm to the mash-tuns." Cider Mother grabbed the stair-rail with her right hand and her spawn with the left. "Up we go now," she said. "Upsy daisy." She sang, "*Hush little baby, don't you babble / Mam's gone to buy you some potable / Of that potable you'll drink your fill / And live long life you surely will.* You'll no drink out of cisterns like Nora did. Tha sha' have potable every day tha draws breath." She drew the spawn close. "Come now. Upsy daisy. Up to watch the Hunt. Hurry, now." She cast a glance at the sun. They'd a good hour yet fore shutter-up. "Hurry," she said, and climbed up the stairs.

# The Rat Hunt Rolls Out

*The sun, well clear of the harbor, sliced sea from sky, thrust hard shafts through shutter chinks, bowled through windows thrown wide to the seagoing breeze. The stones of town and bluff steamed and their steam was sucked harborward by the water's cold, pent breath. Brooms pushed crumbs out open doorways; there the sweepers paused, turned their backs on the sun, rolled their stiff necks and shoulders in the day's new heat. In dens and crevices, grasspiles and rubbage heaps, rats snugged closer to their nestmates.*

IN THE HARUM, the horii shaved with even strokes the half-mast Boys, who lay unmoving neath the razor. Matron walked the ranks, slowing some and urging others on, so's all finished at the same time, give or take a stroke or two. *Next!* The horii began oiling the Boys with unguent they skimmed from tween their legs, hissing urgency at the novae who brought the carboys of oil long the line of couches; never leaving off rubbing, filling every pore with the scented oil. It went smooth as first rains with no gankish nova like Mary Katharine M'Cool to tread Matron's heels, that eager to find out, by asking, what the scent was made of, how infused, what its purpose, how long it'd last unstopped. This nova passel asked no questions where they knew there'd be no answer. They fetched and carried and scurried and ducked their heads did a Boy look them over. The shaven Boys was oiled; the limp cocks rose; Ambrose snapped his long whip at the heels of those few Boys who dared to grab horii — "After Hunt, you clinkbrain toerag; could light a lamp with your earspag as keeps you from hearing what I said a hunnerd times: *you go in after Hunt.*" In the courtyard, the Musicians was tuning atop the Hunt Wagon, A and A and A from Max's viol. The drummers beat *bangarang*, the cymbals rang *samdankissh, samdankissh*, the viol sang *skreelyabach ayheyoh ayheyoh*, the trumpets *popparopped* tripletime, the long horns squealed, the tambors *shack shakrattled*. Limp cocks rose and taut cocks *bangarangled* oiled bellies as the Hunt Boys rose and stretched. Naila and Chrysta and Galyse and all moved tongue and hand and body long a Boy's length *poppoparop* as they buckled corvisers over hairless, slippery chests and bellies. Naila slid a long hand neath the corviser to pinch a nipple; Chrysta cupped ass; Galyse sucked a downdraft cocktip; each to her fancy. "Do as the moment bids you," Matron said as she paced, and the horii obeyed the moment's bidding as they rubbed corvisers to gleam, as they rubbed. Ambrose shouted, "Time, gennelmen!" and the risen cocks *bangaranged* belly and bronze as the risen Boys strode in the procession *samdankissh, samdankissh*, muscling for position back of Hunt Cappen Thursgood, long the pool and down the ramp and out the great studded iron doors flung wide by shabrag coulees scraping their brows on the entry cobbles. The Hunt Boys *skreelyabach naskreel* swarmed round Hunt Wagon, pushed the stokers aside *bangarang*; each thrust a left thumb through the open doors of the Wagon's keel, full into the flames they plunged them, *poppoparoppop*, and each drew his singed thumb long his cheekbones in two long smuts neath the eyes for hunting luck. The Rat Hunt Boys strode to their places round the Wagon and stood soldier. Beaters placed bronze pikes in their hands, bronze butts tween their feet, trident spikes over their heads, and fitted to each a Galanty mask with its stiffhair crest on their brows. Beaters proffered daggers and poniards, hilt first, which each Boy slid in his belt. *Bangarang bang, samdankissh samdankissh, tatapoppa popata popata, shakrittle shakrattle, skreelyabach ayheyoh ayheyoh ay hey ay hey.* Twelve coulees shoved back the outer gates, the horns blared, the shabrag coulees hustled headbent to the carrypoles and *samdankissh samdankissh* lifted the poles to their shoulders, cymbals cymbals crash crash as the Hunt swung through the gates and out to the street beyond, where the rimers waited, and the beaters massed, and every dreg peered tween shutters.

"Galanty Hunt!" shouted Ambrose, his voice cracking as he spied the gold hoop on Morsnal's finger at prow beside Max. "Let the Galanty Hunt begin!" stifled by his tight throat.

Anathematizers bent their whiteskin cowls as the common rimer chorus sang: *The Rat Hunt Boys / With eyes of flame / Came whistling through the howling streets / And slaughtered as they came.* And then the Anathematizers pushed back their whiteskin cowls made from skin of the burned dead, and covered their eyes lest their words strike the innocent, and answered in widemouth chant, *Come death and welcome, come tween the desire and the spasm, come unto the dropping-wells of fire, come to hideous ruin and combustion.*

The beaters stepped out first, shoving blunt poniards at every likely clump of ragweed or nipplewort, stirring rats from cover.

Next the Rimers, chorus and Anathematizers in one voice. *Come, soft noses, come tiny dung-rot feet, come teeth that bite ragged, come two-head little gods that despoil what they do not destroy, come slinking creatures with eyes like the first pits in beauty's smiling face, hither hairless tails you ropes that fasten life to death, come and look into our eyes for you long to be o'ermastered once before you die, come.*

The gleaming Boys strode out back of the hooded rimers and they chanted COME they bellowed COME from the bottom of themselves, they sang COME in one voice while sap spurted from their thick cocks pressed gainst the brass corvisers. The Boys sang COME as they tramped as they howled as the beaters stirred a ratnest to the boil, as the rimers froze the rats mid-scamper. Vagrant coals illumined their oiled flanks as they sank their spears in ratflesh, a pike's three tongs skewered grey-brown rat belly, punctured entrails spilled to dust; the rats writhed once, twice, and no more wriggle and squirm but on spiketip jounced and tumbled this helpless riven dance up and backwards to the cry of *Doors!* in the wagonfire that blossomed from the Wagon keel's open iron portals. Light died slowly from fixed brown eyes as a rat was *poppoparoppop* jonked from the skewer to the coals. As the last shining iris dulled to black, its whiskers burst to fire as the spike slammed shut the oven doors, bloodpus running down spikehaft to handguard. The Hunt Wagon's gilt scrolls was so early smutched with the first gluey smoke of this Galanty Hunt. The Musicians planted their feet gainst columns of gluteous ash, swaying like sailors with the roll of it. At the prow, the viol arced parabolic forward, sawed, screamed, on his ratgut strings. The drummers crouched at the back, their hands flailing free and independent on the skins. Trumpets raised their horn mouths soot-stoppered to the sky and tossed sacks of gold tones over the sides, slid up and down as spitted rats burst in the bowels of the wagon's crematoria. The Rat Hunt poured and stompled long the jetty, pell mell, tric-a-loc, cock-a-leekie, anyhow, *skreelyabach ayheyoh ayheyoh ay hey ay yeeee* from Max at the prow, sweat and the spat of burning flesh dripping off the strings as he played as he plays as he sha' no never stop playing till the Hunt's played out till every rat is spitted.

The Rat Hunt jounced over Charnholm stones, spawn running after to beg for sliced tails; let their mams tell them never so often, they'd still dare to run after. The beaters at the fore poked mong the bare stones and dust-sinks for the look of the thing. Anathematizers chanted on their heels: *Come teeth that bite ragged, come two-headed little gods that despoil what they do not destroy.* The Hunt Boys skirled round the Wagon, pikes raised with spiked carcases, oven doors in Wagon keel swung wide as one Boy after another unthirled a squirming rat onto the coals. As the Wagon juttered over a hole, a few coals spilled to the cobbles. "Hoy Finn!" shouted Thursgood, "Spark-up here!" and Finn M'Cool ran back to tread the coals to ash. "Thanks," said Thursgood, and gave a nod. To a beater he inclined the head. The ashes swirled round Finn's stockstill boots in pure amaze. Thursgood lowered his right eyelid to half-mast, "Boola boola," he mouthed, and turned, and raised high his pike to join his Boys in chant: COME they chanted, COME as they pumped rats a full fathom overhead, COME as blood dripped from their pikes, COME their risen cocks tipped in carmine, COME as each leapt as he rounded the prow and clacked his heels together COME they chanted.

"Coming they coming!" cried Suellen.

"Shutter up now," Cider Mother shifted the spawn in her arms. "You're near too weighty for this," she reached out of window and swung the shutters to. "Time and past time for you to scutter round on your own two feet," she hitched the girl closer to her hip, "so's you can be more hindrance to your mam," she smoothed the soft hair. "I bominate waiting," she told Suellen, who clapped her hands.

"Coming they!"

"Yeah, and we can nobbut wait. It'll work or it'll no work. Want to help me wrap a flask?" Suellen bobbed her head up and down rapido. "Sure and you've no choice in the matter soever," as they crouched by the head of garret stairs.

⟜

"These stairs squeak!" said Chantal. "Like they've been spitted."

"There's no sound to these stairs," said Roger. "It's the wind, perhaps. I've two coulees turning the ventilator fan so it's fresh. For after. Maybe it's that you hear."

Chantal snorted. "Think I can't tell the one from the other? Don't you hear that wail? Like a child crying."

Roger laid a hand on her shoulder as she picked her way down. "No child is crying. There's only the fan blades whining."

Chantal tossed her hair all down her back. "You've invited a dozen of our friends to Hunt Breakfast, after, and none of them will hear themselves *or* the music with that noise caroming round the cave."

"Treesa's hosting twice that, easily."

"Hummph. Thassy always overdoes."

Roger pointed out that Treesa and Janno had a larger cave, and got sniffs for his pains. He reminded his wife that only Gov Don and Lady Mandra had a larger, and received a double helping of sniff and snort in answer. He put his arms round Chantal when they reached the cave proper: "We had some good times down here, remember?"

Chantal giggled. "I remember you pacing all day every day for a decade before you started carving faces in the empty storeboxes."

He held her tighter. "Well, that was daytime, wasn't it? *Declared* daytime," he corrected himself. "I don't remember any pacing at night in our bed, do you?" caressing the tops of her breasts, "Isn't that something we should investigate?"

"I remember asking you to pace yourself," said Chantal, following him through the archway, "but I don't remember you listening to me."

"Would it have been better had I listened to you?"

"No," she said, and fell on top of him, "maybe not."

⟜

"It would have been better had you listened to me," Lady Mandra told Gov Don.

"I've a position to maintain, Mandra." Gov Don looked off away. "Do you hear a wail? Like a whine or a weep? In the courtyard?"

She snapped her fingers in the air between them. "*That* for your position. *All* of them in our cave? Where do you imagine they'll sit? Or void their bowels, for that matter. There's insufficient potpourri in all Charnholm to mask the scent of *their* droppings." She swirled away and back again in two heartbeats: "What were you thinking?"

"That I've a position to maintain, Mandra. Has some dreg brought its puling naked issue kicking to our compound?"

Lady Mandra sighed gustily. "No," she said, "never once yet, and again, no. Position. You could maintain it better were you to *tell* me in advance that you've increased our hosting threefold. We'll need ... yes, I'll summon Mayry Patriza, yes, and all the footmen, yes, and did you tell Collins?"

"We'd a nice round of back and fro on the topic yesternoon, thank you for asking."

She tapped his cheek with one painted talon. "You are a scoundrel (*tap*) a rascal (*tap*) and a rogue (*tap*), Donal. Set the footmen at the gates, mmm, yes, we'll leave a handful there to blow accola, and what to serve that blocks the bowels, hmmm ..." she swirled off, *tap-tap, tap-tap* down the stone stairs to Collins's realm.

Gov Don puffed out his cheeks as her voice descended. Mandra'd see it all sorted. He pulled at the tips of his grey-brown moustache. Careless of him not to have told her. Hmmmph. Well, Mandra always rose to an occasion. He walked to the foot of the shaft-ladder and cocked an ear. The Hunt was howling near the foot of South Point. Best run through this viewtube thing again.

"Let us run through it again, then, shall we? Yes?" said Lady Mandra to Collins. "A kilderkin of cider, a firkin of scrumpy; a keg of smoked fish, a dozen breadloaves with applebutter balls — pressed in the new mold, Collins — and the rest of it, of course, you know well. Now that accounts for beverage and comestible. But what shall we do about their nether ends?"

"Pardon, m'lady?" Collins shifted from one laden foot to the other on the cold kitchen stones.

Lady Mandra snapped her fingers. "Their *bowels*, of course, where will they void their *bowels*? We can dessicate no more than five bowels per day in this cave."

Mary Patricia closed the courtyard door behind her. "Could we no give them night-soil buckets?"

"After the Galanty Hunt, Mayry Patriza, you and I shall discuss punctuality. Yes, we could supply necessary-pots, yes, in two or three curtained recesses, yes ... but how are they to be emptied? Should the Hunt be delayed in its arrival, or there be close skirmishing round the viewtube, the necessary-pots we have will fill in no time. Should any call for encores, we could be here till dusk, with a kilderkin of cider drunk down that must and will go *some*where."

"M'lady?"

"Yes, Mayry Patriza?"

"Could easy scurry topside tween jouts — like when beaters is the only ones moving — and dump the necessaries in an empty hogshead. After Hunt's done, a brace of coulees can lug it to privies." Mary Pat stood with her insteps sput up gainst two lines of stone grout, her hands folded at her amanensis belt.

"Hm, hmm," said Lady Mandra. "Were you unaware, Mayry Patriza, that Governor Donal has most explicitly forbidden any entry to or exit from the shelter cave for the duration of the Galanty Hunt?"

"Why's that, m'lady?" Collins snuck one asscheek onto a corner of kitchen table.

"I've no notion whatsoever," said Lady Mandra.

"Gennelmen can't keep atop all the scurrish details, m'lady." Mary Pat's face was that smooth you could shine silk with it.

"Unseen's unknown," said Collins.

"There's a hogshead near the back ladder, m'lady," said Mary Pat.

"Right." Lady Mandra snapped her fingers at Collins. "Set out three, no, *four* necessary-pots in the storage alcoves; Mayry Patriza, you're delegated to empty them as needed and if the Governor finds you at it, may the wind and the sun have mercy on you. Every denizen of South Point shall be our guest today, scheduled to arrive in an hour's time: look sharp!"

"Look sharp, Morsnal; guests to starboard," said Max, sawing at his viol, "give them the old heave-ho," his hair lank round his face, his ratgut strings sputtering.

"Heave?" Morsnal clutched the prow with both hands, lips twitching in his greygreen face.

"May ratpaws tread in your porridge," said Max. "Hoy Scerzo! Guests to starboard!"

"Guests!" cried Scerzo, waving a brass trump in answer. He slid tween the Musicians to the starboard taffrail, rolling with the motion easy as strolling down jetty. Morsnal eyed him with envy and clutched the prow the harder. Scerzo leaned over taffrail to the trio of spawn who scrabbled at the grease-smutched ledge, their toes blistering in scrollwork openings next the oven doors. Scerzo leaned to them till his hornmouth was a handwidth from their noses and he blew, *popparop, poppata poppata pop paRHEE papapaparop EEErop*, till their fingers lost their clutch and they slid down side of the Wagon to land plop on the cobbles. *Pop poparop pop, pop pop!* the trumpet laughed as they fell behind. One-hand on the taffrail, waving his left arm for balance, Scerzo strolled back to his place with a nod to Max.

Max played a long wail that rang off the prisoning stones, *Can can no canno-o-o get out, ge-e-e-t canno o out o-out,* and returned Scerzo's nod, and laid back bowing waves *ayehoh ayehoh ayehoh* for the horns to roll on, and said to Morsnal as he played, "There's some hears the music like the rats hear it, see? It calls them so they'll swool up the Wagon sides only to be nearer, poor fools. The next batch is yours, young Morsnal," as he rocked on his heels *ayehoh ayehoh,* "no vomit on the Boys, mind, use the ash pail near the figurehead."

Morsnal held his lips tight clamped as he blinked in answer, but grey soft ashgrit come up in the back of his mouth and he was spewing in his hands as he elbowed the lid off the ashpail, heaved till there was nobbut air left in his gut and then he heaved air flecked with pink specks and still he retched, the figurehead's mild pearl eyes watching him the while.

Max's head swayed from side to side *ayehoh ayehoh skreelyabach,* "Prow's no your mam's soft arms, young Morsnal. Grab the handker out my belt when you're done." He skreeled overhead as Morsnal retched neath the mild pearl gaze, pink droolstrings hanging from his lips. "We're coming up on the climb, best clamp a hand to taffrail." *Skreelyabach ayehoh ayehoh, bangarang bang, pop poppa ra poppa pa, samdankissh samdankissh, tatapoppa popata popata, shakrittle shakrattle.* The Hunt Wagon lurched from side to side as it struck the rough stones at the foot of South Point's only wide trail.

"Did the richards no smooth up this road?" gasped Morsnal.

"Yeah," said Scerzo, shaking spit from his bell.

"This is how she rides smoothed up?" Morsnal drew himself up.

"Yeah," said Scerzo, raising his horn.

"Ah," said Morsnal, his smucky hands clutching the taffrail.

"Yeah," said Scerzo, and puckered his lips to blow.

⟨⟩

"Now pucker up pretty and keep those teeth covered or by the swolejaw rat I'll push your nose out the back of your head," said Dingle. "Scrape me with your teeth again and I'll smash your face on this rock," and he wrapped the dreg's pale copper hair tighter round his fist. They was back of the salt-glisten baulk in the shallow pit as gave Dingle his name. He'd found her crouching there when he snuck back for a snort of tarponesse; he'd time enough, the Wagon a good few minutes behind and his cock was taut from the powder and her long back, together, "How *doth the busy bee / improve each shining hour,*" he'd told her as he pulled her to her knees and let down his flap, "get on with it," but she'd resisted — him! a scutman! — so he'd had to give her a bit of the rough, tie her wrists to a baulk ring, well she was tame enough now, a good thing — aaah, he sighed — for he'd no time to mete the discipline she so — aaah, ah now, he groaned — obvious deserved, the Wagon was nobbut — oh, ah, faster, ohhh, ohhh ahhh now, he groaned in rising tones — the Wagon coming faster nor you'd think it — ohhh, slower, oh ohhhh, ohhh — she could no touch him with her hands tied, ah well, he leaned forward over her wide, supple lips as he rubbed his hard nipples with his own soft palms and ohhh, ohhh, ohhh, he sighed as his head jerked back and his throat come apart neath the knife. His eyes started from out their sockets and Dingle fell back on a baulk spike as snapped his lifeless spine.

"Sorry for that," said Lena. "Had to wait till he let loose of your hair."

Deirdre was on all fours in the dingle dust, spitting out the taste of him, her arms swayed behind her with a length of flayrope. Lena undid the knots as she chattered. "Fooling here where scutmen prowl, and you're to come the dreg, are you? Could been mashed to pulp, you dentical fool. There, now's that better? Rub your wrists, rub them now, Deirdre, you'll need the blood in them right off; here's a scutman dead we got to get shut of; come on, rub them up; now raise yourself; there you go. A ratbit fool was Dingle always; any more of his blood on you?" Deirdre shook her head and Lena chuntered on. "I've nobbut a few drops on my overtunic, strip it here, so, and hey presto! clean and neat a housedreg as you could want." Deirdre smiled weak. "There you are, there you are then, come on, come on now," hissing as she set the dazed body on its hams, pooring her hair back from her brow, "Did no lose more'n a few strands here; there's luck, and none ever looks eager for Dingle to return; there's luck again, and the Wagon's coming with Max at the prow; luck a third time. Raise you now, no harm, raise you and let's go cheer the Wagon."

"Hurrah the Wagon," whispered Deirdre.

# Rising Up

*The sun hurled orange rays over the bluffs and down into Charnholm harbor. Thick, blunt, harsh, rays so dry they drew eyes from their sockets. Dregs wet their lips with potable and licked the taste of the spag flaskplug from their teeth; did a drop fall on a leaf, that drop so bent those rays as to blister the leaf's green skin. The seaward breeze blew yet in fits, starts, gusts, puffs, that dawdled in coves, corners, doorways till each puff died singly, exhaling with the dying breath the matty herbs that clung to the blufftops; thyme, rosemary, wild onion.*

WHILE THE RICHARDS DRESSED for Gov Don's viewtube, every dreg who could rise from pallet and walk had already watched the Galanty Hunt mass outside the hall. They now straggled home in threes and fives, clotting at corners to talk over the performance.

"Well if you ask me it was better fore all those tumblers came."

"Jongleurs."

"Jon-klers, is it? Well what they'd to do with Rat Hunt I could no tell, even was you to roll me in spag and set me on the noon jetty. I like to hear the Anathematizers, I do."

"I could hear them fine from where I was."

"*Sure* and *you* could hear them fine, sneck up on the plaza like you was. Augie and me was tucked away behind back of beyond."

Drosh swum up out of nowheres to urge Bedelia Coldhand, calling her Magnificent Delia, to walk long the bankmen with him. To prom a nod together, as he put it. "You'll scuse us," Drosh bowed to Bedelia's friend, "familiar as you maun be with a man's desire," taking Bedelia by the elbow and moving her towards the bankmen.

"What the —" said Bedelia when they was past earshot.

"Bedelia," said Drosh, his large hand round her elbow, "Bedelia." He jerked his head toward harbor, "*Mam Can Cook* is in, sails furled and dawdling round *Hail Janus.* Now why's Fergus no ashore for this of all Hunts?" and tipped a flask to his mouth. "Bedelia."

"Oh, what's towards, Drosh?" she said, tugging away from his hold.

"We need hawser, Bedelia."

She looked past him to greet a pair of bent dregs shuffling upjetty, a third wizened dreg upright tween them, its face turned to the sun. "I see you got granmam out for the Hunt there." The shufflers nodded, intent on keeping the old feet clear of the cobble grooves. Bedelia Coldhand turned back to Drosh, "Now if that's no curious. My hawser line's a wanted item this day. You're third in asking. Who can count for the ups and downs of desire, hmmm? Well I've some store, worth looking on, come along."

"Bedelia," he said, all ploring and furrowed and hands spread.

Bedelia cast a quick look over her shoulder but the three dregs was well past. She hisssed, "How much hawser can one Hunt use, Drosh? Beaters has a few dozen ells; Finn M'Cool took four coils, full, yestereve; Quix come by daily for a week, tapped my scrumpy, and each time left with a big wide belly of hawser wrap. Even Augie Inkwhistle, tottery chaff as he is, been stuffing guide twine down his trous. There's rope enough to wrap half Charnholm tucked mong the Hunt and those watching it this morning. An you was to hold off on the scrumpy till the sun was at zenith, you'd recall these plain facts."

"Gessel says there's a justborn wailing neath Rimehouse annex. A dreg as is nursemaid to a richard-born says —"

"Lena? Deirdre's Lena?"

Drosh's head bobbled. "The same. She seen it. Says she seen the justborn as wails. Sprawled down a deep hole nobbut a handspan wider nor the creature's head, its tiny arms flailing, sucking at the red sand and wailing hard. How're they to bring it up to surface, lacking rope? Hole's too narrow for even a half-size dreg so —"

Bedelia Coldhand grabbed him by both elbows and shook him. "Right aright. A brace of mainlines, hmm, and guide rope they'll need, hmm, now for cradling, the thick net, hmm, and has any brought pap for the justborn? Come long, Drosh, do," her arm tucked through his like any couple hasting to their holsday stew on the hob.

Deirdre and Lena hasted up the wide path in the Hunt Wagon's wake. "Come long now," said Lena. "One comfort, your tunic's so spockled, you look dreg enough to foozle any."

"Have you the —" Deirdre panted, a hand pressed to her ribs.

"Drosh is tending to that. Come long now."

"You ever seen a justborn before?"

"Out of course I have, was I no born dreg?"

Deirdre stopped mid-path. "What do they eat, Lena? Are they adjusted to potable? What do they like to talk about?"

"Justborns has no speech, you dentical fool. They —" Lena's own speech dried up on her. Deirdre had shucked off the events back of the salt baulk like brushing cobweb from her lashes and was thinking on the justborn only. A richard as thought about someone outside their own skin; there was a rare for you; there was a never-seen for you. "You'll see in a bit," she said. "Come long quickstride you'll see."

Finn led the beaters quickstride up to an elderbush thicket. He indicated a faint path with his pike. One by one the ragged beaters crouched, and the locust leaves rustled overhead as they slid tween elder bushes and was lost to view, though still main hearable — inside the thicket there was considerable grousing as twiny branches grabbed beater tunics. Finn pulled the flask from neath his tunic. He'd no looked at it since Mary Pat slid it down her sleeve to him as the beaters passed Dead Horse Moraine. "Cider Mother says you look well today," she'd said, no more, and Finn blinked his left eye a few times for answer. He eased the spag plug from the flaskneck and took a cautious sniff, and gagged, and near spilled the contents as he jerked his hand away from his nose. Valerian. What was his mam thinking? No richard'd drink this thout gagging. He plucked at the wrap, and grinned, for mint leaves was tucked inside. Finn jammed them down flaskneck. That'd sweeten it, could aught sweeten it any. Finn hid the flask and slithered crouching through the elder bushes toward sound of the beaters. They was nearly out from the thicket, he told them. "Mayhap a shorter road but twice the time, M'Cool," one grumbled, and the others hummed accordo.

Finn put down their glumps, and sharpish: "Any rather scramble up the rocks?" he asked, and none had aught to answer.

Dan and Palan scrambled up the rocks neath South Point. "Sure and there's a better way to do this," said Palan.

"Mm-hmm," said Dan, grabbing an outthrust cone and belaying his legs up to the next ledge. "We could trumpet our coming with a handful of musicians," he said. "Think that'd do us better?"

"No," said Palan.

"We could stride up the wide path by side of Hunt Wagon," said Dan, "hallooing 'Here come we / in boots of gold / to strike you down / to leave you cold' — think that'd do us better?"

"No," said Palan. "Sides," he added, "we lack boots of gold," scraping his palm on the outthrust cone and cursing, "likely they'd notice that and come to think we'd nobbut lies in our mouths."

"Ayuh," said Dan, "that'd be the way they'd come to think that."

"What'll they think when we rise up from out of nowhere mong them?"

Dan shrugged, as best a shrug can be shrugged when the shrugger's shoulders are wedged gainst a rock cove. "Think we come to strike them down and leave them cold," he said. "It's mortal hot down the shelter caves, I hear."

"You know, do they see us coming up to them, they can easy send out a troop of scutmen to spike our lives from out our chests." Dan climbed on. "I nobbut mention it," said Palan. Dan wrapped his ankles round a handswidth jut and levered himself up. "On account of we should be making ready for it," said Palan. Dan rested on his new ledge, panting the least bit. His hair was matted to his skull, his left arm wrapped round his kit bag. "It's a thing might happen," said Palan.

"Yeah. Listen, you ever spoke to other lives?"

"What, those as is dead now? No." Palan slid back a full bodylength, and grabbed Dan's hand to crawl up to sink down grateful beside him. He sucked his bleeding knuckles.

"No, no. I mean, ever spoke to any as was no dregs?"

Palan sighed gusty. "Do you no remember, I'm the one as built the viewtube for the richards, eh? Who talk considerable and often."

Dan shook his head. "I mean, ever spoke to them as was no dregs nor richards nor anywise went on two legs?"

Palan stared at him, a bloody knuckle halfway to his mouth. "Course no. Well, I been out to sea for months together when, yeah, I fancied I could chat with seafoam; I conjured fishes to leap from the depths and dance with me on deck. You know. *Hail Janus* been out past horizon for a long trip lately?"

"No, nobbut daytrips with fishnets." Dan looked north to the deeplade dock. "Why's the *Mam Can Cook* fooling round the *Hail Janus*, now I ask you."

Palan spared a short glance. "Fergus trolling for custom, likely."

"He's all times freighted with persevere, give you that."

Palan waved away all thought of his dap. "So there been no long trips where a body starts chatting with the topmast wind. Cause what happens shipboard —"

"Stays shipboard. Right aright. I'm no talking ball of speakful fire, nor lights belowsea, nor mermaids, sirens, dames nor specters of any sort. Ever spoke with animals?"

Palan eyed the ledge overhead. It jutted ten foot out to harborside. Getting up and over should been no more nor climbing up from sea to figurehead, but an you drop from figurehead, you drop into the sea, as he'd done a few times. Off this ledge you'd land in sea, right aright, but it'd be a considerable drop, one as'd end in a mass of Palan crumbs spockled on the crags. He dragged his eyes back up to meet Dan's. "No," he said, "I never spoke with no animals never."

Dan swung his carrysack round. "Nor I," he said. "Up to a few days past, I'd called it impossible. Then I met these two." He pulled out Alpha and Delta.

*First a yellow fog rises behind the ears then a dark and a light and after the fog come the buboes. On first sighting we drive the befogged onto Charnholm verges and there we leave them with sufficient carrion and gutterspill to last them till a Hunt comes.*

Palan's head swung tween Dan's shuttered mouth and the two grey rats in his lap.

*The great stone scrapers fell roof on floor on roof on floor on squeaking kit and rheumy snout alike. The live brown towers as spunk green at their tips come rootfirst out our tunnels our caves our storehouses our meethalls and shitcoves, all, to dust crumbled*

"By the last —" Palan stopped. "May my right hand be clove —" He licked his lips. "What in gorry?"

Dan put finger to his mouth. "Hsssshhh," he said. "Shutter up," and bent to the two rats in his lap. In his lap! Their tusks nobbut a handwidth from his eyes!

*All to dust crumbled as the roots croppled, our paws scrabbling in dust on dust that lay heavy on the dark lively eyes of our nestmates our kits.*

"Can they hear me?" Palan whispered.

"Well," said Dan. "Can you hear them?" Palan nodded. "Well then."

*In that dust we thrashed in that dust we choked, leapt gainless gainst the dust that fell and fell as the tunnel walls shook neath the stones falling and the live brown towers crashed rootlast and skincurled burning all burning above us*

"Cheery little creatures," said Palan.

"This is Alpha." Dan put her on his left knee, where she flattened her whiskers in a bow, "And this is Delta. He was wounded in action gainst Ambrose, go easy on him."

Palan considered. This was Dan, brother to Finn and Mary Katharine and Mary Patricia. He was Cider Mother's blood-spawn. Palan reached out a finger slow as sap oozes from branchbreak. Gently he stroked Alpha's back, who arched neath his touch, her eyes half-closed. I am sitting on a ledge twenty fathoms above the seadepths, stroking a rat's grey fur. Right. Right aright. He petted Delta with more caution, mindful of its bloodcrust necklace. "This the male?" he asked.

"That's Delta. Morsnal called him D, but what kind of name's that for a creature?"

"Delta, now, is it." Delta turned his snout toward the sound of his name, still half in sleep. Any rat sleeps all it can when the sky's full of blaze and heat, rouses at the cool landbreeze. Delta'd been near dead that morning, so he was sleepier nor most. "Alpha here's the female." Alpha licked his fingers as he stretched them toward her; Palan recoiled for a heartbeat at rat tongue on his skin, but he was flexish, was Palan. He brought his heart back down into his chest and stroked Alpha's back. "Morsnal?" he said.

"Mmmm. He's riding prow on Hunt Wagon today."

"Left you his rats for safekeeping, did he?"

"Ambrose had him training up rats to practice Hunt Boys on the close-in. Ambrose told him the Boys'd nobbut spar at them. Stead of that, they spiked them every one."

"How'd these —"

"Alpha she saved herself. Climbed up Morsnal's tunic."

"You think they —"

"How're we to know? Delta they spiked round the neck and left for dead."

Palan considered again. "They're remembering the Great Burning, are they no?" Dan nodded. "As you remember it?" this with more caution, yet Dan nodded again, his eyes on Alpha's tongue warm-rasping Delta's bluddered neck. "Well then," said Palan, "let's go on up," they both eyed the outthrust jut, "soon's we figure how to climb round this —"

A rope dropped down to dangle tween them.

⟜

Cider Mother dropped a rope with a thick packet tied to its end out of window. She closed the shutters slow and come back to sit on her three-leg stool. "Your mam used to dance on rope, Suellen," she said. "How's for that? With a lovely sprat of a boy. Ambrose his name was. We danced on rope and the people gasped and gawked and clapped their hands."

The spawn said, "Hands!" and put her own over her eyes: "Mam, you can no see me!"

"You're right! Where's Suellen? Where's my Suellen gone?"

Suellen laughed. "Here in the garret with you, mam. But you can no see me! I dispeared entire!"

The shutters parted a crack. "There's a tug," said Cider Mother.

"A tug a bug a nug a fug a rug a rug a rug!"

"Lugga mugga here's a hugga," said Cider Mother, lifting the sprat to her lap. "Now we've more waiting to do, right? Let's play at statues, sha' we? Who can sit the longer with no word spoken?"

"You can, mam!" Suellen jumped down and pattered over the bare floorboards in her bare feet.

"Away from window, Suellen." Cider Mother spoke low. "Now, Suellen." She crept back to her mam's arms. "There, there," said Cider Mother, rocking, "we maun be quiet for this next part. Doost like to be quiet, doost tha no?"

Suellen clamped her lips together to show willing, the while she shook her head.

Tomal shook his head. It did no dislodge the rat jaw clamped to his nose. Stead, it drove the tusks home. Blood spurted tween his eyes yet the rat held on. The world went red as the Hunt Boy tried to pike the rat off; only scraped a trench cross his brow. Tomal spun round in tighter and tighter circles. The rat hung on. Tomal piked his own cheek in trying to force it off. The rat swung from Tomal's nose, its eyes pinpricks, its claws scrabbling Tomal's mouth and chin. The Boy opened his mouth to roar for aid and a long grayfur leg went down his throat to the hilt. Tomal gagged as the claws raked the hangflap at back of his mouth, but could no vomit past the rat's strong limb; the morning pap came up and met the rat's grimed talons and clogged there. Tomal's pike flew from his hands as he reached lasthope for the writhing rat, ripped it and half his nose off his face and out his throat, threw it overcliff, and sank to his knees, sobbing for air.

A few Boys stood headdown round him, pikes at their sides. Thursgood shouldered them aside. "Ware ratblood," he cautioned. "Always keep your daggers where you can get at them when you chance the close-in. Othergates, they've time to fasten. Right aright. Once more unto the breach, dear friends." The Boys dragged their feet in following him, still looking over-shoulder at Tomal, a lump of redbrown cartilage tween his eyes and mouth, the whole chogged with blood, with fur, with scrape from tween the rat's hind claws. "Come long now," said Thursgood, and the Hunt Boys went dragfoot away. Their Hunt Cappen caught them up a minute later.

The Musicians had gone quiet when the rat leapt at Tomal. "Summat lively," Thursgood told them now. "We've half a hillside to climb yet." The drummers began to pat the taut skins; the horns lifted mouthpieces but could no just fash their lips round the metal; Max tapped his foot one-TWO three-FOUR and he bowed *skreelEYlaBACH skreelEYlaBACH* and three rimers sang highup in their chests *A glorus glorus / waryor waryor / A glorus waryor death had he / houpla! / What more glorus death can be? / houpla! houpla!* at which the horns brayed *houpla! houpla!* and the Hunt Wagon moved forward as coulees put their shoulders to its wheels, and coulee feet tramped up the hill to South Point, and Max sang to himself and Morsnal at the prow: *skreelEYlaBACH houpLA houpLA*. Morsnal sidled close to Max and whispered, "Tomal breathes yet, why do they sing like he's dead?" Max missed no beat nor note: "Dead by now," he said. "Hunt Captain carries quick death in his belt."

The Hunt Wagon labored uphill, its wheels grinding *pocketa-pocketa-pocketaARRHNK* as the iron rims struck a headsize stone. *Pocketa-pocketa-pocketa ARRHNK* and the coulees sang *"There's no mountain high enough / There's no cliff is steep enough / To keep this Wagon down / Oh no! / To keep this Wagon down."*

Rising, rising, ah now rising, sang Max's viol. *Can can no canno-o-o-o get out o out o-out.*

The Wagon's iron-rim wheels sang *Pocketa GRAHnk pocketa GRAHnk* as they struck the wide path outside the richard compound's high stone wall.

⌐⌐⌐

*Pocketa GRAHnk pocketa GRAHnk*. The rimers stalked fore the Wagon, anathematizing the rats in verse.

COME *greysnout dimeye keennose*
COME *with all your grayfur rose*
COME *on your tensile stride*
COME *with your nostrils high*
COME *with your lashing tails*
COME *on your clicking nails*
COME *to the Wagon's wheels*
COME *to the music's skreel*

COME *to the dance*
COME *to the dance come along*
COME *dance to the Wagon's song*

Mary Katharine M'Cool and Rimshot the drogyne stalked side by side at the left flank of the rimers, the latter chanting round a lump of treesap. The semblage paused on a flat spanse outside the richard gates to whirl in place. "Who wrote *that* drimmel?" said Rimshot. Mary Kath hunched a shoulder toward forefront of the rimers where a whiteskin figure spread her arms wide, rattling a dozen bangles, mouth raised to the dark yellow sun. "Should known," said Rimshot, "got Goodwin's tracks all over it. And Bran's," it added. "She was gone to tend him, no? Well, she'll likely peel off when we pass his shadepatch. This drimmel'd freeze the rats where they live, uh-huh. Was I a rat I'd curl the deeper in my nest, see, lest my blood turn to spag in my veins off hearing such no-count lack-beat verses. Or mayhap I'd rush out and bite the chanters fierce, though it was my own death, lest all my nestmates turn to spag from their ears on down."

"Sacafice yoursen for that?" said Mary Kath, lifting her arms three handspans from her hips and twirling slow, her feet treading BOM-ba-ba BOM-ba-ba BOM-ba-ba in the dust.

"Would indeed," said Rimshot, rolling the treesap round in its mouth.

"Mayhap they do," said Mary Kath.

Rimshot drew up short. "What? Have you —"

A nearby jongleur hissed, "Mary Kath! Look sharp! Your solo!"

Mary Kath spread her arms wide and lifted her voice high:

COME *you sacks of bubo, bags of plague*
COME *your dark blood festers, your skin's aboil*
COME *creep crawl crouch, let us rain our brokehearts on you*
COME *be gulfed in ours the greater sorrow*
COME *for we remember the dead they*
COME *to us and break our hearts again so*
COME *to our songs; bring your deaths*
COME *we sha' lift those weights from you*

COME *lay down your small black deaths*
COME *they sha' be consumed as fire*
COME *surrender your burdens*
COME *lay them at our feet*
COME *you sacks of bubo, bags of plague*
COME *and be cleansed*
COME *and be given over*
COME *to our songs.*
COME. COME.


And the rats crept on their bellies towards her voice.
The rimers stood still as the verges filled with rats.
Their noses to the flagstones.
Their fur flat to their quivering backs.
Their tails dragging in the dust.
Through the elder bushes they crept towards Mary Kath's voice.

In the elder bushes, Finn whispered his beaters to take courage now, to be statue while rats crawled over their boots, tween their legs, over beater flesh they crawled; no shiver nor tremble stirred the elder bushes as rat claws scraped as they flowed in their dozens over the living statues in the thicket to the whirling rimers.

"Some dozens of guests in an hour's time," said Mary Patricia M'Cool.

"Teach your granmam to crack marrow," said Collins.

"I'm charged with providing the necessaries, so —"

Collins lifted the cloth: "Ta-daa! Basins galoro, Dazymare, right here fore your eyes. Going surface while Hunt's on?"

Mary Pat let her copper hair hang in her eyes as she bent. "Might could have to," she said.

Collins batted a yawn with one plump hand. "Me, I take kindly to this whole notion of the viewtube. Clever fellow, that Palan. No wind, no dust, no chance of ratbite; nobbut cakes and ale the livelong day. Lady Mandra she deserves no less."

Mary Pat held the necessaries in her arms. "Lady Mandra said to place these round in curtain alcoves."

"Mm-hmm," said Collins, her eyelids falling. "Go long with you."

Mary Pat walked away soft. As she passed, Collins murmured, "It's Brock and Doole on guard at head of the shaft, Mary Pat. Lady Treesa says they mussed her coif or summat, but oh the graciousness of her; she'll have them back should they make it through the Hunt unbitten. Brock and Doole, mind." Her wide lips closed; her bosom rose and fell in long, regular waves.

The *Mam Can Cook* rose and fell on long, regular waves. Fergus had her at anchor while he brewed fresh tarponesse belowdecks. The Hunt Boys was huge custom for tarponesse after Hunts when they was jump from slaying; after horii sluiced every last drop of foul from their frames, they rose from the oiling couches everywheres empty; put it fore them and they'd imbibe, inhale, devour till every bowl was bone-clean. Was there was one thing Fergus held to, it was that a body maun seize opportunity. Like dap, like sprat. Which would you look at the sprat now. The dreg as fashed the viewtube, aye, and socked it into sheltercave to boot. Oh now Palan was doing fine on land.

Nor no sprat clove closer to his blood duty. Softening the ground for Fergus with that close-in, he was. After Hunt Boys was done with *that*, they'd be unco' prime for tarponesse. A sliver of light pierced the porthole shutters. An hour to go. More if the jongleurs was encored.

Fergus slid a stiletto neath tarpon jaws and teased out the veins. He missed Palan for doing that but it was a fair swap for having the ship so quiet these days; no sprat yammering how he ought do this, ought do that, decks to swab, keels to scrape. Fergus laid the veins with their freight of ichor in the stockpot on brazier and raked the fire closer round it. He snuffed a guttering wick and bent to his alembics, where the first ichor batch was distilling. The vapor was nobbut tinged with yellow. When it turned yellow-orange he'd decant it. Till then he'd naught to do. Fergus brought a made vial to the scoop of his thumbbase and dribbled there a few grains. He tilted his head and inhaled with first his left nostril and then his right. Always done it so. You had to keep steady in your habits so to stay on course.

"*Course* they know," said Morsnal. "They loathe the plague —"

"Avert," said Max tween jaws locked gainst the viol.

"What?"

Max raised his chin a notch, changing his skreel to *BACHala BACHala BACH*. "I said, avert. Leave that word lie."

"The rimers sang it just this now."

"Yeah, well, was you to take rimers for your model you'd end up spag-brain as Bran and Goodwin." Max nestled his jaws into the viol. *SkreelyaBACH skreel sa-sa-skreelyaBA-ACH.*

"The rats hate the - the foul mong them so much as we do. They bring them up to the verge for us to slay. They drive the stricken out the nest."

"Uh-huh." Max rolled his eyes. "Batten down my hat, willa? The sun's unco' fierce."

Morsnal pulled the brim down over Max's brow. "It's true what I say, you know."

"Uh-huh," said Max. "We're coming up on a close-in now."

"See, they know Ambrose been training on the close-in, so they set out some few sacafice rats, rats as play they're mazed, to take down Hunt Boys when the dastards move in close, they —"

Max breathed down his nose, ruffling Morsnal's hair. "Coming up on a close-in right *now*."

"Jump for the eyes. My kits played that way with each other from the first. Jump for the eyes when they're cornered, they all —"

"Coming up on a close-in, shutter *up*."

"Sure, Max. Cause see rats have *huge* hindquarters, the muscle in them's like —"

"Shutter up NOW," said Max. And Morsnal complied. For the most part. He muttered, and he drummed his fingers gainst the taffrail, but Max could rise above it and rise above he did. *SeeYAskreel skreel skreelyabach seeYA YAHA skreel YAHA skreel seeseeYA saSKREE skreeheeheel.*

"Heel and toe, boys, heel and toe. Dance with them! They come to compound gates to dance so dance with them!" Thursgood nor none of the Boys ever seen rats so thick massed on the verges as they was this morning. And every one on the road verge, waiting. You could no step without you crushed one; ah but crushing one was no Hunt Boy work, was it? Never seen them so thick-massed nor yet so still, moving no paw nor whisker. Creeped your spine for fair. This'd make the close-in pretty for the richards, it would and all. "Daggers out! Poniards out! Max! Lead this lot up and through the compound gates!"

And Max skreeled, and the rimers chanted, and Morsnal blew a fine high whistle as only rats could hear. And the rats came on behind, bellies low to the ground, nails clicking the pathstones. From the Hunt Wagon's deck the Musicians announced their coming: the trumps *popparopped* triple-time and the cymbals rang *samdankissh, samdankissh*. The Anathematizers in their white skins of the burned dead sang:

*The Hunt Boys with their eyes of flame*
*Strode up the hill and slaying came*
*For rats they crept and rats they leapt*
*In richard halls fair ladies wept*
*And wrung their hands and sighed*
*As bitten richards died*

A dozen footmen unshouldered their pikes and hooked the door rings. With a great heave and a great creak the gates swung open to the Hunt.

*Then rose up dregs with pikes and rage*
*To save their richards from this plague*
*'We come' they cried 'to save our gov,*
*Our shield, our gracious crown we love,*
*Who shelters us from want and thirst*
*That we may live and breed and nurse*
*With potable to make us able.'*

"Oh lay me down in the road and roll me in ratcrap," said Rimshot. "Shelter us? I should live so long to see it."

The richard compound's outer gates swung wide, and the Wagon rolled through them; the Musicians played atop the Wagon; the rats crawled after, their shiny eyes fixed on Morsnal.

*The Hunt Boys came with edgéd blades*
*They raised against the foe*
*The Hunt Boys slew and cast in flames*
*The creeping paws we loathe*
*Hail Hunt Boys! Great praise!*

"Howsomever dirty these rats," said Rimshot. "So it be quick, I ope my arms to them."

"Shutter up, Rimshot," said Mary Kath, and spat. "Careful what you wish for."

# Close In

*The sun was at its zenith. Every shadow had fled, and every stone sizzled in the blank hot light. The ebbing tide fell lackforce on the shingle. No breath of wind in all of Charnholm town. The locusts drooped, even their long beanhusks hung silent, and dust settled slowly down over every surface, grain by grain. The town held its breath. Behind shuttered doors and windows, in cellars and ground floors, away from the scorching roofs, dregs snatched what sleep they could, sweat baking in skinfolds, crusting in eyebrows, gathering in pools at their throats. Justborns whimpered as they panted. Only a few scutmen moved in all the town; most had forsook it to stand guard on South Point, where the Galanty Hunt was arraying in all its splendor before Governor Donal's viewtube.*

OUTSIDE THE VIEWTUBE, "Where's Palan?" said Governor Donal. M'Donal spat in the dust. Gov Don was no use. "Look at that Wagon. Clean as hands could made it nobbut a few hours since. Now will you look at it. Mmph'm."

"Where's Palan?" said Gov Don.

A brace of smiths as was showing scutmen how the view window carried light down into the shelter cave spun away from the group at this and bowed to Gov Don.

"Palan's no here just this now, sir" said Quix.

"Well, where —"

"Gone up to Janno's for more ratmesh, Gov," said Innsmort.

"He ought to be here. The Hunt is at the outer gates and where is Palan? When a dreg gives me his word, I expect him to keep it. A man's sworn word's his — do you hear that?"

"What's that, Gov," said Innsmort.

"That wailing." Gov Don pointed south. "Coming from that direction. Do you hear it?"

"Wailing, sir? No, sir," said Quix.

"Hush a minute. You — smiths! be still." Gov Don bent his head in listen. "Do you hear it now?"

The smiths dodged away as the scutmen bellied forward. "Chance to serve!" hissed the comper. "Stopple your gab and speak up!" He stepped forward first. "Hear the ventilator fan whirring," the comper offered.

"There's pans clattering below," said Mottle.

"A woman tearing the ear off some dreg," chimed Spink.

"That is no doubt my lady, all times at her duty," said Gov Don. "But none of you hears aught else? A wailing? Keening? Great sobs?"

They all bent the ear and made to listen. Mottle looked at Spink, and Spink looked at Mottle. They both looked at the comper and shook their heads. "No, sir, we none of us hears aught," said the comper.

"Hmm, hmmm," said Gov Don, and shuffled his feet in their pointed boots in the dust. "Well, carry on then, keep it up, as you were, sort of thing. I'll just toddle round to Janno's—"

"You've no time for that, Gov," said Innsmort.

Gov Don whipped round on him. "Who do you think you are, hmmm? Speak to me that way? Here, you, scutmen, rid me of this trouble-some smith."

Mottle and Spink stepped forward, Mottle to hold the smith's two hands to the stone wall, and Spink to raise the axe. "Hold hard!" Mottle said, and Spink lowered the axe. "Need a slab of wood atop that stone," said Mottle, "else you'll ruin the blade."

While Spink went in search of same, Mottle kept Innsmort's hands clamped to the wall, the smith's lower lip trembling tween his teeth.

Quix pulled the handker off his head and bent the knee to Gov Don. "Sir, that's Blay's dap, sir."

Gov Don pulled at the tip of his mustache. "Hmm. Hmmm." And turned to watch Spink approach with a block of wood.

"Sir, he's the netmender, sir," Quix went on.

"And who are you?"

"Sir, I'm shipwright. Quix by name, sir."

"Well, Quix shipwright, we've a dozen netmenders."

"No, sir, you've nobbut Innsmort. At this time. Sir." Quix kept his bare head bent down; even so, he could see Spink's boots clomping to the wall, planting themselves on the stones, leaning back on the heels ...

"Oh well then," said Gov Don. "Hold hard there, scutman." Spink's toes raised a puff of dust as they come down. "Lop his hair for him," he said, halfway to the cave mouth, dusting his hands of the matter.

Spink twisted a hank of Innsmort's hair and chopped it one thumb-width from his nape. "There," he said, and spat, and turned on his heel. "Mottle," he called. Mottle cuffed the smith on the head, "You been lucky," he said, and spun away.

Quix scuttled over to the wall. "Innsmort, you dentical fool, get over here." Innsmort stood soldier, only his lower lip quivering. Quix yanked his hand. "Leastwise crouch down; call you lucky, huh! he called nobbut the half of it; get *down* you lackwit." Innsmort bent his knees, slow, the way a ship sinks, his straight back and stiff arms descending till his fingers brushed the dust, when he fell stiff on his side. "It's aright, now, there, you've all your fingers, there, on both your hands, there, they gone off, it's aright now, innit?"

Innsmort extended the long strong fingers of his right hand and clamped them round Quix's wrist. "You know there's a half-dozen net-menders in my street alone," he said.

"Mmm," said Quix.

Innsmort stood up slow. "Right aright. I'll finish the ratmesh on this viewtube, and you'll to Janno's. Tell Gov Don, Palan just now stopped by with the ratmesh and straight set off to join me."

"But —"

"Tell him, Quix." He clapped the shipwright's shoulder and was off.

"Am I —" but Innsmort was past earshot. Quix re-tied his handker round his head. He wetted his lips at his flaskmouth. He walked to Janno's with eyes straight, back forward, a dreg on richard business, no one to look at a second time.

Daniel and Palan looked at the rope a second time. Palan said it was still there, and Dan agreed. Dan mentioned it was tween them, and Palan said that was a fact. Palan said it was a long way down; Dan replied it was a long way up. Palan said the rope was likely from some friend; Dan said it was a typical scutman trick. Bedelia Coldhand's round face appeared over the clifftop: "By the first rat's tailtip flea, would one of you grab hold this hawser?"

"Ah, now, Bedelia," said Dan.

"A fine lot of jesters aching for you to join them up here, M'Cool," she said. "So would you for the love of air wrap your self round this hawser? I've Drosh here and six other arms to haul you if you'll but leave off chuntering —" and stopped as Dan slid his carrysack round to his kidneys and grabbed the rope in one motion. Drosh hauled on the rope.

"Easy round this jut," said Dan. "Uggh," he grunted.

"All aright?" said Bedelia Coldhand.

"Lovely," said Dan. "I been training my muscles since I was the merest sprat to *uggghh* fend off rockjuts."

"Use your feet to keep off them," Bedelia Coldhand advised.

"Was I no *using* my feet to clutch this *uggghh ahhh* rope that'd doubt-less be a grand *uggghh* notion but I'm *uggghh ohhh ahhhh*," he said, and "Aaaahh," he said as he got his elbows over the clifftop; "mind the carry-sack," as six arms reached for his; "take me up easy and *mind the carrysack!*" this last in a high voice to a pair of pale arms as grabbed his belt, beached him, and dragged him away from the rim. He lay there laughing.

"Is that you laughing, Daniel M'Cool?"

"It is and all," he said.

"I've no seen you laugh since your head topped my waist," said Bedelia Coldhand.

"Dunno as I have," he agreed.

"Well." She rolled him on his back, easing the carrysack to one side. "Arnica," she snapped. One pale arm reached a jar from her belt. "You put it on him," said Bedelia Coldhand, and went to Drosh's side. "Lena," called Bedelia, and the dreg's hands circled the rope behind hers. "Grab hold, goldhead," she hollered down. "With *all* your limbs!"

The pale hands pulled the cork from the jar of arnica. Dan closed his eyes. The hands gentled the tunic up his chest. Soft fingers laid salve on his scrapes. On his knuckles, on his elbows, on his shoulders, on his ribs. The sun danced on Dan's lashes. He closed his eyes tighter. On his toes, on his ankles, on his calves, on his knees. On his gashed left hip. He opened his eyes. Pale copper hair fell over the face bent to his groin. He reached out one hand and drew aside the curtain. Two pale green eyes looked into his. His heart opened in his chest. "O, you wonder," he breathed.

"No wonder, sir," said Deirdre.

"What is your name?" said Dan. She told him. "Miranda," he said, "Mir'd Miranda."

Deirdre smoothed back his hair. "Rest yourself," she said. He took her hand and they were quiet together on top of the world for a span.

Till Bedelia and Lena set up a squawking on the cliffrim. Dan hauled Deirdre to her feet and, handfast, they ran to the noise. Dan lay on the cliffrim and hauled at Palan's belt while Drosh coiled the rope in hanks round the column that anchored it. Palan hooked an elbow on the cliffrim, and then another, and then his toes, till he'd levered himself onto the flat.

After he gasped a while, after Lena slapped arnica on his scrapes and bruises, after he made his bow to Deirdre and watched her cozen gainst Dan, Bedelia explained how there was a wailing justborn —

"A babe," said Deirdre.

"Call it that," said Daniel.

"Well, it's shorter," Bedelia agreed. "There's a babe wailing neath the Rimehouse, and we come to get it out."

"Which how we're to do that's a puzzle," said Drosh.

"Seeing as how the hole's slimmer nor any of us," said Bedelia. She coiled the hawser over her shoulder. "Slimmer nor this leg, to be sure, all swole up the worse from the climb," shaking the milkdrunk limb at them.

Palan snapped his fingers. "Palankeen," he said, "Janno's. Stay here," and was off.

It was three minutes to Janno's. Palan used the walk to rid himself of smiles. Daniel M'Cool with a female! A richard female! He was smiled out by time he got to Janno's, and a good thing too.

"Ah, Palan Goldhead." Janno swept across the courtyard, his state robes trailing in the dust. He peered with small beady eyes perched athwart a long thin nose. "How splendid of you to arrive so timely," casting a glance at the dial next the fountain. The water plashed over the stones, making rainbows of the noon light, falling useless back to its pool; a day's full rations turned to vapor by the heat. "Ah, don't fill your flask at this pool, Goldhead, it is perfumed by toilet water. One of my lady's notions." Janno waved five long woad-dyed talons in the air, as one who knew what notions ladies did take.

"Dregs'd drink it. Water the rye with it." Palan could no keep the words off his tongue, nor his eyes on Janno's.

"Mmmm. The dregs are always eager to excise beauty from this world, claiming always that it is non-utilitarian."

"Sir?"

"Never mind, never mind. Let's certainly plan to discuss this subsequent to the Hunt, hmm? At this present, we've need of your services." He waved the dark blue claws again.

"I'm on Gov Don's business." Palan waved his own long hand, the nails bit ragged, the scars white gainst his bronze skin plotched with acid stain, ground mud, cracked long its creases. He put the hand in his pocket. "Hunt's massing in plaza *soon*, sir."

"Though Governor Donal's wishes are always paramount, of course —"

"Well, Palan Yellowtop, may the dry waves roll me if that's no your shiny face," Quix come rolling up loud. "Morning, Janno, sir, fine morning for the Galanty Hunt. Hey Palan, Gov Don's looking high and low for you, and him having the only viewtube, begging your pardon, sir, I'm sure, and feeling considerable strong that the dreg who made the thing is the dreg as ought to —"

Palan made his apologies to Janno, and stepped away with Quix. "Oh, and by the by," said Palan, "Can you give me the lend of a palankeen for a lame smith?"

"A palanquin? For a dreg?"

Palan pulled his forelock. "Onliest as can fine-tune the Gov's viewtube. You see how my hands has lost their smooth," holding them out, the cracks and seams of them.

Janno looked down his nose at both dregs. "Hmmm," he said. A gust of wind blew fountain mist round his face. He blinked in the spray. "Yes. Go round the side; tell the footmen I approved the loan of the sackcloth palanquin."

The dregs was round the corner fore Janno's cheeks was dry. "What the —" said Quix till he got Palan's elbow in his ribs. "What lame —" and another elbow for his pains. They hefted the palankeen past the guardshack. "What's this for?" said Quix. Palan hummed in answer as they hustled toward the cliffrim.

"There!" he said, and laid down his end of the palankeen by Bedelia Coldhand. "You're a lame smith. Wind this handker round your face, and so to Gov Don's."

"What the —" said Bedelia.

"He's no taking questions just this now," Quix explained. "Hoy, Drosh." He nodded at a few females biddling round and Daniel canoodling with the palest. Quix hoped she was hale; they'd no time for sickening this day. "Palan he's a plan on him."

Drosh stumbled back, the perry flask in his pocket clanking gainst the stones. "Wott'll it, yaymen," he said. It was clear he'd be of little use.

They made their way, Bedelia Coldhand muttering and the rest of them panting neath her weight (cepting Drosh, who nobbut stumbled longside), past the nodding Brock and Doyle guarding the Gov's compound, past the pleached fruit trees of the privy courtyard, past the raked gravel of the parade ground, to the Rimehouse annex, to the gap tween old wall and new where the babe —

"That's what we're calling it now," Palan told Quix.

"It's shorter," Bedelia explained.

To the hole in the gap where the babe wailed. The hole spanned two handwidths. Bedelia Coldhand levered herself off the palankeen. "Drop a line, drop a line," she said. Quix snubbed the hawser and let it down smooth.

"Right," said Lena. "What, and now the babe sha' climb the rope?"

All of them looked to Palan.

"Right aright," he said, and pulled his forelock.

⟵⟶

August Inkwhistle pulled the doorknock twice. No answer at M'Cools. He called, "Lympe! O, Lympa!" A curtain twitched at garret window. He sat in the thin eave-shade like he was befuddled, no great stretch. A swaddled packet come at rope-end to knock the stones next him. The garret curtain twitched again. "Lympa!" he shouted. Naught. August Inkwhistle looked careful upstreet and down. With crabbed fingers he unhooked the packet, looking over his shoulder the while. He prised the cord from off the first layer. Shaking hands unwound layer on layer of swaddling from the packet till a flask shone. In one incautious move he raised the flask to his nose — it was —

"Halt!" A posse of scutmen came round both corners, pikes leveled at Augie Inkwhistle's foldskin belly, who hasty shoved the flask back in its cocoon. "What's this, what's this, what's all this?" said their comper.

"Naught," said Augie. A brace of scutmen stepped up to him.

"Powerful sweet smell off that naught he's got there, eh Bannon?" said one scutman.

"And in prettiest nest ever, Crump," agreed Bannon.

"He's too crepit to hold it safe," said the comper behind them. "He's nobody."

"It's no thiefry, or anywise dunning, to take naught from a nobody, ay, Bannon?"

"Easier nor taking candy from a babe, Crump, and twice the legal."

"Hand over," they said.

"Do it easy, dapple," said one of the posse behind them.

Augie shrank gainst the wall. "I found it but this now," he plainted, "Found it all my ownself. Have I no right to it? The guttered rat knows so much what's in it as I do."

"Hanging off Cider Mother's wall, innit?" Bannon gave the old dreg a friendly shove. "Hung there as present for you, was it?" Augie hung his head and crumpled. "Claiming your own, was you?" Bannon pushed his beak in mong the older's sparse chinhairs. "You'd no least right to it, had you?" Augie shook his head. Crump dug a matey elbow in his ribs as knocked him endwise. When Augie thrust out his hands to stop his fall, Bannon caught the flask midair. "Houp-la!" said the scutmen.

"First fruit," said Bannon, and handed it off to his comper. Eight twitching noses surrounded the comper. The comper took a whiff — "It smells perry," and sipped, "tastes perry, too," and tipped a doubleslug down his gullet. Sixteen squint eyes followed the flask's contents down his throat. "Ayuh. Perry. Which we the only left to bake down here ought swallow. A specific gainst a dunnamany ills, is perry." He slapped his plexus and passed the flask to Bannon, who tilted the flask, and then Crump, and then the next six throats gurgled. When it come round to their comper again, August Inkwhistle fell to his knees pleading, "Tip me a slug now gennamen, the least slug, would you now please," which gave them all to push great laughs, *hoddy hanxh hanxh.* "Willa look at this shuffler?" Bannon tossed the flask behind Augie's back to Crump, who held the flask over the old dove-seller's gaping mouth ... and laughed *hoddy hoddy hanxh.* "You dunna want to weak yoursel, old gip," Crump snatched the flask away and poured a good slug down his own gullet. He nobbut tapped the old dreg's ribs with his boot-toe — an easy tap, a nudge more like, he'd a dap himself, had Crump — as he passed the flask to the next scutman. And so around, and so around, till the flask was drained. "Keep-away!" someone bellowed, and the nine scutman kicked the flask round, the metal bouncing and denting off their boot-toes, off the cobbles, off the house-wall, their flushed faces roaring "Golee! Golee-o!" whenever one kick sent it tween another's legs. They wiped the sweat as sprung from their skin till their sleeves was damp. "A rare scorching day for this," Bannon gave a weak laugh and leaned gainst a wall. "Best snag a likkum shade," said Crump. "Whassa?" said a scutman, slumping next to Crump. "Take five," said the comper, who'd a fine sense of when to give orders: when his dregs was ripe to follow. So now the zausted scutmen obeyed him, sagged into what shade they could find. "Go South Point soon as rested," said the comper, and closed his eyes. Sixteen gritty eyes followed suit. Nine noses snorted. Eighteen hands went lax.

Augie Inkwhistle picked up the flask. "Considerable dinged," he said to the air as rumbled over the snoring dregs. "Gessel could maybe hammer back its shape." He tapped Bannon's arm: "Leave to pass on?" but the scut-man made no move. Augie repeated his question to no effect. "Well, well," said Augie, "they rise early and work hard, do scutmen. Best to pass on and make no noise about it." He sniffed the flask cork he held still in his hand. "May I be tossed mong rats if that's no valerian in this perry." He clucked his tongue. "What a sad mischance, mm, mm." Augie shook the comper's shoulder, "Cappen! Cappen! Duty, duty, duty!" but the only answer he got was a high thin voice calling from above, "Doody doody wanna doody!" that must been too soft to catch his wrinkled ears, for he made no sign. "Hmm, hmm," said Augie, "so this flask was laced, hmm, and so strong, hmm." He stowed the flask at his waist. "Strange doings, these, strange indeed. Hmm, hmm." He looked up at the sky like it'd answer. The garret curtain parted an eye-width. August Inkwhistle lifted a hand, like to balance himself, and the curtain closed. He staggered his way downstreet, hmming, hanxhing, shaking his head, holding back laughs so hard he could scarce see the way clear.

⟨⟩

"Best see our way clear fore we do aught," said Palan. "The Hunt's near the plaza, and I need to be there when they come."

"Now we've but to get this slip noose round the babe and haul it up." Palan gave a final tug to the knot.

"We've arms enough to haul, but how sha' we get the loop round the babe?" said Lena.

Deirdre looked up at Dan, like he could stitch the stars onto the daytime sky, and as easy wipe away this small trouble with a wave of his finger. He put his lips together and took a long breath. "Right aright," he said. He knelt to his carrysack. "These're Morsnal's gifts. Dan pulled Alpha and Delta from their nest. Drosh shrank back and Bedelia come forward with stick raised: "Did you splinter your rudder? Bring rattan here mong us?"

Dan stroked Alpha's soft grey fur. "These is Morsnal's rats."

"Which dears them to us how?"

Dan skritched Delta behind the ears. He put a piece of saltfish on the ground. Alpha waited on his two-note whistle, *Tzee-tzwhoo*, on which she sprang off his leg (Lena screeched), turned a legtucked somersault ("Ooohh," said Bedelia and Deirdre as one), and landed snouttip on the saltfish chunk. And quivered. *Tzwhoo-tzee*, Daniel whistled, and she started in to eat it, dainty as Lady Mandra at tiffin.

Bedelia Coldhand laughed out loud. "So Morsnal's rats'll take your command, eh?"

"Go meet the Hunt," Daniel told Palan. "I've this in hand."

⌐⟶

"Hand me a poniard," Kellock told a beater. "This is our last close-in fore we reach the plaza. Watch this, Thursgood," striding towards the rat-mass, "here's the way of it." Kellock thrust his leg-greaves in mong the rats, who backed, talons clicking on the stones, and backed as he come on, crouched to make a small target, his poniard twisting in figure-eights, laughing, looking over his left shoulder at Thursgood — which is how he come to miss the brace of rats as launched themselves at his right arm a jawlength above the wrist and sank their long foreteeth deep. Kellock had a game heart; he tried to shift the poniard from his right hand to his left, so to stab them off him, but the blood was spurting by then, dark purple coming out his flesh in fountains with each heartbeat. His face went grey and his knees bent double; he sank to the stones with the two rats fastened to his forearm, and so he was sprawled when the last blood pumped away, so quick his eyes was open yet when the rats loosed their hold and scuttled in mong their pack.

"The close-in, ladies and gennelmen," said a voice.

"Come ye, come ye, step right up," said another.

"Who was that? Stampel?" Clarch whirled round.

"Nobbut a musician," Thursgood soothed.

"I sha' —"

"Do naught," said Thursgood. "You canna touch Musicians thout Ambrose by. Kellock was a dolt and there's an end to it." He clapped the other's back. "We can pike three dozen, easy, with how they're feeding on him. Hey? Always looks good to enter plaza with pikes full of rats, right?"

Clarch rubbed his eyes on the crook of his arm. "Right," he said. "Right aright."

On the Wagon above, Morsnal hissed that nobbut thirteen was left.

"Hmm?" said Max, bowing in long swoops.

"Hunt Boys! The half of them gone!"

"Pity about Kellock. He'd a good feel for the drums." Max tuned his A string.

"Boys! To me!" hollered Thursgood. "Pikes only till we come to plaza! We've had unlucky chance this day, what with rimers gone up ahead to thrill the richards, but are we no Hunt Boys?" and they clamored *Yeah*; "We sha' cleave our way to plaza!" and the Boys shouted *Yeah*; "Where the rimers sha' anathematize those rats to jelly, versify their bones to curd!" and the Boys took up their pikes and *Yeah* they shouted.

*Bangarang bang, samdankissh samdankissh, tatapoppa popata popata, shakrittle shakrattle, skreelyabach ayheyoh ayheyoh ay hey ay hey.* Thirteen. He'd a good feel for the drums. Dark purple blood dries quick to black.

"Spike them!" shouted Thursgood. "I'll give Chrysta to the Boy as spikes nine!"

"Nine'll no fit on a pike," said Morsnal.

"Thursgood's cappen," said Scerzo tween *tatapop* and *popata*. "Think that's news to him?"

"*I'd* no give up Chrysta, ha-umm, for all the —"

"Shutter up," said Max. "Horns, cymbals, drums: on two. And one. And —" with a clash and a brass and a *skreelyabach ayheyoh* the Hunt Boys came, with eyes of flame, up the steeply path, *ayheyoh*, and spiked the rats and raised their rat-pikes high, *ayheyoh*, higher nor their eyes, *ayheyoh*.

The spiked rats squirmed round the staffs that spit them. The pack pressed flank to flank and followed after, their crudescent tails lashing the dust.

⌒

"Dust this sconce! Beat this tapis! Scrub those necessaries! Parlogals, stiff your pinnas! Footmen, slick your hair! Collins, when will the crudites be ready for the guests?"

"Right now, Lady M. Fore you take another breath." Collins sat at the wide table stirring a pot you could wash a sprat in. "Dazymare! Where's the big dipper?"

Mary Patricia asked her, sweet, "The one could cup a breast? Or any-how *my* breast?"

"Mayry Patriza, desist from taunting Collins this morning. Never judge a soul by its body's shape," Lady Mandra pulled her breastband the tighter, "rather, bestir yourself to helpful acts. The Hunt is at the foot of the path as we speak; there's no time for repartee. Do you understand me?" fixing Collins and Mary Pat, both, with her stare.

"Yes, m'lady," they said.

When she'd bustled out, Mary Pat plomped on the bench next Collins. "Stir the pot."

Collins made to rap her skull. "I sha' be stirring and stirring, do you get me the necessary."

"Best shun that word today," Mary Pat buffed her nails gainst her pinna.

"Ha! Right you are. Mercator! Spindrift! Punzelmane! Get me the big dipper! Let me see those asses twinkle!" The dregs come hotfoot, pinnas on the flap.

Mary Pat grabbed a necessary while they swirled round Collins, and was half to the door when Lady Mandra swished through the curtains, one brow lifted. Mary Pat had tried and tried to raise just one that way. "Yes'm," she said. "Off to place the necessaries in alcoves like you said, ma'am." Lady Mandra raised the brow another notch. How did she do it? "Like you directed, ma'am." Mary Pat scuttled up the ladder, the necessary tucked neath her left arm.

Lady Mandra watched her from doorway. Mayry Patriza rose light as a leaf on the wind, no sag anywheres about her; she rose from dark to light as easily as fish swam to the surface. Her thighs were slim, her calves were taut, her arches high, but she was only a dreg (Lady Mandra returned to her preparations), who'd putresce and wither in a few years' time. Lady Mandra lifted her calloused feet over the threshold and raised her cracked voice for Collins. Soon all that young beauty would be vanishing, vanishing, vanishing away. "Collins!" shouted Lady Mandra. "Were you aware we are having guests today?"

"Today of all days," said Goodwin.

Bran groaned and retched. "Foozled," he said.

"Of course you are," Goodwin said. No snap to her voice. Snapping was crude. She merely supplied information others might have overlooked. "You've no capacity for strong potions whatsoever. What came over you?"

"Beaters," he groaned.

"Oh, beaters indeed. Did beaters tie you up and force the fluid down your gullet?"

Bran nodded, which made him retch again.

"What were you doing with beaters, any road? You, who always sneer at them?"

"None sha' sneer at beaters after this day," Finn told them. "You stood soldier while rats overran us. You stood soldier when weapons was no use, though all your blood was shouting *Flail Spear Run*. Right aright. When we enter plaza, enter heads down, eyes front, like you was searching for rats, hear?" (and the beaters said, *Yeah*) "Come up tween the gangle of Hunt Boys and the widemouth rimers like tide sneeps up tween driftlogs; face the Hunt and keep your back to the rimers, hear?" (and they said, *Yeah*) "Let no Hunt Boy out from our circle. Let no rimer pass in till I give the signal!" "*Yeah!*" they roared.

Finn led them away uphill, and they behind him shouted *For lack of a nail a shoe was lost*; ba-bum they pounded their flail butts on the stones, *For lack of a shoe a horse was lost*, ba-bum.

Finn retied the handker round his brow as he ran up the hill. *For lack of a horse* — well, what else was the job of a beater but to flush rats from their holes? — *a battle was lost* — he'd back his beaters gainst any passel of Hunt Boys as was always seeking their own cockspan of glory — *For lack of a battle* — Hunt Boys had no feel for the pack like his beaters had, twenty-six dregs who'd crouched as stone in the elder thicket as the rats poured over; couple went pale as his palms but none broke — *a war was lost* — his beaters; had he no made them? they'd learned naught from Ambrose cept to quarter the ground with their flails; his beaters was more nor ready to take on Thursgood and Ambrose arm in arm with all their hordes behind them — *and all for the lack of a trumpery nail*.

"We've no time for that trumpery now," Cider Mother soothed. "Bumpy's down cellar, sitting plush on his own chair. We'll have a tale to tell him when we come home, Suellen. Shutter up now, acushla. We're taking a nice boat ride, is this no nice? Round South Point we go, we go, round South Point we go, tra-la, to beach at Vale of the Bones, aye, to reach the trail on our lones, why, nary a bone sha' we find, aye, they gone to dust where they lie, sigh, their buboes gone dust long syne."

So with clapping, singing, jerky, and fruit leather, they two went round the Point and was lost to view. Only Fergus heard them as he swayed on deck as they sang past; that song, that voice, pulled him to follow. The *Mam Can Cook* was riding low in the water as he steered her out from behind the *Hail Janus* in their wake. The junk hugged the rocks so close as Fergus had skill to bring her. Easy enough to follow the sound of them, *"The bones is all a tale, my sweet, the bones is all but dust."* Fergus took a snip of tarponesse to stave off hunger, and a slug of perry to chase the snuff. He'd a fair wind at his back and all the luck in the world close-packed in his keel.

# Play Out Rope

The sun had come to the middle of the sky and there halted. In the haze of
dustmote, lightmote, the sun was no smooth disc but a raggedy pulsing, a tidewashed
clamshell fringed with seaweed translated to orange-yellow. The tide was at the slack,
drawn back to its furthest extent from the shingle littered with driftwood, kelplengths,
shells and other flotsam that glistened with salt crystals. Any fingerling wave-tossed
on the stones was cooked through, its flesh falling from its bones. A leaf fallen that
morning had now crisped along its main vein, a thumbnail of powder holding its
form by habit. A wind gust might complete its transformation to dust, perhaps one
of the gasps that escaped the exhausted air as it wallowed toward the cooler sea, but
such gusts came seldom, and none penetrated the shuttered windows to ease sweating
dregs who tossed on their pallets, scratching in their doze the bites of fleas and flies
who enjoyed the only vigor in bakestone Charnholm.

On the high plateau of South Point, the Hunt moved to climax. Richards in
a cool shelter cave crowded round the viewtube to watch the Hunt Boys stab, close-
in, the plaguey rats.

A UGUST INKWHISTLE TODDLED from shadepatch to shadepatch tween
Cider Mother's brewcellar and Gessel's shop. Having roused the
sawyer and sent him up the hill to South Point, the old dove-seller lay him
down to sleep in the shop sawdust, whereon he commenced to snore in
steady honks till the seabreeze rose up to flee the sinking sun.

Daniel, hunkered in the lee of Rimehouse annex, played out the rope
easy, easy, till the pomace-soaked tip was at the babe's mouth. It reached
up for it. It sucked. They tossed down milkweed, cloths, grassclumps, whatever'd make a plump for it to sit back on. So they inch by inch decreased
the hole's depth. "Had we more stuffing," Dan lamented, but they'd none,
made do with what was at hand, wiped the sweat off them with the crook

of their elbows, squeezed last season's apples from Bedelia's plackets — "I'll never again taunt you for saving, Bedelia," said Dan — dipped cloth off their own bodies in the mash, twisted the cloth into nipples, and again. At last the babe was nobbut three armlengths down. *Skreelyabach skreelyabach samdankissh samdankissh* jumped over the ridge like so many flea-riddled rats. Deirdre looked from face to face; did they not know the Hunt was nigh? But when her eyes reached Dan's face, she looked no further. The beak of his nose. The curls over his brow. The muscles in his neck. His shoulders as they flexed as he played out rope. *Skreelyabach ayehoh ayehoh.* "The Hunt's come up to the plaza," said Deirdre. Dan pursed his lips. "Pay it no mind," he said, and coughed up dust, and spat.

Innsmort spat on Gov Don's viewtube mesh, at the northmost point of the plaza. It was netted fine as he could make it. Below him, Mary Patricia stood chatting with Brock and Doole at top of the cave's rear bolt hole; at its fore-entry, Palan stood cross-arm watching Finn lead the beaters to the east flank, while Mary Katharine and Rimshot steered the rimer mass to the west. The north side of the plaza was open entire to the Hunt Wagon as toiled slow up the final slope on offal-clogged wheels, viol skreeling in echo of the spitted rats.

"Hold ladder foot, willa?" Innsmort come careful down the rope ladder. Mary Pat dusted his shoulders, friendly, once he was safe down. "Can see the south fence from up there," he said, wiping tar off his hands. "Queer tricks the heat does play. Like the top of it was moving. Like hands waving."

Mary Pat grabbed his sleeve. "Bes' 'hutter up," she said through her teeth. "Whole 'laza a'hind you's 'ull o' 'ichards."

"Mind your hand, there, Mary Pat. Hast a drap of perry about for a dry gullet?"

"Best check the viewtube guyropes fore you go," said Mary Pat, and towed Innsmort to the southmost rope, a good twenty yards from the bolt hole. There, she gripped his shoulder: "Talk soft. South fence was waving?"

"Ayuh. What's amiss with guyropes?"

"Naught. South fence was waving?"

Innsmort plaited his fingers. "Gov Don near took my head off when I told him this morning."

Mary Pat grunted and turned him loose. "Then best be somewheres out his sight for a time, no?" Fore Innsmort could answer, she went on, "Best hide mong the rimers. Go to Mary Kath, now, and tell her I said to put you in whiteskin —"

"Skin of the burned dead on my own! I'd never —"

"Better than tha' own dead skin. Do as you hear. Tell her — mind, now — tell her straight off you seen the south fence waving. She'll likely get a good chant off that, put her in good with Bran and them. Hear, Innsmort?" Again she left him no time to get his thoughts to his lips. "Straight round the plaza to Mary Kath and Mary Kath only." His forehead rucked and he started in with the mouth again; there was no time for that. Mary Pat sent him off with a less than gentle shove towards the west flank where the rimers massed in slow chant.

Once he was fair launched, Mary Pat flirted herself at Brock and Doole. "The old man's brains is fair baked by too many summers. Had he a lash in his eye, he'd make out it was a three-mast fleet in-sailing." She stroked their spines, "Such muscles you two have." They nodded as one, their eyes half-closed. She stroked a little the lower till they was panting, and then she took them, Brock then Doole, into the guardshack for a quick toss, whispering to each how he was the one she craved, only he, but she must pleasure the other so to keep it from milady. They'd their eyes closed, but hers was open to follow Innsmort's murbling progress round to Mary Kath. "Oh!" she cried when he'd made harbor mong the rimers, "Oh good," and whichever footman it was come at that time.

⟨⟩

Time was come. Mary Kath signaled. Finn slouched — all eyes was on the Hunt Wagon — and crouched — the Wagon jolting over the entry stones — and scuttled to rear of the beater flank, where he careless dropped his poniard; he searched, parted grass blades on his knees, and rose with summat in hand to stroll casual round the compound to a cove he could piss in thout frighting any richard lady. Finn shook his cock dry and carried on strolling till he come on Mary Kath. They ran over all the points of their plan, and Finn was about to take his leave when Mary Kath said, "Innsmort seen them waving."

"What? Where?"

"Aflank the south fence gates."

Finn spread his palms and shrugged. "Naught to be done. Best pick up the pace then. Maun beat up rats now. Quarter hour." He was gone fore you could say *Gov Don*.

⌣⟶

Gov Don had fashed three flat rings as could be seen from the view-tube. That is to say, he'd told off dregs to set them up. In the first, tumble krewes spilled from the rimer mass and vaulted over each other, walked on their hands, gathered in four-leg pyramids in shape of a bull that pawed its hooves and charged a loose red tunic who leapt who launched who seized its horns and somersaulted over its back to land, arms outflung, back of its tail; the bull aimed a kick at the redness who twisted easy aside, arms still upflung. Another pyramid formed in shape of a horse who charged the bull who kicked again at the red tunic who slid away like a fish from a hand ... only to turn with telescoping sword as unfurled to fathom-length with a shake of its hilt and snicker-snack tween two legs of the pyramid bull who skewered fell in a tussilade of outflung berry-purple handkers and panting lay on its side while the red tunic and pyramid horse danced in slow col-lected trot three times round the circle, coming wider with each circle till they was nobbut an armslength from the beaters on the east flank and the rimers on the west flank, till they was smack front of the viewtube, at when the dead bull flew apart into tumblers who leapt out, ankles gainst their asses, to cartwheel in and round the circling horse and the circling red tunic, spang up gainst the tube-mesh the tumblers rolled.

In the second ring, seven woad-skin jongleurs tossed stuffed ratskins mong themselves as they circled three tambours who beat *bamp-ba-bam-bam* who beat and beat the stretched grey skins gainst their hips, *bamp-ba-bam-bam* stuffrats flying past their ears, long ribbed tails tangling their hair, rat-whiskers touching ratwhiskers high above tambours *bamp-ba-bam-bam* as they flew from jongleur hand to outstretched hand *bampa-bampa-bam ba-bam-bam* the jongleurs twirled in place, their skirts fashed of daggered color strips as

flew up from their gentals as they twirled; a stomp of the right foot flung
stuffrat to kiss one palm which flung it in turn cross-circle to another, the
jongleurs twirling, catching stuffrats at their backs, a half-twirl to face the
crowd and they two-hand tossed them cross-circle; the tambours *bamp-ba-
bam-bam* shuffling bell-ringed feet in place *bakachatta bakachatta ba ka ka*,
hips swinging as jongleurs sweated blue streaks down chests and bellies
*bamp-ba-bam-bam* and *bamp-ba-bam-bam*; as they spread in wider and wider
rings, the stuffrats flew unerring.

In the third ring, fools in cap and bells *baskacha baskacha* climbed a
pile of rats and slid down a pole ringed by sag-breasts who swiped the fools'
two-foot woodcocks as down they slid and beat the woodcocks gainst their
saggy breasts, at which the fools did cower *baskacha baskacha* and caper
*baskacha* and curl *baska baska.* A fool on another's shoulders barked tween
his cupped hands till a passel of fools grabbed soft pikes tipped with velvet
bells and ran, stabbing the dust, to a Wagon wove of straw, ran round it
and round it, stabbing empty dust while the shoulder-riding fool barked
gabble uncease as the fools stabbed, as they swung their scrim corvisers as
their two-foot woodcocks waggled as they chanted: *The Fat Bum Boys / with
sighs of CAME / hopped blistering through the bowling streets / and whacked off
as they CAME* stroking their woods with both hands as they ran as they
stabbed as they pranced, woods waggle-dangle, round the wicker Wagon till
the sag-breasts come plittery plitter, shuffle toe, to dab the fools to rub them
with fish oil, which sent the Fat Bum Boys to itch and twirl and howl till
the fool beaters come crawling up with poultices they clamped on each
howling stinking Fat Bum. The sag-breasts galumphed round the ring in a
triumphal lap the while, their hori tulle flouncing, their floursack dugs flapping round their waists; till each was caught from behind by a corvisered
fatbum fool and bumpalump bumpalump they was rogered round in whacking thrusts, dangling woods poking tween sag-breast thighs, the joinkered
couples baring their teeth at the crowd as they poked and rubbed as they
galumphed in massy tandem; till there entered the ring a fool so corplent
they'd to wheel her, squatting on her spangled hams, singing *Useless gerruls
hear my song / Suck those cocks till they grow long / And a one suck two suck three
suck four / Now turn your back / Ope wide your crack / And a one swive two*

*swive three swive four / Let them swive you slit you slice you more / You'll feel no pain till they're out the door / Till they're out / bom bom bom / Out the door / bom bom bom* and with four strong arms to raise her heap of flesh, the corplent fool soared high and sang *Useless gerruls / Lap my pubes / That's the best / Of all the lubes / And a one lap two lap three lap four / Till a shudder takes me / Till down I pour / And a one lap two lap three lap four / Then off with you / Away with you / You dirty dirty horii / Till I want some more-ii.*

Even the rimers laughed for fair — once they seen Matron laughing, any road — they like to split their guts laughing, and the richards? down the shelter cave? jostling round the viewtube? Out of course they took their cue from Gov Don. When he started in to chortle, they all chortled likewise. Gov Don and Lady Mandra chortled side by side on gilty thrones, their robes their headdresses their pointy-toe slippers, all, chockblock in mirror rounds, look at them hard as you could you saw nobbut your own self. Back of the chortling, richards muttered as how the sights was but a glimmer and the songs a mere burble. "Need a viewtube for each cave," said Janno to Roger, and Roger said ayuh to that; "For myself, I prefer the bleachers where one can see and be seen rather than this sad crush," said Treesa to Chantal, and Chantal inclined her head a hairsbreadth. Still, Gov Don had chortled; still, each of them owed favors to Gov Don. "Keep mum for the nonce," said Chantal to Treesa; "I can bear it for once in a way," said Roger to Janno; and so ran the murmur mong the sembled richards. They shuffled their feet in their pearlsewn slippers, turned the beads on their wrists, waited. They was main good at that. Time's passing gave them no itch soever.

*That's the moment when the Hunt creeps up / To the trumpeting of the horns,* sang the Musicians atop the Wagon.

The Hunt come hurlyburly shripshrop tricaloc, every Boy at full cock, Max sawing *skreelyabach skreelyabach* the cymbals *samdankish samdankish* the horns *poppoparop,* through the compound gates full wide the Rat Hunt Boys come in bloodsplotched gleam — what was left of them — and the jongleurs and the tumble krewes turned funambulist, walking steady up the stretched hawsers from ground stakes to roofmast, while the fools rose in a spring tide to the roof ladders, all in quickmarch they rose.

The rimers moved forward stately, hands shading their eyes so not to singe any innocent watching. *Boldly strike / where least the blow's / expected. / Raise the pike / on rat so close.*

The beaters pulled cages of rats on long ropes to the center.

Lady Mandra pulled a long breath and looked round at empty cups. She signaled Collins to bring fresh brimming tumblers of perry for all. Collins handed sweating silver ewers to Mercator! Spindrift! Punzelmane! She wasted no breath on Dazymare, upladder emptying the necessaries with Brock and Doole.

Cider Mother heard the horns from South Point landing stage and hoisted Suellen to her shoulders.

Fergus on the *Mam Can Cook* heard the cymbals *samdankish* and pulled fresh tarponesse from its alembic as he tacked round South Point in Cider Mother's wake.

Gov Don looked round on the raptured guests and thought first he'd send a full pipe of potable to Palan Goldhead in thanks for the viewtube, though on second thought a hogshead would be a gracious plenty.

Chantal and Roger slid into an alcove, hands in each other's clothes, their tongues active.

Mary Kath gave the nod to Mary Pat back of the shelter cave.

Palan Goldhead in the lee of the south fence unwound coil on coil of rope ladder from his waist.

Finn gave his beaters the word to advance and slid through the funambulists to hand Palan the grapple hooks. They lashed them to the ladders.

The Hunt come to full stop in the center of the plaza. Every richard eye was glued to the viewtube's optic. The Hunt Boys hoisted high their pikes as they paraded round the Wagon. COME they chanted as they circled, COME they sang as their full cocks spurted, COME the richard ladies could no been pulled from the optics was they given youth eternal, lips open and breathing hard. The rimers encircled the Hunt Boys. The beaters hauled their heavy squealing cages tween the rimers till they touched the Wagon's four irongirt wheels.

Gov Don stirred in his seat. This was the moment to address the Hunt Boys. His Hunt speech; the Boys looked to him for that, depended on his encouragement, waited for it, could hardly start the finale without. Lady Mandra laid her hand on his. "This once you'll stay silent," she said, then stroked his upper arm like he had, still, muscles enough to lift her over threshold; "Galanty Hunt you proclaimed it and Galanty Hunt it shall be. We remain below." Which was right and proper, no contest; Mandra was right, as always, of course she was. Still.

Ambrose strode cross plaza to the Gov's customary spot neath Hunt Wagon's prow. "The Galanty Hunt," he bellowed. "Giving thanks to the richards as brought us these fine musicians" — uppity pesks — "these brave beaters, first in field" — last in hearts — "the Anathematizers, who lull the rousted rats in verse" — which they surely primed themselves on — "today's specialmost Tumbler Krewe: tumblers, jongleurs, fools" — Lady Mandra's twinkle-eye notion to give such slum a chance to show off their amachoor tricks — "and finally, the young males as risk life and limb, blood and skin, to keep Charnholm safe, ladies and gennelmen, dregs and bawds, I give you ... the Rat Hunt Boys!" Tremendous cheers. They was licking it up; well, let them. Olympia was the onliest who'd know what he done and she nowhere about. Her two aboveground, Mary Kath a useless rimer, Finn lifted to Bestest of beaters, what was that, prince of paltry; still with the both of them out on plaza, you'd think Olympia'd show her face. Ambrose lifted his joined hands over his head and shook them once left and once right and the crowd roared *Halloo* in answer. He swept his joined hands down and said, quiet, to Hunt Boys only: "Spines soldier, weight to the balls of the feet, arms loose out from their shoulders, the pike's a *tool*, mind, thrust *through* the rats' bodies."

The beaters stood to the ratcage doors. The Anathematizers stepped forth from the rimers, spread wide their whiteskin arms and called: *You sha' dance on your bone-froze paws*

And the rimer mass chanted in reply:

You sha' go on dancing.

*Move never step from your place*

You sha' go on dancing

*In your bare place in the open*
You sha' go on dancing
*When Hunt Boys come with pikes*
Spikes
*Spears*
Poniards
*As they pounce on you*
You sha' go on dancing
*Your hearts shall still beat when they toss you to the flames.*
Beating yet when first flames lick you lick you lickyoulickyou.

And the Beaters threw wide the cage doors. The rats cowered inside, eyes fixed on the Hunt Boys. No motion, no sound, only one drummer beat with the heel of his hand, slow and long: *Bome. Bome. Bome.*

*Bome.* "Rats ready to leap out their cages," said Mary Kath. Mary Pat took a breath and ran downladder to make sure the drinks was all served right. Mary Kath offered Brock and Doole her special flask, which they drained quick and grateful.

*Bome.* Collins told Mary Pat the drinks was ready to serve "just as you made them, Dazymare, and the necessaries are full to bursting, be so kind as to empty them," they both of them on the broad grin as Mary Pat climbed upladder and down till every necessary was tipped. As she worked, richard chat frothed round her:

"Will you look at the yellow teeth of those rats."

"Have ever you seen them so close?"

"Can you hear the rimers? I can't."

"Next time, let's go back to the Bleachers."

"You can't see as much from there, but you can *be seen*."

"No point putting on gowns to have them mangled in this crush."

"That one ... there ... in the far cage ... look at the tusks on it!"

"Were this my entertainment, I'd serve up something better than cider and pastry."

"Mandra had so little notice."

"So much as we, yet we're here in full array. Dear Mandra, there's no denying she's a touch slackwaist."

On her final trip, Mary Pat asked Collins, quiet, if she'd passed the tumblers round.

"I did that," said Collins. "Each of them downed full measure."

"Right aright. Should hit them a quarter hour after," said Mary Pat. Collins nodded.

A few minutes later, Chantal slid down in her seat. Janno collapsed next her in a tangle heap. Thassy and Roger exchanged a long look that melted into a long embrace of the nearby, suddenly comfortable floor. Cinna and Gaby pirouetted round Ross and Strenal, slide-slide-slide slide-slump-slump-tumble-snore. Gov Don looked at Lady Mandra. Lady Mandra looked at Gov Don. They closed their eyes gainst the force of their exchanged look. Propped on the arms of their sidebyside thrones, their heads slumped back gainst the nappy headrests and they too dozed.

"Now that," said Collins, "is some fine timing."

"Seems they go bone dull for a few moments first," Mary Pat agreed. "Good to know if ever there's a second time."

Collins slapped her rump. "Get on with you, willa? You've nobbut a few hours."

Mary Pat smiled her thanks and climbed the ladder for the last time.

Belowstairs, Collins speckled the sleeping richards with the water from the fouled necessaries, each richard receiving a proper, equal share. She set the basins in their proper alcoves, and plumped herself down on the bench for a nice quiet snooze.

On South Point:

Rope spilled down the shaft from Mary Kath and Rimshot's hands.

Rope spilled down the babe's narrow hole, it now an armlength only from their hands.

Rope spilled from Cider Mother's hands down the south slope in even spools.

Rope spilled down from the plaza's south wall, secured with grapples to its top.

Rope spilled from the *Mam Can Cook,* securing her to South Point landing stage.

Ropes of staggerrats spilled from their cages. Tails lashed to tails, rat-coils spiraled teeth outwards towards the Hunt Boys.

*Samdankish, samdankiish. Bome. Bome. Skreelyabach ayehoh. Bome. Bome.*

# Swing, Swing, Swing

The yolk-yellow sun, broken by its own heat, had run out all over the pan; the hot blue sky paled to green, at its furthest edges crisped to dull grey brown. No sun none you could point to, only the spreading yellow staining the blue sky to green. No wind. Never had been least thought of wind. The air clumped together and pressed down on Charnholm, drawing blood from the stones as it drew sweat from skin. Lungs labored to draw it in, sieving the dust, labored to push out the last silted puff. Where the Hunt had passed, smoke rose grudging from the stubborn flesh of ratpile scraps. The tide at its slack dallied with the saltglisten flotsam, pushing it a few fingerlengths in, and then out, in, and then out, sweeping the trash into crescents that scraped the shingle kariissh, kariissh. Skeletons of fish of leaf of kelp of ships washed back and fro gentle in the slack tide. The rot of their flesh came up full off the shallow pools in the shingle, swelled up and over Charnholm town, and rode the charred fleshsmoke some way up the bluffs that circled the harbor till the stench could rise no more against the heavy lid of grey-brown air.

Some few points stood above the soiled miasma. Reading from north to south: A few of the sour crags in the northerly lee of North Point; the top half of the crumble as once was North Point Light; the boltholes of the smithcaves up atop the sandstone bluffs; the crowsnest of Hail Janus; the topmost four fathoms of South Point; the capstones of the fence round the potable works. Looking south past South Point, mayhap the glint of a few broken crowns of scrapers away south in the silver city; mayhap only a trick of the light.

Few were awake to see. Charnholm dregs snorted through handkers in their greybrown cocoons, raising themselves betimes well-practiced in their sleep to wet their lips with potable and sleep again. Scutmen sprawled snorting on cobbles outside Cider Mother's door. Richards slumped burbling below Gov Don's viewtube. Augie Inkwhistle wheezed in-out in-out through his few teeth on his fleabit pallet.

I N THE SHELTER CAVE MONG THE SNORTING RICHARDS, Mary Katharine pulled out drawers, opened doors, sifted through shelves, Rimshot chuntering and questioning at her the while. At last Mary Kath said, "Shutter up, canna? Is it possible? Hast ever done it?"

"Course I can. Why I gone days thout utt'rance, been mistook for a stone; what's the good of it? Who'd be a —"

"Rimshot. Shutter up for now. *Aqua pura.* That's what we got to find."

They found it in a dried gourd on the top shelf of a kitchen cabinet, like it was nobbut more storage. Inside the gourd, a cylinder rolled in a copper tube sealed with red spag.

Mary Kath slit the seal. She unrolled the parchment within. "Aqua pura," she breathed. She laid it on a stone inlay table where ivory elephants trumpeted cross a shallow lapis lake, secured it with empty tumblers on the corners. "Quit breathing on my neck, Rimshot," she said.

The two rimers leaned over the pages, paying no least notice to the snorting richards all over the room.

⌣⟶

"Room enough for me and my hands," Lena said to Daniel M'Cool. "Yours are too large. Leave off and let me at the justborn."

"Babe," said Dan.

"It's shorter," said Bedelia Coldhand.

Lena huffed. "Grab my ankles an you want to be of use. Easy now. Got it. Pull up ... easy ... oh by the last rat EASY ... slow up now ... its limbs are catching on this ledge slow slow ... there." She plumped the justborn on the hole's rim. Deirdre grabbed the creature by its middle and hauled it away to Bedelia's lap.

"There my precious there my sweet there suck on this willa there," giving it a rag soaked in pomace to suck on. Its wails stopped sudden, and the dregs hunkered round its quiet pock-pock on the rag tween its lips, its twig arms flailing a bit gainst its bloated belly, twig legs fallen apart. Its normous eyes stared wide at the giants round it.

Dan leaned gainst the plaza's south wall, listening to the Hunt. None could heard the babe's wails nor yet the sharp silence after in all the din they made. He could no see the Hunt, for Rimehouse annex jutted tween him and the plaza, but he could hear the Boys chanting COME, the rimers chanting *You noisome clanch of vapors! / Remorseless, treacherous, / Lecherous, kindless scum. / Ulla! / Ullaloo!*, Max sawing away *skreelyabach ayehoh skreelyabach skreel*; then a high sharp squeak like wind snapping the rigging — and again — from the far side of the wall it was — and again — "Do you hear that?" he asked Deirdre in the crook of his arm.

"What?" she said.

"That squeak, that high sharp —"

Bedelia and Lena protested as how they just got done with the one sound, and what trouble it cost them, course it was worth it, surely, yet was this the time to puff up another rare noise? But Deirdre listened.

She listened close. Her skin was pale as his palms, soft as the just-born's, no pock nor crack anywheres. Her eyes the pale green of the sea in foam. "Yes," she said.

They slithered to a low spot in the wall where a capstone'd gone missing, a few courses of stones below it gone to crumble off lacking its protection. Dan made a cup of his hands and she stepped into it, with one boost she'd her elbows atop it. *Skreelyabach ayehoh samdankiish. Bome. Bome.* The voice in his skull said, "Now." Alpha and Delta stirred in the carrysack; an he'd no near forgot them! Deirdre squealed. The high wind in the rigging squeaked in answer. There was whisper overhead. The voice said, *"Yes."* Deirdre said, "Let me down easy, Dan. And be ready." Ready for what? He'd no least idea. He eased her down and she remained Deirdre, the voice had come and gone yet she was still there, flesh in his arms, speaking: "Cup your hands again." He did as she said, the voice ringing in his skull, *"Yes"* and with one scrabble two thin welty legs come down from the topstones backwards, easy, squeaking thin and sharp all the while.

When he'd set the legs on the ground, a wizened creature near its natural end peered up at him through a mop of white hair and said "Yes" and looked round, so thin its eyes clicked gainst its sockets, till it found the justborn. "Yes." How could a creature so starveling scuttle so fast? It took the justborn easy and certain from Bedelia Coldhand's lap and held it to its breast. "Yes." Leaking some from the eyes, it looked up at them, the small creature tight gainst itself, and said, "Yes. This is mine."

They was all of them crouched to rescue the justborn from this crazed being when Bedelia Coldhand heaved herself to her feet and, her palms outspread, no threat soever, come up close to the white mop. "She's the mother," Bedelia Coldhand said. "Have none of you sense enough to pack in a thimble? She needs provender and potable fore any else." She told the mother they'd a dunnamany questions to ask when she'd fed, and the white mop nodded as she tore into a rye slice.

When her mouth was empty, the justborn sucking at her breast, they asked her where and how and why and when, and she swallowed, wiped the back of her hand cross her mouth, and spoke:

"They let us keep the first spawn, the scutmen do. The first is ours; an there's a second they take it. They lay it in the hole outside — outside the Potable Works, course — and let it wail its life away. To discourage us from making more, they say. The man I'm with was main careful, but the scutmen as caught me in the distillation chamber, no. They took it from me three days since." She hugged the small sleeping creature tighter to her breast. "I tried and my man tried to get over the fence but all we got was welting off the scutmen for our pains. They wait till you're near over the fence, then they cane you. Well, that's how they start, by caning you. There's sixty of us, more or less. They come, they go, tween one day and the next." The justborn woke wailing and she petted it back to sleep.

"They take the hale from you," said Lena, and wrapped her arms round her chest. The white-hair said, "Yes." Lena rocked gainst her crossed arms and said, "Sixty, you say?" The mother said, "Yes."

That was when Lena's eyes changed in her face and all the raising she got off the richards turned to curdle in them — they was keeping the Potable Works safe for all Charnholm, was they? Keeping it safe for richards only, more like. "Right aright," said Lena. She jumped up and pulled Deirdre's elbow: "We're cracking the Potable Works and no mistake," to which Deirdre said was she sure? all reasonable, taking herself off Dan for one heartbeat to remind Lena how adamant she had been about protecting the Works. "Yeah yeah," said Lena. "Dan, get Quix and Drosh and hustle them gatewards right this now and no mistake. What a dupe I been. All these years I been hearing lies pour from out their mouths and still I thought they was made of truth on this one. Potable Works for all Charnholm, they said. Glorus future for dregs and richards alike, so long as it was protected. Waiting till it was ready, they said." Dan made to speak and Lena cut him off: "Shutter up and come with me. The gates are round the cliffs to the southeast. Come *long*, Dan. We can ask the whys and wherefores later. Now's our time to move. Come *long*." Dan took two following steps and halted, cupping the carrysack gainst his waist. He kissed Deirdre on the lips, "I'll meet you there soon as I can," he said, and walked away to the plaza. Lena let him go. She saw naught but the memory of Janno tiptoeing a jusborn through the courtyard up the stairs and to my lady's chamber. Lena was to keep shtum about it for it was part of the glorus future as richards was preparing for all Charnholm. Lena shook her head and, in the present, swept up the white-haired creature and her justborn and they moved like froth fore wind to the gates.

The gates creaked neath Cider Mother's fist. Suellen puckered her mouth, on the edge of crying; "Shhha, shhha," said her mam. Rustling and chittering on the far side of the gates. "By the last rat's rotted tooth," said Cider Mother, "willa open these gates or no?" More susurrance her only answer. "I brought you ropes so to climb out from there," she said, "the richards is all sleeping by now."

"Huh." One voice from behind the gates. "You scutmen who've tried this trick on us so many times, do you think to fool us yet? Only you can open these gates. We've lost enough to climbing the walls; we've no more to spare."

"Do I sound a scutman?"

"How's a scutman's sound?"

"Fair enough. Listen. I am no scutman but a plain brewer from Charnholm town, Olympia by name."

"You're dunce as any scutman. Charnholm town. There's no dregs left in Charnholm town."

Cider Mother coaxed and commanded and negatived their arguments while the umber sun bored holes in the sky. The dregs on the far side would have it she was nobbut another scutman out for sport, looking to pick off any Works dreg so temerous as to climb the wall. After her twenty-second protest, a shout rose within: "Ropes on the north wall! Ropes on the north wall!" at when all the rustling shuffled off north. Cider Mother shook her head and chewed her ryetack. "Naught you can do but make the mash and light the coals," she told Suellen. "Mind that when you're grown," and the sprat laughed and clapped her hands in the dust till clouds rose.

Dust clouds rose from Hunt Boys stompling closer and closer to the rat cages in which the rats still cowered within. The rimers chanted, *Old, cold, loathed enemy! / Enemy inveterate! / You herd of boils and plagues ...* Palan and Finn caught the Hunt over their shoulders as they tossed the grapple hooks gainst the sheer stones of north wall, downslope from Gov Don's shelter cave. The eyes meant to be on the lookout for just this, eyes of Brock and Doole, lay closed in the outhouse after their last drink with Mary Pat. The grapple hooks caught, and Finn started up the rope they secured, which loosened and tumbled him back to the dust. They tried a three-hook the next time, and again Finn tumbled into the dust. Palan scratched his head, "Surely those grapples ought —"

"Why do you no hook to the loose stones?" said Mary Pat.

"Steal up behind a body like that," muttered Finn. "Scare the heart right out of a ... what's towards?"

She buffed her nails gainst her pinna like there was all the time in the world. "Mary Kath and Rimshot was fixing ropes to the shelter cave's back entry when I left. Why do you no hook the ladders where the wall's low, by the loose stones?" Finn explained line of sight to her, and how the loose stones was dead visible from southside parapet of the compound: "It's straight downslope!" he told her. Mary Pat thought no eye'd leave the rat cages right then, only Finn was so lamentable cautious. Palan allowed she'd a point there, but Finn held out that scutmen's eyes was always roaming. Mary Pat said, "Scutmen drink with richards fore a Hunt, which is to say their eyes is closed now, certain. Rimers and beaters and Hunt Boys, all, their eyes is on the rats. Now's your time." Mary Pat looked far off and she spoke from the bottom of her plexus, so Finn moved, and quick about it. They tossed the grapples to the topmost loose stones, where they fixed on the first throw. Palan and Finn had climbed up and over in the time it takes to tell it.

Mary Pat stayed below for lookout till they sussed the ground on the other side. From where she stood it was all confusion; Finn and Palan's voices interwove with shouts of "Ropes on the north wall! Ropes on the north wall!" and then muttering, and then screeching and clashing, and then more mutter.

From where Finn and Palan stood, all the dregs in the world had run right down on top of them, waving cloths, skreeling AYEH AYEH at top of their lungs, their skin blue as twilight right down to their toes. Finn and Palan laid their backs gainst the wallstones, which only inflamed their attackers the more. The women come in with their cloths and sticks, the men flanked them with stones poised to throw, their combined skreeling mingled with Max's viol from the plaza: *skreelyabach ayehoh AYEH AYEH skreelyabach AYEH*. Finn stepped away from the wall, his palms outspread: a stone caught him full in the chest and red blossomed on his tunic. Dazed and breathless, he made a bloody path in walking toward them. The blue dregs hung back, as mazed as he, their weapons at their sides. "Scutmen! Scutmen," hissed a woman, and Finn shook his head, no, gestured at Palan, shook his head again and, "Nobbut dregs like you," Finn said loud as he could. The blue dregs huddled some on hearing this and at last a tall male stepped up to Finn.

"Shtark," he said, "Where are you from?" and Finn told him. Shtark said, "Charnholm town," strode back to join the Works dregs, raised his voice for all to hear: "This one too says he's from Charnholm town!" "South lie, north lie, the same lie," someone said and the men raised their stone-throwing arms.

Palan dodged a stone to his temple as sliced his right earlobe, the spoorting blood bringing the red-eyed Works dregs closer. When he ducked again, a slung stone missed his pate by a hairbreadth. The next few did no miss.

Finn was knocked sidewise by a stone to his left shoulder.

Palan was doubled by a stone to his plexus.

Finn walked forward, his palms outspread still, blood dripping from his shoulder, blooming on his chest, trickling from his mouth. The Works dregs hoorled *Ah-weeoorlah Ahweeorlah*, as they slung stones in clothends round their heads, *Ahweeorlah* a stone to Palan's shin, *Ahweeorlah* a stone cracked gainst Finn's elbow.

Finn kept on till he was armslength from Shtark. "We are no scut-men," he said through his swelling lip, "nobbut dregs like you, by my right arm we are from Charnholm." His heart was slamming his ribs consider-able, the Works dregs was no less fierce so close, lips drawn back from yellow tusks; the women hissed the louder as they come on closer still closer to circle round him. The smell of elderbush flower was sharp in his nostrils. "I am Finn M'Cool," he said, to hear his name last of all sounds, "Finn M'Cool come to give potable back to the dregs." The Works dregs come to a halt altogether, the women's hands froze to their cheeks. "Finn M'Cool come to lead you from this place," and they fell to their knees as he did. Finn had always thought he'd somehow make his mark on the world, yet he'd no thought it'd be with his blood. "Finn M'Cool, here with Palan Goldhead" — mayhap Matia's foreseeing had weight here — "we're here to bring you out from this place," seeing as no stones was flying at that dentical moment, he repeated, "Finn M'Cool at your service," and Palan near bit his tongue to blood as the blueskin dregs of the Potable Works stood and advanced on Finn.

A woman folded her pinna round Finn's bloody chest.

A man dabbed the blood from his mouth and shoulder.

"Finn M'Cool," said Shtark, his mouth pulled up on one side like dust'd turned to ryeflour in his palm, repeating that name again and louder till all the blueskins was laughing and crying to once, "We're main glad to see you."

The Works dregs come close, now, to tend Finn and Palan both. Finn figured he'd best seize the day and quick about it, now while they was all kindly. He asked their safe-conduct to the Works, and Shtark was agreeing, when they cut him short with a new hoorl: "Ropes on the north wall! Ropes!" Finn explained, so loud as he could, that it was nobbut his sister Mary Pat, at when the mob sputtered down enough to hear Finn explain how she was keeping lookout gainst scutmen from the wall's far side.

Mid all that hoorah, Mary Pat struck a lacious pose atop the wall.

Palan grinned from neath the wall where he lay getting his breath back. Would you look at that copperhead stretched out on the walltop. Mary Pat could no resist an entrance. "Well, you found yourself a handsome passel of bluebodies," she told him as she eased herself down the stones one-beat two-beat three-beat, each motion poured into the next. The Works dregs stood gape-mouthed. Finn concealed a broad grin in his hand while Mary Pat laid it on for the audience. Laying it on by the ell, she was, down to the point of her painted toes. Shtark was helping Finn tell her how the scutmen had that morning once more tried coaxing the Works dregs to the walltop — like Finn had known this always — and from that coign tried to coax them like always: *Jump down, come now, jump down, who's your friend, eh? we're here to help you;* so forth so on they cajoled. Well, that morning some lackwit Works dreg he believed it, and leapt, and was run through by a laughing scutman's pike. They said scutmen was the only faces they saw from beyond the walls; it was scutmen took the fresh potable and laid a few fish in their place.

Finn closed his eyes. Had scutmen brought Matia's foreseeing? Who, an it was no scutmen? He kept his eyes closed the better to listen.

All this while the Hunt went on *samdaankish skreelyabach ayehoh* COME and COME and COME. Hunt Boys must be circling the rats in their cages for the close-in; what pleasure it'd be to set Ambrose swan in the middle of the plaza all by his lonesome with nobbut a poniard and a kingrat of long yellow tusks creeping up on him; yes and Gov Don ought join him; yes and the richards who thrilled to the close-in, and every scutman as ever was — how could this dreg Shtark keep his eyes in their sockets in telling this new tale? would you listen, now, oh livery rats ought gnaw scutmen's bones as took the hale from them, as come slap through the gates bold as six-month rats to take hale justborns from out their arms. They ought to sweep down to the southeast and meet Quix, Drosh (had to be sobered up by now), Bedelia Coldhand and all. The Hunt was skreeling highest ever he heard it; sure Boys was dropping uncommon rapid, for by this late in a Hunt Max was usual bowing in long strong arcs as put heart in the Boys, cept now he was sawing skreech sharp and quick; for the close-in, must be — they needed to sweep down to the southeast and meet Dan and Deirdre and — in a minute. Soon as Shtark was done telling this. Soon as the chill left his bones. In a minute.

⟳

A minute speck by the landing stage hauled a toy redsail junk gainst the pilings by a thread it coiled round and round a spool. It stood, laid a pinhand to the base of its twig back, walked up the dock on its toothpick legs in lopside stagger neath a carrysack. It swelled as it labored up the stones till by time it reached the Works southeast gates it was the size of a snoopface time-eating sack of crookbones, though that was no what Cider Mother called him to his face. "Ah, Fergus," she said, placid from her square of shade.

The man did his possible to look the innocent. "Olympia," he said, fumbling the carrysack round behind him. "O-lym-pee-ah. Beauty beauty beauty."

"Caught your tongue on summat, Fergus?" Cider Mother inquired courteous.

"My tongue? Now, no," fashing his long fingers through his black curls, the sweat sudden on his cheeks, "what ever'd I catch my tongue on? My tongue is prince mong the oiled, at all times ready to come out and do its proper. I'm nobbut its housing, how I look on it ... but I've give all that up, you know."

"Have you," said Cider Mother.

"Oh yes indeed, change of heart I had entire, seen the error of my ways. Come to help you steal the secret of making potable, I have, yes."

"Have you."

"Remarkable, innit?"

"I remarked on it."

"Y'see, here's old Fergus, scourge of health, maker of tarponesse ... oh yeah I know what all's said of me, my ears is sharp enough ... and it come on me earlier this day when I saw August Inkwhistle slip a flask from out a bag as hung from your own dwelling and slide it down the gullet of the lone passel of scutmen left in Charnholm town; they snorting on the cobbles still, likely," he waited for her to make answer, but she did no, "so I said to myself, I said, there's a woman with spunk enough about her, I said, by the last rat I'll help her steal the secret of potable from out the Works, by the last rat's dead eyes I will."

"Did you."

Fergus was sweating hard by now. He made to move into the shade near Cider Mother but something stopped him. Mayhap the knife she pulled from her waist, how she easy sliced the ryetack with it. Fergus stayed his ground. "Sure," one eye to that thin blade, "sure I did," palms wide spread; "What've I done, I ask you, Olympia, what else have I done ever but seek a better life for all dregs? Yes," warming to it, "every dreg's my brother," as he bowed, one eye to her flashing blade, "or sister, for mine's a life devoted, I tell you, Olympia, devoted to easing pain," again with palms widespread; "Olympia, I ask you, is it no best to ease pain? For dregs could no never rise up on richards. No." Her regard placid, unmoving, she drove the knife into the dust. Its thin blade shimmied in the heat. Fergus shuffled forward, back, ended on the same square of dust. "We could no. I count myself a dreg, you see."

"Are you no?"

"Course I am, course I am, dreg as dreg. I only go mong scutmen cause they has the dosh. I've a motherless sprat to care for, think on, yes and taking from scutmen's been all times my revenge, yes," now even the spawn in Olympia's lap was giving him the same unblinking gaze. "I weakened them," this clear to him now, "that's what, weakened them with tarponesse. Why, you could say it was I prepared the ground for this great Galanty Hunt. It was Fergus as put the scutmen and no few Hunt Boys, too, on the steady tarponesse nod, and why? So we dregs can recapture our destiny; like Promthus stealing fire we sha' steal the secrets of making potable, yes, and here's what it is," the curls plastered to his skull with the sweat, "you're reasonable, Olympia, a far-seer like myself. We got to take care of these dregs with short sight," moving on cautious feet towards her, an eye to that knife, "the ones as, see, the ones as might guzzle up all they can, no thought for the morrow; the most of those dregs is that way. Well, can you blame them; all the years on years they spent scrabbling for crumbs they'll need time, I tell you, time to adjust to having all the potable they need, and in that time," he was nobbut an armslength from her by this, and she still regarded him quiet and steady; Cider Mother was listening to him, to Fergus, "till they modificate their ways why they'd maybe damage the secrets, so what we got to do is, are you listening?" she give a slight nod but a nod natheless, "Take supremest care on the secrets; we got to guard this precious resource well, keep it to our own selves; you and me we've the years and the acumen to think for our people which they've, no blame to them, never had the scope to develop. So let us now, quick while the Works dregs is away, slide through the gates and rescue the secrets for the good of all dregs now living and those yet to come forevermore. My junk's tied to the landing stage and we can away with it fore any notices, round the point —"

"Fergus." Curious it should take no more to silence him entire. "Fergus, you work with stoppered vials in making tarponesse, do you no?"

He'd come to believe it entire by now. "Course I do, course, in my unrecognized untiring effort to weaken scutmen I —"

"Well, I've a stoppered vial." She pulled it from her carrysack and held it fore his eyes. "Floating in salt-pack alembic. When my Nora died I lanced her buboes and filled this vial with her lymph. Is it potent or has it withered? There's a question. Here's another. Shall I crack it gainst your eyebones or force it down your maw?" Cider Mother stood up. Her eyes was close on Fergus. "Give me that rope." He cowered in on himself like a November leaf. Cider Mother unhasped his carrysack and drew from it a long smooth diamond-plait. Cider Mother shook out the coil as she'd shake out her nighttime hair. She wound Fergus's rope round Fergus's limbs. "The clove hitch," she told Suellen, "is your knot for any shifting load. It lets you loosen or as now tighten your hold by hairs; you loop it so, and slide it, so, and where you've slid it, there it's fixed." Cider Mother coiled and knotted the leftover diamond-plait and coiled it — no point cutting a good rope like this — and dragged the trussed Fergus to a shadepatch.

His eyes was fixed open. "Do you plan to slay me?"

"Oh think a notch less on yourself, Fergus," she said as she replaced the vial in its alembic. "A rat, sure, when necessary. But you? I've neither the time nor the inclination. Ah, and grapple hooks in your carrysack, now that was thoughtful. But you'll no take the potable secrets, Fergus, all to keep them in the hull of your junk. Aqua pura's no another gift from the stars to keep Fergus in idle sniff forevermore." She took the spawn by the hand. "Come long, Suellen. We'll send back for you once we settle this," to Fergus over her shoulder. She knotted a grapple hook to the diamond-plait, and caught it on the gate's newel. The other end she wound on a cracked pillar — "See, here's your clove hitch working, Suellen," tightening the line till it twanged. She hoisted the spawn to her back. "Cling," she told her, and Olympia stepped onto the line like it was solid jetty and started up it to the newel. Fergus's eyes followed her, cursing, but his curses took no hold; Suellen's grip and Olympia's soles was equal steady. She glided up the rope soft as *Hail Janus* coming into dock. *Sha sha sha*, her feet on the rope the only sound. She reached the newel and straddled it and tied a second rope round its neck and tossed her hand in the air at Fergus fore she slid down the rope and disappeared to the far side of the wall.

From the far side of the Works, Ambrose stopped mid-spiel. Though the rats was still in their cages his hands fell to his sides, his mouth gaped, his blood rose, his eyes fixed on Olympia gliding long a rope in the middle of the sky — which was impossible. The Hunt Boys slacked round him; he gave it no mind soever. Olympia. He fell laughing, there in the middle of the Galanty Hunt, with all the Boys looking up to him he fell helpless laugh-ing — Ambrose! — the tears falling on his knees and the Galanty Hunt dis-solved to a passel of wristy boys, their cocks shriveling in the heat.

It was Max as looked away to spy Daniel M'Cool stroll up from nowhere, a carrysack cradled in his arms. Dan give Max the wink, and Morsnal jobbled him in the ribs: so it was now, was it? Max paused a mo-ment as Dan kneeled to the plaza stones and laid down his carrysack nob-but a foot or two from the cages full of staggerrats twitching their long tails. The carrysack bulged. Its mouth opened. Max picked up his bow. The sun was broiling the clouds to wisp; there was a crisp smell off the Musicians sweating globules; as the rats shifted from paw to paw their nails made the softest of clicks gainst their cagemesh; he tasted metal in his mouth; Morsnal's jabber stirred the hairs on his forearm. His cock rose and his bow rose and do you want to die on your knees? or meet death on your own two feet? he played it out loud on the skweering viol: The long note of the timbers falling and the short *pfaff* of the windows blowing out and *skaaarllll* the pillars cracking and *dthud shangg* the stones falling and *thonggk* the bodies dropping and the high *skreeeeleeyaaah* the trees exploding from their own rootballs and *arrrgggghh awooorrhhhh* the flames eating. And then the silence. The ashes wafting in the silence. After the silence, the wail, all the small wails plaiting into one wail as rose as smoke and wavered as smoke and filled the last crevice of every ear. As smoke.

*As smoke rose in our caves. As our pups burned.*

Dan pressed his palms gainst his ears. He wrapped himself round his bent knees and rocked on his heels.

*We burrowed deeper in our holes. We lived in fear, hiding, ducking from sight, hunched, scurrying for the next meal.*

Alpha and Delta looked at the thick grey rats and the rats stared back through the mesh. The two clawed their way up Dan's legs, they burrowed neath his tunic. Their whiskers quivered gainst his chest. They hunkered on his shoulders.

*The taste of burnt flesh. Savory. Salivatory. It draws us from our caves. Cooked spuling flesh. Yes.*

The thick grey rats poured from the cages, bellies low to the plaza stones. The rimers intook breath. The Hunt Boys shuffled in place, dull-eye, pikes loose in their hands. They fumbled poniards out their belts. The beaters whallyhooed, brandished their pikebutts, the only vigor on a gelid stage, and their shouts drove the rats towards the Hunt Boys. From the Hunt Wagon come a clear whistle: G-G-G-E-flat, and: G-G-G-E-flat-F-F-F-D; G-G-G-E-flat-F-F-F-D; it'd turn your brain to spag, G-G-G-E-flat-F-F — and Alpha and Delta leapt down from Dan's shoulders. They sliced through the ratpack. Some rats they herded toward Hunt Boys —

*Use them use their pikes use them to kill the pestlent —*

The Boys fell on those rats driven gainst their boots, fell on them with their blades, severed their lives from them with spike to backs of their necks, one thrust and the rat eyes dimmed and the fleas leapt off them —

Morsnal's Alpha and Delta running back and fro the while, baring their yellow tusks at those rats with pus-swole jowls, driving them onto the knives of the Hunt Boys —

*Drive the misgotten to them —*

Fraser threw himself down on his left hand and right toe, stabbing a rat mid-spring, suffering nobbut the gentlest of nips from a female Delta pushed at his heel —

G-G-G-E-flat-F-F-F-D G-G-G-E-flat-F-F —

Had the Musicians atop the Wagon oped their eyes, they might seen Morsnal's two trained rats driving only pustulated rats closer and closer to the Hunt Boys; those below on the plaza stones could see nobbut scrummage. The richards could seen it; each close-in stab and gush was all smack center of viewtube, but richards was snorting still, packed in the shelter cave in droolish sleep.

Morsnal saw it with gladness: Fraser. Tomal. Doyle. Bannon. He wanted those four close as he could get them.

G-G-G-E-flat-G-G-G-E-flat —

Fraser limped hamstrung through the beaters, past the rimers, out the plaza. Tomal was nowhere to be seen. Doyle and Bannon alone stretched their necks for the blade.

Alpha waved her tail and looked over her back as she made off to the shelter cave's shaft; the hale rats followed her to a stash of food, *a lovely rotting heap*, she promised as she ran. Delta herded from behind and so they two got the hale rats to the ladder's top.

The rats poured down ladder in Alpha's wake. Collins woke, and screeched, and flailed the stewpots off the long table into the next room. A cubit length of rat leapt to the table and sunk its teeth into a loaf of rye. Collins houffed and screamed and tossed that loaf and its fellows through the doorway, knocking a necessary on its side. The rat bared its teeth and galloped off the table to the feast she'd spread for them. The whole passel set in. They squeaked as they ran to draw the rest of the pack down below, and again the ladder was dark with rats, and again, till Collins had thrown the last speck of food out the kitchen, when she plumped herself onto the bench and threw her pinna over her face.

The rats had been caged for six good hours. They bit down the provender in great lumps. Where stew fell on sleeping richards, they bit the food off them. Richard flesh fish flesh; all the same to hungry rats. Paws as slipped in the fresh blood formed a bridge for the next surge; hunger drove them on. They scrambled and vaulted from one lump to the next. Their whiskers clogged with fat and blood and face-talc.

Richard skin underlay the chunks of stew and the rats ate the stew and the plate it came on. Hale rats swallowed the richards' sterile flesh. Their blood lapped that barren meat and carried it to their organs to root there. The rats ate what forage there was in the room of snorting richards to the last drap, when they fell asleep in alcoves and under chairs in coiled heaps, their now-fruitless blood beating at the tips of their ears.

But that infertile stain spread soundless. The silence lengthened. Collins drew her pinna off her face. A sleek grey rat eyed her from the table. She opened her mouth to scream but fore she could start in, the rat stood on its hind legs, crossed its front paws, and kick-danced down the table's length, where it turned, flung out its thin claws, and bowed. Alpha had got dainty in her lifetime of treats from Morsnal's plate. She looked up, expecting dried pomace, or runny cheese, or nut butter; what she got was a small saucer Collins poured from a tin bottle. "There now," said Collins — Collins! — and sat back so not to fright the small creature — Collins! — it must be said again. Had the world turned inside out? Would the moon's dark side now appear? Rain fall upwards, the sea teem with fish, other lands be heard from? Alpha, free of these large questions, lapped the potable, her eyes half-closed with pleasure. Collins reached out a hand to stroke her, and Alpha arched her back gainst that caressing hand.

Belowground, the quiet snorting of richards sleeping where they'd dropped, according to plan.

Aboveground, the slaughter went on according to plan.

Hunt Boys wheeled, stooped, struck, spiked the remaining rats in fine choreography, tossed them so many so quick into the Wagon oven that flames licked its taffrail. Musician sweat rained on the drum skins, swelled hornvalves shut; the wet cymbals rang *samdanploff samdanploff*. Ambrose had wiped the laughter off his face and he was up and shouting, "Gorry dripstaffs *get* in there call yoursel' Hunt Boy where you get the nerve I've *no* idea you've all the hunt in you of kelp I said *get* in there, think you'll best please richards by mimic of jetty wall get *in* there and get in *closer ...*"

From Morsnal's perch in the Wagon prow it was nobbut smoke and sound. Max was bowing a keening whine that held the wail of the walled justborn, the spatter of ratfat in the fire, the long sigh of Bannon as rattusks met in his eye; Max bowed high thin sharp and louder, oh now louder, a wail louder than all from somewheres past the shelter cave past the wall on the plaza's south, from everywhere to nowhere; the air so fetid his own hand was gone from sight but there, again, a higher, thinner, sharper cry than any rat ever, or than any justborn, and another yet another plaiting into a great wail to burst your ears, oh now louder as Max waved the Musicians to play louder; Morsnal cocked an ear toward the shelter cave; the plaited wail rose up, sank its teeth into his ears; his fists pressed into them no use; he melted to the floor.

Max nudged the lump of him off his foot. He'd no time for Morsnal just now. The justborn and summat more was wailing out of his viol. The great beak of Max's nose presided over the viol's long high wails. He sawed a series of sharp queries *are you are you are you are you* near the bridge, and — how could a creature that small moan so loud? — and the justborn wailed in response *I oh I oh I oh I oh / Can no can no canno-o-o-o get out, ge-e-e-t canno o out o-out*, the notes spatting off the strings softer and softer till they was mewing at each other cross the plaza in pitch so high the rimer chants fell from their mouths as they bit their backteeth gainst its icy points, till blood-slick poniards slipped through Hunt Boy hands as their earshells coiled gainst their skulls; Max's chin near down to his breastbone, the bow quivering his high cheekbones, his breath rasping tween his gaping lips louder than the skweering viol, louder than the soft mew of the justborn — that every woman in the plaza felt tween her legs — as froze every rat to be slaughtered where it stood, the plash of their claws in the bloodrun stones louder than the viol's dying ululation — and now softer, ah now softer, and rising now, ah now rising ...

The seabreeze rose soft, soughing through the marshgrass, whistling gainst their rough blades; it riffled bloodpools, lifted neckhairs.

# In the Works

*The sun swole orange in fury at its imminent plunge into the harbor, hurling javelins longwise at the sandstone bluffs that flamed under this barrage. The waves were shot gold at their crests by the same weapons, pushed higher and higher by the rising tide and the seabreeze, falling on their own necks in roil, smashing the shingle to drown the next serried wave in flume, tossing flotsam like so many dice to the table, only to snatch them back before they could be counted; the ponderous sea always a beat behind the land, its waters heating to boil even as the land bent its cheek to the seabreeze. The sea gulped the day's long heat and exhaled from its cold depths a chill fricate breeze onto the land. First the locusts quivered, their compound leaves on flat petiolules flustered by any least barometric change; next the futtock shrouds of the Hail Janus stirred round the crowsnest; last the napehairs trembled of those dregs who slept incautious near their shutters. They woke, rubbed their eyes, sipped their potable, and cracked their shutters on a new Charnholm; unnoticed by virtue of its most ordinary ordinariness, since the world is made new each time a body opens its eyes. They slipped into their dried-sweat tunics and set to work hauling scraping shaving scrubbing gutting before the light should fail.*

*As the seabreeze rose it thinned the grey miasma that had wrapped the town through the long afternoon. The dregs breathed an inch the deeper into their lungs. The harbor flung spume; the rigging creaked off the ships; but the spawn gathering kelp heard a high note missing, and spoke of it; the women grinding rye missed a high thin note in the evening chorus, and spoke of it; the men binding fardels in the ryefields heard some lack in the evening's noise, and spoke of it; but the absence was passed over in the rush to get the day's work done before darkness flooded in.*

A CIRCLE OF DREGS HAD GATHERED beyond the plaza wall, listening to the absence of the high thin wail. In the weedy dust at the foot of the wall, beaters tapped the flat hot stones as they chatted mong themselves. Who'd know better than beaters when the prey was well and truly fled?

Finn sent them down to Charnholm to collect any macery from the drugged scutmen fore the potion wore off. He knew they'd spread the word how Potable Works was taken. When the beaters was gone, Finn returned to the Works, where most all the other dregs sat crossleg.

In the plaza itself only the musicians sprawled in the locust shade, shippering drumskins soft, shaking spit from their horn valves, draining scrumpy by the carboy. Max sat apart with Morsnal, running a dry cloth over and over his fingerboard neath the viol's strings.

Rimers, hands in their sleeves, paced the plaza's circumfence, chanting slow some funerary songs.

One longleg spawn climbed the wall from the Works side and raced back to prattle to its elders how there was only whiteskins pacing round a huge red wagon wreathed in smoke.

All the spawn inside the Works scuttered up to the wall in packs, in twos, urging each other on, giggles splitting their mouths, *go on go on no you go on no you right aright you then, you scared? who's scared, I'm no scared, well go on then, aright I will,* wheeling back to their mams *did you see did you see did you — mam! — did you see I climbed the wall?* Their mams brushed their hair with shaky hands and put them aside, *that's fine, are you no the brave one, now run along.* The spawn rushed back to their play while their elders resettled their crossleg thighs and craned forward to hear the talk.

"So we'd no notion, all these years," Shtark marveled, "that there was any hale dregs left in Charnholm but scutmen only." Bedelia, Quix, Drosh, Cider Mother, and a handful of the older Works dregs passed round a carboy of scrumpy, telling their lives since the Great Burning. Daniel and Deirdre had wandered off somewheres. Those who'd still any spring to their legs was walking the Potable Works.

⟅⟆

The Potable Works was six and twenty long coops, each a dozen paces long with crawl-doors either end, their roofs of glass, their glass roofs steamy.

"*Aqua pura,*" breathed Mary Katharine. This was the design on the leathern pouch, this trove of riches.

A one-leg woman and a tall, pocked man was explaining the Works. "You draw up the sea water," said Varnay, leaning on her crutch, "here's the windlass and buckets, here, their holes plugged with spag as scutmen bring when they come for pick-up. You fill these troughs with seawater, here." She bent through the crawl-door and they followed after.

"What material's this?" said Palan. "It's denser nor wood, stone is heavier, does no ring like metal." He tapped it with his knuckles, "What's this made from, then?"

The tall man said, "Every few years they take us out the southeast gates, down to the sand." He coughed long, hollow, spittleless, hand to his side. "We gather shells and grind them, add sand at two to one, mix the grit grains with seawater, one to one, line a mold with spag, pour in the mixture and let it set a night and a day, unmold it —"

"The spag lets it to slide out, then, so?" asked Palan.

"Ayuh," said the man. "Then you let it set for a fortnight or so, then billagat gran, you've yourself a new trough."

Palan shook his head. "You maun show me just how —"

"Ayuh," said the man, and houffed into his palm. "Well, first you —"

Varnay raised her hand. "Thern." She told Mary Kath, "The seawater sits in the troughs, heats by sunrays as comes through this," indicating the roof; fathoms of slanted glass set at a steep pitch above and athwart the long troughs, the whole tilted long the downslope to face south, "till it rises as steam —"

"Rises up as steam," said Mary Kath. "My sister's seen that."

One brow lifted. Mary Kath wished she could do that. "Has she," said Varnay. "The steam condenses gainst the glass ceiling and runs down the slant sides to these troughs here, long the outer walls; runs down through them to these closed hogsheads here, and there's your potable."

Mary Kath's breath was thick in her throat. She pushed out the crawl-door and leaned on the windlass. All these years dregs worked bent-back twelve hours a day and all that while these works was pouring out the potable with barely a hand turned. *Aqua pura!* here she'd been thinking she'd aught to bring to the table. The pin-pricked leathern purse? Worth no more than a glance; "Nice drawing," Varnay'd said, "zactly same as ours." So what point to it? Why'd they done it at all; broke open the Potable Works and cowed the richards and made the rats to flee; when here at the end of all was nobbut these technicans, no more grateful than beached cod, and about so eager for rescue as Hunt Boys to fondle Matron's sagbreasts.

Thern and Varnay had come out behind her, the woman's one leg shivering neath her. They did no see Mary Kath crumpled over the windlass. Varnay said, "They'll wake from their stupor and they'll come for us and what was the use, Thern, I ask you, all these years keeping the scutmen tame when now it turns out these Charnholm dregs has so riled them with their potions that they'll rampage mong us so long as we live?"

Thern laid his mangled left hand on her shoulder. "Varnay, my dear, the wall was breached. It's over. The scutmen is broke forever." She shuddered neath his hand, turned gainst his shoulder, wept. "The wall was breached and we're safe now," Thern repeated. When she wept the fiercer he said, "No waste, no want; mind you cry over the trough to save hauling." At which she laughed, harsh, unused to it, her face runneled like first rains on bluff soil. Mary Kath gave her a handker, and Varnay put out her hand to Mary Kath and said, "Had you only come a week sooner," and wept again. Thern hushed her, "They come so quick as they could," and spoke to Mary Kath: "Scutmen caught Varnay's man hoisting their eldest over the wall. They lashed him to walltop. Five days he was lashed there, no potable nor naught, till at last he stiffened and died. Scutmen been giving the eldest interruption lessons twice a day since then."

"Interruption lessons?" said Rimshot as it slid out of crawl-door.

"Do they no give them down in Charnholm? They bind him to a stool and take it in threes to question him: what's your name, how old are you, why do you plot gainst your betters. You know. An he does no answer, they stripe his back for him; does he answer, they cram their nightsticks down his mouth, *Suck on this, that'll learn you to interrupt.*" Thern shrugged. "Scutmen like their prey young and smooth, females for preference, but they're no so delicate in their tastes."

"Scutmen's all on them foul," said Rimshot. "And who made them scutmen? Richards."

"No, you're wrong there," said Thern. "Richards *protect* us gainst scutmen, vile pirates who landed here and started straight in to stealing our spawn, having their play with us; they'd all times vault the wall, dance us at maypole with their cat-o-nine-tails; we was well on the way to stinguishment. Then richards struck a deal with scutmen: to take only every second spawn and stay to their side of the —"

"Scutmen was planted by richards, and it's richards feed and water them daily," said Rimshot. The Charnholm dregs told the Works dregs how richards turned dregs to scutmen; referring them, did any doubt, to the elder dregs still sitting by the stove-in wall.

"Well well," said Thern at last, "that'll take some thinking through," but Varnay grinned. "No," she said, "sounds right. Walk long of me to the south slope. I've a thing to show you there."

The spawn wheeled round them as they walked south at Varnay's one-leg pace, a good five minutes till they reached a rubblekarp just over the ridge. "There," said Varnay.

"Rubblekarp, eh? There's rare for you," said Rimshot.

"Shutter up," said Palan. "What's this?"

"A spring," Varnay said.

They waited for her to say what a spring was and when she did no, peered into its umbrous recesses.

"What's that sound inside the stone?" said Mary Kath.

"That's the spring."

"Paint me pink and call me scarlet: what's a spring?" said Rimshot.

"Water," said Varnay. "Potable water. Come up in a trickle a few months back. When rats drank it and took no harm, a few on us tried it. None died nor even sickened. It's a hogshead a day, now."

They said naught for a few moments. Then Finn grabbed Mary Kath and jigged her round and round.

"Grand till it fails," said Rimshot.

"Oh shutter up," Mary Kath suggested, falling to the dust. "Should it fail, we've still the aqua pura. Think on it, Rimshot. Think on it."

"So I am." Rimshot thrust its jaw forward. "Where's it come from? How long'll it last?"

"I care no whit and who does?" Finn jigged round the rubblekarp on his lonesome. "Potable for the taking, enough for every dreg in Charnholm and to spare. Kelp might wither, the sea go dry, the winds lie pent in their knotted sacks, this spring could fail, a rat flea could bite me as I speak, yes and scutmen and richards alike might suck up Cider Mother's valerian potion and fall into swoon while we valiant leap the high stone walls of Potable Works, yes and rats might speak —"

"If there's one certain in this life, it's that rats lack power of speech," said Rimshot.

Finn chortled, "Rats might speak and choose us dregs to be their friends; it's possible —"

Mary Kath grabbed his hands. "Finn M'Cool, you can no more make up a tale like that than you can fly, so —"

"It's no their tails can speak, you rod of fortune, light conductor, bolt channel, one foot in ouranos and one on solid earth," his hands on her forearms swinging her round; "an rats can speak; an we can overcome richards; an potable can spring from the stony earth; why then anything's possible. The moon perhaps will give down milk, horses sha' tire of their lives in crumble-book pictions and sha' leap from wavecrests and snortle through their saucer nostrils and tromple the jetty cobbles; *since mornings a billion years from now are nothingness, we can behold them;* there's for your crumble books," he snapped his fingers; "we'll set the richards to spag diving and with every crumble book they recover they sha' bow down, yes, like this, and lay them at your feet and humble ask, *will that be sufficient madam?* and then back away from your awesome presence, and yes! every tree sha' bear a thousand fullblush apples and every mouth sha' guzzle scrumpy from dawn to dusk and then burp *bawwwraaampp* and then uncork the perry, yes!" He swung her round ... smack into Palan.

"Hmmm," said Palan.

"Oh why ever no?" Rimshot flip-flapped forward onto its hands, then back. "The Potable Works sha' —"

"There's a passel of dead to burn out there in plaza." Quix loomed up back of Palan. "Up and doing," he said, "Cider Mother says we've nobbut an hour, mayhap two, fore the richards wake, and there's a tidy lot of work to cram in that time."

While they straggled out the southeast gates and down the narrow trails, while they gathered phrag-grass from the brackish cove, while they bound it in long fascines, while they lugged the fascines back up the trails, they talked without let. There was so many tales, and gaps in tales, and every speaker was whole-skin or good enough and the seabreeeze risen. They did, true enough, dawdle through the veg gardens, assailing Thern and Varnay with questions. They answered slow, the change still new on them, their mouths still stiff from long disuse — "Peppers, beans, tomatoes; no, these'll no harm you; zucchoes, aubergines, lavanda, corn, have you no seen corn till now?" — and so forth. But the dead and the sun and the potion's effects had their own inexorable pace, so they labored on, peering through white eye-masks of dried sweat, stubbing their zausted toes with every fourth step.

"A long day, this," said Finn to Palan, who ran off in answer. "Where's Dan?" he flung over his shoulder.

"Off with that Deirdre, why?" Finn huffed next him.

"Got to find Dan," was all Palan answered. The seabreeze licked their knees as they ran through the Potable Works to the shady lee of the stovein wall where a thick shadow clung to the rubble. Palan shouted: "Dan!"

Dan was wrapped in Deirdre. He turned slow, his eyes half-lid, to a voice from far away, "Yes?" he said.

"Daniel M'Cool!" said Palan. "Where's they rats?"

"Yes," he said again, "Yes, they're right here," feeling for their bodies in the carrysack, "No," he said, waking some, "They're gone."

"Right aright." Palan was brisk. Dan gone treacle, and Finn a capering bussum; "Has every dreg mong you gone stark staring? We need those two soonest. All our futures depend on it."

"Depend on what?" said Deirdre, waking slow from trance.

"On finding two rats," burst Palan.

Deirdre offered that there were many rats in the plaza.

"Two *particular* rats." Palan shook Dan by the shoulder. "Think. Where'd you last see them?" but Dan remembered naught.

Finn held his brother by the elbows and stared down his eyes. "Daniel. Morsnal's rats. Alpha and Delta. Where are they now?"

Dan said, "Alpha has eaten the fruits of the richards; she shall stay below the half of every year. Delta roams the surface salt-faced with weeping; he has forsworn the light of day."

Considerable silence followed. "But where *are* they?" Palan hissed at Finn who shrugged his shoulders and tried again, getting nobbut more of the same nonsense for his pains.

"By the last rat, have you naught to do at this hour but chunter on?"

Palan greeted the newcomer with nobbut a raised hand but, "Mary Pat!" said Finn.

She kissed Palan full on the mouth, which stopped him entire, smoothed her clean pinna and settled her hands to her hips. "What all you males get up to when I leave your sight for two minutes together. Daniel, your powers to hear beyond must mussed soggy off all this nearby potable — Alpha's in Gov Don's kitchen right this minute napping on Collins's lap; Delta's found his way back to Morsnal and he's in great danger, to be sure, lest Morsnal pet the fur off him. As for the rest of your augury — did you ever in all your puff know a rat as loved to scamper in 'boveground daylight? Have all your wits drained to your cock? Deirdre, was it you brought him to this pass?"

"But they come out in daylight, Mary Pat, they do, they must, else how do Hunts slay them?"

"Rats push their plaguey fellows to the verge," she said, "Dan'll tell you on it, likely;" and turned polite to the blueskins. "You maun be Works dregs," she said, and she and Thern and Varnay bowed and smiled and swapped names till Quix rose from a comfortable stone to remind them in weary voice that there was a tidy lot of dead needed burning in plaza fore the richards woke. They chuntered on as they walked to the stove-in wall, Mary Pat marveling over the spring, the Works dregs wide-mouth at thought of houses of stone, theirs for the fixing. There was some delay when they reached the plaza, when Thern and Varnay was struck dumb by the view of Charnholm town and the ships at anchor and the sun falling into the water, but Mary Kath's urging draggled them on to the deadheap till the horii shrieked, uncommon high and long. Mary Pat and Mary Kath disladed their fascines in a jumble at their feet and all the others followed suit.

The horii shrieked again. A forest of pikes was stomping up the path from Charnholm town. They shivered and froze. It's when the sour rises up on your tonsils that you realize how sweet it is to be out from neath a

grinding heel. They shivered and flushed and trembled, ready to spit themselves so not to lose the sweet taste in their mouths; to die rather than go
back neath that heel. The olders stood shoulder to shoulder to protect the
sprats, and in block they stood so. The pikes come closer, and closer still;
they was within the gates when their leader shouted, "Give you good even!"
and August Inkwhistle shouted again: "Aught left for us?"

So, out of course, there was more converse round the plaza, more
hands to aid the lamby work.

Finn helped his beaters dislade all the scutmen's macery they'd emptied out of armory into one massy pile. The olders pushed up their sleeves
and proceeded to divvy up the gear.

"Greaves, now, line them with soft flannel and you can kneel to garden
all day long," said Bedelia Coldhand.

"Those pikes'd frame a shade awning long the jetty," said Quix.

"Delia, here, she'd weave us the cloth." Drosh squoze her shoulders.

"This cat-o-nine-tails'll macerate the apples to a fine pomace," said
Cider Mother, who'd come up quiet and promised them a tale, later, up
the orchard.

So the macery dwindled to naught and, when it was clear, they
stripped the dead of their corvisers for bakepans and pikes for picnic shade,
scooped up a poniard here or a dirk. In a short time the pile was down to
nobbut a handfull of worn greave-lacings, which Bedelia Coldhand swept
thrifty into a sack. "Might come in handy," she said.

All the while, the work of stacking the dead in a pile for burning went
on. Beaters gaffed the bare corpuses and drug them away off up-slope, one
by one, so long as they could bear it, when another took their gaff and
sumed their burden.

The horii stood round, shifting from foot to foot, posing their curves
this way and that with no effect on the zausted males. "Othel's occupation's
gone," Finn whispered to Palan. Dregs lounged in the shade listening to
the musicians pluck strings, tootle horns, tap drums. They tapped their feet
light on the plaza stones, their blood rising in despite of all. Olders fidgeted
as their own blood rose, it being new to them and they unprotected on that
side of the demesne. "It'll take some getting used to," as Bedelia said to

Drosh. Rimers, old and young, spouted chants, fell silent, stretched their mouths in smile.

In all this swirl, the remaining Hunt Boys jaunkered on their hams, hands dangling tween their legs, gentals crinched up inside them. They stared straight ahead, dull as spiked rats. When the first yawning richards stumbled from their shelter caves, the Boys nobbut trailed their thumbs in the dust.

Rest of the dregs was on the jump immediate. When Gov Don opened the door for Lady Mandra, they jolted up like a lightbolt struck them. Cider Mother and Bedelia Coldhand scunned cross the plaza to greet them, a sight as even drew Dan and Deirdre. They four met the richards as their beaded slippers hit the threshold. They swoored over Mandra *ah good even gracious lady,* waved their handkers at the suppurate ratgashes astrake the richards' flesh, *stigmatic flora blooming on their skin ah grace hath much marked thee,* tugged their forelocks, curtsied in the dust and generally carried on till Lady Mandra batted them away. "Where's Mayry Patriza?" she said to Deirdre. Cider Mother clasped her hands in fierce delight neath her pinna: changed, changed, fearfully changed, all while the old frail slept. Ha!

Lady Mandra's question drowned in the flood of thankyous that dregs poured over richard heads by the hogshead, by the kilderkin, by the pipe: *oh the gift of potable thank you, and breaking down the wall thank you, and the crops within the Works thank you, and dissolving the scut patrols thank you; every babe born in Charnholm forever and ever sha' thank you, gracious and generous we do thank you, had you no raised us up so careful we'd never rose so high, like careful parents you guided our steps till we could walk on our own thank you ...*

They chuntered on that way till the richards was near mazed to belief. Indeed, nobbut their sleep-stiff joints kept them from patting themselves on the back: How kind in us to light the dregs to a new life! they said to one another. How grand in every way! They was a little puzzled that they'd no memry of it but put that aside as the words flowed from the ever-increasing circle of dregs, so the only air the gaping sleepthick richards had to breathe was the dreg circle's warm exhalations, *never sha' we leave off praising you, good and gracious, kind and noble, tell us more of how the plan first come to you oh great ones.* The richards inhaled it till they was dizzy, pressing their gashes to others' in stigmatic kisses as they gulped down praise as sprung parthenogenic from the mouths of dregs. At the last, the richards was chock-full of pride. How they'd schemed! How they'd honed the plan mong themselves! How hugged themselves anticipating this day!

Many dregs had to turn away to laugh up their sleeves, but Bran and Goodwin over-rode that noise by leading the rimers in a new chant of praise which Rimshot shoved in their hands:

*Sing to the Governor, greatest we call,*
*Bulwark of Charnholm gave potable strong.*
*O great mong richards, our strength lay neath a pall,*
*To save us you gave it in glory lead us on!*

"That'll quench 'em," said Rimshot, and it did. A few rimers huddled round Bran and Goodwin after the first run-through of that song; the rest wandered off like they just recalled some important duty. "The richards'll swallow it faster nor blinking, though," said Rimshot, and they did. Could no get enough, like to split themselves cross-face with grinning; even Treesa on Janno's arm inclined her head gracious to the left and right as they strolled forth, even they grinning.

Lady Mandra was no grinning. She'd a rosebud rictus on her, long as your thumb. "Ah, Mayry Patriza," she ran her eyes over the dreg from toe to head, "how very clever you do look." Mary Pat courtsied. "I applaud the sense you show in keeping your top lip firmly planted over your bottom. I have been wondering: do you, perhaps, recall the leathern purse I gave you on your first day as my amanuensis?" Mary Pat nodded. "That was slipshod of me," Lady Mandra said crisply. "I hope you'll bestir yourself to find me a new parlogal, Mayry Patriza. One with expertise in these little scratches," raising the cloth square to reveal a two-inch raggedy rat-gash seeping orange, then quickly replacing the cloth, holding Mary Pat in gaze the while. "We're all a bit scratched in this manner, so do exert yourself, Mayry Patriza," carrying her small smile away to join Gov Don in mounting the plaza dais.

Palan watched them mount the dais. The Gov kept rubbing at his wrist slashes, absent, till Lady Mandra pressed hers to his and raised their soldered hands high in triumph: *Hail Gov Don! Hail Lady Mandra! Beneficient Grandiocious!* The seabreeze carried the stench of them up-bluff. Those few Hunt Boys left standing, from all the cocksure band as left the barracks that morning, was torpid, raising no hand to wipe dustswirls from out their eyes. Finn directed his beaters to lay the last fascine round the deadheap; he and Palan saluted one another cross the heap then lowered their torches to the dried reeds and stepped back. The fire grunted and hissed as the flames roared up in a thick column of cloth and hair, stretched red-orange tongues as licked fat, as sputtered, hissed, bubbled, then skreeled high and long as it turned flesh to spag. Bones cracked. The skreel dropped in pitch, thrummed low as it sank its blue talons into marrow.

Any face'd come out in damp. Any nape'd drip chill. Any eyes'd tear. Heat and smoke extract these liquids.

Dan shook Finn and Palan out of trance. "Go on," said Dan, "Up the orchard in an hour's time," and pushed them in that direction. He drew a long breath and a long pike and pushed the corpy masses deeper into the flames. The fire roared the deeper.

The fire roared and Gov Don boomed. The Hunt Boys roused up at the sound. They cantered to the dais and raised him to their shoulders and carried him, still booming, away downpath. Lady Mandra followed after as far as their two-mast caravel, where she stopped, and raised a hand in farewell, and turned her face. They sailed away into the sunfall, tacking into the wind, nobbut a few Hunt Boys their escort.

Lady Mandra's vanishment snapped some cord as held Mary Pat's feet to the plaza stones. She brushed a hand cross her face and went down ladder to the shelter cave. Collins was swatting rats out the door with a large broom, they nobbut snarling a bit in their sated drowsiness. Mary Pat untied her pinna and flapped it at the last few rats and Collins slammed the door to behind them. They sank to the bench.

"Ah there, Dazymare. Taken good care of the richards?" said Collins.

"They was bit up and suppurate. But they walked off fine," said Mary Pat. "Seemed powerful set up to have give dregs the gift of potable."

Collins brayed. "Who come up with that one? Mary Kath? And Olympe? Brilliant. Tell you, those richards was skirmishing for the rear as they clumb out, sure the dregs was going to slit their throats, screeping for a parlogal to help them, but those slackwaists hid in closet." She raised her voice: "Mercator! Spindrift! Punzelmane! Stir your stumps! Safe to come out of your dens now." Collins settled her bulk on the bench. "And you, Dazymare, get along. They're waiting for you up the orchard."

"How do you —"

"Think I've eyes only in back of my head?" Collins swatted the air. "Go on now. I druther your space than your company; best swing that rump of yours out of here sooner."

"But what'll you —"

"Mercator! Spindrift! Punzelmane! Going to slub the day away? This kitchen's thigh high in rat fecal and I know none of you thinks *I* sha' clean it. Brooms, mops, buckets, lye — *stir* those lazy stumps or I'll know the reason why; leave off your blubbing, Spindrift, we use no salt to clean *this* kitchen as well you're 'ware; Mercator, you've to *scrub* that floor, petting it's no use soever — give me that pinna, Dazymare, you've no need for it any longer, go on — are you thinking this is a *lie-down*, Punzelmane? for I tell you straight it's no —"

She was railing still when Mary Pat joined Dan and Deirdre by the deadheap fire. The seabreeze lifted the last ashes, and swirled the heavy dark grey smuts up-bluff. "Come long, then," she told them. Deirdre craned her head over her shoulder as her foot struck the gatestones: "Look back and you'll turn to salt," said Mary Pat.

The Musicians sang the ashes into the air, the horii crossleg round them, rapt, their faces smoothed. The rimers had shucked their white skins and was knocking back scrumpy flasks as they chanted with the drums. A few broke off from that happy band: Max, Morsnal, Galyse, Chrysta, Rain-cats, Mary Kath, and Rimshot. A limping Fraser trailed them, as far from Morsnal as he could keep. They passed through the gate unspeaking.

The drums beat long into the night, the soft chants sang the moon up and then down again. Horii leaned back on their hands, careless of the seabreeze as plastered dark grey flowers to their oiled skin.

# Up the Orchard IV

*The soothing dark swept down from the clifftops, its breeze turning leaves on their stems, ruffling the surface of the calm harbor, lifting the hair and clothing of the quick and the dead. The moon rose blunted, a good thick slice of its full shape pared away by time in its revolution. In its light, Charnholm town was one wide movement of bonfires, torches, dancing; on the harbor, barges and curraghs and dories, lit by swinging lamps at the prows, slid through the quiet waves as they took on silver from the rising moon; and from Charnholm town rose too the sweet groans of coupling between the voices raised in song, below the pulses of drums in their dozens. High above Charnholm, in the crescent cove open to the north, the night's cool wind skimmed the upper boughs of the apple trees and the brambles round them, blew coolness against the hot flesh of the weary group beneath the orchard boughs who sprawled upon the dusty grass in silence.*

THEY SPRAWLED ON THE DUSTY GRASS for a good while in silence, breathing with pure stonishment that their ribs and lungs and limbs was all attached and working; that those they loved best was living yet. For a long while that was enough and to spare. Deirdre leaned back gainst Daniel, his face buried in her pale hair. Palan and Mary Patricia sat a little off, their shoulders just brushing. Mary Katharine held one of Finn's hands and Cider Mother held the other. In silence they watched Alpha and Delta play on the grass.

"We could done it thout those two," said Finn M'Cool.

"We done it better with them," said Cider Mother.

"Victory came cause we told the truth and we told it straight," said Mary Kath. "Dregs rose up soon as they learned the truth."

Cider Mother raised an eyebrow. Mary Pat said, "Oh our Mary Katharine will no ruin a good tale with accurate and punctilio. We told it to them straight, right aright, but I was longside you for try and try again, do you no recall?" Mary Kath nodded slow. "Well, Charnholm dregs did no just leap out their lives first time we showed the bait, now did they? Took a time or three and then some."

Cider Mother said, "Victory, hmmm? I misdoubt that's the way of it. A good solid day's work, I'd say."

Mary Kath said, "We told it so they could hear it."

Mary Pat added, "So they could see what they heard."

"And they was ready to hear it. The close-in took too many," said Finn.

"It was the show they wanted to see," said Palan. "The ship they wanted to sail in."

"All elements did conspire," Mary Kath intoned.

"Give the intonation a rest," said Cider Mother.

Dan muttered, "Justice like a mighty sword shall flood forth from mountains; iniquity shall vanish like smoke and error be no more." They all looked at him, long and level. Dan shrugged. "Nobbut repeating what the Voice I got from James A said."

"Pretty to think so," said Mary Pat.

Finn nipped in fore Dan and her started wrangling. "That prophetry, now, come in mazing helpful," said Finn, "though how'd my name get mixed up in it?. Way I heard it, supposed to be the goldhair come from the sea. Hoy, Palan. Rouse up and look the hero, willa?"

Palan shook his head. "I've nobbut one small notion: one time I heard Matia's prophetry, on a northern island, and in that telling, Finn M'Cool was the hero; it was he as'd slay the dragons and save the pressed-down. Did you never hear it so?" But they none of them had.

"You was all heroes," said Cider Mother.

"You was a hero, too, mam," said Mary Pat, "Was you sliding down the rope as stounded the Works dregs, stopped Ambrose in his tracks," and the others hummed daccordo.

Cider Mother laughed. "Right aright, we was all heroes, and so deserve hero provender," which she passed round; rye and apple butter and smoke-fish in kelp wrap. Mary Kath brought a serving to Morsnal, who shared it with the tummock rats at top of orchard. Max sat crossleg gainst an apple tree, playing the seabreeze mong the boughs on his viol, and smiled away the proffered food. Chrysta promised they'd be down in a few; she was showing the orchard to Galyse and Raincats and the drogyne Rimshot, who was clean stounded by the living trees. "Kept theirselves alive, they have," said Rimshot; "no pampered richard darlings. Rooted in time and the sweet-water web far belowground."

Seeing as Rimshot was making song, Mary Kath put smokefish and rye aside. She wrapped portions for Thursgood and Fraser as well, who crouched downslope by cliffedge, too shamed to come mong them yet.

As they ate, they spoke quiet of who'd been where and done what since the morning. "Some of those prophetries come to naught," Mary Pat said. "Like that bloody wall I kept foreseeing."

"Like the aqua pura." Mary Kath was still bitter on that one. "Those Potable Works dregs known it all this time."

"Never mind," Palan comforted her, "it vigorated us. Sides, some of them was whang in the gold. The rats did run nose to tail cross the plaza; there was indeed a dark grey sea of them."

They passed round the carboy of potable. "Ours, now," said Mary Kath.

"In the main, our plans worked out mighty," said Finn, "cepting the moments when the Works dregs was trying to slaughter us entire." They passed round a carboy of perry to celebrate their fine plans; and another to praise Alpha and Delta; and once more to toast the future.

"Day on day and year on year we can no foresee," Mary Kath gloated.

"Full of unknown," Mary Pat agreed.

"To the unknown," said Deirdre, and they toasted that.

Palan asked what had come to Fergus. "And Sganal," Finn added.

Cider Mother said Fergus'd likely come sniffing round soon or late; sooner, likely, an she remembered to send someone to loose his bonds.

"I'll be glad of the Mam Can Cook," Palan allowed.

"And Sganal?" Finn asked again.

Dan roused up from Deirdre's lap. "That Sganal, he fell down-cliff," he said. "Lamentable far." Finn asked was he sure, and Dan replied, "His bones was shivered."

Into the silence, Cider Mother proposed a toast to his death, "Though I seldom laud a passing, that Sganal was vile clear through."

"Was richards made him so, mam," said Finn.

"He'd been vile in a smaller sphere had there been no richards never," said Mary Pat.

"We thrown off the richards; we sha never throw off the mean, the petty, the carelack," said Mary Kath.

"Fair enough," said Finn. "That'll make use of your rage."

Mary Kath laughed. "True for that. I'm customed to it, after all."

They let the silence return a while thereafter.

As the moon swung above the clifftops to silver them, Quix come out of the brambles with a roll of cloth neath his left arm. "Evening," he said first to Cider Mother, then "Evening," he said to the rest. "Got it, Olympe." Quix raised a corner of the cloth to show the bronze skin as covered the features of the justborn from Thassy's fountain.

Cider Mother got to her feet slow. "Thank you, Quix. Dan, grab the spades. We'll lay it by James A's tree."

They took it in turns to dig. "More ceremonial-like," Mary Kath said. It needed nobbut a few spadefuls from each to tuck that small bundle safe in the earth. Round the open hole, each tossed some token on the shroud. Mary Pat laid down a fish-spangle thong: "No need for this no more," she said. Mary Kath gave her bell-hung Rimer's cap. Cider Mother tucked a salt-pack alembic mong the folds. Finn gave the taff-end of the rope as breached the Works for them. Palan sprinkled a few drops of potable over the figure. Deirdre pulled the raggedy doll from her pocket as was all the childhood she'd had and laid it by the justborn's right hand. Quix wove a small cradle from a few apple twigs to place by the left hand. Dan's pockets was empty. He poured the grieving Voice down into the earth: the ringing in his ears, the endless longing, the helplessness as all was reduced to ashes, to ashes; all that he gave to the small creature cased in some foul smith's metalwork.

Mary Kath sang a wordless song as they filled in the grave, as Cider Mother planted a sapling at its head, as they tamped down the earth, as they cleaned the spades.

And then they sat there while the moon rose on the new-made world, and their hearts was light within them.

Troubles would come round of their own accord, and none could see how the future'd shape itself; it was no matter to them soever, that night as they sat high above the sea with the singing and the bonfires coming to them faint, as Alpha and Delta sported in the grass, as the waves shissshed gainst the shingle, as the cords they'd woven mong those present and those absent fressled round and round the column of what they'd that day done, unbreaking.

⌒ **The End** ⌒